A COMEDY OF MURDERS

A COMEDY OF MURDERS

George Herman

Carroll & Graf Publishers, Inc.
New York

Copyright © 1994 by George Herman

All rights reserved

First Carroll & Graf edition July 1994

Carroll & Graf Publishers, Inc.
260 Fifth Avenue
New York, NY 10001

Library of Congress Cataloging-in-Publication Data

Herman, George.
    A comedy of murders / George Herman.—1st Carroll & Graf ed.
       p.   cm.
     ISBN 0-7867-0064-5 : $23.95 ($32.50 Can.)
      1. Leonardo, da Vinci, 1452-1519—Fiction. 2. Artists—Italy—
Milan—Fiction. 3. Dwarfs—Italy—Milan—Fiction. 4. Milan
(Italy)—Fiction. I. Title.
PS3558.E677C65 1994
813'.54—dc20   94-4670
                                                                                  CIP

Manufactured in the United States of America

For Kurt
partner, companion, friend
and first-born son

Chapters

1. The Duke and the Dwarf 1
2. The Countess and the Court 43
3. The Madman's Tower 85
4. Flight and Fantasy 125
5. Fear and Festival 161
6. A Plethora of Plots 195
7. The Little Wars 229
8. A Medley of Murders 263
9. The Old Man 291
10. The Flight of the Fugitives 319
    Epilogue 347
    The Cast of Characters 353

A COMEDY OF MURDERS

Chapter 1
The Duke and the Dwarf

*"I shall endeavor,
without disparaging or . . . defaming anyone . . .
to satisfy you,
partly with theory and partly with practice,
sometimes showing effect from causes,
sometimes affirming principles
with experiments . . ."*

Letter from Leonardo da Vinci to the Signori padri diputanti of Milan Cathedral c. 1488

"*Commedia!*"

The beanpole in the black half-mask hurled the word at the townspeople like a summons to dine, and the laughing approval and the roars of welcome from those gathered in the Piazza Palestro in Cremona echoed from the stone walls of the Palazzo del Comune and reverberated up the narrow side streets.

Simone Cario, the tall, rangy Arlecchino of I Comici Buffoni "the mischievous comedians," jigged his way around the small wagon stage. The company had been in existence less than a year attempting a new form of comic theatre which the people had labeled *commedia dell'arte*.

Workers stopped in their noonday meal to watch the cavorting beanpole in the cloak of brightly colored rags. The spectators, including wives and tradesmen, clerics, children, and guildsmen, stood shoulder to shoulder or sat on the lip of the common well, and the young whores watched from the open windows and the small balconies lining the piazza.

Children were lofted to the shoulders of their fathers or clutched the skirts of their mothers in curious fear of the skeletal man who danced before the curtains as if there were only rubber bones in his body.

"*Commedia!*" Arlecchino screamed again. "Come see! See Pantalone, the grasping old miser of Venice, lose his fortune because of greed and stupidity! See the lovers, Francesco and Isabella, foil the attempts of their parents to extinguish the fires of their passion! See the braggart French Captain Bombardon trip over his cowardice and impale his lies on the lance of truth!"

The people roared as Piero Tebaldeo, dragging an absurdly long sword, and with his pillow-stuffed uniform bulging in odd places, suddenly appeared through an opening in the curtains to announce: "Everybody loves me, everybody fears me! I'd as soon chew up a prince as an onion."

Met by a barrage of insults and threats from the Italians, who remembered the recent invasion by the French, the Captain trembled violently and fainted, falling behind the curtains to the laughter and derision of the townspeople.

Arlecchino came center and held out his hands in mock salute. "Come! See Scapino of Bergamo struggle to give birth to twins while his wife, the cunning songstress, Lesbino, cavorts in the closet with Doctor Graziano!"

The crowd shrieked as a naked derriere appeared through a break in the back curtains and wigwagged at the audience.

Arlecchino struggled on. "See pretension and pomposity shredded! See wealth and power ridiculed and stripped of their velvet robes! Laugh as the clever servants mock their masters as they connive, plot, and lie to snatch a few ducats! Chuckle as the bumbling assassin becomes the victim of his own weapon, dancing the vendetta to his own destruction!"

The performer did a sudden cartwheel and ended miraculously seated on the very lip of the stage to the delight and applause of the townspeople under the bright, autumnal Italian sun.

"Come!" he called again. "Watch Colombina, our own Prudenza of Siena, cook a porridge of old shoes, dead cats, and snails to feed your humble narrator, your own, poor, hapless, hungry Arlecchino!"

The audience mock-wailed at the misfortunes of the man in patches as he took a large white linen handkerchief from his tunic, wept in it, and then squeezed about a liter of water from it.

Hell's fire! Arlecchino thought to himself as his quick, professional eye judged the wealth of the audience. There isn't a soldi in any of their pockets. It's watered soup and unbuttered bread again tonight.

He jumped to his feet and again spread his arms wide in welcome with a cry of *"Commedia!"* which flushed a covey of pigeons that fluttered into flight and soared above the square.

The starving actor mentally, and momentarily, feasted on pigeon pie and roast rabbit.

To the west, on the rolling plains of Lombardy, death rode the wind's back, but the hare below could only sense it. The small, gray rabbit, in its fear and confusion, darted to the left and then abruptly to the right, uncertain as to which direction the menace waited for him. He scurried among the fallen gold and scarlet leaves of autumn, raced around the base of the elm trees, paused momentarily under a sheltering berry bush, his heart pounding and his eyes desperately scanning the gently rolling hills for the killer stalking him. Then he bolted from the shelter, trying desperately to reach the safety of his burrow before the threat materialized

Overhead, the black and gray falcon folded its wings and plummeted, striking the fleeing hare like a fist from heaven. The hapless animal, stunned and disoriented, was thrown to one side by the blow and struggled to regain its senses, but the falcon banked and swooped, sinking its sharp talons into the rabbit's head and killing it instantly.

It carried its prey aloft and then descended some distance away in a single smooth and graceful movement, dropping the bleeding hare in the gloved hand of a bearded horseman in a black tunic, hose, and a brocaded cape. It perched on the leather pad fastened to its master's right forearm and awaited its reward, and the rider lowered the bird to Guarino Valla, his head falconer, who fed the bird a scrap of raw meat, placed a pearl-encrusted hood over its head, and returned the bird to its covered, wicker cage. Then the warden untied the leather guard from the master's arm as two servitors rushed to remove the hare and deposit it in the thick, canvas game bag.

"Blood, Your Highness."

"What?"

"I'm afraid, Your Highness, there is blood on your tunic," observed Guarino.

His Highness, Ludovico Sforza, duke of Milan, examined the stain and brushed at it as though he could make it disappear with a wave of his hand. Guarino believed it possible, for he was well aware that a gesture from the duke could easily exile a man from northern Italy or dispatch him from life.

The duke of Milan possessed a fair complexion, although throughout Europe he was known as Il Moro, the Moor, and was often depicted allegorically as a black man or a blackberry. He reveled in this image of a man of tenebrae, so his customary wardrobe was black as a starless night. His face, still smooth and blemishless in his late forties, could easily be that of a man a decade younger, and his posture and lean build remained that of a young athlete. Now, beneath his velvet cap ornamented with a diamond the size of a walnut, he brushed back the black bangs that he had taken to dyeing following the death of his wife eight months earlier, and his dark eyes surveyed the large hunting party gathered apart from him.

A messenger arrived at full gallop, his mount panting and covered with froth. They plodded their way between the members of the hunting party. The man's red-white-and-blue livery was covered with mud and wet leaves, and his own fatigue was evident in his eyes and the bend of his shoulders.

He rode directly to the duke, reined in his weary mare and handed a folded parchment to Il Moro.

"Thank you. See to his needs," the duke instructed his servitors. "Feed and rest his horse."

He broke the red wax seal which bore the crest of Girolamo da Tuttavilla, senior diplomat at the court of Milan, unfolded the document and scanned it.

"September 20, 1498. Confirmed: assassin is in Milan. May be traveling with your hunting party. Take care. T."

The duke noted that the message bore the initials, "B.C.," which indicated that it had passed through the hands of his chief of security, Bernardino da Corte. He folded the message and slipped it inside his tunic.

Another assassin, he sighed to himself. The third this year. And who sent this one?

He looked at the slate-gray sky toward the north.

Yes, he reflected, quite possibly the damned French.

In an elaborate bedchamber in Paris, the tall and sinewy Louis de Valois, formerly Duc d'Orleans and now newly crowned king of France, sprawled in the red velvet chair near the bed of his cousin's old advisor, the exiled Prince of Salerno, Antonello di Sanseverino. The septuagenarian moaned and made suffocating, guttural sounds which segued into deep, soul-racking coughs that shook the old man's body. The young king halfheartedly listened to the crescendo, pulled a grape from its stem, imagined it to be the left eye of Ludovico the Moor, and chewed it with enthusiasm.

"You know this Italian usurper has no legitimate claim on the duchy of Milan," Louis complained.

The aged councillor struggled to focus on his new king, but his eyes were moist and his vision blurred. "I hate to intrude upon your musings with the obvious fact of my dying," he wheezed, "but I do have other things on my mind at the moment than your claim to Milan."

"But I do have the better claim," the king continued,

brushing at a drop of blue liquid that had fallen on his tunic. "I carry the blood of the Visconti through my grandmother. The Sforza are only commoners, ruffians who seized Milan by force of arms. At this very moment I could make an alliance with the pope and the doge, cross the Alps, and drive the usurper back into the arms of his niece's husband, the Hapsburg emperor."

"So simple, eh?" growled the old man, and then he turned on his side. "You shouldn't trust that lecherous Roman or that greedy Venetian and his Council of Ten! Did you learn nothing from your cousin's Italian campaign? The Italians cheered *his* arrival, too; and then, as he was attempting to leave, they banded together and cut his retreating army to pieces! Never, never trust an Italian!" He moaned softly. "Now, please, please, my lord," he whined. "Go away and let me die in peace. I'm dying! Dying, damn it!"

"It is simple enough," the young king persisted. "Even now I am considering a treaty that would give the Venetians the Cremona and the Ghiara d'Adda, and the pope the Romagna for his bastard son. Then I could send my Swiss and Gascon pikemen through the Alpine passes and take my rightful place as duke of Milan."

The dying advisor moaned and tugged the red satin bedcloth around his head, almost disappearing within its folds. The old man wheezed again, erupted in a series of violent coughs which left him gasping for air, and then turned his face into the pillow. "Then, go and do it, sire, and let me expire quietly."

The dark-haired young man rose and smiled at the bent, gray-bearded apparition huddled in agony and despair in the great canopied bed. "Very well, old friend," he said. "But under what pretext? The Italians well remember my cousin's campaign, and a claim to the duchy of Milan, however just, would not satisfy them." There was no comment from the mountain of covers, and the young king smiled, drew closer to the bed and almost whispered, "And what shall I tell the prostitute waiting in your antechamber? Should she stay for your funeral or seek another client?"

"Prostitute? Which prostitute?" inquired the old man peering out from his pillowed sanctuary, his voice suddenly clear and resonant.

The king shrugged. "Their names are legion. How can you expect me to remember them all? This one has a beauty mark high on her right breast—like a signpost pointing to the nipple."

"Shara!" Antonello crowed, suddenly throwing back the coverlet and slipping his thin, birdlike legs over the edge. He shuffled into his fur-lined slippers and wobbled toward the young king. "Leave me, sire," he pleaded. "Leave me to be consoled by my beautiful Shara in these, my final hours!" He smoothed his nightshirt with a bony hand, darted quickly beside the headboard and jerked the bell cord. "Go and plan your return to Italy. If you lack a motive that might seem more reasonable to the Italians, have the Moor assassinated and then march into Milan claiming you came to prevent any rioting and looting that might endanger our French merchants doing business in Lombardy."

"I knew I could rely on you for a political explanation," crowed the young man. "But assassination. How? No one gets near the Moor but his own hand-picked guards and his chief of security, Bernardino da Corte."

The old advisor smiled. "So this old fox may know a trick or two that the young lion does not, eh?" he cackled "For your information, we have someone in the Moor's court who could kill the bastard any time we choose."

"We do?" queried the king. "Who?"

At that moment a stiff-backed servant pushed open the tall doors of the bedchamber and stood to one side as the whore wafted into the room on a cloud of overpowering perfume and a high-pitched giggle. A few steps from the bed, she stopped, smiled, and gave a deep curtsy that revealed the shadowy valley between her breasts.

"Your Excellency," she cooed.

"Yes, I certainly am," the old advisor agreed. "Come!" He extended a bony hand to the buxom young woman loosely wrapped in a riot of colors and textures with a linen headdress that split into two horns. "Please, sire!" he whispered to the young king. "Your cousin-king specified that the assassins' identity be kept a secret. But, while I do not know his name, he knows mine. Whisper it in the circles of the court, and it will be a signal that you are ready to march and that the moment has come for the murder of the duke."

The ancient quickly began untying the laces of the whore's bodice, his bony fingers suddenly facile and strong.

The young king pondered: Whisper his name? Sanseverino?

Sanseverino? pondered Il Moro. Could he be the one sent to murder me?

The duke of Milan studied the tall and muscular man in black armor who was leaning from his saddle to whisper something in the ear of Madonna Valentina, an amiable and audacious lady of the court who was rumored to be the soldier's current mistress.

Galeazzo di Sanseverino was thirty-two, the captain-general of the armies of Milan and the duke's son-in-law. His armor bore the family crest, a shield divided in half with alternating yellow and red horizontal stripes. The handsome officer carried a few small scars on his cheek and nose with pride and grace, but his dark eyes, Il Moro considered, were those of a hunting hawk, penetrating and cold.

And I am to be your rabbit, Galeazz? the duke wondered. Possibly. A man unfaithful to his wife might prove unfaithful to his lord.

Il Moro slowly urged Neptune, his great stallion, toward the main body of the hunting party. The army of women and wardens, princes of the church, courtesans and pages, all elaborately attired, greeted him as he approached, bowing or nodding and bestowing warm smiles upon him. The ladies, he observed, were poised delicately on their sidesaddles, mantled in damask and wool to protect themselves from the autumn chill, and their jewels caught the rays of the dying sun and flashed their rainbowed lightnings. His courtiers and nobles wore the fashionable embroidered short capes lined with fur over their multicolored tunics and hose, while the cardinals insisted on wearing their symbols of power: the long robes, the purple capes, the heavy gold chains with jewel-studded crosses on their breasts, and the round-brimmed hats that made rapid riding impossible.

Very wise, he smiled to himself. Always remind the nobility where the real power of Italy resides.

The nobles and clerics, princes and parasites, sat erect, smiling and patient, waiting to demonstrate the prowess of their own hawks. The beaters flushed quail and hares from the underbrush, and one by one, the hunters hurled their predators into the air and watched as the killers snatched the smaller birds in midair or swooped to seize the fleeing rabbits.

Il Moro was suddenly forced to pull back on Neptune's reins as a doe, flushed with the smaller animals, dashed across the clearing and disappeared into the underbrush. The duke had endorsed his father's restriction that does were never to be killed.

Only dukes, he thought.

Il Moro was not especially disturbed by the warning that an assassin had been dispatched to kill him. The litany of the murdered dukes of the Italian city-states, their allies, and their enemies would fill a large library, and Il Moro himself often considered a swift assassination more expedient and effective than diplomacy. The challenge to identify the potential killer was little more than an amusing game, an intriguing mystery rooted in the genuine possibility of his own death, more entertaining than the amusing puzzles constructed for him by Maestro Leonardo da Vinci.

Milan is crowded with men, women and, perhaps, even

children who would like to see my head mounted on a pike, he reflected. No one even suspected the two young men who stabbed my brother to death at the door of his own cathedral.

"Imagine!" he murmured to himself. "Killers awaiting their victim at the very door of a church!"

The two quarrymen ascended to the observation platform on the roof of the Certosa monastery in Pavia like two wraiths rising from the dark passageway below, moving stealthily and silently, each carrying a long metal bar with a curved end. The lean face of the taller one was trimmed with a dark beard, the mustache and the goatee meeting at the corners of his mouth. The second quarryman, much smaller and clean shaven, looked quickly around at the empty rooftop and turned to peer toward the horizon.

"There's no sign of them, Alfredo," said the smaller man.

"They'll come," the taller man replied. "You saw the message. The duke's hunting party will be directed to the Certosa today. All we have to do is prepare." He worked his metal rod under a large block of marble. "Are you going to lend me a hand, Luigi, or just stand there scratching your skinny ass?"

Luigi picked up his long rod and began to assist in prying and nudging the large, uncut marble block toward the lip of the scaffolding. "I don't like it," declared the smaller one. "Some money is left outside a window and a voice from the shadows says 'Go to the Certosa and join the quarrymen working on the new cupola.' The voice commands us to wait there. We're told someone called the Griffin will contact us with further instructions. Well, here we are. But how do we know this isn't some sort of trap, eh?"

"A trap? Hell's fire! For whom, Luigi? Me? Or you?" The giant laughed as he judged the distance to the edge of the roof. "Nobody cares what happens to us, little friend! We mean no more to Il Moro or to this Griffin than a horse's turds, expendable, offensive to their delicate nostrils, but of some value even if only as manure. It doesn't bear thinking about, Luigi. We are the professionals. We receive a commission. We carry it out. We take the money and spend it quickly, while we're alive, and we don't ask too many questions." He grunted, and picked up a heavy wooden wedge. "Tip it," he ordered the smaller man. "I'll wedge it so a single hammer blow will cause it to topple." Alfredo watched as his associate pried up the edge of the block and quickly slipped the wooden triangle into place. The tall one jogged the marble to permit more of the wedge to slip beneath the block. "That should do it," he said. "One strike from the hammer, and it should drop right where we want it."

"I don't like it," said Luigi. "I like to see the face of the man who hires me. I don't like messages whispered in dark corners or strapped to the legs of pigeons or slipped under a door or inserted inside an apple. I like everything straightforward."

"Listen," Alfredo snapped, "this is the way things are done these days. Codes. A slip of paper here, a whisper from the shadows there. If something goes wrong, and we're tortured, we can't say who employed us, can we? Because we don't know, do we?" He placed a hand on the large marble block. "Yes," he murmured, "that's good." He made one last examination of the tipped marble. "Now remember. As soon as I tip the block, we run downstairs and mingle with the other workers in the refectory. There will be confusion, but nothing to point to us. It was an accident. God's hand. A marble block slipped from the scaffold and fell. Then, as soon as the court leaves, we take two dray horses and the cart, tell the sutler we are going to pick up more marble waiting at the docks, climb aboard a waiting boat, and we get the rest of our money." He motioned Luigi toward the passageway. "Come. We'll be ready when the hunting party arrives."

Luigi came up beside him. "What the hell is a griffin, Alfredo?"

Alfredo put a massive arm around the smaller man. "I don't know, Luigi," he said softly. "Some sort of bird, I think. Like a hawk."

* * *

Il Moro pulled the stallion to the left to better watch the hawk in flight. His attention was then diverted to the solitary figure on the edge of the clearing also studying the bird.

Maestro Leonardo da Vinci, his long beard streaked with gray at only forty-six, had mirrored his patron and had dressed entirely in black, his long cloak covering not only the artist but the flanks of his mount. Like the duke, Leonardo's head was crowned with a soft velvet cap, but he was ungloved, no hunting hawk perched on his arm, and no servants attended him. Instead the painter studied the hawks in flight and made swift, liquid sketches in a leather-bound book, quickly attempting to capture, Il Moro knew, the curve of the wing, the positioning of the clawed feet, the bend of the neck.

Still the court engineer and artist never failed to amuse, so the duke nudged his mount toward Leonardo. "Well, Maestro," the duke greeted him, "and what have we observed today?"

Maestro Leonardo did not look up from his sketchbook. "The shadows and lights of the countryside take on the hue of their sources, Your Highness, because the darkness caused by the density of the clouds, combined with an absence of direct sunlight, tints whatever it touches. Note, too, that a horse, when trotting, has almost the same fluid movement as a horse running free; and I've noticed that the Spanish mare of the cardinal of Modena has a beautiful neck and a very fine head, while the captain's white stallion has finer hindquarters."

The duke smiled. I'm sorry I asked, he thought.

The painter continued to sketch rapidly. "The feathers of birds produce beautiful colors as they move, similar to those found on the ancient glasses, or in the roots of turnips left at the bottom of wells or other stagnant water, in which each root is surrounded by a rainbow."

The duke laughed lightly and shook his head in wonder. "I refuse to ask when and how you encountered turnips left at the bottom of wells, Maestro Leonardo, but I remain fascinated, as usual, by what you see." He gestured to the rest of the hunting party. "What about the human element, eh? For example, if so commissioned, Maestro, how would you paint me?"

The painter glanced at his protector. "With spectacles, in Justice black, as Good Fortune, protecting youth from poverty, threatening that monster with a gilded sceptre."

Il Moro chuckled at the description. "Indeed? And Galeazz? How would you paint our captain-general?"

Leonardo knew that the duke's reference was to the gentleman in black armor now slowly approaching them on his white charger.

"I would paint him as an ermine speckled with mud."

"Indeed? Why?"

"Because an ermine is a symbol of purity. The ermine would rather die than soil itself."

"And the mud?"

"The captain is a man of the world."

Indeed he is, the duke mentally agreed, and he turned his horse away to face the approaching captain-general.

"A splendid hunter, your Astorelli hawk." Galeazzo di Sanseverino commented. "Although I still prefer the Alfanechi."

"Oh, Russian hawks are unpredictable, Galeazz," the duke replied. "Like the Russians themselves. My falconer, Guarino Valla, keeps two Alfanechi, and says they attacked him." The two riders slowly turned their mounts toward the waiting company, and the duke lowered his voice. "I have received a warning. It seems that another assassin has been sent to kill me, and da Tuttavilla thinks he may be traveling with our party."

"Another, eh?" Galeazzo growled. "God's blood, there must be an academy somewhere graduating assassins waiting to have at you. Well, I told you before, Highness, and I say it again: behind these attempts there will probably be some damned Venetian!"

"Possibly," the duke silently acknowledged. "The only member of this hunting party that I have no reason to suspect is Maestro Leonardo."

"Oh, don't eliminate those damned artists," advised the captain, glancing over his shoulder at the dark artist. "They're a useless lot who adore money. They might well consider a murder or two between commissions. Look how they charge exorbitant fees with no trace of conscience. Ship them to Florence, I say, and let the crazy Dominicans burn them along with their paintings."

"Galeazz," Il Moro laughed lightly, "a little respect."

"Respect, my backside!" snapped the officer. "Consider Maestro Leonardo. He never completes anything. The jest of the court is that if he ever slept with a woman, his mistress's hair would be as gray as his own before he finished. You brought him to Milan to design the biggest statue in the world, a tribute to your father, didn't you? And it has yet to be cast, right? And, mark me, his damned wall painting in the Santa Maria delle Grazie will never be completed in your lifetime!"

"I didn't bring him to my court to make the statue," corrected the duke. "He wrote me that he could design and build portable bridges, mortars and cannon that he said could hurl stones like a hailstorm. He said he knew how to construct mines and secret passages without noise of any kind, and covered vehicles that could penetrate the strongest enemy line, and armored ships that could resist all cannon fire. And these are precisely the skills I need if the French decide to cross the Alps again. God only knows what new type of cannon Louis has waiting for us beyond the Bernard Pass. It was only as an afterthought that the Maestro informed me that in painting, he could do as well as any other. Those were his very words."

Galeazzo drew abreast of the duke's horse. "Well, I still

say it's some damned Venetian bloodsucker who is yelling for your head. Those hook-nosed, skinny-assed money changers in their silly turban hats and brocaded coats sit in their clammy palaces, inhale the stink from those open sewers they call canals, finger their mountains of gold florins, and plot murder. They're jealous, you see. Florence has the better artists. Rome has the power of the church, and Naples has the most imaginative whores, but the best guns crown the kings who support the whores, the artisans, and the church, and we make the best guns."

"Even so, we must not underestimate them," the duke repeated. "Consider the fact that the Venetians love their doge. He has given them free medical care, provided homes for the orphans and jobs for the elderly who want them, and has licensed and regulated their whores."

He shook his head.

"While I have a million enemies," he murmured.

"Pantalone believes he has a million enemies," announced the tall man in the uniform of a captain of mercenaries.

In Cremona, the assembled members of I Comici Buffoni began to laugh and offer suggestions. The company stood or sat on prop barrels and crates in the curtained area behind and beneath their platform stage and prepared their costumes and masks for the first performance of the afternoon.

"Arlecchino plots with Scapino and Colombia to convince the old man that the only place he would be safe is locked in his room," continued the mock captain. "That frees the servants to drink his wine and eat his food and have a party."

"Good!" exclaimed Prudenza, the portly, red-haired woman who played the role of the servant-wife, Colombina. "We can begin with me bringing him a plate of sweetmeats and some wine!"

"But I, as Arlecchino, will grab them!" cried Simone Corio. "I eat them and immediately go weaving around the stage and finally collapse at Pantalone's feet! That makes the old man think his food is poisoned!"

"Then I'll take a sip of his wine and collapse, too," suggested Prudenza. "And I'll fall on top of you!"

"Good! Good!" their balding leader, Piero Tebaldeo, agreed. "Then I will stagger in as the Captain with a knife sticking out of my belly and cry that someone in the street mistook me for Pantalone and stabbed me!"

"And I'll enter as Lesbino, eat one of the sweets and expire on top of the pile!" laughed Anna Ponti, the dark young woman who was the principal songstress and the performer specializing in bawdier servants.

The young man billed only as Turio of Verona and the company's old miser, Pantalone, adjusted his black cape. "I like it!" he laughed as he slipped his feet into the Turkish slippers. "Then I'll do my weeping act and go to lock myself in my room."

Francesco, the handsome young man admiring his face and figure in the polished metal plate that served as a backstage mirror, fixed a black curl in the middle of his forehead. "Then Isabella and I will announce that we are running off to get married despite her father's objection!"

Isabella Corteze, the beautiful, feminine half of the team of lovers, ran a hand over her silk hose and adjusted the ribboned garters around her pale thighs. "And as we leave, I'll take the bag of gold Pantalone had hidden behind the picture of his mother!"

Rubini, the short, acrobatic young man who played the black-masked servant, Scapino, was busily practicing his handstands, but added, "Then I will run off with the painting itself, describing my affection for the old lady depicted in it, saying she reminds me of my pet dog or something."

"Good!" Piero cried. "Then Doctor Graziano can come in, join the party, and then, finally, go into the locked room and tell Pantalone that he has been deceived."

"But I'll first pretend he's imagined it all. Then examine

him!" cried Marco Torri, the lanky man dressed in the short black robe suggesting the academic costume of the university teachers of Bologna or Pavia. "I'll stick my thermometer up his ass and make him bob up and down for a while!"

"But be careful," snapped Turio. "You handle that prop like a damned sword. The last time I thought it would come out my throat!"

"What are you complaining about?" Marco snapped. "It telescopes!"

"Then lubricate it!" Turio persisted. "It's rusted!"

"Lubricate your ass," Prudenza sneered, "and we'll all have fun together."

"How do I look?" Francesco asked.

Prudenza, Anna, and Isabella circled the handsome young man. "As tasty as a ripe peach," declared Anna.

"And as fuzzy," Isabella laughed. "Loosen the ties on your tunic, Francesco, and your curly-haired chest will have every fishwife wetting her underlinen."

Piero stuffed a small pillow under the tunic of his uniform. "I hope the people like us," the troupe's leader said, sighing.

Simone peeked around the curtain at the crowd assembling in the piazza. "They look like they want a good time. Farmers and townsmen mostly. Wives and children. Some masons who have slipped away from their work on the bell tower. Three or four fat merchants. A covey of whores there to cheer for me, their Arlecchino. Even a priest." He turned away from the curtain. "The priest may not care for it," he added, "but then again, our theater is a complete break from the morality plays of the guildsmen. The clergy doesn't know what to make of us."

Piero buttoned his tunic around the pillow, transforming himself into a potbellied captain of mercenaries, a popular character with the people. He hooked his long sword to his sash.

"Well, winter is at hand, and we have only a little money left. Unless we earn some gold or at least a few more ducats, perhaps we should consider turning north. Perhaps we can play in the courts again as we did in Milan, where we could be warm and provisioned."

"We have to be invited," Anna reminded him, taking a swallow from a small flask she drew from under her voluminous, scarlet petticoats. "And Il Moro didn't know how to take us."

"His chamberlain knew how to take me," cooed Prudenza, "and did rather well, too."

"That trouble following the last performance was not my fault," declared Rubini as he performed a triple cartwheel across the dressing area. "How was I to know the wine was so potent?"

"Yes," said Piero unhappily. "In general, we did not impress the nobility in Milan."

"Well, I think I impressed a few," said Anna. She corked the flask and hid it again in the folds of her underskirts.

"But not with your acting, darling," said Isabella, grinning.

"When was she acting?" Prudenza tugged at her bodice to reveal just enough of her own breasts to win the admiration and the coins of the men in the audience. "I must have missed that performance."

Anna stuck out her tongue at Prudenza.

"You best keep that tongue warm in your mouth, dear," the big-bosomed woman retorted. "You wouldn't want your only talent to freeze and break off."

"Why turn north, Piero?" Marco interrupted as he crossed between the two women glaring at one another. "If we continue down the Via Emilia and through the Romagna, we can play Parma, Modena, and Bologna before the snows. Lots of money in Bologna, what with all those rich, spoiled university students."

"Not to mention those miraculous Bologna sausages!" exclaimed Rubini, rolling his eyes and rubbing his stomach. "I could eat a million! Spiced with peppercorns! Wonderful! Wonderful!"

"And the spaghetti Bolognese!" sighed Prudenza, remembering. "With that sauce of onions, carrots, pork and veal, and butter and ..."

"Stop it!" Anna demanded. "I'm starving! How long has it been since we've had real food?"

"I suggested turning north to the courts of the nobility, because our style of theater is more familiar there," argued Piero. "We have only a little money left, and the increased taxes have left the peasants in the Emilia with little more than the clothes on their backs."

"True," Rubini said as he put on his black mask and performed a quick cartwheel. "North or south, the sooner we get out of the Emilia, the better."

"Rubini's right," Francesco said, continuing to admire himself in the polished metal sheet. "At least in the north admirers offer you a glass of wine. In the Emilia, it's water— if anything."

Piero added his Captain half-mask with its bulbous red nose and peered at the sun. "It's time," he declared. "Everyone understand the outline of the plot?"

Everyone assured him that they understood the scenario for the afternoon's performance, but Marco as the Doctor stopped just before entering and asked, "We don't have a setting. Where does this play take place?"

Piero considered the question. "Who in Italy is most likely to have a million enemies? Someone who is unpopular even here in Cremona?"

Prudenza gave a small laugh, looked at the others, and they all chorused as one.

"Il Moro!"

"Look at them," the duke of Milan exclaimed quietly as he surveyed the hunting party. "What do you think, Galeazz? Who here would want me murdered?" His eyes focused on a young woman in a bright red velvet coat. "Perhaps the beautiful countess on the gray gelding?"

She is still as radiant and lovely as in her portrait that Maestro Leonardo painted nearly eight years ago, the duke reflected. Now she is a Bergamini and a countess, and she wears that title with the same grace as she wears that single, flawless jewel dangling from the black sable band on her forehead.

The Countess Cecilia Bergamini saw Ludovico staring at her, and she smiled and nodded to him.

"The countess was your mistress when she was a Gallerani," Sanseverino commented. "And she is the mother of your son, Cesare. Maybe she wants to return to the source of her old power, your bed."

"Unlikely," Ludovico considered. "The countess has proven herself amiable and generous, but completely faithful to her husband."

Now, reveling in the lady's beauty, Ludovico remembered the da Vinci portrait in which she held an ermine, the animal that Maestro Leonardo had labeled a symbol of purity. He remembered, too, that when he had taken the ermine from her, the animal had bit him.

Yes, he thought, jealousy is a strong motive for murder.

"Then consider her husband, Count Bergamini," the condottiere suggested as he watched the aristocrat cautiously stroking the head of the falcon, and he laughed as the bird, annoyed, suddenly pecked at the count's finger. "You did force Countess Cecilia to marry that bloodless, ball-less aristocrat." He nodded to the gentleman in the short cape and scarlet hose who rode beside the lady.

Ludovico considered the possibility. "No," he said softly. "She knows it was Beatrice who forced that marriage on her."

"The count still has a good reason to murder you. You shared the same woman," Galeazzo insisted. "He has to act as father to your illegitimate son. To put the horns upon a man is an insult to his honor. He may want to avenge that slight. And to an Italian, a man's honor, as we know, is everything."

"Yes and no," Ludovico replied. "The count would have a motive if I were still sleeping with his wife, but, as I told you, she won't permit it. Besides, I pay the count a large monthly endowment for Cesare's upkeep and have proposed the boy for an archbishop's hat. He would never kill the goose that lays so many golden eggs in his nest."

"Well," Galeazz sighed. "I don't envision the assassin being a female."

The duke bowed his head to Madonna Dorotea as the lady dismounted, removed her gloves, and fed a strip of raw meat to her pet cheetah, adorned, like his mistress, with a velvet collar studded with diamonds. Il Moro smiled to see that the claws of both the mistress and the cheetah had been painted a bright and bloody red.

"Nonsense," the duke argued. "The virago is the feminine ideal in Italy today, Galeazz. God knows my late wife was a match for any assassin, and my niece, Caterina, put down a rebellion at Forli by dragging the ringleader by his hair through the piazza. Then she went directly to her bed and gave birth within the hour."

The captain-general nodded. "And she also believes you poisoned her brother which might make her a possible assassin."

Il Moro shook his head. "No," he said softly. "I recently pledged her funds so she didn't have to sell twenty-five thousand ducats worth of her jewels to Venetian money lenders who offered only six thousand. She, too, wants me alive and prosperous."

The hunters were beginning to turn their falcons over to their handlers and had dismounted to exchange gossip and polite, veiled insults. Madonna Gaddi stroked her short riding whip and smiled at Cardinal de Celano who had helped her dismount and had taken the opportunity to caress the lady's trim ankle.

"Perhaps the assassin is someone from the church," suggested the captain-general. "Cardinal de Celano has a reputation for lechery. Perhaps assassination is another of his vices."

"Ah," breathed the duke. "Quite possible. The Roman Catholic clergy, from the Borgia pontiff down to the lowest sacristan, are not above committing murder if it serves their own ends."

It was at that moment that the duke realized that there were no less than five cardinals riding with the party this brisk September afternoon. He noted their standards flying in the rising wind from the north: an assortment of sunbursts, lilies, chevrons, gules, mascales, and a menagerie of the exotic: the winged lion with the eagle's head, the rampant leopards with enormous tongues, the dark wolves with long, tufted tails, and the gray dogs with exposed, sharp teeth. He watched with some amusement as one of these cardinals, his own brother, Ascanio Sforza, rested his hand on the thigh of a beautiful, flame-haired courtesan.

"Surely not your own brother?" the captain asked, seeing where his lord had focused his attention.

"Why not? Ascanio's spent enough time at the Vatican to acquire a knowledge of the exotic poisons preferred by the pope and his bastards." He again placed a reassuring hand on the neck of his mount. "And if one seeks an enemy," said the duke, "first consider your own family."

"My own family hates me," whined Pantalone as he bit into the small silver coin that someone had thrown on the stage in Cremona. "They don't understand. Money is vital to life. It is blood and sinew. It is hope and reason. Money cannot buy happiness, true, but what it does to alleviate misery is a small miracle." He pretended the coin was counterfeit and glared at the audience who laughed. "Money cannot buy a woman's affection, but it can buy the package it comes in, and that's enough for me!"

He did a small dance and tripped off the stage. The audience roared, and the crowd rained coins on the wooden floor of the platform.

"Just scudi," commented Piero Tebaldeo still in his captain's costume. "Not a ducat or a florin. Nothing of gold."

The duke threw a coin to the lean falconer, Guarino Valla, who, in turn, fed the duke's second Astorelli hawk a scrap of raw meat. He patted Neptune's thick neck as the stallion nervously pawed the earth and nuzzled the nose of Galeazzo's mount. The duke sat silently, shadowing his eyes against the bright sky as he watched a falcon soar, quicken its pace with a flutter of wings and then drop on the smaller pigeon. He turned his attention, then, to the mounted assembly. The hunting party had built a small fire in the clearing, and the hunters and handlers curved around it, warming their hands and faces, and one or two of the courtesans, imitating Madonna Valentina Gaddi, turned their backs, lifted their skirts to their waists, and toasted their posteriors, to the delight of most of the cardinals and the servants.

Suddenly, to his right, the beaters flushed an enormous black boar that cut across the clearing, squealing in fright and anger, his tail held erect as he searched for the cover of the underbrush, his thick neck swinging his murderous tusks from side to side in a futile attempt to locate his enemy. The duke's mount reared in surprise, and Il Moro tumbled from Neptune's back. Instantly the boar turned, his red eyes glittering with his fury, and he charged the fallen duke who quickly jumped to his feet, wheeled, and drew his dagger from its sheath. Before the enraged boar took another step, however, a rain of arrows sang through the air and lodged themselves in the animal's thick hide. Momentarily the stricken and confused beast paused, looking like a mutant porcupine, and squealed his pain. Then he collapsed at the duke's feet.

The duke sheathed his dagger and brushed away the damp earth and the dead leaves from his cape as he avoided the groping hands of the dozens of servants who came running to assist him. He adjusted his cap and waited until a mercenary returned Neptune to him. The stallion, quieted but still nervous, pawed the earth and waited for his master to mount. The duke embraced the muzzle of the beast to reassure him and then he settled into the saddle and studied the dead boar.

"You see?" Sanseverino declared. "You have nothing to fear. See how quickly my archers protected you?"

The duke smiled and turned his mount.

"If they were aiming at the boar," he said softly.

The two men had remained a small distance from the others as the hawks were hooded and caged. Now the duke nodded amiably as he was approached by the lovely countess and two of the cardinals.

"We are not far from the Certosa, Ludovico," his brother observed. "Shall we pay them a visit? The Carthusians boast a splendid cellar."

"An excellent suggestion, Ascanio," the duke replied. "The sun is beginning to drift behind those clouds, and the air chills. A warm fire and a warming drink would be welcome. Besides," he added, "I ought to see this new facade Omodeo is building that is costing me a small fortune."

The duke pulled his mount's head around, followed by the entire army of courtiers, servants, and guests, and the hunting party turned toward the walled monastery beyond the hill to the north.

With a single exception.

Behind them, Maestro Leonardo da Vinci, his long beard and hair blowing in the autumnal wind, remained studying the pattern of shadows and light upon the clouds. He continued to be absorbed in his observations until, suddenly aware that he was alone, he closed his sketchbook, and abruptly turned his horse's head to follow the others.

His last notation in the book read: "A hawk in flight is an

allegory for fame. Fame flies and rises heavenwards, because virtue finds favor with the Creator.

"My lord the duke, unfortunately, has no wings."

The black, noisy rondines soared and circled high above the open observation platform beneath the unfinished cupola and the new facade of the Certosa monastery. They swept past the four misshapen, carved-stone gargoyles that stared sightlessly at the distant, advancing hunting party. Then another profile joined those of the grotesque stone faces, his right eye pressed against a spyglass.

After a moment the young dwarf, Niccolo, nineteen, telescoped the instrument and put it in the leather pouch slung from one shoulder. He finished the last dregs of the wine stolen from the refectory earlier that afternoon, placed the empty container near the overhang, and scurried over the rooftops until he reached a point where he could look down on the gateway that led to the inner courtyard. The early evening air chilled, so he pulled his fur-lined tunic around his shoulders and buttoned it.

The young man's face was handsome and well defined with a strong chin, a straight nose, and dark eyes, and his curly black hair cascaded down to his shoulders. His teeth were white and straight, and his arms and chest were muscular. He was, in short, not deformed nor disproportionate, merely small, more properly classified as a midget, but in this time and this place, he was grouped with all others of dimunitive stature, and was labeled by his peers as a dwarf. His legs were strong, and he could scuttle about with speed when it was necessary to dodge the angry kicks of the cooks whose sweets he frequently stole in the monastery kitchens. But he realized without understanding that, despite his facial beauty and his keen intelligence, he was different, and somehow this difference made him less than other men.

Niccolo had been left at the door of another Carthusian monastery when he was three, and it had become evident that he was not like the other children. Over the years he had tried to imagine what and who his parents might be. Was his intelligence and handsome face of highborn origin? Was his father a wealthy lord who could not handle the disgrace of an unusual child? Or were his parents, like him, small and different? He knew he had been given the name of the saint upon whose day he had been abandoned, and, at fourteen, he had been brought here to the Certosa, because this monastery possessed a better library and the monks were skilled in Latin and Greek. It was evident the young man had a quick mind, and his rare ability to memorize whole pages, word perfect, had suggested that perhaps there was a place for the young man among the monks or, perhaps, at the university in Pavia. So his duties were principally attached to the library where he indexed the books and kept the reference files. The scholars found that he could, given the title or the general nature of the text, call to mind the exact location of the book among the hundreds of dusty, leather-bound volumes that filled five rooms.

Although the monks sometimes wished to consider Niccolo as a candidate for their order, both the young man and the Father Abbot knew the dwarf did not have "a vocation." His fantasies, fired by drawings and texts in the forbidden section of the library, rejected any capacity for abstinence, and his propensity for petty theft was a questionable asset for a man of the cloth. He was continually slipping sweets from the refectory and wine from the cellars. He reveled in the bawdy tales and songs exchanged by the quarrymen and the construction workers who were working on the new facade, and he insisted on repeating them to the shocked monks without invitation.

In short, as the Father Abbot often sighed over the little man, "The world is too much with you, Niccolo."

Now more visitors are coming, he thought.

On the one hand, the young man disliked visitors to the monastery, because they disrupted the disciplined, quiet routine which he enjoyed. Furthermore, he was sometimes paraded before the travelers as some sort of exotic creature that both fascinated and repelled them. Members of the nobility were especially cruel and occasionally made obscene speculation about his sexual abilities. One or two of the more brazen courtesans even petitioned the Father Abbot to see the young man nude, but the monk had quietly refused, saying such an action would be, at best, impolite, and, at worse, immoral. Consequently, in the past six years, as Niccolo had developed into manhood, the Father Abbot had approved the young man's request that he be permitted to stay in his cell or on the roof when visitors arrived, and Niccolo had appreciated this singular kindness.

Despite his reluctance to be showcased with the monastery, the curiosity of the nobles concerning the dwarf was occasionally matched by the little man's curiosity concerning the nobility. From his perch on the observation platform, Niccolo was always the first to see visitors arriving, and then he would sometimes scramble over the rooftop, down the narrow, winding staircases to where large, elaborate tapestries were hung before arched doorways to assure maximum privacy for the monks. He could peek around the edges of these tapestries without being seen and marvel at the embroidered silk and satin tunics of the noblemen and the elegant, ostentatious, high-waisted dresses of the ladies. These gowns always revealed more of the ivory shoulders and breasts of the ladies than deemed necessary or modest by the Father Abbot, but Niccolo found them exciting. He would gape at the abundance of jewels, glittering under the golden light of the candles and the oil lamps, and, in his dreams at night, he imagined himself adorned with the same silks and fur collars, ornamented with gold medallions and ruby rings, being fondled and clutched to the fair, bare breasts of the ladies.

But when he saw the duke's hunting party approaching, Niccolo decided he would have nothing to do with this particular assembly. He would avoid direct and personal contact with the duke of Milan whose serpentine standard was even now being advanced before the approaching company. He had heard terrible stories about the dark man and his court. He had heard the monks whisper accusations of how the duke, whom they all called Il Moro, had murdered—or ordered the murder of—the previous duke in order to be invested with the duchy of Milan by the Emperor Maximilian.

The Father Abbot had also recounted lurid stories of the Milanese court, hoping to teach Niccolo moral lessons through parables. He told of the strange doings of the artist-in-residence, Maestro Leonardo da Vinci, who would cut open the bodies of dead paupers for purposes the Father Abbot called "diabolical." He had been both fascinated and repulsed by the tales of the deep corruption and blatant immorality of the ladies and the courtesans, the intrigues and the deceptions and the secret crimes committed to gain a little power here, a small fortune there. These stories were considered a part of the dwarf's instructional program and were always linked to moral judgments and condemnations of the secular world of the aristocracy.

In addition to his regular lessons in Latin, Greek, and the "vulgar tongue," Italian, Niccolo was also being fortified with a strong moral sense of honor and propriety, although the Father Abbot himself admitted that he had no idea what future awaited the dwarf. The abbot knew that the intelligent and mischievous young man was considered imperfect and lowborn in a society where physical perfection and courtly manners were vital to social acceptance. He also knew that, beneath the court's polished and polite veneer of gentility and morality, there were ravenous worms of corruption and decadence, but he prayed that Niccolo, somehow, might be spared that revelation.

Earlier that afternoon Niccolo had snuck some of the new wine from the monastery cellars and had finished it. Now his muddled vision and thinking were urging him to ignore the approaching party, stay on the roof, and, perhaps, sleep, dreaming of ivory-skinned ladies who doffed their filmy chemises to dance for him. But there was a sound from the doorway, and Niccolo quickly nestled himself in his cozy, private corner under the thick canvas sheet near the unfinished cupola where he was hidden from anyone searching for the kitchen thief.

As the hunting party approached the monastery, the trumpeters and drummers heralded the arrival of the duke. The sudden cacophony caused Niccolo to peek out from his refuge beneath the canvas canopy to see which of the cooks had come searching for him and the missing wine. To his surprise he saw two quarrymen standing on the edge of the parapet, their backs to him, next to a large marble block. He slowly realized that the hunting party must be just outside the walls, so he was confused and surprised to see the taller of the two men suddenly take his hammer and pound a wooden wedge under the block, causing it to slide and tip.

Alarmed, Niccolo stood and screamed, "Stop!" He hoped he could make the two men aware that the block was in danger of falling on the hunting party just entering the Certosa below them, but his scream startled the shorter quarryman who wheeled abruptly, backing into the taller man who was thrown off balance. The heel of his right foot descended on a wedge which slid along the inclined scaffold. For a moment the tall man teetered between earth and sky, frantically groping for something with which to balance himself, but then, with a scream, he fell back and out of sight.

A fraction of a second later the marble block, freed from the bond of inertia, slid, tipped and fell.

Niccolo could not see, from where he was, if the marble or the quarryman had fallen on anyone, but from somewhere below he heard shouts, horses whinnying in fright, and vivid curses. His full attention was focused on the smaller man who had wheeled to find the source of the disruptive shout and now quickly drew a dagger from his sash. Niccolo did not clearly understand what was happening, but the sight of the quarryman with a weapon pointed at him caused the dwarf to prepare himself for an attack. The short man raced across the roof and hurled himself on the dwarf. Niccolo's strong arms managed to stop the blade from descending, and with a quick twist of his right leg, he turned the quarryman over and reversed their positions with the dwarf straddling his attacker. Then there was a cry, a sharp pain, and Niccolo was hurled into blackness and oblivion.

He regained his sight to find a circle of faces looking down at him, and he realized that he was prone on a table in the refectory.

"Lie still," said the Father Abbot. "You have been hurt."

Niccolo put a hand to his head and felt the sticky warmth of his own blood, but he managed to lift himself into a sitting position. Before and around him was a small congregation of monks, a man in black armor, a nobleman, some soldiers and a single lady. Beyond this group, gathered by the archway and held back by a line of mercenaries, was the rest of the hunting party.

Niccolo slowly focused on the tall, bearded man who was bending over him. The Father Abbott stood beside the table, looking worried and dismayed. There was also a nobleman, all in black, with a large diamond on his velvet cap whom Niccolo assumed to be the duke of Milan. The dark ruler had removed his falconing gloves revealing a ruby ring on his right index finger that was fitted with a cameo profile of Caesar.

"I found him on top of the other man," Sanseverino declared to all who listened. "There was no one else on the roof, and I had no way of telling who was with the assassin, so I hit both of them."

The bearded man dabbed at the dwarf's wound with a wet cloth. "A small laceration of the membranes," said Maestro Leonardo. "No sign of damage to the cord or nerves."

"Can you stand?" asked the duke, and Niccolo, trembling, a little sick from the wine and the realization that he had perhaps caused the death of someone, managed to get his feet under him and to stand on the table before the assembly.

The tall bearded man continued examining Niccolo. He put his two massive hands on either side of the dwarf's head and peeled back his eyelids with his thumbs. "My opinion is that there was merely a little bleeding." He released the dwarf and turned to the duke. "Still, I imagine Maestro Ambrogio would say the blood was 'bad' and prescribe a legion of leeches."

"Let us be gracious, Maestro," advised Il Moro. "Pray, do not insult my court physician when he is not here to defend himself."

The Maestro shrugged. "Still, my lord, it should be necessary for doctors, who are the guardians of the sick, to understand what life is, and what health is, and in what way a balance and harmony of these elements maintain life and health, and how, when these are out of harmony, they are ruined and destroyed. It is obvious that whoever has a good knowledge of these characteristics will be better able to heal than he who lacks them. When these elements are well understood, that is: what man is, what life is, what constitutes the temperament and health, he will also understand . . ."

Il Moro stopped the flood of explanation with a wave of his hand and concentrated his attention on the dwarf. "Yes, yes," he said. "But I am more concerned with what happened on the roof. Fortunately the marble fell on the very man who was attempting to drop it on us." Seeing the fear and anxiety in the dwarf's eyes, the duke took the opportunity to inquire gently, "Young sir, what were you doing on the roof?"

"I always go to the roof when visitors arrive," the dwarf replied.

"There was this empty wine container near him," Sanseverino declared, taking it from a guard and handing it to the Father Abbot.

The old monk shook his head in recrimination. "Niccolo, Niccolo. I've told you a hundred times . . ."

"Yes, Father Abbot," sighed the young man. "I know."

The old cleric shook his head again. "What happened up there, Niccolo? Were the two men alone?"

"I saw only the two," he murmured. "I saw the hunting party coming with my spyglass, but the wine—I finished it all, I guess. And, well, I thought I heard someone coming for me, so I hid. Then I saw the two quarrymen, and one of them was tipping this great marble block from the parapet. I thought, 'He doesn't know what he is doing. He's going to kill somebody below!' So I shouted to warn him. I didn't intend to hurt anyone. I just wanted to draw their attention, to make them realize that the marble was in a dangerous position." He looked around at the assembly. "I'm sorry." He looked pleadingly at the Father Abbott. "I'm not lying, Father Abbot," he said. "I swear before the Virgin . . ."

"He's not lying," intoned da Vinci. "It is common sense that if you wanted to kill someone by dropping a block of marble on them, you certainly wouldn't conscript someone so diminutive. I believe he did hide under the canvas used to protect the marble, because his hair, skin, and clothing are covered with Carrara dust."

"I sent four of my best men to Milan with the surviving assassin," the captain declared. "A few hours on the rack will have him singing for us. We'll find out who sent them."

"Are you certain you saw no one else on the roof, Niccolo?"

Niccolo still trembled, but he struggled to think, to work his way back to reality from the alcoholic haze. "No, there was no one else. When I first came—about two hours after midday—there were three or four quarrymen who had winched new marble to the roof. I didn't want to share the wine with them, so I waited until they were gone before I drank it, and then, when I heard someone coming, I thought they were after me, so I hid." Suddenly something flashed in the young man's memory. "But I've seen the tall one before, the one with the short, black beard. I remember, because he was unusually tall. There was no one as tall among the other workers." He glanced at da Vinci. "I am particularly conscious of heights," he explained.

Da Vinci nodded but did not smile.

Duke Ludovico stroked his beard. "Does anyone know the name of the dead assassin?"

"Alfredo Coelci," Niccolo announced.

The Father Abbott smiled at the young men. "Then that assuredly is his name. Niccolo has a remarkable memory, Your Highness. He remembers every word he reads and every word he hears."

"Ingenious," the Maestro quietly commented.

"Coelci is a quarryman, hired upon recommendation of the foreman who had used him on other projects," the boy offered. "I remember that from the workmen's register."

"Oh?" said Sanseverino. "And can you remember which master mason supplied the recommendation?"

"A master of Venice," Niccolo replied instantly.

"Ah," the condottiere exclaimed. "I knew it!" He wheeled on the duke. "What did I tell you? Venetians!"

Il Moro was silent for a moment, and then he said, "Galeazz, return to Milan and tell Bernardino that I want him to question this second assassin. Find out all you can about who may have sent him and this . . ." The duke turned again to Niccolo.

"Coelci," the boy declared at once. "Alfredo Coelci."

"Coelci," repeated the duke. "Have him question the second man, but do not kill him. I may want to put a few questions to him myself."

Sanseverino saluted and strode from the refectory, gesturing to two or three of his soldiers to follow him. The duke turned again to the dwarf, who, by standing on the table, was nearly of equal height. "I owe you a debt, Messer Niccolo," the dark ruler said softly. "I apologize for having dragged you from your rooftop retreat, but I will somehow make it up to you."

"Why not bring him to Milan?" the soft feminine voice

spoke again, and the duke turned to see the Countess Bergamini smiling at him across her sable muff. "The Gonzaga have introduced dwarfs into their courts, and they have proven themselves to be amiable and loyal servants. It is really quite fashionable for a beautiful woman to be accompanied by her dwarf. It makes the woman seem more beautiful by contrast, and some of your court women can use all the help available to them."

She saw the flash of annoyance in the duke's eyes. "Are you interested in acquiring a new servant, Countess?" he asked drily.

"Not I," the beautiful woman replied. "I could never support him on my poor husband's income. I thought he would be better received among your own court ladies. And the young man is handsome in his own right and would attract visitors to the court. Indeed, he would reduce Madonna Dorotea's cheetah to a mere curiosity."

The duke turned to the Father Abbot. "Who are the young man's parents?"

"Unknown, Your Highness," the monk replied. "He has been with our order since he was three. He is now nineteen."

"He is educated you said?"

"He is exceptional," the Father Abbott responded. "He has, as I told you, a remarkable memory, and he can read and write in Latin, Greek, and Italian."

"Indeed," said the duke as he smiled at Maestro Leonardo, "he betters you, Maestro." He turned back to the dwarf. "Our divine Leonardo comes from a small village in Tuscany. He is fascinated by subjects as varied as the flow of water over rocks to which muscles in a hand can be severed by a single stroke of a blade. He is a mathematician, sculptor, painter, musician, inventor, an amusing storyteller, and a dignified jester. He can also bend horseshoes with his bare hands. His god is logic, and his weapons are patience and perseverance. He has only two faults. He designs tricks and amusing games, but I have never seen him laugh, and he is only now beginning to teach himself Latin, the language of all civilized humanity. In this last regard, you surpass him."

The bearded man in the black cloak smiled and gave a slight cough. "Perhaps you could apprentice him to me, Your Highness. Rather than submit the young man to the humiliation of the court ladies who will tease and torment him, I could teach him the rudiments of perspective, both natural and accidental, and he could tutor me in Latin."

"I know perspective," snapped the dwarf, "both natural and accidental."

The duke smiled at the retort and waved his hand in dismissal once more, his ruby ring flashing in the candlelight. "You already have two young assistants, Maestro Leonardo, and Giacomo Salai gives me enough trouble with his thievery and debauchery. You also enjoy the company of Giulio Tedesco and Maestro Tommasso and a score of other parasites who constantly come to visit and work with you and inevitably stay half the year and devour my food and wine."

"Please, Your Highness," Niccolo suddenly pleaded. "Let me be a companion to one of the court ladies. I won't mind the humiliation. I promise you! I have heard of Maestro Leonardo. He will want to cut me open to see why I am so small."

"I know why you are so small," the Maestro replied, "both naturally and accidentally."

The duke laughed. "You have an ominous reputation, Maestro."

The bearded artist bent over the dwarf. "You should understand, young man, that there is the same difference between the representation of corporeal things by the poet and painter as between dismembered and intact bodies . . ."

Once again the duke interrupted. "Obviously this young gentleman would be happier as a companion to one of the ladies of the court. Let it rest at that."

The Father Abbot did not like Niccolo being discussed as if he were some commodity that could be bought and sold, and the dwarf read the anxiety in his eyes. "My lords and ladies," the cleric said softly, "any decision should be Niccolo's. He is not an animal or an artifact to be bartered for. If he is to leave the Certosa, it will have to be his decision."

Duke Ludovico nodded and again turned to the dwarf. "Young man, how would you like to enter my service? You will sleep in a soft, warm bed on linen sheets with woolen blankets and pillows of down. You will be provided with a splendid wardrobe especially designed for you: satins and brocades, leather boots, embroidered cloaks and tunics . . ."

"And a sword?" Niccolo pleaded. "A small one, of course, suitable for my size? If I had had a sword on the dome roof, I could have defended Your Highness better."

"A sword of course," smiled the duke. "It is only fitting that my protector be suitably armed. And perhaps a small jeweled dagger made especially to fit your hand—with a gold scabbard. You will eat the same food as I, dine from the same plate. You will be given a mount proportionate to your stature. You will be subservient only to your lady and myself, and only we will punish you if you disobey or annoy us. Is that pleasing to you?"

"Punishment of any kind is hardly pleasurable," Niccolo complained.

"The duke's wine cellar surpasses the Certosa's," the countess quietly observed.

Niccolo smiled at the lady. "Then it is satisfactory," he said softly. He caught sight of the Father Abbot from the corner of his eye and turned to him. "With your permission, Father Abbot."

"You have it, Niccolo," said the cleric. He frowned at the duke. "He will continue his studies?"

"Of course," heralded the duke. "We will return to the Castello Visconteo and then home to Milan. Have the young man ready to travel by week's end."

Impulsively Niccolo leaned toward the duke, raised Il Moro's hand to his lips and kissed the ruby ring.

"Ah, Niccolo," sighed the duke with a broad smile. "Perhaps I may finally have someone in my service who has no reason to kill me."

And he added with a laugh, "Yet."

During the next few days Niccolo prepared for his transfer to Milan and into the service of Ludovico the Moor. He said his farewells to those among the brotherhood whom he especially admired and loved, gathered and packed what few personal belongings he possessed, and received gifts from the Father Abbot, from the librarian, and from the principal cook.

Brother Pax, the librarian, presented the young man with two leather-bound books: a New Testament recently translated into the vulgar tongue, and a Greek text, *The Golden Sayings of Epictetus*.

"Epictetus was a slave," the aged monk informed him, "and deformed, a cripple, which some say was a result of bad treatment at the hands of his master. But he had some splendid advice for young men." The librarian opened the book but recited from memory: "Lose no time in adopting a standard of character and behavior for your own, Let silence be the general rule, or say only what is necessary and in few words. Enter conversations sparingly, avoiding such common topics as gladiators, horse races, athletes, food and drink. Above all, avoid talking of persons, either in praise or blame, or comparing one with another. Turn conversations your way by your own discourse, but if you find yourself among strangers, be silent."

In short, thought Niccolo, I should keep my eyes open and my mouth closed.

Brother Antonius, the overlord of the kitchen, gave him a basket of his favorite smoked meats and cheeses from the Certosa's supplies, and, at the same time, regaled him with tales of the culinary delights he would find in the duke's kitchens. "The venison," he declared, "will be cooked to rags and powdered with an exquisite ginger. Veal will be boiled with sage and suffocated under a glaze of cinnamon, cloves, and saffron, stiffened with eggs. There will be pastries . . ." The old kitchener stopped, and his tired eyes misted at the thought of what he himself could create with bottomless supplies and an unlimited variety of utensils. Then he walked away, murmuring to himself of "pate of carp" and "roasted whale tongue."

The abbot gave the youth a silver crucifix on a chain and assured him that the talisman could protect the dwarf from "vile temptations, seductions, and bodily harm."

Niccolo could not bring himself to inform the gracious and gentle superior that he fully expected temptations in the Milanese court, would probably succumb willingly to the seductions, and could handle himself fairly well when threatened with bodily harm if he received the promised dagger and sword.

In fact, he had only two genuine concerns about becoming part of the court of Il Moro.

The first was the duke himself who seemed to Niccolo to be a man possessed with a shadowed soul, mysterious and unpredictable to even those who knew and loved him. While his new master seemed to like him and would doubtless protect him, there was something about the man that suggested the winds could change direction in an instant and blow him away.

The second was Maestro Leonardo da Vinci. Brother Theophilus referred to the famed, notorious, bearded man as "the devil's consort," and Brother Pax said the court painter held "blasphemous and heretical notions," had twice been tried for homosexual activities and twice been exonerated, and had dedicated his life to exploring "the dark secrets" of magic and witchcraft.

Tangible threats did not frighten the young dwarf, but magic terrified him. Like most men, he was reluctant to challenge the unknown, and when Maestro Leonardo had examined his hands and skin, Niccolo felt that the tall man was seeing things within him that the dwarf did not want revealed. He imagined that the Maestro had some remarkable ability to see beneath the skin, the flesh, into the very core of light that was his soul.

Then he remembered a warning of Brother Fraternum. "Some men, appearing like all others, have the ability to suck the soul from the young and impressionable, and make them slaves to their diabolical ends."

He did not sleep that night.

Chapter 2
The Countess and the Court

"Do you not see . . .
that it is a very beautiful face
which arrests passersby
and not their rich adornments? . . .
As you adorn your figures with costly gold . . .
do you not see the resplendent beauty of youth
loses its excellence
through excessive devotion to ornamentation?"

Leonardo da Vinci "On Painting"

On the third day following the duke's departure, a quartet of tailors appeared at the monastery door, took some rapid measurements of the dwarf, and immediately disappeared. They reappeared on the fifth day with a squad of mercenaries in the livery of the Sforzas. They brought with them four pairs of woolen hose, six chemises of silk, three doublets of brocaded satin, a velvet cap, laces for belts, a traveling cloak, two pairs of shoes, and a pair of fine, knee-high leather boots. They picked and pulled at the new wardrobe while Niccolo dressed himself, a right he had insisted upon, and they complained and bickered and shook their heads as they made an adjustment here, took a tuck there, and labored over the entire procedure. Finally the dwarf smiled as they buckled a wide leather belt around his waist, attached a sword and scabbard exactly proportionate to his size on the right side, and, as promised, a jeweled dagger that was fastened to his left. The remaining clothes were packed in two leather cases bearing the serpent crest of the Sforza.

"The fashioners must take pains," explained the tall captain of the mercenaries to the newly adorned young man. "The duke once had a tailor imprisoned for three years for spoiling a doublet of crimson silk."

Finally, Niccolo was mantled in the velvet cap and the traveling cloak lined with fur, and he was escorted, amid tears and huzzahs and last-minute warnings, to the impressive coach and four that awaited him at the entrance of the monastery. It was a magnificent dark carriage riding on great curved metal springs with large wheels trimmed in silver and circled with iron, but the insignia on the doors was not the Sforza serpents but an apple tree on a mount to which was tethered a hound.

"It is the crest of my lord's father, Francesco Sforza," explained the escorting officer. "You remember the old poem? 'Let the sleeping dog lie,' said Sforza . . ."

The dwarf finished it. " 'If you touch him, he will tear you limb from limb. Too late, then, to cry.' "

The officer laughed, but Niccolo felt himself tremble.

After a repetitious litany of prayers and supplications by the Father Abbot over his bent head, the young dwarf climbed inside the velvet-upholstered carriage and had a large fur throw tucked around his legs. The escorting captain seated himself opposite the young man, struggled to position his polished scabbard and sword so it would not push up against his ribs and finally decided to remove it from his sash.

Nested warmly, if not comfortably for his feet did not reach the floor to give him stability, Niccolo bounced between delight and dismay as the coach began to sway and bob violently along the old Roman road.

The coach raced into Pavia, past the duomo, past the huge bronze equestrian statue in the piazza before it. It sped past the church of San Teodoro and the convent of Santa Margareta.

"It is also a brothel you know," Niccolo informed the captain.

"The convent is a brothel?" echoed the captain. "How do you know? Who told you?"

"The monks at the Certosa," Niccolo explained.

The captain smiled and said nothing, but the unspoken thought hung heavily inside the small coach.

How did the monks know?

Niccolo gasped at the brief sight of the huge Castello Visconteo, the duke of Milan's home when he was in the city, and the dwarf remembered that the Father Abbot had once told him the castle contained a two-story kitchen and a large indoor bathing pool. The coach stopped at the docks where the boats and barges traveled east or west on the Po, or northwest to Lake Maggiore or to the east fork of the Ticino, and here the horses were unhitched and the carriage was loaded aboard a barge with its escort of mercenaries.

The river transit was boring. Niccolo drew the damask curtains and drifted into a brief sleep.

It was nearly sunset when he awoke to find the coach at the Darsena docks outside the Porta Ticinese, the southern gate to Milan, a muddy marsh at the head of the Naviglio Sforzesca. A fresh team of four horses was harnessed, and the coach rattled off the barge and under the gateway cut into the great wall of russet brick. Niccolo stared from the coach window at the battlements and the tall bell towers now summoning the faithful to vespers. They stood like gigantic sentries silhouetted against the twilight sky. The young dwarf tried to absorb everything as the coach raced through one square after another. Occasionally he caught glimpses of the noses of the bronze cannon that jutted into the street from the porticoes of the arms factories.

Everywhere there were three and four-story buildings, taller than the old, magnificent trees surrounding the Certosa. There were shops of perfumers and confectioners, their aromas scenting the air with flowers and sugar, now being closed for the day. Groups of wicked-looking men still gambled at cards before the basilica Sant'Ambrogio, and sharp-eyed women, readied for their evening merchandising, stood in clusters of two or three and glared at the coach as it passed. One yelled something that the dwarf could not hear, but the comment drew laughter from the whores and the gamblers as the coach raced on. Niccolo caught brief views of the numerous arcades of goldsmiths and potters, separated from the arched entranceways by heavy iron chains strung between stone columns to keep dogs and other undesirables from blocking the approaches.

Now and again Niccolo caught sight of small clusters of brawny young toughs hired by the shopkeepers to keep order and to warn away peddlers and panhandlers. They stood ready to accompany to their homes their masters whose purses bulged with the days receipts.

Niccolo gasped as the coach rambled past the facade of sculptured marble of the duomo, the largest in Italy, and like the Certosa, still unfinished. Finally the coach turned from the Piazza del Duomo, passed through a short tunnel connecting the two gatehouses, and entered a cobbled courtyard. A great wooden portcullis, pointed and capped with iron, closed behind them, swallowing the carriage, horses, and passengers whole.

The young man was assisted in embarking from the carriage by the captain of the mercenaries and two servants who rushed to his side. He had only a moment to look about him at the gray stone walls that embraced the inner court and did not recognize the carved crest above the tall doors of the palace. He was quickly escorted through a large foyer ablaze with candles and dozens of oil lamps, up a circular staircase and down a corridor lined with silent sentries of burnished armor and files of live guards who stood as rigid as the empty metal sentinels. The dwarf had only a moment to glance at the frescoes depicting near-nude gods and goddesses cavorting under olive trees.

At the end of the corridor, illuminated by two elaborate, crystal candlebra, was a portrait of the beautiful young woman whom Niccolo immediately recognized as the outspoken lady at the Certosa. In the portrait her long delicate fingers held a restless ermine, and her face was turned as if she were looking at someone who had just entered the room to the right of the painter.

Niccolo suddenly realized that the livery of the stiff-backed sentries and the accompanying servants did not match the colors of the mercenaries or of the captain who had escorted him to Milan, but the dwarf was not given time to consider this observation as the two servants pushed open a tall door decorated with ivory-colored frescoes and propelled him into a small antechamber.

The lady in the room was attired in a loose-fitting dressing gown of burnished gold that revealed her ivory shoulders and, Niccolo observed, an immodest amount of her breasts. Her head was circled by a gold velvet band that had a large ruby brooch centered on her forehead. Two gold rings, one containing a diamond and the other a ruby, winked at him in the candlelight. Her small feet were encased in scarlet, fur-lined slippers, and her scent, lilac, permeated the small room.

"Welcome, Niccolo," said the Countess Bergamini as she came toward him. "Welcome to the Palazzo del Verme."

In the kitchens of the Castello Sforzesco at the other edge of Milan, the tall, gaunt servant glanced cautiously around him and then stepped into the shadows with the ragged vagabond who was devouring food charitably supplied by the duke's chamberlain.

"Dino, your cousin is dead," whispered the vagabond.

"Where?" asked the servant. "How?"

"It has something to do with an incident at the Certosa," the vagabond explained. "No one is saying what happened, but it involved your cousin and another. The accomplice was brought here three days ago. He must be in your dungeons."

The skeletal servant gave a small moan. "Poor Alfredo," he mourned. "He was the pride of my mother's sister. He used to carry me on his shoulders when we were children." Suddenly the tall kitchen servant grew angry. "Alfredo would never kill anyone unless he had been insulted. There is more to this than meets the eye, eh? You know what I think? I think the Moor had him murdered for his own purposes!"

"Why?" the vagabond asked and bit into the shank of meat.

"How would I know?" growled the servant. "Who knows what craziness the rich dream up?" He crossed to the archway and lifted the key to the wine cellars from its peg. "Poor Alfredo," he said quietly.

At that moment in the Palazzo del Verme, the countess glided across the thick rug toward the dwarf, took his right hand, and led him to a chaise placed near a table containing a flagon and two silver goblets.

"You must forgive me for abducting you this way," the lady pleaded, "but there are some important matters I need to discuss with you." She gestured to the two servants who exited the room, closing the tall doors behind them. "You are not expected at the Castello Sforzesco until tomorrow morning, and I thought you might like to refresh yourself, have a good night's rest and a little nourishment before you were formally introduced to the court, so I bribed the captain to bring you here first."

"This is not the palace of Duke Ludovico?" asked Niccolo.

"Oh no, dear boy," the countess enlightened him with a warming smile. "The duke's castle sits within the protecting arms of a semicircle of elaborate buildings and faces a park of four hundred meters on each side. It is as big as any four palaces placed together. It is surrounded by high walls and moats as deep and as wide as rivers. It contains enormous courtyards, marbled stables, and a zoo filled with wild and exotic animals. The duke's private park is nearly as large and as verdant as the Lombard countryside, and his castle has towering, white-columned arcades with pink terra-cotta bordering white windows." She gestured briefly, and Niccolo thought, unhappily, around the room. "No, my dear Niccolo, this is my husband's own little, humble palace, modest and unimposing, but—comfortable enough."

Servants appeared with silver trays laden with sweets and small cuts of meats, cheeses, and delicacies which they placed on the table beside the chaise and then backed from the room. The countess placed large downy pillows around the dwarf seated, nervously, on the chaise. Then she, herself, served him as she talked.

"Master Niccolo, you are going to be in a position where you might be of great service to your lord, the duke, and to me," the countess said softly. "I have learned that you will be placed in the service of Madonna Valentina Gaddi, mistress to Galeazzo di Sanseverino, and I would be remiss in my duty as a virtuous woman if I did not warn you against this whore who is shameless."

Niccolo was surprised to hear the word "whore" from the delicate lips of a fine lady.

"Like a sapling," the lady continued her warning, "Madonna Valentina bows and bends to any passing wind that wishes to caress her. She wears no underlinen, and her bed has entertained more gentlemen than the duke's banquet hall. Even before the death of the 'Illustrissima'—which is how my lord referred to his late wife—Madonna Valentina was reported to have serviced the duke himself, once on a library desk, twice in the water closet, and occasionally in the chapel confessional! It was an open scandal and undoubtedly contributed to the duchess's demise."

The countess noticed the look of shocked surprise on the dwarf's face. "But you must also understand, Niccolo, that there are different standards applied to a duke. He is above the laws of morality that are imposed on lesser men, and, in spreading the bowed legs of Madonna Valentina, he cannot be considered to have been dishonoring his wife. Indeed, he worshipped the lady. Even now he uses Beatrice's symbol, a carnelian, as his own official seal. You must understand that the moral code of the Milanese court is, how shall I put it? Unusual."

She fed him another delicacy. "The real reason you were brought here is that I wished to inform you that the duke is in great danger." She raised a goblet of wine to the dwarf's lips and continued. "The attempt on his life at the Certosa was merely an overture. The real threat will come from someone close to him, someone within the court. I do not know, as yet, who that traitor may be, but my own agents say it is someone who romantically refers to himself as the Griffin. Very melodramatic, and a bit too theatrical for my taste, but, for reasons of my own, it is imperative that I protect the duke from this assassin. You see, Il Moro has proposed an archbishop's mitre for our ten-year-old son, and I am determined to keep the duke alive to protect and promote Cesare."

Niccolo was surprised. "A ten-year old archbishop?"

The beautiful lady laughed. "Oh, of course. You've been in a clerical world, haven't you? I hate to shock you so soon, my young friend, but any clerical position in Italy is for sale. The price currently for a cardinal's cap is, I believe, one hundred thousand ducats. We are inundated with the scarlet. Anyone, absolutely anyone, can be a prince of the church if he has the means to pay for it."

Niccolo was mildly surprised that his monastic world of the Certosa was so unlike this domain of unethical and worldly clergy, but he had been warned. He also did not understand what precisely the countess expected of him, but he accepted another sip of the dark-red wine which was stronger and more full-bodied than that from the Certosa cellar. The countess placed another dainty between the dwarf's lips, and he surrendered himself to the ecstasy of exquisite chocolate.

"I will do anything I can," he said slowly as he chewed the soft sweetness, "to protect my lord."

"Good!" the countess exclaimed. "I knew you were a man of superior intelligence. Now, I am going to tell you a little secret. There is a hidden passageway running through the castle. It can best be described as, well, as a path of discretion. When he designed the building, the first Sforza, Francesco, included this narrow, secret corridor stretching from his own chambers to the public square outside. It was to be a quick means of escape if the castle came under seige, and Duke Francesco used it to leave with no one knowing. Ludovico only discovered it when the contractor presented an unpaid bill that his father had neglected to honor. He had the contractor extend and enlarge the passage, added spy holes set low into the wainscoting so they were almost invisible from the opposite side, and then he had hidden doors constructed in—ah—certain rooms. Frankly, he used this passage to visit the court ladies who caught his eye. Late at night Il Moro would suddenly appear at the lady's bedside. Later, when the women were asleep, he would as magically disappear although the doors remained barred and guarded. It contributed a great deal to his reputation, suggesting he had made a pact with the devil and had been given the power to appear and disappear at will. As you may imagine, this was an ability which titillated the ladies and made seduction even easier. Ludovico also wisely kept the passage secret, because he knew the ladies and gentlemen of the court would use it to better judge the naked physical attributes of prospective lovers, and the rise in traffic would pose problems. So, to the best of my knowledge, its existence is known only to Ludovico; his chief of security, Bernardino da Corte; and myself. Il Moro doesn't know that I know of it. I discovered the passage, because once, when he thought I was asleep, I saw him move the medallion on the walls of my bedchamber and a door appear. Later, I explored and used it."

Niccolo was rapidly drowning in this sea of talk about secret passageways and anonymous assassins, purchased cardinalships and the indiscretions of Madonna Valentina, but more insights flowed from the countess as she fed him bits of dark chocolate and cinnamon.

"You will find the doors to these passageways marked by

large medallions of the Sforza symbol, a coiled serpent. Turn the serpent, and the doors will open. Remember. Trust no one, no one at all, in the Castello Sforzesco. Only I have the duke's interests at heart, and only I am in a position to protect him without his knowing it, because I am removed from the court and the Whisperers. I can take action from here without arousing everyone and warning the assassin."

Niccolo wanted the lady to explain why she was removed from the court and who the Whisperers were, but the countess wiped the dwarf's mouth with a linen cloth and replaced the goblet on the tray. The young man was both excited and wary of the lady and her reception, but he reasoned, as well as he could under the enticing circumstances, that any service that helped protect his new master would be in keeping with his new position at court.

"It is better for everyone," the countess continued, "if my role in this little game is kept secret. If the real assassin knew of my interest, it could put both me and my son in jeopardy." She placed another tidbit in his mouth. "Do you understand what I am saying, Niccolo?"

"Yes, Countess," he replied, savoring the tang of the cinnamon.

"Good," the lady smiled at him. "You will be rewarded, of course. The chamberlain of the castle considers departing with any of the duke's wealth equivalent to having his penis shortened; so, although you will wine and dine well, have comfortable quarters and wear exquisite clothes, there will be a scarcity of florins for your own use. The duke prefers his court to be dependent upon him. However, I have one or two friends in the court who remember and respect me, and through them, I will see to it that you receive a suitable purse every fortnight."

Niccolo, confused and floundering in the flood of information, lied. "I understand," he said.

"Every second Sunday you will go with the court to attend Mass at the basilica Sant'Ambrogio. One of the court ladies will share her hymnal with you. You will insert whatever information you have for me within the pages, and the lady will see that it is passed to me. Write down anything unusual that you may see or hear, no matter how trivial it may appear to you. Do you understand?"

Niccolo nodded, and then suddenly, to his complete surprise and momentary alarm, the countess took one of the small cakes, placed it between her own teeth, leaned forward and placed it between the dwarf's lips. At the same time, the dwarf felt a hand groping between his legs.

"My," the countess exclaimed as she quickly drew back. "You have come armed, my small friend! And with such a delightful little sword!"

Then she gave a small laugh, suddenly rose, and swept from the room.

In the antechamber at the Castello Sforzesco the great doors swung open and the duke sailed into the room, dismissed the small army of courtiers following him, and anchored at his large, dark desk. After a moment, the door opened again and a perspiring, bearded gentleman in a gray tunic and hose entered behind a cardinal in full clerical regalia. Il Moro rose, came around the table, nodded to his two brothers and genuflected to kiss the ring of the cardinal.

"Eminence," he intoned solemnly.

"Ludovico," replied the cardinal, drawing the duke to his feet and embracing him.

Il Moro motioned the cardinal to one of the two chairs placed before the desk and turned his attention to the other guest whom he embraced.

"Giovanni," he smiled.

"Brother," murmured Giovanni.

The duke motioned Giovanni to the other chair and then seated himself behind the desk. "I sent for some refreshments."

Giovanni did not acknowledge the courtesy. In a moment

he was on his feet and before the desk. "I know you are very busy, brother, so I will come directly to the point. That lecherous bastard on the throne of Peter wants to use his daughter, my wife, to advance his causes. He had at least three suitors waiting to hop into bed with her, including an Orsini, a Riario, and even that antique, Antonello di Sanseverino, exiled prince of Salerno and uncle to your own captain-general."

"You might mention the pope's preference," added the cardinal. "It is Alphonse of Aragon, and the union would establish a bond with Spain and the Catholic rulers."

"But first the old lecher must arrange some grounds for declaring my marriage to Lucrezia invalid," Giovanni whined.

"Can he?" asked the duke.

"Of course not," Giovanni insisted. "We were married under the strict tenets of both Church and civil law! But that won't stop Rodrigo Borgia. He has already prepared a canonical court to pronounce Lucrezia a virgin! Imagine! A virgin!"

The duke tried to hide his smile. "Is she—virginal?"

"Don't be ridiculous," the lord of Pesaro exploded. "The lady wasn't a virgin when I married her! You've heard the rumors! She supposedly has slept with her own brothers as well as her father!"

The seated cardinal raised a gloved hand to his lips and gave a small cough. When he had the attention of his brothers, he said quietly, "In deference to my position in the Curia, brother, I would appreciate it if you did not give credence to these infamous lies against the pontiff."

"Lies?" roared Giovanni wheeling on the cleric. "Lies? God's blood, Ascanio, the Vatican orgies are scandalous!"

"We are family here," the duke said softly. "And I am raising my own children to give due reverence to the holy pontiff, the vicar of God." He then turned to the cardinal. "But I think, Ascanio, we can acknowledge that the current pope is not a saint. What was it Machiavelli recently said? 'The Church has deprived Italy of religion'?"

The cardinal shrugged. "There is not one single witness to any alleged incest between the pontiff and his daughter. Let us give the devil his due."

"Of course there are no witnesses," bellowed Giovanni. "Where could they be? Hiding under the bed? And who would come forth to say they witnessed such a thing?"

The duke raised a hand in restraint. "The pope's perversions are innumerable but irrelevant," he said softly. "You say he wants your marriage to Lucrezia annulled, Giovanni. How does he propose to do that?"

There was a long pause before Giovanni quickly resumed his seat and murmured, "Impotence."

The duke leaned across the table and placed a hand behind his ear.

"Please?"

"Impotence!" bellowed Giovanni. "He wants me to plead impotence! That would make his daughter at least technically a virgin, and she would be free to marry someone more suitable for the Borgia ambitions!"

"Impotence?" the duke repeated to his brother's obvious discomfort and annoyance. "Is that possible, Giovanni?"

Once again the lord of Pesaro was on his feet. "What do you take me for, Ludovico? Of course not!" He turned to appeal to the cardinal. "My god, my first wife, Maddalena da Gonzaga, died in childbirth! How does the pope imagine she became pregnant? Another immaculate conception?" He turned again to Il Moro and leaned against the table. "The Gonzaga themselves realize the absurdity of such an accusation. They have even offered me another woman of their family if Lucrezia divorces me!"

"Very generous," smiled the cardinal, "since they have a dozen bitches in their kennels, salivating for a stud."

The duke dismissed the comment with a stroke of his hand. "So what do you intend to do about all this, Giovanni?"

"Fight it, of course! The old son-of-a-bitch really only wants his daughter for himself . . . !"

"Giovanni . . ." warned the cardinal.

"It's true!"

"It's possible," corrected the cardinal, "but absurd. Why would the pontiff need to bed his own daughter? You know yourself he has his choice of literally hundreds of women, and there is always his favorite mistress, Vannozza Cattanei, who mothered most of his illegitimate children. Why would the Holy Father want his own daughter?"

"Why does he want the Romagna?" stormed Giovanni. "Or the estates of the Orsini? Or Naples? Because he wants everything! Everything! He wants power! I really think he ordered his bastard, Cesare, to murder me as he murdered his own brother . . ."

"That was never proven, Giovanni," the cardinal insisted.

"Of course not, Ascanio!" Giovanni wheeled on him. "Who would dare to testify against Cesare? He'd have them killed within the hour! But I know the same night Juan was murdered, Lucrezia sent word I, too, was in danger, so I immediately fled to Pesaro. Indeed, in retaliation for warning me, the pope sent Lucrezia into confinement at the convent of San Sisto."

"Well, I remain confused, Giovanni," said Il Moro. "What do you wish me to do about all this? Do you want me to sign a testimonial affirming that my brother can still raise his prick?"

"Do whatever you can!" pleaded the duke's brother. "You are duke of Milan! You have been invested in a fief of the Hapsburg emperor! Your own niece is empress!"

"The Hapsburgs would most certainly stand clear of this mess, Giovanni. And, to be blunt with you, the French king has negotiated accords with France and Spain which have freed him to attack me. The bastard has drawn up a treaty with Venice which partitions Milanese territories. The point, my brother, is that war is inevitable. You must understand that, under these circumstances, I need all the friends I can muster. I do not wish to antagonize the pope, because I may very well have need of his armies."

Giovanni paled and wiped at his forehead with a linen handkerchief. "But—what am I to do?" He fell back into his chair.

"My god! Impotence!"

Far to the south, the small wagon stage of I Comici Buffoni had been erected in the Piazza del Duomo in Parma. The troupe's wheeled two-story structure was anchored between the large stone lions that guard the great doors to the cathedral. The plot outline for the afternoon was based on a legend that the Benedictines of Parma created potions in their pharmacy that could cure anything and work miracles.

On the stage, Turio, as the aged Pantalone, wobbled and wheezed his way around the small playing area, comically coughing and hacking to the amusement of the townspeople gathered there. After a moment, the curtains parted behind him, and Marco Torri appeared as Doctor Graziano, a tall, thin apparition in professorial black. Unseen by Pantalone, the doctor glided silently toward the old miser and suddenly bellowed in his left ear, *"Obscurus fio!"*

It was doubtful that many in the audience recognized the quotation from Horace, but the effect on Pantalone, and the crowd, would have been the same had the good doctor announced, "Your upper lip has been sucked into your left nostril!" The old miser leaped in alarm, and the viewers shrieked with laughter, and when Pantalone turned and began to beat at the physician with his soft cap, the crowd urged him to even bloodier reprisal.

Finally the laughter faded, and Turio glared at the doctor through his green-tinted half-mask with the large drooping nose and grumbled, "Yes, doctor? What do you want?"

Doctor Graziano drew himself up to his full height and intoned, "I have come at the request of your wife, Colombina."

"Is she ill?" inquired the old miser. "It's so hard to tell from her customary pallor."

"No," declared the doctor. "She is complaining of you."

"Well, the feeling is mutual."

"She says you do not sleep with her anymore."

"She's right. She farts in her sleep and snores like a camel."

"I don't mean that," the doctor continued, searching noisily through his bag of outlandish instruments and emerging with an absurdly large bellows. "She says you—well, you haven't been doing your duty."

"What?" asked Pantalone, suspiciously eyeing the bellows.

"She says you haven't been servicing her."

Pantalone shrugged and inched away from the doctor and the threatening bellows. "Well, it's true." Almost in a whisper he added, "I'm impudent."

"No, no, no," Doctor Graziano insisted. "You can't service her. Therefore you are impotent."

"I can but I won't," Pantalone countered. "Therefore I'm impudent!"

The skeletal physician shook his head and extracted a huge container of brackish green liquid from his bag. "Colombina says you can't."

"Well, I can," the old man snapped. "If you doubt me, go ask the Widow Basalari."

"The Widow Basalari is dead," announced the mock physician as he filled the bellows from the jar of green liquid.

"What do you think killed her?" responded Pantalone. "I was too much for the dear, generous woman. Six, seven times a day!" He made an obscene gesture that was immediately recognized by the audience who howled in both amusement and derision.

"The widow died of stomach distress," intoned the doctor, now stalking Pantalone with the bellows.

"Because I spent so much time pressed upon it," Pantalone crowed.

"She ate tainted meat," insisted the physician.

"Women who die of eating tainted meat, don't expire with a smile on their face."

The doctor continued to back Pantalone around the small stage. "Colombina says you can no longer salute the flag."

"Not when I'm bored with the band," wheezed the old man. "It's difficult to be patriotic when the music is a dirge."

"Colombina says your willow is bent," Doctor Graziano persisted.

"I'll bend my willow up her bony ass!" roared Pantalone. "I'm as good a man as I ever was!"

"Yes," agreed the physician. "That seems to be the problem."

Suddenly Pantalone stopped backtracking around the stage and stood his ground. "But, even if what she says is true, what do you propose to do about it, you breeder of imbeciles?"

Marco grinned beneath his pale half-mask. "I have an elixir created by the Benedictines of Parma," he said, and the audience responded with cheers and applause. "It will make a new man of you."

"I don't want to be a new man," whined Pantalone. "I'm not finished with the old one yet."

But his pleas were in vain, as the doctor leaped, pinned the poor old miser to the stage floor and squirted the liquid into Pantalone's mouth and over his masked face, neck, and chest.

"Hell fire!" erupted the old man when he was freed and sat upright on the edge of the stage. "I'd rather have the disease than the cure!"

A wave of laughter swept over the small stage and a shower of coins clattered at the feet of the actors. Piero, the professional, quickly glanced at the small denominations.

Again no gold or silver, he said to himself. We'll never make it to Bologna. We should reconsider Milan.

In the Castello Sforzesco in Milan, Giovanni Sforza wailed that he did not deserve such treatment at the hands of the

Roman pontiff, and the duke rose and came around the desk to face his brother.

"The pontiff of Rome says you are impotent. You say you are not. Very well. Prove it. Send word to your wife, Lucrezia, to meet you at some neutral place. Nepi perhaps. Sleep with her, and I will see to it that representatives of both families secretly watch."

"Are you mad?" murmured the pale supplicant. "What will you do, Ludovico, sell invitations? Am I to perform for an audience of Borgias and Sforzas? And what if I can't—I mean, what if—?" The duke smiled. "God's blood," pleaded Giovanni, "how can I be expected to—to be—aroused—when I know there are a dozen eyes watching behind the tapestries? And probably making wagers!"

Il Moro shrugged and returned to his chair. "Well, how about this? Sleep with one of my ladies of the court, and I will have one of the Borgia family watching. I presume you can have an erection with only a single set of eyes watching? You've done as much at my festivals."

"One Borgia?" Giovanni asked. "Which one?"

"I don't know. The surviving Juan. The cardinal of Monreale."

"Unhappily, no," the cardinal interrupted. "Juan Borgia has syphilis and has been sent away until he is cured. I understand it will take about two years." The cleric stirred himself and rose unsteadily to his feet. "But the Holy Father, himself, has suggested a compromise. If Giovanni will only claim a—temporary—deficiency due to—oh, I don't know—an evil spell, the pontiff will permit him to retain all of his daughter's dowry."

The duke gave a small chuckle and asked, "An evil spell? My god! Cast by whom may I ask?"

"Who cares?" snapped the cardinal. "Pick a potential witch. Isabella d'Este perhaps."

"The marquesa? Why the marquesa?"

"Why not? It would cause trouble for two of our enemies,

the marquesa and Venice, because her husband is captain-general of the Venetian armies. The fact that the pope believes the marquesa is a witch might make the doge think twice about invading our territories from the east."

"I don't think we can make anyone believe it."

"Who has to really believe it?" declared the cardinal. "If Giovanni signs a pledge to an evil spell that rendered him temporarily impotent, and the pope sanctions the annulment, who cares if anyone believes it?"

Il Moro shook his head. "I have a better idea. Why not say the marriage was invalid, because Lucrezia was already betrothed to Cherubino Don Juan de Centelles? I recall such an arrangement having been formally announced and a dowry of one hundred thousand Valencian florins being exchanged."

The cardinal shook his head and returned to his chair. "Yes, but two months later the pope changed his mind and betrothed his daughter to Don Gaspare d'Aversa. Then that was cancelled before the year ended while the pontiff considered higher bids."

Giovanni, who had remained silent during the interchange between his brothers, now suddenly murmured, "How much?"

"What?" asked the cardinal.

"You said the pope would let me keep the dowry if I swore I was under an evil spell. How much?"

The cardinal shrugged. "What was the dowry? Thirty thousand ducats, wasn't it?"

"I know that!" snapped the lord of Pesaro. "Damned insulting! If I'm to plead to impotence—even temporary—and caused by a witch—the pope will have to salt the stew a little."

The cardinal smiled. "How much?"

Giovanni approached the table. "I hear he is offering one hundred thousand ducats if Alfonse of Aragon marries my wife. He can afford ten thousand more florins to have his daughter's marriage annulled. I mean, how much is my honor worth?"

"To the pope? Nothing."

Giovanni's face turned into a mask of suppressed anger and insult. "Really? Then perhaps the old bastard can be persuaded to offer a little something for my silence."

There was a momentary lull. After a while Il Moro leaned on the desk and inquired softly, "Your silence, brother?"

"I am not as stupid as they think," Giovanni said smugly. "I have my own sources, and I happen to know that if Lucrezia is examined by a canonical court to prove she is still a virgin, they will have a hard time of it." He waited, pleased with the expressions on his brothers' faces, before he finished his declaration. "The lady is pregnant."

The duke threw up his hands. "My god, Giovanni! If she's pregnant, then you are saved! An impotent man can't have a pregnant wife!"

"He can, if the child isn't *his*!" snapped Giovanni. "And it isn't! When the pope sent his daughter away to San Sisto, she had the liberty to engage in a little lechery of her own. It seems there was a young Spanish chamberlain whom the pope used as an intermediary between the Vatican and Lucrezia. From all reports he is handsome enough, if you like the swarthy, greasy-haired type who reek of violets. They call him Perotto, and, as emissary from the pope, he had access to my wife's private apartments as well as her privates, and now the bitch is with child."

The cardinal and the duke exchanged glances. "Mother of God!" the duke said softly. "Does the pontiff know?"

"Of course not," replied Giovanni. "Otherwise, would he prepare a canonical court to inspect the lady?"

"Are you certain this information is correct?" pressed the cardinal.

"My source is Madonna Maria Chigi, a young Genoese lady-in-waiting of your own court."

"Madonna Chigi?" echoed the duke. "How did she learn of Lucrezia's pregnancy?"

"She was at the convent, too," the pale man informed him. "I thought you knew. Your late wife sent her there on some sort of pilgrimage, I suppose, just before she died."

"A pilgrimage?" inquired Il Moro. "And so long ago? Why? To whom? There are no relics to my knowledge in the convent of San Sisto. What was the nature of this pilgrimage?"

Giovanni shrugged. "I have no idea. The girl stayed there through the summer and just recently returned to your court. But it's not important or relevant to my problem, Ludovico. What are we going to do about this forced annulment?"

"I don't like being linked with this situation at San Sisto," Il Moro snapped angrily. "If Lucrezia Borgia is pregnant by a Spanish chamberlain that will ruin the pope's plans for a canonical court decision of virginity! Do you think that will remain secret? My God, when they examine Madonna Lucrezia, they'll know at once that someone had her at San Sisto, and they'll learn a young woman of my court was there at the same time! That ties her indiscretion to my court. The pope may even consider me an accomplice to Madonna Lucrezia's seduction, and they'll paint my court as a bacchanalian cesspool! That's all the pope will need to join with the French to overthrow me! And I told you I needed his friendship!"

"But I didn't . . ." mumbled Giovanni. "I wouldn't—"

"I'll tell you what you'll do, Giovanni!" roared Il Moro pounding the table. "You will sign this paper declaring yourself impotent, and you will keep the pope's money and retire quietly to Pesaro. You will affirm there is no more steel in your sword, for whatever reason provided, and you will keep your mouth shut about everything you're heard about your wife's pregnancy! Am I clear?"

"But—"

"Am I clear?" thundered the duke.

"Yes. Of course, brother."

"I better return to Rome," grumbled the cardinal rising from his chair. "I should be there when the pontiff learns of this."

"Yes," the duke agreed softly. "Go immediately and reassure the Holy Father that neither I nor any member of my court had anything to do with this seduction of his daughter! I have an audience with my envoy to the French which will take up most of my afternoon, and then tomorrow morning I am expecting the arrival of a new addition to my court, but I will send da Tuttavilla to the Vatican as soon as possible to reassure him."

With that the duke streamed from the room, gathering the cardinal and the disturbed brother in his wake.

That night Niccolo slept in a large, pillowy bed in a small room of the Palazzo del Verme where a fire was kept roaring in the grate until the morning light. From time to time he was dimly aware of a parade of young women floating silently into the room, feeding the fire, refilling the pitcher with fresh water on the table beside the bed, checking the chamber pot, and bending over him briefly, theoretically to determine if his breathing was regular and if he appeared to be resting comfortably.

Always, long after the servants had departed, he was aware of the scent of lilac in the small room, as if the countess decreed that her presence should pervade every corner of the palace.

At morning's light, a trio of young and laughing women servants invaded the bedchamber, drew back the heavy damask drapes to let the autumnal light stream into the room, stoked the fire to renewed life, and presented the dwarf a tray of food which also contained a goblet of Venetian glass filled with a warmed and warming beverage. He was propped against a cloudbank of pillows and feasted on sausages and rolled, buttered pastries stuffed with cream. There were containers of varied jellies, a mound of roasted chestnuts, and small wedges of cheese. There was a tiny custard cake and, to Niccolo's amazement, a relatively new, solid-gold, three-tined eating utensil.

After devouring only a portion of everything on the tray, the young man was bathed and dressed, despite his protests, by two male servants. Then he was escorted down the corridors to an antechamber where the countess awaited him.

"Ah," she smiled, "You've broken your fast, bathed and are ready. Good!" She bent suddenly and kissed the dwarf on his cheek. "It is only a short distance to the Castello Sforzesco. I cannot accompany you. Do you understand all this?"

Not understanding at all, Niccolo nodded.

"Good," caroled the smiling countess. "Farewell, my little friend."

She left the room, and Niccolo sat waiting for someone to escort him from the palace. He had carried the Epictetus with him, and now, bored, he opened the book and read.

"Remember that you are an actor in a play, of such sort as the divine Author chooses. Play it appropriately. Your duty is to act well the part assigned.

"The crafting of the plot, however, is another's."

As the coach and four raced through the streets of Milan, Niccolo marveled at a huge statue of a equestrian mounted on an arch before the south wall of the cathedral. Since he had not seen it the previous day, he assumed he was now on the opposite side of the duomo.

Across from the dwarf, the same captain who had brought him to Milan explained. "It is a clay model for an equestrian statue of Francesco Sforza designed by Maestro Leonardo. It is as tall as a four-story building, but, as with many of the Maestro's works, it is impossible to complete. There is a problem with casting the bronze for it that I do not completely understand, but there, at least, is the clay model."

The coach and four rattled under the great gate that opened on the square and entered the courtyard of the duke's castle. The escorting officer stepped down onto the flat paved area and turned to assist the dwarf.

"Where are we?" asked Niccolo.

"The courtyard within the Rochetta," replied the officer, "the stronghold of the Castello Sforzesco. Come."

The tall officer led the young man up the stairs where two female servants curtsied and indicated that Niccolo and his escort should follow them. Silently they led them up another staircase, down a series of corridors where they again bobbed a curtsy to a man dressed in blue velvet who peered at the dwarf through a loupe. This man led Niccolo and his escort into a small antechamber half-filled with men standing in small groups who glanced briefly at him as they entered and then returned to their conversations. The man in the velvet doublet gestured to chairs decorated with the Sforza serpent worked in blue thread and instructed them to wait. He disappeared through two doors that reached nearly to the high ceiling.

Before the dwarf could ask about the assembly, the officer was whispering in his ear. "This is the antechamber to the Salla della Palla where the duke receives petitions and visitors. You see that stately gentleman in the dark blue uniform with the golden sash? The one with the French lily on his breast? That is Count Belgioioso, Milanese envoy to the French court. He is probably here to report that the new French king has decided to invade Italy to support his claim to Milan. It will come as no surprise, because the French have been arming for months."

"How do you know that?" Niccolo asked.

"I keep my eyes and ears open, and my mouth shut," replied the smiling officer, and Niccolo immediately recalled the instruction of Epictetus: "Let silence be the general rule."

He felt both embarrassed and exhilarated at actually being in attendance at the court, and he studied the faces and clothing of the assembled men when the man in blue velvet appeared again and addressed himself to the escorting officer.

"His Highness will receive the young man shortly. You may return to your other duties."

The officer stood, bowed smartly and saluted the dwarf and then executed a quick turn and was gone. Niccolo struggled to his feet from the high chair and followed the man in blue velvet. His escort paused outside a door, swung it open and gestured Niccolo into the next room.

It was a much smaller room, more intimate, with a warm fire in the hearth. There were three or four chairs placed before an elaborate, handsome desk on which Niccolo observed a decanter of wine and some glasses. As the door closed behind him, the dwarf realized he was not alone. A pretty serving girl stood by the side of the desk, downing a glass of wine. When she wheeled and saw the dwarf, she instantly curtsied, replaced the glass on the tray, and then, embarrassed at being caught, she dashed from the room through the opposite door.

Niccolo smiled and wanted to reassure the girl that stealing wine was also his own avocation, but as the door closed, the handle of the great portal behind him rattled and turned. Instantly the duke entered with a woman of the court.

"Ah! There you are, my young friend," the duke cried and crossed to him. Niccolo saw the duke glance at the tray of glasses and the decanter, and the dwarf thought that perhaps he had noticed the one upright glass still contained a little of the wine. But the duke gave no sign of having noticed the irregularity, and he turned to the lady. "Madonna Valentina, I have decided you deserve a small reward for your loyalty to the court and to your lord." Il Moro rested one gloved hand on the shoulder of the dwarf and smiled at the lady who curtsied to him.

Madonna Valentina Gaddi, an overly painted, dark-haired woman of above-average height with large bosoms and wide hips, smiled without enthusiasm and studied Niccolo. Niccolo, in turn, took note of the lady's formal gown, decorated with narrow decorative ribbons, a fashion with which he was familiar, but he had never seen anything like Madonna Valentina's headdress. It was stiff, with three points like a gable on a roof and suggested that sometime in the past a giant hand had descended to squeeze the lady's temples. Over it was draped a white lace veil that trailed down the Madonna's back to her waist.

"His name is Niccolo," explained the duke, "and he is an exceptional young man who can read and write in Latin, Greek, and the vulgar tongue. He apparently has an astounding memory and can accurately repeat anything he reads within a few minutes of reading it."

The faint smile froze on Madonna Valentina's face. "I thank you, Your Highness," she murmured. My god, she thought, what am I supposed to do with a dwarf? And especially one with an exceptional memory?

As if to answer the unvoiced question, the duke continued. "I understand that dwarfs are quite fashionable in the courts of the Gonzaga, so I think this little gentleman will make you the envy of the other ladies."

"I'm sure," the lady agreed. Or the butt of their jests, she reflected.

"Now take him and show him about the castle," the duke commanded. "Acquaint him with our rules and regulations. I have had rooms prepared for him adjoining your own in the women's wing."

The lady nodded. "I understand, Your Highness," she said. "I am most grateful."

The emphasis only added to the irony, thought Niccolo. The lady appreciates the gift, but would prefer a diamond clip.

The dwarf was aware of an increased pressure on his shoulder and understood that the duke was passing him to the lady, so he obligingly stepped forward and stood beside her.

"One warning," said the duke with a smile and a small

gesture toward the table and the decanter. "The gentleman likes his wine."

Niccolo blushed and silently thanked the duke for his graciousness. He wished to defend himself, but the lady forced a smile upon him, curtsied to Il Moro, and then held out her hand, like a mother summoning a small child. The young man smiled, took it in his own, and they left the room together.

As they proceeded down a corridor to the women's quarters, the lady said drily, "I am pleased you have been placed in my service, Master Niccolo, though I am confused as to why I have been so honored."

As they glided down the wide passage open on both sides to the gardens, they were approached by a stocky, bearded gentleman dressed entirely in black. His handsome, athletic legs were wrapped in silk hose, and a small soft-crowned hat with a wide, turned-back brim rested on his chestnut hair. There was a heavy, golden chain of office suspended from his shoulders, and the medallion carried the Sforza serpent. His overdoublet was made of brocade with a large pattern worked in silver, and it had wide slashes that enabled the pleated cuffs on the gentleman's sleeves to protrude.

It provides a splendid hiding place for a dagger or some other weapon, thought Niccolo.

"Ah," breathed Madonna Valentina, "here is a gentleman who could better acquaint you with the restrictions of the court." The pair paused before the bearded man who gave a quick, courteous bow to the lady, and Valentina responded with a quick curtsy. "My lord," she declared, "may I present to you my new ward, Messer Niccolo? He is a gift to me from the duke and will be residing in the court." She turned and looked down at the dwarf. "Niccolo, this is Messer Bernardino da Corte, assistant castellan of the Castello Sforzesco and the man responsible for the security of our lord, the duke of Milan."

Noting that the bearded man did not extend a hand, Niccolo made no move but smiled and nodded.

"Yes," da Corte hissed. "This must be the young man who saved the life of His Highness when an attempt was made to assassinate him at the Certosa. The gentleman with an incredible memory. Very reassuring." Now he focused all his attention on Niccolo, and, in a gesture of friendship, squatted to be on a level with him. "You may prove very valuable to us, young master," he said softly.

"I have been given that impression," Niccolo replied.

"Indeed?" probed the dark man. "By whom?"

Niccolo suddenly realized that this was his first encounter with the intrigues of the court, and he wisely decided not to mention the countess.

"By His Highness," said the young man.

Da Corte studied the dwarf's face, and then he slowly rose and said, "Of course." When he was erect, the dark man announced, "Well, Messer Niccolo, our rules are simple. You should never be outside the women's quarters unless accompanied by your mistress or on a specific mission for her. You must be in attendance at the court when ordered, with or without Madonna Valentina, and especially when we have visiting dignitaries. You are not to be beaten or punished except on specific orders from Madonna Valentina or His Highness, and only then by the lady or someone of her choosing. Is that satisfactory?"

Niccolo nodded as another man, shorter and stockier and dressed in the livery of the Sforza appeared at da Corte's elbow. The new arrival whispered something, and the security man nodded and turned to the lady.

"I am needed elsewhere," he said. "It seems a servant girl has just collapsed on the north stairwell, and there are signs she has taken poison." He started to walk away, but turned to say, "You see, Messer Niccolo, there are a great many dangers lurking in the court. My instructions were for your safety, not to impede your freedom." He smiled at the Madonna. "I trust you will also warn our young friend of the madman's tower."

Madonna Valentina nodded and curtsied once more as the two men wheeled and swept down the narrow corridor. "That other gentleman was Messer Salvatore Cossa, the captain of the Whisperers."

"The Whisperers?"

"The duke's special agents. God only knows what they do precisely, but you will encounter them constantly. They suddenly appear and then disappear as quickly, and they always seem to be scuttling about, passing a folded message here, whispering something there."

Niccolo was suddenly aware that the poisoned servant might have been the same one he saw sampling the duke's wine. He felt he should tell his mistress that the duke should be warned, but he remembered the advice of Epictetus, and remained silent. After all, he thought, it is a matter for da Corte, and he seems capable. He watched the two men vanish around a corner of the passageway.

"What is the madman's tower?" he asked.

The lady gave a small laugh. "That is a jest of the court. My lord refers to Maestro Leonardo da Vinci as the 'madman.' His workshop is on the upper floor of the tower in the southwestern corner of the castello, and the entire court has been ordered to leave the man alone. One must never go there unless you are explicitly invited by the Maestro himself or ordered to do so by the duke. Under no circumstances are you to go there when the black banner is displayed from the tower window."

"The black banner?"

The lady bit her lower lip and hesitated before she answered. "The Maestro has permission to, well, to investigate or examine, how shall I put this? He is sometimes—provided—with the bodies of dead vagrants or a mercenary slain in a tournament. The Maestro, well, he and his assistant, Ser Salai, they, ah, they cut them open and study the inner—organs. The Maestro draws them and keeps sketches of them in large notebooks. I know it sounds absolutely morbid and barbaric, but the Maestro argues that it enhances his knowledge for painting and sculpture. When a body is up there, a black banner is hung from the tower window, plainly visible to anyone approaching the staircase to his workshops, to warn them, lest some sensitive soul stumbles in by mistake and finds him at his grotesque pursuits."

At that moment Niccolo saw a gaunt servant carrying a carafe of wine rush hurriedly down the adjoining corridor. Ah, he thought, Messer da Corte has discovered the poison. He sighed with relief.

"Who is this Salai?" he asked.

"The Maestro's assistant," the lady whispered, "and a malicious, arrogant swine. Have nothing to do with him. He steals anything that is not part of the structure, alternately insults and fawns upon the ladies of the court, lies with an expertise beyond anything known to civilized man, and occasionally will provoke a quarrel between members of the court with his cunning half-truths and gossip and then revel in the pain and humiliation he causes. He will ridicule and mock you when he thinks I am not nearby, and, above all, he will try to catch you doing something—inappropriate. Then he will threaten to use the information unless you do what he wishes. I forbid you to have anything to do with him."

Niccolo shook his head. "I'm sure we have little in common, my lady," he said. "He does not sound very trustworthy."

"Very good," said Madonna Gaddi. "One you may trust is Francesco da Bicocca, captain of the guards of the women's quarters. He models himself after Captain-General Galeazzo di Sanseverino. He is as strong, as handsome, and regarded by many as the most irresistible man in Italy."

Ah, Niccolo reflected, what a marvelous assembly of thieves, extortionists, murderers, and adulterers. Then he remembered a brief epigram from Epictetus.

"Try to enjoy the great festival of life."

❖   ❖   ❖

Why is it that we try to hide our most barbaric and horrifying acts in the darkness? wondered Bernardino as he and a companion descended the narrow spiral staircase that led to the dungeons under the Castello Sforzesco. Do we really imagine that God cannot see in the shadows?

He strode as quickly as he could manage over the burlap and straw strewn over the puddles of slime and moisture on the floor of the narrow passageway. The torches lining the walls were placed far apart, but their light reflected from the surface of the pools and enabled the two men to sidestep them.

Behind the black figure, Salvatore Cossa struggled to keep pace with his superior. Gingerly the thin security man stepped around the bags of salt that lined the passageways and realized by the increased moisture and the fetid air that they were now under the moats of the castello. Before him, Bernardino took a torch from the iron rings in the wall and turned down a stone corridor that barely enabled him to stand erect. Salvatore followed close behind him, cringing from the occasional brush with a scampering rat frightened by the firelight. Eventually, he heard the clang of a bolt being thrown and he followed the chief of security into the small room.

The floor of this room, heavy with moisture-laden straw, was also slippery with fungus. There was the overpowering stench of feces and urine, and the two men quickly put their linen handkerchiefs to their noses and mouths. Bernardino lit two more torches on the walls from the one he carried, and the light revealed the great wooden rack centered in the room. The naked, broken body of Luigi, the smaller quarryman from the Certosa, was still suspended on it, his arms and legs grotesquely elongated from the torture, his chest a bloody smear from a series of small cuts that been inflicted upon him to gain information. The broken man had clearly lost control of his bowels.

"You're certain he is dead?"

The leader of the Whisperers nodded. "Galeazzo himself

saw to the torture. The man said nothing more than that he had been hired by someone who whispered from the shadows that he was the Griffin. Nothing else. The torture continued, and the man expired."

Benardino tread carefully up the small stone platform that supported the rack and seized the dead man's hair. He pulled back the head and looked into the open, unseeing eyes.

"Who the hell are you?" he whispered. "Who sent you?" There was no response of course, and he let the head fall back on the bloody chest. "Galeazzo was ordered to keep the man alive until Il Moro himself interrogated him. The duke will not like this."

He descended the stone platform and crossed to Salvatore. "However, this could not be the one who allegedly poisoned the duke's wine. That had to be someone in the court. Any sign of the carafe of wine missing from the duke's salon?"

"No. The assassin probably removed it himself when he heard of the unfortunate death of the servant girl, this Anna Spinolo."

Bernardino shook his head. "There is more to this than I can fathom. Something, something is very odd here."

Salvatore shrugged, holding the torch higher to guide Bernardino toward the small doorway. "He is the second one to name this Griffin."

Bernardino took the torch from him and started through the narrow corridor. "Yes, and that is part of my dilemma. If there is such a man, why haven't we heard of him before? Code names imply organizations, and the larger the organization, the more probability of a weak link, someone who can be reached, someone with his palm out and his tongue ready to wag. But none of us heard a word of this Griffin until last month, and yet his arm can reach into the castello and, presumably, poison wine."

They emerged through the stone corridor into the damp and the cold again, and the black-garbed man replaced the torch in the iron ring attached to the wall. They removed the handkerchiefs and inhaled the cool, musty air.

"These men were Venetians. Do you think this Griffin is a Venetian?" asked Salvatore once again skipping to keep pace with Bernardino.

"Tuttavilla says it is someone in the court," Bernardino responded. "I have had my agents peering into every corner and closet. I know all there is to know about the members of the court, and I have come up with nothing." He stopped suddenly and turned to Salvatore. "Have your Whisperers heard anything?"

"The usual. Who is sleeping with whom. Who is spreading gossip about the last festival. What new skill the courtesans have developed to attract the duke's attention. But nothing about any Griffin."

"Well, keep everyone alert," the security chief commanded. "And tell them to pay special attention to this new addition to the court, this dwarf from the Certosa. If I find he can be trusted, he might prove a valuable agent. If not, he may have to be isolated."

"You think the dwarf may be the Griffin?"

"Of course not," snapped Bernardino. "But I know nothing about him." The two men ascended the spiral staircase and stepped into the small antechamber in the castello. The hidden entrance closed behind them, once again becoming a large paneled segment of the wall containing a portrait of Il Moro's father, the condottiere, Francesco Sforza.

"Oh. One other thing," whispered Bernardino. "The late duchess sent one of her ladies-in-waiting to the convent of San Sisto before she died on some sort of pilgrimage. No one seems to know what it is or why she was sent, and that has aroused the curiosity of Il Moro. The girl, Madonna Maria Chigi from Genoa, has returned to the court, and I want you to find out all you can without letting her or anyone know that she is being investigated. Do you understand?" Salvatore nodded, and Bernardino started to walk away. He reached the door of the antechamber before he turned. "And keep an eye on that damned apprentice of Maestro da Vinci. My gold belt is missing."

Niccolo's first few weeks in the Castello Sforzesco were filled with new sights and sensations that raised a million questions that the young man hesitated to ask. His initial report to the countess through the hymnal pipeline was short and rambling. A servant girl had died of poisoned wine, but the poisoner was not found. Madonna Valentina had been observed in the late hours of the morning slipping from her rooms and past the dwarf's door. Someone had attempted to poison the raw meat fed to Madonna Dorotea's pet cheetah, but this was attributed to female jealousy and had nothing to do with the attempts on the duke's life. The arrogant apprentice to Maestro Leonardo was seized and beaten one night on returning from a rendezvous with some nameless servant girl in the kitchens, but no one acknowledged beating him.

The first of the countess's promised purses appeared on Niccolo's desk as if by magic one early morning, and the dwarf buried the gold florins under his clothes in the lower drawer of his chest.

To his delight, Niccolo found he was given more liberty than he expected from the initial warnings. Madonna Valentina frequently sent him on trivial errands to various parts of the castello like a common messenger, and she gave no indication that she was concerned if the assignment took three times as long as it would had the lady performed the mission herself. Indeed, more and more Niccolo felt his mistress deliberately contrived some of these little excursions to free herself for secretive and, presumably, more pleasurable activities.

These small assignments were always accompanied by a brief and hastily scrawled passport that enabled the young man to wander almost anywhere in the castello, and, when challenged, he had only to present the document to the guard.

The Castello Sforzesco was everything Niccolo imagined

from the stories told him by the countess and the monks. It was a fortress within circles of moats which were spanned by no less than sixty-two drawbridges. In every corner of the parks and courtyards were massive machines of war, and Niccolo was told there were more than eighteen hundred such instruments secreted behind bushes and hidden within buildings. It was obvious that this was the court of a warrior, because there were twelve hundred mercenaries living within the walls of the castello. There was even a full company of Marmelukes captained by a count. They were everywhere, lining corridors and stationed near every doorway. The duke also supported forty chamberlains; platoons of subchamberlains; regiments of choir singers; battalions of artists-in-residence; enough secretaries to populate six villages; and entire nations of cooks, gardeners, maids, grooms, and ladies-in-waiting. The duke's secretary, Bartolomeo Calco, had no less than eight secretaries under him, plus seven assistants, a keeper of the seals, four recorders, two archivists, and squads of treasurers and doorkeepers.

The castello itself had square ports on a defensive rooftop gallery that ran completely around the ducal court and a new round turret from which Niccolo could see nearly across the entire city or down into the courtyards and ducal gardens. The park contained an artificial lake, formal gardens with a variety of flowers and hedges from every part of Europe and geometrically shaped bushes, carefully groomed gravel paths, and, best of all, a menagerie with an elephant and lions and a poisonous Egyptian snake which both fascinated and terrified the young man.

Niccolo was more comfortable in the stables which were actually a series of greek temples with arcades of tall, white columns and arches. The ceilings were vaulted, and frescoes lined the walls. Fresh, cool water was piped into each stall, and long lines of clay conduits removed the waste of the hundreds of horses. Uniformed grooms would parade the animals among the surrounding trees daily when the weather permitted, and occasionally Niccolo was permitted to sit astride one of the stallions which was far different from his occasional morning rides with the Madonna Valentina when he rode his small pony which was the color of bronze with a glistening white mane.

There were, of course, two areas of the castello that Niccolo never investigated. One was the old dungeons beneath the moats which, according to the court lords and ladies, were used more often in the days of the Visconti, but which were, today, used primarily to store the salt whose trade Il Moro controlled.

The other, of course, was the madman's tower. Indeed, since his initial contact with Maestro Leonardo at the Certosa, Niccolo did not encounter the resident artist. He was told that the painter spent much of his time at the little Dominican church of Santa Maria delle Grazie where he was creating a fresco for the refectory. Every day, Niccolo was told, the Maestro would walk the four hundred meters to the church and remain there until after dark. Some said he did no work there at all, but would sit and stare for hours at the cartoon etched on the wall, and then make a few quick sketches in his notebooks and return to his workshop on the upper floor of the southwestern tower. Others said that he spent more time quietly judging the work being done by the stonemasons under Cristoforo Solari who was constructing a joint tomb for the high altar in which the late duchess and Il Moro would rest side by side eternally.

Niccolo's own quarters, two rooms adjoining those of Madonna Valentina's, were small in comparison to those of his mistress, but much more expansive than his cell in the Certosa. The lady's suite of rooms on the upper floor, just beneath the brass cupola of the central tower of the Castello Sforzesco, were, according to rumor, "inherited" from the Countess Bergamini after the duchess had forced her into marriage and out of the castle. The rooms looked out on the pines and elms and oaks of the ducal park, and her bed with its white satin bedspread nestled under four thick brass columns supporting a canopy of gold cloth.

Niccolo and the Madonna Valentina shared a common

water closet, a small chamber containing two arrow loops, an armoire, and a small fireplace near the bench which had a hole cut into the capstone to serve as a toilet seat. This stone latrine had been constructed, as most of the others in the castello, on stone supports that either projected beyond the face of the wall or opened on a long deep shaft that terminated at ground level in the cesspit.

One day, when his mistress had departed for one of her mysterious assignations, Niccolo examined the lady's rooms and located the gold serpent on the wall medallion which had been described by the countess. He remembered what the lady had told him about the secret passageway, and he slowly turned the serpent a quarter of a circle to the left. A hidden door opened and revealed a dark, narrow walkway sandwiched between two sets of walls. A wave of cold air, reeking of stagnant water and mold, swept into the room, and the dwarf cautiously entered to explore the hidden corridor.

To the left, it led upward, presumably to the madman's tower, and to the right down to the antechambers, the Salla della Palla, the kitchens, and into the piazza outside the castello walls. The young explorer found oil lamps hanging from pegs at intervals along the walls. He lit one with a taper from the Madonna's room and that enabled him to work his way along the entire length of the right passageway. He found there were more of these hidden corridors that branched out from this one and spy holes cut into the walls at his own eye level that enabled him to see and hear what was happening in many of the rooms in the castle. He tried to envision the countess bending over to peer through these small openings, and he imagined the passageways suddenly flooded with the delightful scent of lilac.

Niccolo reasoned that Madonna Valentina did not know of these passages. Since the lady was linked with both Galeazzo di Sanseverino and Il Moro himself, she would not have risked nocturnal transit down open corridors of the castello if she knew the secret of how Il Moro magically, and infrequently now, appeared at her bedside.

Niccolo was a little afraid of the hidden passageway at first, and ventured into it only twice in his first two weeks at the court. The first was when he suddenly developed a hunger in the early hours of the morning, awoke and dressed himself, and then slipped down the walkway to the dark and silent kitchens. Here he scurried about, examining cupboards and bins, barrels and sacks until he found a small cache of sweet pastries which he brought back to his own quarters. He could, of course, have waited another hour until the cooks and apprentices appeared to ready the fires and prepare the morning meal, and then ordered something brought to him. But the idea of sneaking through the walls and stealing what he wanted revived pleasant and thrilling memories of the Certosa, and, for a moment, his separation from the monks and from his favorite pastime of kitchen raiding was not so heavy a burden.

His second exploration began when he heard the slippered feet of his mistress glide pass his door the end of his second week in the castello. It was only the fifth hour of the night, and there was still movement and activity throughout many of the rooms, so Niccolo was surprised that Madonna Valentina was daring an assignation when her chances of being discovered were likely. He decided he might do a little adventuring himself. He slipped into the Madonna's bedchamber, turned the medallion and entered the secret corridor.

It was dark, of course, but he did not light a lamp. His fingers groped the cold, damp walls as he inched his way toward the first bay to the right of the passage. He noted a sliver of light, and slowly slid the covering from the spy hole and put his eye to it.

It was Il Moro. He paced before the small delegation of advisors gathered around him.

"Are you certain?" asked the duke.

Bernardino da Corte nodded. "One of the court ladies confessed that the duchess had confided in her."

Il Moro sighed. "Why not me? I was her husband. Why couldn't she confide in me?"

Niccolo could not hear the response of the security chief, and finally the duke moaned, "Are you sure she said, 'the old man'?"

Bernardino nodded. "Salvatore heard her. She said the man was 'the old man,' and once she said, 'father.'"

Francesco da Casate, one of the oldest advisors to the Sforza family, put a hand to his head. Cardinal Ascanio Sforza, appearing totally disinterested in what was being discussed, fed bits of pastry to his parrot which was perched on the back of his chair, and Count Girolamo da Tuttaville, envoy-at-large and fifteen years older than Il Moro, removed his spectacles and wiped them with his linen handkerchief. Salvatore Cossa, the captain of the Whisperers, nodded.

"That's what she said, my lord," Cossa affirmed. "She said it was 'the old man.'"

Il Moro turned to face the man responsible for his security. "But what does that mean? Did she provide a name?"

"No," Bernardino shook his head. "She was terribly frightened, and it is entirely possible she did not know the name. She did not think her secret would come out, and now we were questioning her, and she was afraid she might be tortured."

"'The old man,'" Il Moro repeated, "and 'father.'"

"Old is a vague term when applied by one so young," volunteered da Casate. "To someone that age, a man of thirty might seem old."

"And 'father' is equally ambiguous," said the cardinal. "It could mean her own father, the plea of a child, or she might refer to someone clerical. She might mean a priest."

"Unhappily true," Il Moro agreed. "And the 'old' might pertain to someone in the elevated priesthood."

"A cardinal?" asked da Casate.

"Possible," shrugged Ascanio. "There are several who are notorious in such matters. Cardinal de Celano and Cardinal Albizzi to name only two."

Il Moro threw himself into the red velvet chair behind his

desk and fingered his blackened hair. "Salvatore, compile a list of possibles," he said.

Suddenly Niccolo felt a wave of cold air brush past him, and he instantly thought: someone else has entered the passageway! He let the spy hole cover slip back in place, rushed up the narrow corridor, slipping in the blackness until he reached the bay that was the entrance to the Madonna's bedroom. He peered through the spy hole first to make certain that his mistress was still absent, and then he opened the paneled door, entered and closed it behind him.

He rushed to his own room, removed his clothes and climbed into bed.

It was an hour before he could drift off to sleep, and even then it was a restless night with terrifying dreams of Bernardino da Corte and Maestro Leonardo cutting him into small, edible squares.

The next morning, soon after he and the mistress had broken their fasts, he was sent to fetch a book requested by Madonna Valentina from the library. The mercenaries were everywhere, and he overheard two of them saying that the king of France was rumored to be arming, ready to move against Milan. Everyone had been alerted, and some of the war machines had been openly wheeled into plain view. The scent of battle was in the autumnal air. Still the morning was very cool, promising winter and snow, but bright with sunlight, and Niccolo felt free and alive as he scurried down the columned arcade to the library. He paused momentarily to watch the flight of some large black birds that swayed and slid on the invisible wind currents, wings extended and as graceful as court dancers. It was only after they flew away over the ducal gardens that the dwarf turned his attention to the article dangling from the tower window.

A black and ominous banner.

There was a fresh body in the madman's tower.

Chapter 3
The Madman's Tower

"Lest bodily prosperity should stifle a flourishing talent
the painter . . . should be solitary.
If you are alone
you belong entirely to yourself . . .
You must forego companions
who are disinclined to your studies,
and have a brain capable of reacting
to the different objects
that present themselves before it."

Leonardo da Vinci
"On the Life of the Painter"

"And now we are sending you to Rome to spy; but no one sends a coward as a spy, for if he hears a noise and sees a shadow moving, he loses his wits and comes flying to say, 'The enemy is upon us!' "

Niccolo considered the passage from Epictetus and thought about his commission from the countess which, to his mind, was really only an affirmation of his sworn duty to his patron, the duke of Milan.

No one sends a coward as a spy.

He tossed on his bed and considered what he was feeling after his sight of the black banner earlier in the day. The countess had said that everything unusual was to be explored and reported in order to protect the duke. He had never seen the black banner unfurled before, but Madonna Valentina had said it signaled that there was a body in the madman's tower.

Whose body was it? What happened? And isn't this precisely the type of information that the countess would need? And, most importantly, was Niccolo afraid to enter the domain of the master of the dark arts, Maestro Leonardo?

Definitely.

Was it any concern of his what Maestro Leonardo did in the madman's tower?

No.

Was he content, then, to let life go on as usual within the Castello Sforzesco and accept what he could not change?

Like hell.

Within the hour, Niccolo found himself once again between the walls of the hidden passageway, this time working to the left, the path upward to the tower. He lit one of the small oil lamps and carried it with him, occasionally stumbling over a cross beam partially exposed in the pressed dirt floor of the walkway. Something brushed by his left foot, and he almost made an outcry, but he remembered the warning of Epictetus and bravely murmured to himself, "It is only a rat or two. You've dealt with dozens of them in the Certosa kitchens. Don't be afraid. They won't bother you. Continue."

The upper passage was longer than the downward path to the antechambers and the kitchen, and the floor seemed made of packed earth rather than the stone walkway that led down from Madonna Valentina's chamber. It seemed to the dwarf that he had been climbing for hours. He became conscious of the extreme narrowness of the passageway, the cold, the smell of stale air and waste, the damp condensation, and a greenish mold that covered the stone wall to his right. The ceiling of the passage began to lower, and the floor of the passageway and the right wall slowly turned to wood. There was more warmth in this section of the narrow corridor, and the footing was easier. Niccolo reasoned that he was in the area of the tower itself, because, he reassured himself, hot air rises. He had reached a semicircular area, a sort of bay, ballooning to the right, and he extinguished his lamp, because he knew that if the madman's workshop should be dark, a sliver of light would be enough to expose his hiding place. He located one of the spy holes and carefully raised the round wooden disc in the right wall. Immediately a soft light from the workshop poured through the small hole, and Niccolo put his eye to it.

From what he could see, the room was empty and dimly lit by three oil lamps and a soft diffusion of light through the tall windows to his left. He gently turned the bar that paralleled the serpent on the opposite side of the wall and pushed the door open. He cautiously stepped into the room, closing the panel behind him.

The Maestro's workshop in the Castello Sforzesco was a very large, square room that comprised one complete floor of the southwestern tower. Sections of the room were curtained off and shadowed. Windows were inset about two or three feet apart in the four walls, large arched windows, some of them now blinded by heavy damask drapes. From the windows to his left, Niccolo could look down on the ducal gardens and the panorama of trees now turning autumnal gold and scarlet, the maze of hedges and pathways, the menagerie and the stables. He opened the draperies on the windows to his right and found he could see into the courtyard and beyond the rooftops of the inner walls. He was surprised to find he could see the enormous paved area inside the main portal, large enough to accommodate a fleet of coaches and carriages, with grassy triangles bedded between wide boulevards of crushed stone that led to the surrounding buildings. From this height he could see the two round towers on either corner of the outer walls, the tall central tower that rose above the main entrance to the courtyard, and the bend of buildings arcing beyond the castello's walls.

It was nearly twilight, the sun suspended just above the Milan horizon, and Niccolo trembled in the cold wind that embraced the tower.

If this madman has an orderly mind, thought Niccolo turning to survey the room, he also has disorderly habits.

The room was chaotic. Strange wooden structures filled most of the open areas, and the walls were lined with shelves of huge, leather-bound books. Others were piled around the floor like small mountain ranges. Near the northern windows were three or four easels containing, Niccolo reasoned, paintings or sketches, each covered with a dust cloth.

The dwarf cautiously lifted the corner of one of the coverings and revealed an unfinished sketch, part chalk, part tempera shading, depicting two women and two children. The central woman restrained a squirming, chubby child on her lap as the infant leaned toward the other child, a youth of about seven or eight, who rested an elbow on his mother's knee and studied the baby. Niccolo found himself smiling at the active infant trying to break away from his mother's grasp, as any child of that age might do. There was an unfinished, sketched hand with the forefinger extended and pointing to the skies, but it was impossible at this stage of the painting to determine to whom the hand belonged Niccolo marveled that the painter had achieved depth using only highlights and shadows, the faces and upper torsos of the two women projecting from the canvas.

He replaced the cloth and looked around the workroom. There were five or six tables, one stained with oils and pigments, another containing an open book, two inkwells, a knife for sharpening quills, a covey of feathered pens, three fat candlesticks, a collection of rolled parchments, and a large, upright mirror. Two of the tables each supported something draped in white linen sheets, and Niccolo found himself trembling at the sight of them. He instinctively and deliberately turned away and began to examine one of the stacks of books. He recognized many of the standard works available in the Certosa library. One stack, however, contained a copy of the Caballa, a text that had been kept under lock and key in the "forbidden" section of the monastery. There were also other old and equally "forbidden" books, all of which contributed to the legends of "nefarious" activities by the artist-scientist. Niccolo smiled as he renewed acquaintances with these texts that had contributed a great deal to his own private education at the Certosa. One entire stack of the books was completely devoted to mathematics, and it seemed to the dwarf as if the Maestro might be obsessed with Euclid.

Niccolo turned his attention to the wooden machines centered in the room. One was a flat wagon whose bed contained two large horizontal gears and four massive, bent springs. The flat frame was connected by a series of three gears to the back wheels of the wagon, and Niccolo reasoned that it might be a vehicle that could propel itself if the springs were wound tightly.

A toy, he thought.

Beside the wagon was another vehicle in two separate sections. The first unit, basically a three-wheeled cart, had a single wheel maneuvered by a wooden handle like the rudder of a ship. The second section was another flat frame mounted on two wheels that contained a pair of upright gears that meshed with small pegs placed around the periphery of each of the two wheels.

There was another device which, Niccolo assumed, was for making files, incorporating a dropped weight that would trip a hammer and cause it to strike a blank metal bar at precise intervals. There was an instrument containing a thin, razor-sharp strip of metal that seemed designed to saw wood when powered by a steady stream of water. There was a lathe of sorts, the kind Niccolo had often seen in the carpentry shop at the Certosa, but this one seemed intended to cut screws. There was a windlass and a pile driver, and, suspended from the ceiling above the instruments, a giant pair of dragon wings that seemed to incorporate a small seat and a leather harness.

His attention was drawn to the table covered with books and rolled parchments. He pulled a small bench over to it and stood upon the bench to study the books. The pages of the big text were covered with scrawls and slanted images that made no sense to the young dwarf.

Hebrew, he wondered. Or Arabic perhaps?

He remembered the duke's declaration that Leonardo could not yet read Latin, so it was unlikely, he reflected, that the painter had mastered other languages. The images seemed closest to Greek letters, but Niccolo could not decipher them. He glanced in the mirror, and to his astonishment the scrawls and scribbles on the large pages suddenly became recognizable Italian.

Mirror writing, Niccolo marveled, so that the notes can only be read by reflection!

And he read: "Alessandro Carissimo of Padua for the hand of Christ."

And farther down the page: "Pleasure and pain are twins, because there is never one without the other so they should be joined together, but back to back, because they are also opposites."

The margins of the pages were crowded with quick sketches, some no more than a single fluid line that nevertheless suggested a falcon in flight. There were images of trees and mountains over which the Maestro had imposed precise arcs and interlocking lines. There were hundreds of mathematical equations that seemed to apply to the perception of distant objects.

The young man smiled and whispered to himself, "Perspective."

There were sketches of the most grotesque, frightening, and bizarre human faces imaginable, portraits of gnarled, wrinkled old men wrapped in what appeared to be Roman togas. Their jaws projected in such a way that their lips almost collided with their noses. Some of these horrendous apparitions wore what appeared to be laurel-wreath crowns as if they had just won a major award for ugliness. There were also sketches of human arms and hands in every possible position, of naked men bending and twisting in an assortment of poses, of a human leg, the outer flesh stripped away to reveal a network of sinews and muscles stretched from the individual toes to mid-calf.

Something about this sketch alarmed the dwarf and reminded him of his purpose in coming to the tower. He stepped from the bench, summoned his courage, and crossed to one of the covered tables to gather the information that would most interest the countess.

What was beneath the linen sheets?

Slowly, and with a rising sense of danger, he pulled the small bench to one of the tables, mounted it, and drew back the sheet to expose the head and shoulders of the body beneath it.

It was the body of the quarryman who had attacked Niccolo at the Certosa. Now, naked and white as chalk, his open eyes staring at the ceiling, the Venetian appeared more frightening than when he came at the dwarf with a drawn blade. There was something distorted and repulsive now about the body. Niccolo drew back the sheet a little further. The arms and legs were angular, broken and bent and dislocated from the torso. There were deep lacerations of the chest, but no sign of blood. Obviously the unfortunate man had been tortured.

Suddenly a hand was pressed against the dwarf's mouth preventing him from screaming, and an arm was an iron band around his waist. Niccolo was seized and lifted him from the bench.

"What are you doing here, grotesque?" inquired a voice at his ear. "Nosy, eh? You like looking at naked men, eh? Is that what you like, you little monster?"

The attacker suddenly hurled the dwarf away from him, and Niccolo drew his dagger and wheeled to face a youth, stocky, about twenty with a handsomeness that bordered on female beauty. There was a crooked smile on his face, and he slowly slipped his own dagger from its sheath at his waist.

"Oh," he laughed, "you want to play blades, eh, monster? Come, then. Come."

Niccolo was both frightened and excited, but he knew he could not fight the young man whom he knew to be the Maestro's assistant, Giacomo Salai.

"I don't want to fight with you, Salai," the dwarf murmured. "You just step aside and let me go, and there'll be an end to it."

"Sheath your dagger first," the boy commanded.

"You first," Niccolo responded.

For a moment the dwarf expected the youth to charge him, but, after a moment, Salai nodded, still smiling, and put his dagger back in its scabbard.

"Thank you," Niccolo breathed, and he sheathed his own dagger.

"I've heard of you," said Salai, circling to the right of the dwarf. "You're the grotesque the duke brought back from his hunt. You sleep with the women in their own wing."

"I sleep alone," Niccolo replied, countering to keep the boy at a distance.

"Then you're certainly not a part of this court," laughed Salai. "Why, eh? Why don't you sleep with the women?" he pressed. "Are you still a virgin, grotesque? Have you ever been with a woman?" The dwarf did not answer. "You are a virgin!" heralded Salai. "I'll bet you've never even seen a woman naked, have you?" Again Niccolo kept silent, but the boy's circling movement had brought him to the edge of the second table. "Then here, monster!" Salai crowed, and he whipped back the linen sheet.

On the second table was the body of a girl, and it took the dwarf some time to recognize the servant girl whom he had caught sampling the wine. At the first sight of her, that day in the antechamber, Niccolo had thought her pretty, but now the pale-green pallor and the blatant nakedness seemed obscene and repugnant, and he instinctively turned away. But suddenly and violently the strong arms encircled him again, lifting him from the floor and whirling him around to face the table.

"Here's your chance, grotesque!" Salai barked. "She won't fight you, and she's about as lively now as any of the bitches in this dungheap."

Niccolo realized that the boy was trying to force him to lie on the naked body of the dead girl, and, enraged and frightened, he struggled with all his strength, pushing with his feet against the side of the table, but the Maestro's assistant was deceptively strong.

Relief came like a thunderclap from somewhere behind him, and the dwarf suddenly felt the strong arms release him. Niccolo wheeled, one hand on the table edge to support himself, the other again drawing the dagger, but he saw the tall, black figure of the Maestro hovering over Salai who had both hands cupped to his left ear. A thin stream of blood was running between his fingers, and the youth was moaning and slowly sinking to the painter's feet. Niccolo sheathed his dagger.

"You disgust me," the deep voice murmured.

Salai struggled to his feet, his eyes glaring at the bearded man who had just struck him. "I was just having a little fun with the monster."

"The monster?" the Maestro growled. "Is the grape a monster, because it is not a plum or an apple? I'll tell you who's a monster here, Giacomo! It's you! What you need, scoundrel, is a little of the discipline this young man has known all his life. Pack your things and go to the Santa Maria delle Grazie. I'll arrange for you to spend a few weeks in a Dominican cell. You'll take your meals in their refectory, and you can repay the monks by assisting Bramante. Now get out of here, before I lose what little patience I have left and hurl you from the tower."

The boy stumbled to the door, still clutching his hands to his ear, and turned there. "You'll pay for this, old man," he grumbled softly, clearly intending it as a threat. "I'll make you pay! Wait and see! You need me! You need me!"

And he was gone.

Niccolo was both relieved and trembling at the sight of the imposing, bearded artist who now collapsed into a chair and hid his head in his hands in anxiety, but he could only think of himself.

Please, he pleaded silently, don't throw me from the tower!

"Forgive him," the Maestro murmured through his hands. "Giacomo came to live with me on the feastday of Saint Mary Magdalen, eight years ago. He was twelve years old then. On only the second day, I put four lire aside for clothes for him, and he stole them from my purse. That should have warned me. Within a month he stole a silver point worth twenty-two soldi from Marco who was living with me, and I had to face the conclusion that the boy is an irreparable thief and a liar. Nothing I can do will ever change him." He looked up from his hands. "So—I love him. It is the only weapon I have left."

Niccolo, both frightened and confused, said nothing.

"What are you doing here, Messer Niccolo?" the Maestro asked quietly after a moment. He slowly rose and began to draw back the drapes, permitting more of the twilight to seep into the room. "Weren't you warned about coming here? Didn't you see the black banner at the window?"

Niccolo nodded, saying nothing, still afraid that the madman would work his magic and throw the hapless dwarf into an eternal void of some sort.

"How did you get in here?" the Maestro continued as he lit more of the candles and the lamps around the workroom. "Or, more to the point, what brought you here?"

It seemed a long while before the dwarf could find his voice. "Curiosity," he whispered.

No other answer could have elicited the response Niccolo wanted. The Maestro stopped in his lighting and stared, unsmiling, at the young man. The short wax taper in his hands almost burned down to his fingers before he quickly extinguished it in a small container of sand. The Maestro continued to study the dwarf as he crossed to the tables and replaced the linen sheets over the bodies.

"Curiosity, eh?" the Maestro echoed. "Yes. But to what end? Do you find the dead interesting? Is it their nakedness that attracts you?"

"No, Maestro," Niccolo whispered. "I—I just wondered—well—why you find them so interesting."

Leonardo stroked his beard and even managed a small smile. "Indeed?" he said. "That is a reasonable question." He beckoned the dwarf to come beside him. "And I will attempt a reasonable answer."

As Niccolo crossed to him, the Maestro again slowly folded back the linen sheet until the dead quarryman's upper torso was revealed.

"Here," the Maestro commanded. "Tell me what you see, and remember: there are ten functions of the eye. Consider both darkness and light, body and color, shape and location, distance and proximity, rest and motion—although, under the present circumstances, I imagine we can dispense with the latter."

The dwarf, more afraid of the tall painter with the bushy eyebrows that shadowed his eyes, mounted the small bench so he could examine the body.

"It's a man," he said drily, merely glancing and not touching the cold corpse. "It's the quarryman who tried to kill me at the Certosa."

"He is not a quarryman. Why do I say that?"

Niccolo turned his attention back to the corpse. He forced himself to look closer, and, finally, summoning his courage, he began to examine one of the arms. He was surprised that the skin texture was dry. His imagination had somehow conjured up a vision of something more of slime or crystalline crust, like rime on a cold stone wall.

"His hands," said the dwarf after a moment. "They are smooth. No callouses as one might expect of a man who worked the quarries."

The Maestro slowly worked his way to the opposite side of the table, never removing his eyes from the dwarf. "Good, but obvious," he murmured. "Also note what you do not see. The gentleman lacks the upper body musculature essential to a man who spends his life cutting, sawing, and moving stone."

The Maestro continued around the table, his eyes focused completely on Niccolo. "How old is he, do you think? Where does he come from? And, more to the point, of what did he die?"

The dwarf looked up. "According to the rolls of the purveyor, he was twenty-three, and he came from Venice."

"That is what you remember from the purveyor's rolls," commented the Maestro, "but that is not absolute truth. Memory is never reliable. Time colors it. Further, the young man could have lied about his age and his homeplace, and the purveyor would have merely recorded the lie." The Maestro drew closer to the dwarf. "How did he die?"

The dwarf shrugged. "Torture."

"Too obvious," the painter sniffed, "though he was obviously tormented since men do not walk about with their wrists at the level of their knees. Do you assume, then, as Maestro Ambrogio da Rosate does, that he died of the cruelty inflicted on him?"

Niccolo forced himself to look at the body again. "Yes," he said.

"Then what do you make of the hole at the base of his neck?" the Maestro asked.

The dwarf focused again on the body. "Hole? What hole?"

The Maestro raised the head of the dead man and revealed a small red mark, no more than half a centimeter in width, beneath his hair. "There. See?"

Niccolo shrugged. "What does it mean?" he asked.

"It means that a small, thin instrument with a round shaft, but smaller than a stiletto, was plunged into a place where it would cause instant death." The Maestro lowered the head and leaned closer to the dwarf. "This is the work of someone who knows how to kill quickly and efficiently. Under torture, who would have noticed another hole, eh? Especially under the man's long hair? The weapon, however, confounds me. It wasn't a stilletto. Too large. It would have to be strong, because it is not as easy as you may imagine to penetrate skin, muscles, and tendons. It would have to be fairly long, not necessarily more than twelve to fifteen centimeters. I can't imagine what it was."

The dwarf was fascinated but confused. "But—why? Was it part of the torture?"

"Obviously not," the Maestro replied softly, "since the purpose of torture is to inflict pain but not kill, and the killer must have realized that such a penetration would terminate the pain. Either someone was frustrated that the torture was not working, so the procedure was hastened. Or the torture was working too well, and the murderer did not want any further information revealed." The Maestro replaced the sheet over the body. "In any case, the condition of this man's body would offer us no new knowledge, so I will have it returned to the salt cellars until he is buried. Salt is a good preservative for the dead." He turned and crossed to the other table and gently folded the sheet down to the girl's breasts. "But the girl, ah! We can learn a great deal by examining her."

Filthy old man, thought Niccolo.

"The cause of her death is obvious," the Maestro continued, "and doesn't merit much consideration. Discoloration of the nails, a swelling here and here, death by poison, although I have not yet been able to determine which poison. I do know that it was nothing exotic like those favored by the Persians or the Borgias. It is something more—natural. Something easily available in the gardens or in the woods. Perhaps some crushed berries from the lily or mistletoe, or the blossoms of yellow jasmine, oleander, or autumn crocus. They are all poisonous. So, too, are as few as two berries from the castor plant. It could well be belladonna, also known as nightshade. That's abundant in the gardens. But the poison aside, the body is really in excellent condition. No damage to the chords or nerves, or the membranes, as in the case of the tortured man. No, the girl has much more to teach us than the male."

"Will it tell us who put the poison in the wine?" asked the dwarf.

"Why do you assume it was in the wine?" Maestro questioned. "It's true that Messer Bernardino cannot find the carafe, so he assumes that is how the poison was administered. But it could well have been in something else, something the girl consumed earlier, and perhaps it worked slowly."

"I saw her sneaking a glass of the wine," Niccolo responded abruptly.

"Did you?" the Maestro murmured. "Well, that is still not conclusive. It could have been accidental, or, if the girl knew the wine was poisoned, she may have committed suicide."

Niccolo was annoyed at the painter's refusal to accept the obvious. "Why should the girl commit suicide?" he snapped.

"Because she may have been the one who poisoned the wine," replied the artist. "She heard you entering and became frightened that she had been found out, and wishing to avoid the torments of our friend on the other table, she took an easier path to her death."

Niccolo was exasperated. "Ridiculous! Why can't you be content with the simple explanation? Why must you always look for another possibility?"

The Maestro stared at him. "Because," he said softly, "there is always another possibility."

Dino Spada, the tall, thin kitchen servant, tied the drawstring of his hose around his waist, adjusted his codpiece and his tunic, and stepped into the corridor from the dark water closet. He was surprised to see that the corridor was also dark, but he assumed the wind had extinguished the fat candle he had placed on the ledge outside the doorway. He did not have time to consider another possibility, however, for the blow from the heavy metal rod smashed into his collarbone and sent a stab of pain through his body. At the same time four huge hands were encircling his waist and at his mouth, stifling all sound, and he was lifted from the floor and carried back into the small chamber. Guarino Valla, the falconer, and his associate, Mino Spinolo, mufflers wrapped around their lower faces to both disguise their features and to filter the stench, worked quickly and quietly, carting the tall kitchen worker to the bench and then turning him so his head entered the opening in the stone.

"He will have to be stuffed," murmured Valla.

Dino heard no reply, but another excruciating wave of pain swept over the thin servant as his arms were pulled back, and his broken shoulder bent grotesquely behind him. The strong arms folded him like a roll of parchment, as his head was lowered through the opening. He was free to scream then, and he did, as he was forced through the hole and plummeted thirty meters through the darkness to the base of the castello and into the black and suffocating pit of human waste.

Then Mino took a ring from his finger and dropped it into the pit.

The ring, bearing the single letter "S," drowned in the darkness.

In the tower workroom, the darkness surrendered a little to the candles and oil lamps as the Maestro ignited them. However, for Niccolo, the warmth and light did not dissolve the overwhelming sense of unknown and terrifying things lurking in the shadows. The dwarf felt a breath of cold air brush against the back of his neck, and he trembled. Then, not wishing to expose his uneasiness to the Maestro, he shuffled through a sheaf of sketches on the desk before him and pretended to study them.

"It must be wonderful to be able to create such art," he said.

The Maestro crossed to stand beside him and examine the sketches. "Technically speaking," the artist said, "painting is not an art, but a science, based on a rationalization of sight. All things true and beautiful are, at the base, *scientia*."

"Maestro Ambrogio would disagree," Niccolo argued. "He considers himself a scientist, but he cannot paint as you can."

"That is because Maestro Ambrogio is not only a poor artist, but also a poor scientist," the painter snorted. He drew some blank sheets of parchment from a pile and opened a small wooden chest that contained a dozen sticks of charcoal. "Why do you think painters are members of the apothecary guild? Because the apothecary and the painter both grind substances; one to make medicines, one to make pigments. At the base: *scientia*. The business of delicately mixing elements in careful portions and ratios. Mathematics."

Struggling not only to understand want the painter was saying but to decipher the terms he was using, Niccolo suddenly realized that the painter did not literally mean "science" when he used the word *scientia*. For the Maestro it seemed to have another, more expansive meaning: a base of knowledge for intellectual activity. The dwarf congratulated himself on defining the term, suddenly realizing that he wanted this tall bearded man to recognize and appreciate his own intelligence.

"Mathematics?"

The Maestro nodded. "Why does that surprise you? One item and another always make two, whether we are in China or Russia or Italy," explained the artist. "The terms may be different, but the results are always the same. One and one equal two. Applying that fact to what I have just shown you, someone was murdered. Someone had a reason to murder. The killer's identity will be the sum of those two factors. Truth, ultimately, cannot be hidden." The Maestro shuffled through the sketches, apparently lost in a search for something. "And absolute truth is always provable by mathematics," he murmured.

"I can't believe you mean it," the dwarf argued. "How could your mathematics apply to something sociological? Or political? Or spiritual?"

"Watch!" the artist commanded. He took one of the blank

parchments, drew a square, and then, as rapidly, sketched a nude man standing in the box, his head touching the top and his feet centered on the bottom line. "This is the duke of Milan." He quickly drew the man's arms outstretched, the tips of the fingers exactly touching the sides of the box. "Note that the head, the torso, the length of the arms are in perfect proportion. When a man stands with his arms outstretched, the distance will equal his height. That is mathematics being applied to art. It can also symbolize a political fact. The duke is in a box he created around himself. Outside, a million enemies, inside, order and precision. Now . . ." He suddenly placed one point of his compass in the navel of the nude figure and inscribed a circle. "This," he explained, "is an application of an Euclid proposition in geometry." His charcoal darted around the parchment, depicting another set of arms and legs on the nude figure, the fingers and feet precisely touching the circumference of the circle. "This is the duke as perceived by the world outside, arms and legs extended, vulnerable; but a circle, you see, is eternal, no beginning and no end. It is strong, because if you succeed in breaking one side of a square, the entire structure collapses, but an assault against a circle bounces away. These are called tangents, and there are rules for determining where they meet the circumference of the circle. Further, if the circle is punctured, the ends simply meet again, forming a circle of smaller circumference but still intact. This is mathematics applied to military tactics. You see?" He smiled, sitting back. "Art, life, war, politics, they are all derivative from mathematical laws, and such laws allow for no exceptions. None. Absolute truth. Nothing, nothing is true unless it can be proven by mathematics."

"These are games," grumbled Niccolo, thoroughly confused and half convinced that the old man was being amused at his expense. "You are simply applying one set of principles to something completely alien."

The Maestro turned his head to look at the dwarf, and for

the second time that Niccolo could remember, he smiled. "You think so?" he said after a moment. "Well, consider this, small friend. There is a painting by Piero of the French mother, della Francesca, that depicts the baptism of Christ. At first view, it seems simple enough: Christ erect, centered; John pouring water on his head while a dove, wings outstretched, hovers over them." To Niccolo's amazement, the bearded artist began to sketch figures, his charcoal stick darting over the parchment. "To the left is a white tree and gathered around this tree, watching the baptism, are three disciples. But if you apply Euclid's proposition sixteen to the piece, and impose a pentagon over an equilateral triangle, Christ's feet are the apex of the inverted triangle which perfectly centers Christ, and the hovering dove is perfectly aligned with the base of it." Suddenly the sketch became a web of lines and angles. "At the same time, the pentagon exactly encloses all the peripheral figures of the painting, including a bent male in the background donning a robe after the ritual."

"So?" Niccolo murmured, amazed at both the rapidity of the sketching and the torrent of explanations.

"You don't see? You don't understand?" The Maestro quickly sketched an inverted triangle. "Three sides, my boy! The trinity! And the pentagon!" He quickly imposed a five-sided figure over the triangle. "Five sides. Christ's five wounds."

Niccolo grimaced. "Oh really . . ."

"Don't be so quick to mock!" thundered the older man. "You think great art is spontaneous? That it erupts in some mystical fashion from a gifted soul? No! It is plotted, planned, wrought like iron until it meets all the requirements placed upon it by the artist himself!"

"A man looking at the painting will never see a triangle and a pentagon!" Niccolo insisted. "But he can still admire the painting."

"But there is so much more to great art!" the bearded

painter groaned. "Look! The pentagon and the triangle are only a method of constructing a circle divided into five arcs, each arc containing three equal segments!" The Maestro's strong hands began to sweep around the sketch, inscribing a circle, then marking three equal divisions with his compass within each arc formed by the pentagon and the circle. "Don't you see? Can't you understand? Each of the fifteen segments spans twenty-four degrees." He extended the compass to Niccolo for affirmation. "Exactly twenty-four degrees. Twenty-four! Don't you see? Christ was supposedly baptized on the first day of the winter solstice! And where is the sun at the winter solstice? Twenty four degrees below the Equator! Twenty-four! Della Francesca has mathematically made Christ the source of light, the sun! And what is more, every figure in the painting is in exact proportion to the basic segment of an arc. The height of the Christus, for example, is three times the length of a segment. Three! Again the Trinity!"

"But no one looking at the picture is going to know that!" Niccolo insisted. "No one is going to stand before the painting, remember the probable date of Christ's baptism, compute it astronomically and then mentally draw pentagrams ...!"

"Pentagons," snapped the old master, throwing down the charcoal. "A pentagram is a five-pointed star used in witchcraft."

"That's what I mean," Niccolo snapped back, embarrassed but determined to continue the debate. "It's all mystic mumbo jumbo! No one would ever think to draw these—geometries—on top of the painting to learn that della Francesca was saying Christ was the source of all light!"

"I did!"

"Yes. But you are not normal! You are—well—exceptional!"

"Yes!" thundered the Maestro. "And that is what constitutes great art! To the simple man it says something. To the complex man, a little more. And to the exceptional, it speaks volumes! It does not matter if everyone—or anyone, other than the artist—perceives all that is in the work. The element of greatness is that it is in the work at all!'

Niccolo sighed and found himself surrendering a little to the Maestro's arguments. He stared at the bearded apparition, completely wrapped in black and almost indistinguishable now in the twilight from the shadows behind him. "I—don't understand, Maestro," he said. "What good is all this talk about triangles and the Trinity and the arcs and equal segments? Why can't you simply look at the painting, and see it for what it is? A beautiful picture?"

The Maestro stared at the dwarf for what seemed an eternity. "Because the more you understand the work, the more you understand the maker," he replied softly. "A beautiful sunset leads to an appreciation of the maker of so many wonderful things, and ultimately to a love of so great a creator. Great love, you see, is born of thorough knowledge. If you do not know much of the beloved, you can only love a little, if at all. You are like a dog who wags its tail when given a bone. If the animal could understand the goodness of the man who offers him the bone, it would love the giver even more—if the concept of such goodness were within his understanding." The Maestro sighed. "In other words, if you would know God, look at what He has created. If you would love Him, ask yourself why He created it."

Niccolo suddenly found himself in a strange empathy with the bearded artist, and at the same time he felt as if the Maestro had reached his huge hands into his small body and gripped his heart, as Niccolo imagined he might when dissecting one of the corpses. It was, at one and the same time, the thing he had feared most when he had left the Certosa and an experience of such exhilaration that the young man felt he could spend a lifetime living with and learning from such a master.

"All right," he mumbled, stepping down from the small

bench. "Fine. But I still think these are mental games, Maestro. What does all this—mathematical magic—have to do with what is happening here and now? How does all this affect real things, well, like the duke's troubles?"

"Perception! Perception!" the painter prodded him. "The duke's power and strength is less dependent upon reality, than on how it is perceived, especially by his enemies! Is it the square or the circle? If the French or the Venetians see him as vulnerable, then for their purposes, he is vulnerable. Further, if he begins to perceive himself as vulnerable, he is doomed."

"But he is vulnerable! All men are!"

"But that should not concern him," the artist retorted. "If a man concentrates upon his weaknesses, he will devote his time and energies to guarding those weaknesses from his enemies. He becomes defensive. But if he perceives himself to be invulnerable, he will not look at his situation as defensive. He will attack. And our chronicles are filled with stories of vulnerable men who dismissed their vulnerabilities, attacked, and won. The enemy doesn't expect an attack from a vulnerable target!"

Niccolo's fascination with Maestro Leonardo blossomed into open admiration over the next few weeks, and the bearded artist began to assume a new vitality, a sense of purpose that was immediately evident to everyone at the court. "The madman has taken a new apprentice," was the report of the Whisperers to Salvatore Cossa who, in turn, passed the observation to da Corte, and he to the duke.

The response of the duke was unpredictable. He advised Madonna Valentina to let the youth have as much liberty as possible, and the conclusion reached by the members of the court was that Il Moro had actually planted an agent in the tower from whom he could gather information on Maestro Leonardo's activities and opinions.

"Only an idiot would fail to utilize a genius," the duke was reported to have told his advisors, "even if the man is mad."

But the opposite was true. Niccolo, his confidence and trust in the tall artist growing stronger with every day, confided the heavy secret burdens he had been carrying for his months at court. He told the Maestro of the overnight abduction by the Countess Bergamini and the existence of the hidden passageways.

The response of the master to the revelation concerning the countess was to confirm that the lady was above suspicion.

"If she said she wished to protect the duke," the Maestro commented, "then that is her true intention."

His response to the secret corridors was to explore the narrow passages with the dwarf that very evening.

The artist had to sit on the floor to peer through the spy holes with Niccolo standing erect beside him, and what they saw and heard was another meeting of the duke with his advisors in the Salla della Palla, the duke standing centered in the circle, obviously agitated and annoyed.

"There are further complications," sighed the gray-haired, Girolamo da Tuttavilla. "Word has reached Genoa, and a delegation is preparing even now to travel here."

"God's blood!" thundered the duke. "How did they hear of it? Who told them?"

"It's obvious, brother," said the cardinal sipping his wine. "I just returned from Rome, as you know. The pontiff has decided to convene the panel to annul Lucrezia's marriage to our brother, virgin or not. But what is more important, the Holy Father has decided to release his son, Cesare, from his priestly vows, and that could only mean that the young man has his eyes on a principality of his own. Probably yours. So you can be certain that if there is someone out there stirring up the Genoese, it is Cesare Borgia. Either he or one of his agents."

The aged diplomat nodded. "I concur," he said softly.

"The question is," replied da Corte, "what shall we tell this delegation from Genoa when they arrive?"

"I suppose we will have to take the—inevitable—action," sighed the duke. "Then we will have to come up with a story that will satisfy the delegation. Something—sensitive. Something of gentility."

Bernardino reflected on these instructions. "If I understand you, sire, it will also have to be something that Maestro Ambrogio will accept and verify."

"That shouldn't be difficult," replied Il Moro, and Niccolo heard a small chuckle escape from the Maestro spying beside him.

"What of Maestro Leonardo?" asked da Casate, stroking his short, trimmed beard.

"What of him?"

"He will want to have a hand in this," grumbled the advisor. "You know how he is. He'll argue that his science could profit from it, and he'll argue and confuse everyone until he gets his way."

Once again the Maestro made a small sound, and Niccolo pondered whether to warn the artist to be careful.

The duke sat quietly for a moment, then he said, "Then, if necessary, we'll permit him to have a hand in it. What harm could it do? It might even serve our purposes, because Maestro Leonardo is known throughout Europe as a man of integrity. If he affirms what we say, it will be accepted without question."

"Of course," Bernardino whispered, nodding. "Of course." He stood and bowed to the duke. "With your permission."

The cardinal rose abruptly. "I must leave you, too, Ludovico. I am expected at a late dinner with Cardinal Ippolito d'Este and Galeazz," he said. "The captain-general's new palazzo is nearing completion, and he has asked me work with Maestro Leonardo, Marchesino Stanga, and Messer Calco to arrange a grand festival to celebrate its completion. It will be a gala affair in the great ballroom of the new palace. Costumes. Merry dances. Pageants and games." He headed for the door with Bernardino. "You will be surprised at the size of Galeazz's palace, brother. It is now the second largest private residence in Milan, second only to the Palazzo del Verme."

Francesco da Casate and Girolamo da Tuttavilla rose together. "If Your Highness will excuse us, there are also matters that we should attend to immediately."

The duke nodded, and the four men bowed their heads in unison and left the room. The great doors had no sooner closed behind them when Il Moro leaned across the desk to Salvatore Cossa.

"The list of possibilities?" he asked.

Salvatore handed a rolled parchment across the desk, and the duke quickly scanned it.

"Interesting," the duke said. "I am going to give you complete authority in this matter. Bernardino will have his hands full trying to reveal the identity of this 'Griffin.' That is his prime responsibility. Your responsibility will be to proceed against these probables, and I will not interfere with what action you take. Indeed, the less I know of the matter, the better." He rolled the parchment again and placed it to one side. "I have an additional little commission for you, Salvatore," he said softly. "One more appropriate to the Whisperers. Yesterday when I returned from Vigevano, I had occasion to visit Madonna Valentina. It was a somewhat—late hour, and she was not in her bed."

Niccolo felt his chest tighten. So the Madonna's nocturnal wanderings had not gone undetected! If the duke had gone to the lady's quarters, he probably had used the hidden passage. The dwarf swore silently to himself to be more careful in trekking the secret corridors.

Cossa dared not smile. "I understand, Your Highness," he said drily.

"I have been given to believe that perhaps the Madonna has taken a lover," the duke said quietly, sitting back in his chair. "I have also been given to believe that this lover might be my son-in-law, Galeazzo di Sanseverino. What think you?"

The chief of the Whisperers shrugged. "I have heard—some gossip to that effect, but—it is only gossip."

The duke nodded. "Of course," he murmured. "But I should know with absolute certainty what is happening under my own roof. Try to identify the man, but if it is Galeazz, I do not want any action taken. In that case, report to me, and I will do something about it myself."

Salvatore nodded. "And the woman?" he asked.

"Nothing must happen to Madonna Valentina," he demanded. "I want her punished, but in my own way. Let her live with the knowledge that I know everything she does, that nothing is hidden from me. And what to expect should she take another lover without my approval." He smiled across the desk as he rose. "Besides," he said, "this is partly my own fault. I have been neglecting the lady shamefully of late. A man should never leave a, what shall I say, a—vulnerable—woman to her own devices, eh?"

And at this, Salvatore dared to return the duke's smile.

Behind the curtained stage in the Busseto piazza, Piero Tebaldeo presented his last instructions before the *commedia dell'arte* troupe went onstage. He rubbed his hands together to ward off the cold, and as he spoke his breath made small clouds of vapor in the chilled air.

"I hope everyone is prepared! Remember the outline! The Captain returns home after a trip to Milan. He has been but newly married to a much younger woman, and he is wisely concerned that he should not have left her alone."

With that the false captain turned and bolted onto the stage to the applause and cheers of the crowd who had anxiously been waiting for the afternoon performance to begin, dancing about and slapping their arms around their sides to keep themselves warm.

"Home at last!" the Captain bellowed, throwing wide his

arms and knocking over the coat tree to soft laughter from the audience. "You may think me foolish to have gone off and left my very young and very innocent wife alone in this wicked city; but I gave strict orders to my servants that no one, especially no man, was to be admitted while I was in Milan. And although they are stupid, like most servants from Bergamo, they are very afraid of me and will always do as I command." Then he delivered what was an onstage cue since the days of the Roman theatre. "Ah!" he heralded. "Here they are now!"

At that moment Rubini as Scapino and Anna as Lesbino seemed to be hurled onstage as if by an offstage catapult. They stared at the Captain, both screamed in unison and tried to hide behind one another.

"She did it!" shrieked Scapino. "I didn't!"

"Don't listen to him, sire!" countered Lesbino. "Whatever we did that we shouldn't, he did it first!"

The Captain glared at the servants and then delivered an aside to the audience. "This sounds ominous." Then he turned his stony stare back on the two cringing servants. "What have you two been doing?"

"Nothing!" they declared in unison.

"But she did it, not me!" added Scapino.

"After he did it first!" screeched Lesbino.

"Did what?" snapped the Captain.

"Whatever we did to offend you!" whined Scapino.

The Captain bellowed, "What did you do?"

"Nothing!" came the chorus.

"But he did it before I did!" Lesbino declared.

"You're getting me angry!" snapped the Captain.

"Please don't bite off my nose!" pleaded Lesbino dropping to her knees.

"Please don't sever my head from my body!" begged Scapino, trying to hide behind the crouching girl.

"Please don't feed me cockroaches and slugs!" squealed Lesbino.

"Please don't sew my lips together!" Scapino implored his master, grasping his legs and making it impossible for the Captain to walk.

The Captain seized the luckless young man by his collar and pulled him to his feet. "What are you going on about?" he snarled. "Have I ever done any of those things to you?"

"No, but you might!" Scapino wept.

"Now that we've suggested them," added Lesbino.

"Listen to me!" the Captain roared as he hurled Scapino back into Lesbino's arms. "The only thing I am concerned about is my beautiful young wife! Has she entertained any young men while I was away?"

"Yes!" shrieked Scapino at exactly the same time that Lesbino wailed "No!" The servants then glared at one another, and then quickly wheeled on the Captain. "No!" declared Scapino as Lesbino yelled "Yes!"

Scapino became more visibly afraid as the audience rippled with laughter. "Probably!" he murmured.

"Perhaps!" said Lesbino.

"Occasionally!" Scapino declared a little louder.

"Absolutely!" Lesbino pronounced loudly and clearly.

"Repeatedly!" roared Scapino.

"Violently!" Lesbino topped him.

There was a beat as Scapino realized what they had just confessed to their master who was, in turn, scowling and clenching his fist. Once again the black-masked comic servant began to shake from head to toe.

"Define 'young,' " he suggested.

"Have there been any men in this house while I was away?" demanded the Captain drawing his long sword with some difficulty.

"None at all!'" the two quaking servitors chorused. Then, after another beat, Lesbino whispered, "Well—one."

"Two!" moaned Scapino.

"Some!" Lesbino admitted.

"Several!" Scapino wailed.

"Many!" shrieked Lesbino.

"A regiment!" roared Scapino.

"Half of Bologna!" Lesbino bellowed.

"All of Venice!" Scapino thundered.

"Northern Europe!" Lesbino heralded.

"Africa!" Scapino boomed.

Then, once again, he realized that the Captain seemed about to strike.

"But only the males!" he wailed.

"Stop!" bellowed the Captain, waving the large sword in all directions to the delight of the viewers. "I'll get to the bottom of this!" He then attempted to sheath the sword, a task which required all three to maneuver the weapon into its case. Then the Captain marched to the center of the stage and yelled, "Desiree! Desiree, my sweet! Come here at once!"

From behind him, Isabella entered with small mincing steps as though her feet were encased in tiny China cups. "You bellowed, my sweet husband?" she cooed.

"Look at me, Desiree!" demanded the Captain.

"So soon after dinner?" the lady asked.

The Captain began his inquisition as the two servants cowered silently in the corner. "Has anything happened while I was away at Milan?"

"No, husband."

"Nothing at all?" he pressed. "Answer me truthfully."

"Nothing happened."

"Nothing?"

"Well, the kitten died," she offered.

"I'm sorry to hear it," he sympathized. "How did it die?"

"The dog fell on it."

The Captain's eyes widened as the audience laughed. "The dog fell on it? How is that possible?"

"It lost its footing on the roof," the young woman explained, "and just sort of—slipped off."

"On the roof?" inquired the Captain. "What the devil was it doing on the roof?"

"Chasing my parakeet."

"Your—parakeet?"

"It flew out of its cage when it was kicked over."

"Who kicked over the parakeet cage?"

"I did, my love," she smiled at him. "But it was an accident. He tickled me."

"The parakeet tickled you?" asked the Captain.

"No," she laughed. "The young man on the horse."

The Captain began to sputter with rage. "There was a young man on a horse in your bedchamber?"

"Of course not."

The Captain sighed. "I'm relieved to hear it."

"The horse was tied in the street."

"I should hope so."

"The young gentleman stood on the horse so he could reach my balcony," she said with an innocence that confused her husband.

"Was a young man admitted to your presence while I was away?" thundered the fat military man.

"No, dear," the young wife added quickly.

"Thank heavens!"

"He wasn't exactly admitted," she smiled.

"What does that mean?"

The young woman took a deep breath and then began her explanation. "I was on my balcony drying my hair which I had just washed with that perfumed soap you brought me from Naples last month. You know the one scented of jasmine and heather combined in the blue silk wrapper with the black band around . . . ?"

"To the point!" roared the Captain. "Was a young man here?"

"Let me tell you!"

"By all means!"

"I was on the balcony," she began, "drying my hair . . ."

"Forget your hair!" her husband roared.

"I couldn't do that," Isabella whined. "If I don't wash it every other day, the curls just straighten and . . ."

"Tell me about the young man!"

"Well, I was on the balcony, and I noticed him in the street noticing me on the balcony noticing him, and then he sort of bowed to me; which was very genteel of him, so I naturally returned his bow; and then he sort of smiled and bowed again, and I thought 'How polite', so I bowed a little lower to him; and then he bowed even lower, and I . . ."

"Forget the bowing!" the Captain screamed. "What happened after the bowing?"

Isabella pursed her lips in annoyance and declared, "He became impertinent."

The Captain paled. "How so?"

"He winked at me and blew me a kiss."

"The scoundrel!"

"My thought exactly," she nodded. "I thought: I am a happily married woman, and it is not proper for me to accept a wink and a kiss from a stranger to whom I've never been introduced!"

"Very good!" the Captain declared. "You are a virtuous young woman!"

"So I introduced myself."

The mock captain's eyes rolled back into his head, and he looked as though he had been impaled. "What?" he roared.

"I told him my name, and he told me his," the young wife explained.

"In the name of God!" boomed the Captain to the delight of the assembly. "What happened then?"

Isabella adopted a pose that she imagined would suggest modesty, one arm across her breasts, the other at her crotch. "Well, I thought to myself, 'This is highly improper for a happily married young woman to be seen on her balcony clothed only in her shift speaking to a young man in the street.' "

"Quite correct!" sighed the Captain. "So?"

"I invited him in, so no one would see us and be scandalized."

By now the two comic servants had dissolved into a mound of quivering fear, and the Captain, anxious to alleviate some of his rage, suddenly wheeled and kicked Scapino who, in turn, shrieked and tried to hide behind Lesbino.

The Captain turned back to his young wife. "You admitted him?" he snarled. "After I told you to lock the doors and let no man through them?"

"The doors remained locked, my dear," Isabella cooed, "just as you commanded. He came over my balcony."

The Captain wheeled to kick Scapino again, but saw Lesbino there, whereupon he pulled her aside so he could take a good swing at the hapless Scapino who was trying desperately to dig his way through the stage floor. After a kick at the poor servant, the Captain wheeled again and faced his errant wife. "This is unbearable! This is scandalous!" he screamed.

"Not at all, dear husband!" Isabella replied with innocent astonishment. "The young man was, after all, wounded and dying. It was the proper Christian thing to do! It was an act of charity!"

This declaration stunned the Captain. "He was wounded and dying? Why didn't you say so in the first place? Who wounded him? What was he dying from?"

"Love of me, he said. He said my eyes had wounded him to his very heart, and he was expiring with his passion for me!"

The Captain became a storm cloud of supressed rage. "He said that? The blackguard! The rascal!"

Finally he took a breath and asked, "So what did you do?"

"I cured him," she said brightly.

The Captain roared in frustration and anger as Isabella tripped merrily from the stage to the laughter of the audience and a small rain of coins.

The mock officer turned on the servants once again and

bellowed, "You are responsible for this! My innocent young wife couldn't have gotten such ideas from her convent school! Who educated her to the ways of love? What immoral wretch has been in attendance on her and gave her such improper ideas? Who? Who?"

The two servants cringed and began to speak rapidly.

"No one!" shrieked Scapino.

"Someone!" wailed Lesbino.

"A woman!" cried Scapino as Lesbino declared "A man!"

"A manly woman!" Scapino cried as Lesbino offered, "A feminine man!"

Suddenly Scapino threw himself at the Captain's feet and began to confess "An old woman who wears her hair heavily powdered and coiled around her head and ears like a turnip in heat, and with a beauty mark just beside her left nostril— because that's the only part of her face that doesn't look like she is dying of apoplexy!"

There was a long beat as the Captain glared at his servants, and then he turned to the audience, his face a mask of misfortune and disbelief. Then his voice became a moan of pain and anxiety.

"My mother!" he wailed.

The small audience responded with a shower of coins, but Piero, exhausted, stumbled off the stage to find Turio waiting for him with a uniformed courier.

"Signor Piero Tebaldeo?" asked the courier.

"Yes," the fake captain murmured. "What is the problem now? I assure you, signore, we left the money for our reckoning on the table when we . . ."

"Sire," the courier replied, "I come from the court of the duke of Milan, His Highness Ludovico Sforza . . ."

Piero began to formulate some alibi for whatever obscure insult the company may have given Il Moro in implying that the fake captain had been in Milan while his young wife dallied, but before he could speak, the courier continued.

"His Highness invites your company to return to Milan to perform for the festival celebrating the completion of the palace of his captain-general Galeazzo di Sanseverino. Do you accept?"

Isabella Corteze and Anna Ponti, the songstress, entered through the curtains and handed Piero the small coins collected from the stage. He glanced at the collection and smiled.

"You may inform His Highness that nothing would please us more."

"To Father Abbot, Certosa, Pavia."

The young dwarf sat cross-legged on his bed in the Castello Sforzesco, a fur throw wrapped around his shoulders, and his fingers wrapped in flannel gloves which made it somewhat difficult to manipulate the pen.

"Dearest Father Abbot . . ." the epistle began. "It is very cold in the castle. My fingers are numb with the heavy chill even as I write these words, and I must pause from time to time to blow the warmth of my breath on them to keep them supple. It is especially cold in my rooms here in the women's quarters. I freeze, although I am seated on my bed with the heavy fur skin of a black bear wrapped around my shoulders and a cheering fire in my small fireplace.

"It is cold in all of Milano, and, for all I know, it is frigid through most of Italy, but it is especially cold here in the Castello Sforzesco. It is a silent, suffocating chill that invades even the darkest corner and fills every corridor and tower. It prowls with the winds along the columned walkways and the arched halls. It squats like a great frigid cat in every high-ceilinged room where the warmth from the hearths rises to heat only the heavy wooden rafters while the bottom half drowns in the chill. It is in the crystal rime that clings to the cold stone and is only partially blocked by the heavy rugs and tapestries.

"It is a cold of the heart and of the spirit. It hangs heavy on the lids of the mustached and bearded men in dark colors with daggers at their jeweled belts who roam the corridors to listen and look and report everything they see or hear to the master of the house. It is evident in their thin, bloodless lips and their hungry, angular frames. The chill pervades the rooms of the women of the court as they compare each other's clothes and paintings and mannerisms and quarrel over trivialities. The frost glistens on their eyelids and in their powdered hair. It produces the chill melancholia reflected in their sullen and bitter tirades against one another.

"The cold is most evident, however, in what they call the madman's tower, overlooking the gardens, where Maestro Leonardo keeps his amazing and awesome devices designed to make men fly like birds or walk on water or, unhappily, kill other men in war. In the back, shadowed portion of the great room there is another area which can be curtained off. It contains tables. Here the Maestro occasionally has the bodies of recently deceased men and women brought to him to be cut open and their insides sketched on great sheets of parchment. He does these things, not to invoke magic or to indulge in any blasphemous activity, as Brother Pax believes, but to learn more, for Maestro Leonardo believes that knowledge leads to a greater understanding of the nature of God, and understanding leads to love.

"It is here, too, that the Moor's occasional mistress, Madonna Valentina, now under suspicion, spends hours and hours having her portrait painted. I presume at the duke's request. I imagine he has ordered it to keep her occupied and away from her new lover. There is no threat of scandal in the lady spending so much time in the tower, however, because many in the court persist in their belief that the Maestro's taste runs to handsome young boys like his assistant, Giacomo Salai, but I believe this to be blatantly false and insulting. More and more, the Maestro has sent Salai to assist the other artists in the Santa Marie delle Grazie, and, happily, spends more time teaching me.

"But at this moment something as chilling as the winter's breath hangs heavily over the castello. It began with the death of a Venetian assassin whom, according to Messer Bernardino da Corte, expired from torture, but Maestro Leonardo has demonstrated to me that the man was murdered by stabbing.

"Then a young servant girl died from poison that some say was meant for the duke, but they have been unable to find the suspected decanter or to identify the poisoner. The Maestro feels this was either a tragic accident or a case of suicide.

"But their bodies were no sooner removed and buried when a search for a missing kitchen worker ended with the discovery of his body in the cesspit at the base of the castello near the mercenaries' quarters, and both Maestro Leonardo and Maestro Ambrogio determined that the man had been beaten, his shoulders broken, and then pushed through one of the openings in a water closet.

"And only this afternoon, one of the court's ladies-in-waiting from Genoa, a Madonna Maria Chigi, was reported missing, and no one seems to be able to find her. Some say she has run off with a suitor, and others insist this was not in her nature. One day she was seen speaking with Salvatore Cossa, captain of the Whisperers, and the next day she did not report when summoned by the duke. Everyone is afraid that she, too, has become a victim of some mysterious killer stalking the corridors.

"All this discord has been attributed, either directly or indirectly, to an agent of the Venetians who supposedly lives here in the duke's court and who has been identified only as 'the Griffin.' Everyone speaks of this mysterious fellow in hushed tones, yet no one has advanced a theory to explain why such an agent would want to kill servants or kidnap a lady-in-waiting.

"The only bright spot on the horizon is a festival to celebrate the completion of the new palace of Captain-General Galeazzo di Sanseverino in the eastern end of Milan. The celebration will take place some time after twelfth night. The process is proceeding much too slowly for the captain-general. The duke, however, has been busily arranging for a series of parties and performances to alleviate some of the gloom of the castle. He has announced the return of a group of mummers called I Comici Buffoni who apparently play a new type of theater called *commedia dell'arte*. They performed at the court about a year ago, and the duke, reportedly, was fascinated by them, although Maestro Leonardo says the company drank too much and behaved outrageously. My mistress says, a little jealously I think, that the chamberlain was much taken with one of the women, someone known only as Prudenza of Siena.

"The company will reside in the castle but perform at the new palace. I visited the new residence once with my mistress and Maestro Leonardo who is designing costumes and elaborate stages for the festival. There are big arched windows in the second-floor dining hall that look out on the Alps. The distant mountains are very impressive and beautiful, capped in snow.

"But they do not seem as cold as the mood in the castle."

The following Monday was the feastday of All Saints, and, in custom, the entire court attended Mass at the basilica of Saint'Ambrogio. All, that is, save Maestro Leonardo who made a quick journey to Vigevano, his "model city" near Pavia.

Niccolo, accustomed to the sonorous chants of the monks,

the overpowering scent of incense, and the deep solemnity of services in the Certosa, once again found himself mildly amused and shocked that so few of the army of courtiers in the basilica paid any attention whatsoever to the celebrants or the massed choirs, but gathered together in small groups and exchanged gossip and favors. Silence had been the rule in the monastery, save for the chanting, but here the exhortations of the deacons and subdeacons could not even be heard above the din of conversation and animal noises.

Madonna Dorothea's pet cheetah, straining against a gold chain and a gold collar studded with rubies, was causing a furor among the other pets, the monkeys chattering shrilly and leaping, unfettered, on the backs and shoulders of their owners, and Cardinal Ascanio's pet parrot erupted in his singular talent: reciting the entire Creed of the Apostles.

Suddenly a hymnal was pushed into the dwarf's hands. Niccolo, by standing on the upholstered kneeler, was on a level with the head of the genuflecting court lady in the velvet gown with loops of gold woven into the silk pile. He inserted his folded sheet of parchment between the pages and passed it back to the lady who smiled, bobbed her head, blessed herself, rose, and disappeared among the elaborately dressed and disinterested members of the court.

Niccolo was surprised to find that the courier on this occasion was not the same lady to whom he had handed the three previous epistles for the countess. He also noted that when the lady stood, she made an adjustment to her headpiece which required her to remove and then replace the long pin that anchored the starched linen to her scarlet hair.

It was, Niccolo observed, a small, thin instrument with a round shaft, strong, but much smaller than a stiletto.

An hour later in the Palazzo del Verme, the Countess Bergamini silently read Niccolo's report in the presence of her secretary, a thin, bored, spectacled young man dressed entirely in lavender. When she was finished, she folded the parchment walked to the window, and stared through the curtains of falling snow as if trying to discern something behind the immaculate whiteness.

"Galeazzo," she said softly, and the secretary, his pen poised over the parchment and awaiting his instructions, said nothing. The countess turned from the window. "Galeazzo," she repeated.

She crossed to the waiting secretary. "Have you the letter from my cousin in Venice?"

The secretary turned to a small bin of documents, selected one that was folded, its wax seal broken, and handed it to the countess. The lady took it, read it, and returned it to the scribe.

"Write this," she commanded. "Galeazzo di Sanseverino. Proceed as instructed as soon as possible, but time is essential. It must be done before twelfth night."

When the secretary had inscribed the message, the countess took it from him, folded it, dropped the hot wax from the red candle on the fold and pressed her signet ring against it.

Within an hour, the seal was broken and the message read by a burly, yellow-bearded man in the stables of the Castello Sforzesco. He whispered instructions to two other stablemen who, in turn, nodded and immediately disappeared into the shadows and the falling, blanketing snow.

Chapter 4
Flight and Fantasy

"My Most Illustrious Lord . . .
I shall endeavor,
while intending no discredit to anyone else,
to bring myself to the attention of Your Excellency
for the purpose of unfolding to you my secrets . . .
and if any (of these) things seem impossible
or impractical to anyone,
I am most readily disposed
to demonstrate them in your park . . ."

**Letter from Leonardo da Vinci
to Ludovico Sforza
c. 1494**

As December wore down there were a series of religious feasts and a slight lifting of the somber mood at Il Moro's court. Soon after the feast of the Nativity Niccolo was delighted to learn he would accompany Madonna Valentina to the still-incompleted palace of Galeazzo di Sanseverino and view the preparations being made for the great festival. For weeks there had been delegations from the court sleighing through the falling snow to view the decor being prepared by Maestro Leonardo. Always in attendance during these excursions were Marchesino Stanga, the stiff-necked Milanese Minister of Public Works who always seemed to be smelling something unpleasant, and Bartolomeo Calco, the duke's personal secretary, who walked meekly in his shadow. On this occasion, however, several ladies of the court were invited to visit the new palace since they would be participating in the pageant.

It was Madonna Valentina's decision to take Niccolo with her. She knew Madonna Dorotea would be present with her cheetah, and Cardinal Ascanio with his parrot, so the lady outfitted the dwarf in satin brocade that combined more colors than the parrot's plumage and with a heavy diamond pendant suspended from a black ribbon to rival the cheetah's ruby collar.

Also present in the vast room of the new palace this cold winter morning was Maestro Ambrogio da Rosate, a venerable gentleman who served as Il Moro's court physician and astrologer. Niccolo had met the aged master on one or two brief occasions, but he had detected a hostility toward him when the physician learned that the dwarf had become a favorite of Maestro Leonardo.

There was also a trio of cardinals accompanying the duke's cardinal-brother, Ascanio. These princes of the church included the tall and imposing Cardinal Castagno, whom Niccolo had never before seen at court; Ippolito d'Este, an athletic and handsome cardinal who enjoyed a reputation as an expert lover according to reports that the dwarf had heard whispered among the court ladies; and the shorter and more obese Cardinal Albizzi whom, it was rumored, practiced daily to achieve the status of d'Este.

Galeazzo di Sanseverino himself was present, of course, as he had been every day since the construction began, resplendent now in silver armor trimmed in gold. He strode behind the duke who had turned from convention and was even more glorious in a pearl-white tunic flecked with gold with a grape-size diamond on his black velvet cap. The impatient captain-general would pause occasionally, poke at this drapery, finger that lace border, question Maestro Leonardo about the price of everything, and complain to Il Moro that nothing was being accomplished with the speed and frugality he wished.

"My lord," Maestro Leonardo explained to the warrior once again, "quality demands time. I am taking particular pains to make certain the pageant and the procession draw the admiration and delight of the spectators. I strive to be universal, because there is a lack of worthiness in doing one thing well and another badly. Everything must be precise. I once attended a banquet where I saw a tableaux depicting the Annunciation, and the appearance of the angel was such that Our Lady looked as though she might throw herself from a window in fright and disgust."

"Yes, yes, yes," the captain-general repeated. "Spare me another treatise on the necessity of order and symmetry, and just explain to me this billing from the aviary."

"Peacock feathers."

"Two hundred peacock feathers? What will we do with them, stuff a mattress?"

"They are for the grand procession preceding the allegory," the Maestro explained quietly. "There shall be six white horses with riders. On the left sides of each of the animals there will be a wheel whose center will be placed in the center of their respective hindquarters. Each horse will be mantled in plain gold cloth studded with peacocks' eyes. Each rider shall be similarly attired with their crests and chains of peacock feathers on a gold base. On the helmet of each rider there will be a half globe which symbolizes our hemisphere, and on top of this, a peacock with its tail fanned, richly decorated. Each shield carried by the riders will contain a mirror to signify that he who truly desires favor should reflect his virtues to those around him. Then, as they pass before the guests, the grand drapery embroidered with the theme of the pageant, 'Always of Service,' will be raised on the platform that the horses are pulling. There will be revealed our own Madonna Valentina as Prudence, center, attired in bright red velour. Madonna Dorotea as Charity will be sitting on that bright throne over there with a laurel branch to symbolize the Hope that comes from serving well. On the opposite side, Madonna Terese as Fortitude will stand with a pillar in her hand, all in white silk."

"I see little fortitude in Madonna Terese," complained Madonna Dorotea. "How did you choose the women for these allegorical figures, Maestro? For example, I would imagine that anyone of intelligence and taste can see more of the virtue of prudence in me than in Madonna Valentina." The red-haired woman nodded slightly to Niccolo's mistress. "I trust I am not offending you, Madonna?"

Madonna Valentina returned the nod. "Not at all," she whispered. "But I am afraid that I cannot agree with you. I think Maestro Leonardo has chosen exceptionally well. I can well understand, for example, why you were chosen to depict Charity, my dear. You've given so much of yourself to so many for such a long time."

The stately and reserved Cardinal Castagno could see a storm approaching and chose to smooth the seas.

"Maestro Leonardo," he interjected, "would it not be better to have the allegory spring, shall we say, from sacred text? From biblical figures? I mean, there is something to be said for staging one of the miracles of our Lord, something symbolizing the generosity of His Highness and our captain-general? Perhaps, oh, I don't know, the multiplication of the loaves and fishes?"

Maestro Leonardo pretended to be engrossed in adjusting a drapery. "To be precise," he murmured, "the loaves and fishes were not multiplied."

A gasp went through the assembly, and Maestro smiled as the fat little Cardinal Albizzi stepped forward. "Careful, Maestro," he said quietly. "The story of the multiplication of the loaves and fishes has been related to us by men of God. You skirt heresy to deny this."

"Indeed speak carefully, Maestro Leonardo," warned the duke. "I'd hate to lose you to an ecclesiastical court."

"My source is the same as His Eminence's," the artist replied turning to face the four cardinals. "Mark, Matthew, and Luke all say the same thing: Christ divided the five loaves and two fishes. There is no mention of multiplication. Anything can theoretically be divided into an infinite number of portions. That is a simple mathematical truth. But it is not a miracle." Another gasp echoed through the long room. "The miracle," the artist quickly continued, "is that each member of that vast assembly took a portion of what was offered and was satisfied."

Niccolo smiled and hid his smile behind his hand. The fat little cardinal on the other hand sputtered and stammered and turned to the duke for support. "Your Highness, I plead with you! Judge this heresy."

Il Moro tried to hide his own amusement, but intoned, "I am afraid, Eminence, that I must judge for Maestro Leonardo. When anything satisfies the rabble, that is a genuine miracle."

The laughter of the court lightened the mood, but Niccolo noted that Maestro Leonardo, plainly the victor, did not join in the laughter but returned to adjusting the drapery.

Galeazzo sighed as he glanced once more around the ballroom. "I really don't care whether the pageant is an allegory depicting the ten commandments, the seven deadly sins, or the four elements! All I require is that my palace be completed soon and with a little less expense." He turned to face the duke who strode across the room, his hands locked behind his back. "I am spending as much on this construction as a damned Venetian might spend on his daughter's dowry."

"I sympathize, Galeazz, but you are misinformed," smiled Il Moro. "First: dowries require much more expense. I sent Bianca Maria off to Emperor Maximilian with a dowry of four hundred thousand ducats, and another hundred thousand in jewels, plate, linens, and tapestries. And my niece, Anna, is promised to a noble family of Ferrara, and I have promised her future husband a dowry of one hundred thousand ducats. Furthermore, the Venetian doge, whom you scorn, Galeazz, has proven his wisdom by recently capping all dowries. Venetian dowries are now limited to sixteen hundred ducats."

"Hypocrites!" snapped the captain-general. "The doge capped their dowries, did he? But they still spend small fortunes on the festivals following the weddings! Almost as much as I am spending on this pageant!"

Il Moro paused by Niccolo and smiled at the dwarf. "Ah,"

he said, "but everyone enjoys these festivities, captain, whereas only the newlyweds profit from a dowry."

He turned and spoke to the assembly as he strode toward the Maestro. "Most of you do not understand the demands put upon my treasury. For example, only yesterday my niece, Caterina, petitioned me for a loan so she won't have to sell twenty-five thousand ducats' worth of her jewels to Venetian money lenders for only six thousand, and last year I had to pay incredible sums for the artifacts owned by the late Lorenzo de' Medici which our beloved Maestro Leonardo here urged me to purchase."

"They belonged in the hands of nobility, Your Highness," the artist said turning to face his lord. "The purchase symbolized the passage of power from one prince of Italy to another."

"Perhaps," the duke said. "But these elegant gestures are costing me a fortune. Consider the exorbitant fees demanded by Romano for carving busts of my family. Or Bramante's demands for 'improving' Santa Maria delle Grazie and Solari's subsidy for preparing the decorations on the tomb for my late wife in the same church! Sometimes I think I've poured more money into that insignificant little Dominican chapel than the pope has poured into the Vatican!"

The court seemed not to know whether to laugh or sympathize, so silence ruled. "If I were you, Il Moro," Sanseverino finally declared, "I would offer these elite bastards the opportunity to do these pretty, petty things for nothing or cut off their balls."

"No, Galeazz," Il Moro replied softly. "Maestro Leonardo is right. Patronage represents power among the courts of Europe. I am simply saddened to see artists demanding exorbitant fees without a corresponding rise in quality."

"If that is true, my lord," the Maestro quietly insisted, "they are not true artists. A true artist hopes to leave behind works which will bestow upon their maker some little honor and does not work to earn money for their creation. Money, after all, is celebrated only for its own sake and becomes a magnet for envy. How many emperors, how many princes have there been of whom no memory remains? And why? Because they strove only after territory and wealth to secure their reputations."

Il Moro studied the face of the bearded master. "And for what should a prince strive, Maestro, if not for territory and wealth?"

"Knowledge," Leonardo replied. "Acquire that which will repair the damage of old age. Old age feeds on wisdom."

Again it was difficult for Niccolo to know whether Il Moro was pleased or annoyed at the answer. Finally, the duke smiled and said to the court, "Why do I feel I have just been sermonized?"

Again the mood lightened, and there was another wave of laughter through the court.

"Well," growled Sanseverino as he crossed to stand beside Maestro Leonardo, "to the point: I have been passing out ducats and florins by the bagful for capes for the servants, small Venetian glass for the wine, little gifts of noisemakers, confetti, masks, and fees for musicians who can play for the dancing. At this rate, we are both going to be left without a ducat to our respective names, Your Highness. Then perhaps you'll give the word for our armies to sweep to the east and 'borrow' a little from the Venetians before they bring their courage to a boil and attack us."

This comment also elicited a small laugh from Cardinal d'Este and Cardinal Castagno, and the rest of the court took their cue from the ecclesiastical princes and laughed too.

"In the meantime, Maestro," Galeazzo continued turning to Maestro Leonardo, "I would appreciate it if you keep your damned apprentice with his thieving hands away from this palazzo. I miss something every day he comes here!"

Then, glancing around at the bales and crates and scaffolds, the captain-general took a large ornate, golden pin with a pearl head from his tunic and picked at his teeth.

Maestro Leonardo nodded quietly, and replied that he had again sent Salai to assist Bramante at the Santa Maria delle Grazie, but Niccolo saw him glance and take note, as Niccolo did, of the officer's dental probe.

A small, thin instrument with a round shaft.

That night Niccolo was aroused from a deep sleep by a muffled noise from the quarters of Madonna Valentina. The young man blinked his eyes to rid them of sleep and struggled to listen, but now there was only silence. He briefly considered raising himself from under the four blankets and the fur throw that warmed his bed, but he soon dismissed the noise as a fit of imagination or nothing more than a falling faggot in the Madonna's fireplace. He turned on his side with a hope of returning to his beautiful dream, in which, nude beneath his toga, he frolicked with Madonna Terese suggestively fondling the Maestro's "pillar of Fortitude" as her impudent breasts slipped from behind her white silk.

But suddenly Madonna Valentina, totally naked, hurled herself into the dwarf's quarters and made strange, gurgling noises as she snatched at the blankets and furs on Niccolo's bed. The young man sat upright, struggling to separate this real and equally naked woman from the one of his dreams. He seized the lady by her shoulders and tried to speak to her.

"Madonna! Madonna! Please! What is it?" he demanded. "What are you trying to tell me?"

The lady responded by breaking the dwarf's grip and retreating to the open doorway, and Niccolo realized that she wanted him to follow. As he pushed back the blankets he felt the sticky moisture along the edge of the covering and knew instinctively it was blood. As he quickly wrapped his fur robe around him, he realized that Madonna Valentina's hands were dripping with the dark liquid.

He pushed past her as she stood, trembling and incoherent, in the doorway. The Madonna's quarters were dark and shadowed, but there was enough flickering light from the fire in the hearth to reveal a human figure spread-eagled on the rumpled bed. There was blood everywhere, on the floor, the walls, the tapestries, the sheets, the body. Niccolo approached slowly and carefully, noting the bare, muscular arm that projected over the edge of the bed as he mentally cataloged the possible victims.

Il Moro?

Galeazzo?

The dwarf took a burning faggot from the fireplace and held it aloft as a torch to illuminate the figure in the bed. Madonna Valentina, in shock, oblivious to her nakedness and splattered with blood, remained whimpering at the open doorway. The head of the figure in the bed was turned away, but Niccolo circled and held the burning brand high enough to identify him.

It was the man he had seen every day since his arrival in the castello, the man entrusted with the safety and security of the women of the court, the man whom Madonna Valentina had described as "the most irresistible man in Italy."

Francesco da Bicocca, captain of the guards.

At the moment that Niccolo identified the dead man, deep in the cavernous dungeons below the moats of the castello, another naked woman leaned over the nude, smiling man lying prone on the wooden table.

"You see, Mino?" she whispered in his ear. "Do you see how your helplessness makes the pleasure stronger, eh? The straps seize your wrists and your ankles tightly, don't they? You can't get up. You can't turn away. You have to lie there, naked, and let me do whatever I wish to you. How does that feel, Mino? Tell me."

Mino Spinolo, the short, muscular carpenter, smiled and moaned

"I feel—everything, Vanozza," he said. "I am open to everything. It is a sweet feeling, you know what I mean? A sweet agony, like the moment before you bite into the apple and let the delicious liquid flow down your throat."

"That's right," the rotund, big-breasted woman whispered to him. "That's exactly the feeling. It is the helplessness that arouses, isn't it? There is a fear in it, too, isn't there, Mino? Do you feel the fear?"

"Yes," the naked man murmured, smiling. "Yes. A little."

"That's because you aren't sure what I might do," Vanozza de Faenza, the castello pastry cook, replied. "It is what I felt when you strapped me to the pillar a moment ago, when you masturbated, because my helplessness aroused you, didn't it? It is what a woman feels when men grab her, throw her down and strip her, just before the act, before the sudden stab of penetration, even before the hungry mouths are at her nipples. Do you like it, my love? Does it excite you, Mino?"

Mino's body glistened under a thin blanket of prespiration, and he did not even notice the cold dampness of the small room, illuminated now by only two torches suspended from iron rings on the walls. He turned his head to watch the scarlet-and-gold of the flames reflect and dance about the breasts and bare belly of the woman like long, probing, obscene fingers. He continued to smile and muttered a low, "Yes. Yes, it excites me, Vanozza."

"Then we have no more need of conversation, do we, my love?"

The naked woman bent and lifted the man's woolen blouse from the floor. She brushed at the dirt and fungi that clung to it, tore it into strips, and rolled one into a ball.

"No! Wait! Not that blouse, Vanozza!" the man suddenly complained. "Damn it! That's my best blouse! I . . . !"

His words were stopped by the wad of wool Vanozza suddenly pushed into his mouth. He choked momentarily, tasted the foulness on his tongue and tried to spit it out, but the woman quickly began to wrap the other strip around his cheeks and lips to hold the suffocating stuffing in place.

"What do you feel now, Mino?" Vanozza interrogated him.

"Are you frightened a little, eh? Are you confused? Do you begin to wonder now if I might harm you, eh? Perhaps even kill you? Do you feel a little lump of terror rising in your throat, you worthless pile of shit? Is that coldness you feel merely the damp of the room or the arousing of terror, eh? What do you think, you foul-smelling toad! Are you feeling what Dino felt when you and that bastard, Guarino Valla, held him upside-down in the shitroom? Do you know what pain and anxiety he must have felt? My lover, my friend, my sweet companion? God knows why you did it, you bastard! But whatever reason, now you are going to pay for it."

Vanozza bent and recovered her own clothing from the damp floor. She donned the underlinen, feeling the cold against her flesh, and then she slipped the dress over her head, let it fall upon her shoulders and began to button it.

"But I'm not going to do what you did to my Dino, you thin-assed son-of-a-bitch. I'm not going to drown you in shit and piss. I'm not going to do anything."

She sat on the edge of the rack and slipped the dark stockings over her bare legs. She recovered the two garters from the edge of the table, zigzagged them up her thighs and folded the tops of her stockings over them. She looked up to see her victim's head raised to watch her, his eyes pleading.

"You see, you bastard," she growled, standing, "the duke has closed off this section of the dungeons until after the festival which is more than two weeks away. You might live that long, but I doubt it." She turned to let him see the metal object in her hand which she slipped in the shadowy valley between her breasts. "And just to make certain, I will see to it that this key disappears for a while. There are plenty of other rooms in these dungeons, and one more or less won't be missed."

Suddenly the naked man began to struggle on the cold table and mumbled what she took to be curses.

"That's right, you turd," Vanozza bent and whispered to him. "I'm going to leave you here. I'm going to seal the door again and leave you here in the cold and the dark. I'm going to leave to you die in your own shit, with the rats who are even now waiting in their black holes to come and dine on you, gnawing at your eyes and fingers and toes. How does that sound, Mino? Does that sound just, eh? There's a poetry in that, don't you think? It is the proper punishment for the crime."

The buxom woman sat again and stuffed her feet into the heavy shoes. Then she rose, picked the apron from where it was suspended from the handle of the rack and tied it around her waist.

"You didn't expect this when you fondled my behind in the kitchen, when I came in tonight to start the ovens, did you, you bastard? You didn't know what Dino was to me, and you certainly didn't think it would end this way when I suggested we come to the dungeons for a while, did you? Your rotten little imagination drew different dirty pictures for you, didn't it?"

She crossed to one of the torches and quickly doused it in the pool of stagnant water on the floor. Mino increased his struggles on the table but the woman paid no attention to him.

"The darkness doesn't help, does it? Imagine the darkness you drowned my Dino in, you pig! Think about it when you're alone here, when the hunger begins, and the cold lies down on you like a great cat and sucks your breath! Think about it as you know this is the way the world ends for you, assassin!"

And with that final curse, the woman took the last torch, stepped through the opening and closed the heavy wooden door behind her. The small room was plunged into a void, and she smiled as she imagined the silent scream that traveled after her down the corridor.

The murder of Francesco da Bicocca, captain of the guards, the "irresistible," caused another major disturbance to the tranquility of the Milanese court, and as dawn arose over the city, Salvatore Cossa and Bernardino da Corte were closeted together.

"The duke said nothing was to be done to Madonna Valentina's lover, didn't he?" Bernardino snapped at the thin captain of the Whisperers. "Damn it! He was quite clear on that matter, wasn't he?"

The captain of the Whisperers nodded and rubbed his hands together. "I assure you, Bernardino, this was not of my doing. My orders to my men were explicit. Identify the lady's lover and report to me. Nothing more. I assure you . . ."

"You assure me? The only thing anyone can assure me about these days is that the sun will rise! A serving girl killed by poison probably intended for Il Moro! The captain of guards butchered in the bed of Madonna Valentina! A kitchen worker dropped into a mountain of shit! What in hell is happening, Cossa? I was the one usually associated with murder in this castello! Has that power somehow been relegated to another? And what does that mean? Am I next on the list?"

"Calm, Bernardino," sighed Salvatore. "We must stay calm."

Bernardino made a gesture of hopelessness. "I can't seem to grasp anything concerning this damned Griffin! There are so many possibilities. Nothing is ever written down. Instructions are apparently whispered along the corridors . . ."

Cossa's face flushed, and his voice took on an icy sharpness. "If you are implying that my men have been . . ."

Bernardino raised both his palms to suppress any further objections. "I imply nothing. I am simply saying that it would be easier if there was a scrap of paper, a recognizable hand, anything. All I have to work with is the fact: two or more assassins killed Captain Francesco when he was most vulnerable."

"But that may tell us something," Cossa declared softly. "The captain was not without enemies. Shouldn't we start by looking for those who had a grievance?"

"What constitutes a grievance in this court? His tunic replicated that of another officer's? A lady of the court was angry that he chose Madonna Valentina over her? What constitutes a motive?"

"We know one person who would want Madonna Valentina's lover murdered. And what better way to reprimand the lady then to have her witness the execution?"

"You don't mean . . . ?" Bernardino lowered his voice. "You better pray no one overheard that, my friend. My God, we start by trying to locate a man who is plotting to kill the duke, and now you imply the victim is the one with the strongest motive!"

"You have to admit there is a brilliance behind it," Cossa whispered. "While everyone is dying from attempts on the duke's life, he takes advantage of the situation to remove an obstacle of his own."

Bernardino drew a large linen handkerchief from his tunic and tapped his sweating forehead. "My God, that is treason you're talking! For the love of God, try another tack."

Salvatore shrugged. "All right," he murmured. "Consider this: the assassins weren't trying to kill Captain Francesco. He wasn't the one they expected to be in Madonna Valentina's bed."

Bernardino's eyes brightened. "Ah!" he hummed. "Now that is something I could bring before Il Moro. It was the work of this Griffin, who thought his men would be killing the duke himself!"

Cossa shook his head. "No, no, no. You misunderstand. They didn't expect the duke to be in her bed either. They expected her usual lover."

Bernardino's eyes widened. "Galeazzo Sanseverino?"

The thin leader of the Whisperers nodded.

"But—why?"

Salvatore sighed and sat down. "Yes. Well, that is the problem, you see, because the only one with a strong motive to kill Galeazzo is the man whose place he had usurped."

"Are you back on that again?" roared Bernardino. "My

God, will you stay off that track! The duke is above suspicion! Absolutely! I prefer to think that it was an attempt on Il Moro's life!" He headed for the door, again mopping at his forehead. "And that is what I am going to report. This mysterious Griffin sent assassins to kill Il Moro while he was bedded with Madonna Valentina. By the grace of God, he was not in her embrace that evening. That is the conclusion, and that is the way it must remain."

As the door closed behind him, Salvatore Cossa rose, a slight smile on his face, and he blew out the candle as the early morning light slipped into the small room from the arched windows.

Bernardino da Corte immediately reported to the duke that it was the considered opinion of his guardians that Captain Francesco had been mistaken for Il Moro himself. Consequently he ordered the duke to be constantly surrounded with four armed and trusted men, despite Il Moro's argument that he must have his freedom within his own castello. The duke, in anger and frustration, ordered Bernardino da Corte to intensify his search for the mysterious Griffin who was theoretically responsible for this murder-by-mistake.

To everyone's surprise, Cardinal Ippolito d'Este doffed his clerical robes, donned sword and armor and volunteered to serve as a special protector to "my lord and benefactor," trailing after the duke whenever he emerged from his chambers.

Consequently, for the following three weeks whenever Il Moro came into a room, a small army flooded in and around him, to his annoyance and the quiet amusement of the court ladies.

Bernardino da Corte began a systematic interrogation of every guard and inhabitant of the women's quarters, although he openly acknowledged that it was simple enough for the killer to have slipped past the Marmaluke sentries in the dark corridors while the guards sheltered from the cold in their great fur-lined cloaks in the shadowy archways. Niccolo, of course, knew of another way of reaching Madonna Valentina's quarters without being seen, but he wisely said nothing of it during his own interrogation, but he began to suspect, as Cossa did, that the duke himself had slipped down the hidden passageway, found his rival in the bed of his mistress and extracted his own vengeance, and now pleaded innocence in order to put the blame on the mysterious Griffin.

"There you go, assuming things," the Maestro argued with the dwarf when he revealed his theory. "If the duke wished to do away with his rival, there are other ways that would not agitate the court and require this ridiculous masquerade. No, Captain Francesco's killer was most certainly not Il Moro. Furthermore, the wounds indicate that the soldier was stabbed with at least two blades, and from the difference in the depths of the wounds, the killers were of different heights and strengths. There are bruises around the mouth and right wrist which would indicate that someone, perhaps a third assassin, stifled the man's screams and held his right arm immobile so the other two could slash and stab."

"The captain of the guards was killed by mistake by three men who were sent to kill someone else."

"The question is: Who?"

The chief of security agreed that there had been more than one murderer involved.

"Francesco da Bicocca," he reported to Il Moro, "was a big man, a strong man, nearly in size and power to Sanseverino. Even in sleep following a night of vigorous coupling, he would have been a match for a single assassin."

The greatest change at court, of course, occurred in the daily patterns of life of Madonna Valentina and Niccolo. The dwarf's lady was, at first, isolated in a bedchamber near the duke's own and supplied with an almost constant escort of four armed mercenaries, but, after a week of this, she came under the exclusive protection of Sanseverino who swore to his lord that the lady would be protected "with my own life" and "at every hour of the day."

This response produced an envious wave effect among the other ladies of the court who began to report unnatural and frightening nocturnal activities outside their own doors and to wail of their fears of "a madman roaming the corridors." Cardinal Albizzi proclaimed that the murder was divine retribution for "da Bicocca's illicit and immoral carnal knowledge of a vulnerable and innocent woman whom he was specifically assigned to protect," and the portly prince of the church pompously advised the younger and more attractive ladies of the court that he would be quite willing to spend the "early hours of the evenings" in their antechambers, crucifix and holy water at the ready, to guard them against the demons of rape and rampage that might be stalking the darlings along the dark and silent corridors.

Amid all this guarded activity and confusion, Niccolo was nearly forgotten, and, when Madonna Valentina was removed from her own quarters, the dwarf was free to roam the hidden passageways. He was careful, of course, to choose his time and destination, now aware that the duke himself might be using the same roadway with increased regularity in order to slip away for a while from his squadron of guards.

Niccolo chose to spend more time where he much preferred to be.

In the workshop of Maestro Leonardo.

There, four days after the murder of Captain Francesco, the dwarf was surprised to find the Maestro sprawled in his great, high-backed chair, a hand to his eyes as if he might have been weeping.

"What is it, Maestro? What's wrong?"

The bearded artist looked up and stared at the youth for a long time. Then he rose and crossed to one of his tables, and Niccolo realized that there was a body under the linen sheet.

"Is it Captain Francesco?" he asked, aware that by now the body would have decomposed, and he would be sickened.

Maestro Leonardo lifted the covering cloth and revealed the nude and ashen body of a young and beautiful woman. Niccolo, already appalled at the multitude of recent deaths in the castello, gave a quick gasp and sat on the small bench at the foot of the table."

"Another?"

"This was Madonna Maria Chigi," the bearded artist sighed. "Her body was recovered from one of the outer moats this morning. She apparently suffered a seizure or swooned and tripped or fell from the castle walls into the moat where she drowned."

"Tripped or fell?"

"Our resident genius, Maestro Ambrogio, first deduced that she had died of fright," the Maestro commented drily. "He assumed that something she saw from the castle walls frightened the lady. She expired of fright and fell to her death in the moat. He is an ass, of course. First: fright alone does not kill. You have been frightened, haven't you? Of course. And so have I. And yet we did not die from it. The terror must induce some malfunction within the body, such as a sudden change in the pulsing of the heart, or, as in the case of gentlewomen, they might swoon and strike their heads against something. That is what kills, not the apparition or the event. But there is no sign of any wound to the head. There are no bruises or signs of injury on any part of her upper body, yet there should be if she fell from the walls, because she would most certainly have struck the salients at the base of the castle before her body rolled into the moat. Secondly, if the physician had taken the time to examine the lady's body, he would have noticed what I did."

The Maestro drew the small bench to the side of the table

and ordered Niccolo to mount it. "Come here," he demanded. "Look at the bottoms of her feet."

Niccolo forced himself to look at the dainty feet. "They're—they're dirty," he observed.

"Idiot," snapped the master. "That's not dirt. It doesn't wash or rub away." He motioned the dwarf closer. "Well, see for yourself. Touch her. Touch her."

"I don't want to."

"Then you'll learn nothing! Look! Look! It's not dirt!" He rubbed at the dead flesh. "That is a discoloration. Those are the only bruises on her body!"

"She had been walking in her bare feet?"

"Ridiculous! A lady of the court with four dozen slippers in her closets? No! She has been beaten! On the soles of her feet!"

Niccolo was stunned. "Beaten?"

"Effectively," grumbled Leonardo. "There are nerves that nest in the soles of the feet. Punishment applied there is particularly agonizing and pain runs like a river through the entire body."

"But—why?"

"Think!" demanded the master. "It is perfectly obvious why she was tortured."

The dwarf thought. "Information?"

"Of course."

"But who—?"

"Ah! The primary question! Who indeed? Obviously someone who needed some information, and who knew how to get it without marking the body. Someone who knew the girl's body would be examined. Someone who knew that no one would look at the soles of the feet. Someone—"

"Sanseverino."

"Absurd," snapped the master. "Why do you just blurt out things like that without thinking? Galeazzo di Sanseverino is a killer, not a torturer. That's not his way of operating."

"Not his *modus operandi*," nodded the dwarf.

The Maestro stiffened. "Knowing Latin doesn't make you any brighter, does it? The killer has signed this body as surely as if he had written his name in blood on her forehead. A man who knows torture. A man who deals in information."

"Bernardino da Corte."

"Finally," sighed Leonardo.

"Why?"

"Ah! A corollary! I would say . . . honor."

"What?"

"This young lady has recently been delivered of a child. A large child. See these marks around her lower abdomen? And there are other indications as well."

Niccolo looked but was instantly overwhelmed with both shock and embarrassment.

"Unmarried," the master murmured as he traced the stretched patterns of the skin. "This poor unmarried daughter of a Genoa family and a ward of the Sforza had been impregnated by someone. That is justification in Italy for murder. Familial honor. And, to compound the problem, the girl is not from just any family, but from the Chigi."

"I've never heard of the Chigi."

The Maestro lowered his voice and put an arm around the shoulders of the young man. "You should have," he said. "The great families of Italy are not in the impressive castles in Milan or Florence or Venice or even Rome. They have smaller, more modest palaces in Piacenza and Asti, in Siena and Lucca. Their names are not inscribed in the histories or in the Vatican chronicles like those of the Medici, the Visconti, or the Piccolomini. They are scrawled, almost illegibly, in ledgers and account books and at the bottom of contracts and deeds. They are the families who control the banks of Italy. They are the Bardi and the Peruzzi, the Frescobaldi of Florence, and most important of all, the Chigi who control the Bank of St. George in Genoa. Their founder was Agostino Chigi of Rome who was so wealthy that Pope Leo X came begging to him for enough funds to maintain the Vatican.

Without the support of these families, the great castles of the nobles would crumble and fall. No ships would sail from Genoa or Venice to trade in silks and spices from the east or to discover and exploit new worlds beyond the horizons to the west. Without their funds, which are the lifeblood of all commerce, there would be no universities, no art, no science. There would also be no wars, for it is their money that arms the populations and pays the wages of the cannon molders. Without the support of the Chigi family, Il Moro cannot pay his mercenaries or prepare his defenses. If that family does not support him, and if the Vatican turns its back on him, Milan will most certainly fall to the French."

"What can be done about it?" asked the dwarf.

The Maestro stroked his beard and returned to his seat in the great, high-backed chair. "Let us consider. From what we have learned and overheard, Maria Chigi was seduced and abandoned by someone while she was a ward of the court of Milan. The duke's late wife, Beatrice, realizing the magnitude of this scandal, and to spare the child embarrassment and possible punishment, sent her on an alleged 'pilgrimage' to the convent of San Sisto where she was delivered of a child whose adoption the nuns must have arranged. The duke himself was not aware of this until recently."

A memory and a question rose in Niccolo's mind. *A child left in a monastery or a convent by a woman of a rich and noble family. Could this have been my own origin?*

"We know that the Borgias want the marriage of Lucrezia Sforza to the duke's brother annulled so she can marry Alphonse of Aragon. From what you have told me, and from what we have overheard, I deduce that Cesare Borgia learned of Maria's pregnancy from his sister when she and Maria Chigi were both sequestered in San Sisto. Cardinal Cesare reported the pregnancy to Maria's father and to his own father, the pope, in order to discredit the Sforza family. That would permit the pontiff to free Lucrezia from her marriage to the duke's brother, Giovanni, and win Cesare the Romagna from the grateful and generous French invaders when they take Milan. Even now, as we both overheard, the banker Chigi is about to descend upon this court to verify what he has been told."

"But you implied the girl was murdered. What will Papa Chigi say to that?"

"Oh, there will be no evidence of a murder," the master explained. "The duke shall tell Messer Chigi that his daughter, a sweet young lady of gentle temperment and delicacy, swooned while walking along the castle walls, fell into the moat and drowned. A tragedy, most certainly, but I imagine he will have documentation signed by Maestro Ambrogio to affirm the cause of death."

"But if they ask you—would you sign such an article?"

"No, and they know it, so they won't request it of me. And they know I will not volunteer the information for fear of losing my privilege."

"Your privilege?"

"To dissect bodies," explained the artist. "You must have realized from your days in the Certosa that dissection is banned by ecclesiastical law. Monks and nuns, even those responsible for the health of their respective communities, are forbidden by church law to study anatomy or to practice surgery. Even the universities of Padua, Bologna, and Salerno cannot permit such studies, so, to the best of my knowledge, they still believe the stomach is something like a stew pot into which food falls and is kept boiling by heat from the liver before it dissolves and is digested. They also continue to graduate superstitious montebanks like Maestro Ambrogio who call themselves physicians."

He sighed and passed a hand over his forehead. "But Pope Sixtus the Fourth was enlightened enough to permit the dissection of bodies provided they were licensed by a member of the church hierarchy. I am granted this privilege by the duke's brother, Cardinal Ascanio. If I do not do what the Sforza want me to, or if I lodge a complaint that offends Il

Moro, my privilege would be revoked, and my knowledge, recorded in these books, would probably be destroyed. And so, likely, would I be."

"Besides," the artist continued, "by the time the delegation from Genoa arrive, the girl's body will have been wrapped in linen dipped in aloe vera which was used, they say, to embalm the body of Christ. She will be dressed in rich robes and a jeweled tiara, and a great requiem mass will be held for her in the basilica Sant'Ambrogio, celebrated by no less than half a dozen cardinals."

"Will that satisfy the honor of the family?"

"It will help. But bankers have ways of uncovering the truth that would impress even da Corte, and most certainly agents will be sent to interrogate Lucrezia Borgia and the nuns of San Sisto. To prepare himself against such an occurrence, the duke must be the first to uncover the identity of the seducer and, if possible, have him at hand to present to the Chigi family. That might possibly put him back in the good graces of the girl's father—especially if he has the seducer subjected to the most terrifying tortures imaginable. That could restore the honor of the Genoese, and, as I said before, in Italy, family honor is all."

"And if the duke can't find the seducer?"

"A possible candidate will be provided. Dead of course, so he cannot be forced to tell the truth."

"Who is the seducer? Do you know?"

"An unknown variable," the master shrugged. "From what you told me, I would assume that, under torture, the girl said she did not know the man's name. Perhaps because she had imbibed too much of the wine at the festival. But, from what you told me, the girl apparently referred to her seducer as 'the old man' or, perhaps, as 'father.' Even now, da Corte and Cossa have their agents considering all possibilities."

The bearded artist smiled and said softly, "And I am happy to say they number me among those probables—which is certainly a change of attitude."

The dwarf returned the smile. "Is Cardinal Castagno on the list?"

"Why?" Leonardo stared at him. "Have you observed something?"

"When we visited the new palace, the cardinal was wearing his family coat of arms on his scarlet cloak."

"So?"

"His crest is a scarlet eagle-headed creature with the winged body of a lion encollared by a coronet. It took a little time to remember what the creature was. I had seen it years earlier in a book of heraldry in the Certosa library."

"And?"

"It is a mythical animal. They call it a griffin."

In a small antechamber of his unfinished palace, Galeazzo di Sanseverino handed the ragged peasant two gold florins and accepted the small vial. The peasant was obviously frightened and crushed his plain felt cap in his hands.

"You promise this is cantharidine?"

"Do I look like an apothecary, my lord?" whined the peasant. "All I can tell you is that the man who sold it to me swore it was what you asked for."

"If it does less than I expect," snarled Sanseverino, "you know what I will do to you—and your supplier?"

The peasant gave a swift, curt bow of his head. "I promise you, lord, it is a true powder for arousal. It excites women as well as men, and will ignite fires in the loins of even the most virginal lady. A pinch of this, and she'll—well, she'll do whatever you want her to do."

"And what does your little mind imagine I want her to do, you illiterate crock of piss?" grumbled the captain-general. "Dance?"

The peasant forced a laugh, feeling that was the response expected of him, and Galeazz tucked the vial within the folds of his tunic. "Now get your skinny ass out of here before I kick you down the stairs. And remember! Not a word of this to anyone, including your pimple-faced cow of a wife! I know where to find you!"

The worker backed away, nodding with every step, and was gone.

The members of I Comici Buffoni gathered inside their curtained wagon and celebrated their new commission to entertain the Milanese court. Everything had been packed away, and, on the morrow, they would take the Via Emilia to the northwest and to Milan. Now, warm and confident, they drank the rich wine and dined on the roast fowl that been purchased with the advance monies the duke had sent with his courier.

"It was a shock to me, I'll tell you," laughed Rubini. "Another week of poor returns for our performances, and I saw myself having to go back and dance the high wire at the fairs. Now I can look forward to passing the rest of the winter with some comfort and with real food in my belly."

"Did you really consider that, Rubini?" asked Piero. "The high wire? Would you really consider returning to the fair?"

"Yes and no," sighed the company's Scapino. "To the fair, yes. To the high wire, well, I don't think so."

He picked up a lute that rested beside him and began to strum the strings and sing.

"I yearn to return to the fair, my friends.
I yearn to rejoice in the laughter that's light,
from the ladies of night
with their dark perfumed hair
and their eyes of deceptive despair
at the fair.
But I will not return to the wire, my friends,
balanced aloft between death and the dream
for the song of the stars
is seductive up there
at the fair.

Way up there
pains of earth disappear,
ev'ry torment and fear
of your life.
Way up there,
ev'ry star winks its eye
and sings softly, 'Come! Fly!'
'Come and try!'
goes the lie.
No,
pleasures abound on the ground, my friends,
in this world of deception and tinsel and tricks
where life's shallow as sin,
and you never can win
for the gaming's been set to the fix.
It's chaotic, my boys,
but I long for the noise
and those treacherous joys
of the fair."

Simone Corio, the company's Arlecchino, snatched his lute from Rubini's hands.

"You dance on the wire much better, acrobat, than you sing on the earth," he grumbled.

"The court, my lord, is in turmoil. We are experiencing a slight break in the winter, so I thought it might be amusing to—perform a certain experiment."

The duke of Milan sat with his chin in his hands, studying the tall artist that stood before him in the Salla della Palla. "An experiment, Maestro Leonardo? What sort of experiment?"

The artist came nearer. "Flight, Your Highness."

"Flight? What do you mean, flight?"

"I would like permission to test a set of wings that would enable a man to fly, Your Highness."

Il Moro straightened in his chair. "Is it possible, Maestro?"

"I think so. I would like to attempt it."

The duke envisioned a new weapon. In his mind's eye he could see full regiments of Italian mercenaries soaring from the sun and falling upon the astonished French in the Alpine passes.

"Is it dangerous?"

"I will take precautions."

"That's what you said when you sent Salai on the lake with your water walkers. You took precautions then, too, but that was unsuccessful!"

"There was no lasting harm, Your Highness," the artist insisted. "Salai lived."

"Precisely," snapped the Duke.

It was three days later when Niccolo found himself at an open window in the madman's tower, terrified and confused, as the Maestro strapped him into the great dragon wings.

"Stop trembling, my friend. You should not be afraid."

"It's absurd!" shrieked Niccolo. "I'll kill myself!"

The Maestro tightened the belts that strapped the dwarf's body to the harness supported by struts beneath the dragon wings. "Not if you do as I told you. You are the perfect weight, with good upper-body strength, and if you lie prone, relax and use these ropes to change direction, I promise you that you will fly, Niccolo. You will fly like a bird."

The Maestro's request to Il Moro to permit the dwarf to attempt a flight with his dragon's wings depended on the promised break in the winter weather. Realizing that the court was in a state of fear and anxiety, and after repeated assurances that Niccolo would never be in danger, the duke had finally agreed. It took some time to convince Madonna Valentina that she should permit it, since the dwarf was in her service, but her recent scandal was fresh in the duke's memory, and the lady saw she had an opportunity to erase the mark against her if she pretended to surrender her servant for

Il Moro's amusement. He, on the other hand, promised to replace the dwarf with something more expensive and glittering if the experiment came to an unfortunate end.

Niccolo's permission was not really essential, but out of common courtesy he was approached on the subject, constantly assured by the Maestro that the entire venture would be exciting and not at all harmful, and the young man, after receiving and absorbing a bottle of wine, finally agreed. The Maestro pointed out that he had adapted his original design to accommodate Niccolo's small stature and that the dwarf would be attached to a long safety line for the initial, dangerous minutes of the attempt. If the wings appear to be failing, Niccolo had only to hold on and let the wings slow his descent into the gardens.

Now he stood frozen with fear and confusion, flushed with the wine and the constant reassurances of the Maestro, while the great dragon wings were being fitted to him. Below him, far below, far, far below, the duke and his entire court were assembled to watch the attempt at temporarily freeing man from the gravitational pull of the earth.

"We are up so high, Maestro. Can't we try this from one of the lower floors?" Niccolo pleaded.

"No," insisted Maestro Leonardo. "It is the height we need, Niccolo. Remember, when it is a question of flight, the sky is your best friend. It is the ground that threatens you. The more height the better."

"Why can't we experiment with some other invention, Maestro?" the dwarf persisted. "Why not the large shoes and the support poles that permit one to walk on water? I wouldn't mind swallowing a little water for the sake of study."

"I'm not satisfied with the water walkers yet," the Maestro argued. "My last two attempts were—unsuccessful."

"How successful were your last attempts at flight?" probed the frightened dwarf.

"This is the first."

Since his arrival at the castello and his first meeting with

Maestro Leonardo, Niccolo's admiration and confidence in the tall bearded artist had grown and magnified. The artist had a plausible explanation for everything, from the necessity of shading to suggest distance in landscapes to the proper allegorical images to portray moral virtues. The dwarf had stood, amazed, on his small bench as the Maestro bent over his books and revealed the secrets of geometry and mathematics and applied these principles to the questions of movement and portraiture.

But what did he know of flight?

The artist had explained the details of the great wings a dozen times, sketching the angles and the curvature of the thick canvas covering over the wooden framework. The Maestro had drawn triangles and arcs and transcribed pages of numerical markings as he told Niccolo how the wind acts on curved surfaces and spoke of thermal updrafts as opposed to the colder air that mantled the city from the Alps.

"Think of it, Niccolo," the Maestro continued as he finished strapping the young man to the harness. "You are about to do something that man has dreamed of since time began."

"A quick death?"

"Amusing," replied the Maestro with no trace of amusement. "Do exactly as I told you. Stretch your body out. Have faith in your wings. These two cords can turn the wings in such a way that you can change direction. Believe, Niccolo. Believe, and you will fly."

"And if I don't?"

"You'll be able to know that in an instant after you launch yourself. If the wind does not move you forward and up, then stay absolutely still. You will simply be a deadweight attached to a supporting canopy. The wind will sustain and lower you gently to the earth."

"I don't like the sound of 'deadweight.'"

The dwarf felt his mouth turn dry, and his palms moisten. He clutched the rings of the two cords that were to change his direction as if they would save him from plummeting to his death. He was lifted to the sill of the window and made the mistake of looking down and out at the ducal gardens and the assembled court below.

"I'm going to die," he wailed.

"No," the Maestro snapped. "No! Do you think I'd to anything to harm you? The mathematics are correct, Niccolo. I have adjusted the wings for your body weight and your height. You are perfect for the experiment. I have gone over the equations a thousand times. Everything checks. You—will—fly!"

Niccolo opened his mouth to protest again, but the Maestro gave the young man a sudden shove, and the dwarf, absolutely frozen with fear, found himself between earth and sky. He began to fall, but, as the Maestro had predicted, the wind billowed above him in the great wings and the descent was slowed.

The accuracy of this prediction reassured the dwarf, and he slowly, cautiously, drew up his legs behind him and draped his feet over the support bar in the rear of the structure. He no sooner accomplished this, when he experienced a sense of forward movement. Not only forward, but slightly upward, as the rising air pushed against the young man and his wings and lifted him once again to the level of the tower windows.

"Good! Good, Niccolo!" the dwarf heard the Maestro call from somewhere behind him, and gaining confidence, he slowly pulled one of the wings and found, to his utter amazement, that he turned in a smooth, swooping, banking movement to his right.

My God, he marveled. I'm flying!

And he went over the wide expanse of the gardens. He saw the panorama of the castle, the stables, the entire city of Milan stretch out below and around him. He swooped up to momentarily see the gray sky that beckoned him higher, and he banked and swirled like an eagle. He was vaguely aware that his flight had caused a flurry of agitation and wonder in the watching court, and that at least one of the more genteel women had swooned in her excitement.

He banked again, feeling the wind supporting him like a

giant, invisible hand. He soared over the outer walls of the castle, over the piazzas and past the dome of the duomo. Below him the townspeople were seized with the rapture of the moment, vicariously flying with the youth, cheering and waving their hands in their excitement. He saw crones bless themselves and kiss the crucifix of their rosaries as he flew high above them. Workers in the cannon factories stopped at their forges and their anvils and stared in dumb amazement.

He wheeled again, circling back over the castle, narrowly avoiding the towers. He could see the paved courtyards, the coaches and carriages being cleaned and gilded after their winter hibernation, the pockets of gathered snow. He saw the horses in the open courts of the stables, frightened and neighing at the apparition of the flying man. He imagined that he heard the animals in the ducal zoo screaming and bellowing and growling with alarm and curiosity, but all he could really hear was the wind hissing past him as if urging him to be silent and listen.

For Niccolo, it was a frequent dream come to vivid reality. He was supernatural, supreme, one not only with the wind and the cloud but with the eagle and the hawk. He was cold, but the thrill of the flight kept his heart beating so hard inside his chest that he could almost hear it. He imagined that he could lower his legs from the back support and drop on any of the assembly below, snatching at them with great clawed feet and then ascend again, up, up to where the angels awaited him with open arms.

Then, as it is with all power, he did not want to relinquish it. He sensed he was slowly, slowly descending to the gardens in narrowing circles, and he wanted to cry out against the earth and its power to subdue the dream. He tried to maneuver to stay aloft, but the pull of gravity drew him ever closer and closer to the ground, and he suddenly realized that he had not been instructed on how to land with the wings.

Should he keep his feet in place and scrape his belly against the earth to slow his speed? Should he lower his feet and run?

He knew above all he had to look for a suitable place to land. Not in the still-bare trees that raised their pointed boughs like spear points or on the hedges or on the roof of the stables or in the middle of the lake. The gardens, he reasoned, would be perfect, especially the landscaped area around the marble fountain where there were no trees or shrubbery to impede or impale him.

As he circled the fountain for the third time, carefully evaulating his rate of descent and trying to choose the right moment to lower his legs from the support and run with the wings, he saw a beautiful woman watching him with a tall falconer from behind the hedges near the aviary. She wore a hooded cape, but the hood had fallen back to reveal her dark hair bound tightly around her head by a velvet band. Even at this distance, Niccolo could almost feel the warmth of her smile, and he imagined the scent of lilac and her soft voice whispering in his ear, "Well done, my little spy."

By this time he was forced to concentrate all his attention on the rapidly approaching earth. Suddenly he twisted his feet free of the back support and held them out below him, bending his back to keep the wings parallel to the ground. And suddenly he was running, the wind pushing him along until he was afraid he would fall and be dragged.

But, at that moment, he felt the strong hands of Guarino Valla, the head falconer, wrap around his waist and draw him to a stop. Almost simultaneously he was surrounded by the duke and the lords and ladies of the court, and a dozen hands began to undo the straps that harnessed him to the dragon wings. In a moment they were lifted away, and the dwarf could stand erect. In that moment he discovered he had no legs at all and had to be supported by his admirers.

"See!" crowed the Maestro suddenly appearing at his right and clamping a heavy arm around his shoulders. "I told you that you would fly! I tested the mathematics a hundred times! You couldn't possibly have failed!"

Niccolo wanted to protest that his own courage and intelligence had also been brought into play, and those qualities could not have been predetermined by mathematical formulae, but he simply smiled, and the court cheered and shouted "Bravo, Niccolo!" And some of the ladies, still flushed with excitement, bent and kissed him, and the dwarf glowed.

But there was no sign of the countess.

"Incredible," heralded the Moor, turning to the Maestro. "Incredible! Can we use it in battle?"

"Only if you have an army of dwarfs, my lord," sighed the Madman. "Niccolo is the ideal weight and configuration for the machine, and, even then, I fear he was dependent upon the whims of the wind. Even if the wings could be strengthened and adapted for a man of normal size, there is the necessity of high launching places. And even if we convinced an army to jump from ledges and mountain pinnacles, they would be, I'm afraid, helpless before the bolts and arrows of the enemy who would shoot them down like pigeons."

"Well," murmured the duke, turning away with a sigh, "at least it was amusing."

It took hours for Niccolo to recover from the thrills and wonder of his flight and even longer for him to escape from the Maestro and his corps of admiring young ladies. He had returned to his quarters and had undone his tunic to let his heart beat wildly and freely when something fell to the floor. He bent to recover it and found it was a message, folded twice and apparently slipped into his tunic in the confusion of his landing.

Then he remembered the strong hands of the falconer that slowed him. The hands of Guarino Valla.

He opened the paper and read: "You may be in danger. Stay close to Maestro Leonardo."

The warning was unsigned, but Niccolo raised the paper to his face and inhaled the unmistakable perfume of lilac.

Chapter 5
Fear and Festival

"On the 26th
I was in the house of Messer Galeazzo di Sanseverino
to organize the festivities,
and while some of his footmen were undressing
in order to try on some costumes of savages
that were called for in the performance,
Giacomo went up to the purse of one of them
which was on the bed along with other clothes
and removed such money as he found in it . . .
thief, liar, obstinate, glutton!"

**Note of Leonardo da Vinci
Household of Accounts**

Some experiences merit repeating, like a first kiss or the first payment for services rendered, or both, if they occurred at the same time. Niccolo's brief encounter with flight only served to whet his appetite for soaring again above the earthbound, but the Maestro grew progressively solemn following the successful experiment and would turn the conversation to other topics whenever Niccolo introduced the subject of renewed flight.

The great festival to celebrate the completion of Galeazzo di Sanseverino's new palace was delayed more than a month as the Maestro struggled with fabrics and fancies, and the Milanese Minister of Public Works, Marchesino Stanga, attempted to arouse the enthusiasm of the people for a celebration that not only excluded the lower classes, but was being financed with their taxes which were now being increased.

There was another lengthy delay when Bartolomeo Calco, the duke's personal secretary, informed the captain-general that a third of his guests were hesitant to make the journey to Milan until winter relaxed its grip on the Lombardy plains. The break in the weather that had ennabled Niccolo to test the Maestro's wings had proved to be an exception. The winter finally departed, dragging its feet, with a whimper of frigid air, and spring arrived on a flood of birdsong before Galeazzo was able to name a precise date for the festival.

The *commedia* troupe, however, had arrived with the second great snowfall and had taken advantage of the delay in the construction to sharpen their skills and to fill their bellies at Il Moro's expense. The irrepressible company brought a new vitality to the court that almost succeeded in blotting from memory the murders, attempted assassinations, mysterious deaths, and the shadow of impending war that waited in the Little St. Bernard Pass.

The duke himself was seen to actually smile on occasions, although he was still unusually nervous, and rumors arose that he had resumed his nocturnal adventures with Madonna Valentina, restored to her more spacious quarters in the women's wing of the castle. He had even agreed to finance the construction of a small balcony outside the lady's window where she could sun herself when the weather improved, and, with the spring, scaffolding sprouted around an opening in the outer wall. Ropes and pulleys dangled from the hole like broken webbing and a hand-driven winch on the ground below served to raise mortar and stone to the working area. This new construction, which was to take no more than a month, stretched on and on as the workers were siphoned away to work on the Palazzo di Sanseverino or lured by the balmy spring weather to the rivers and waterways with their fishing gear. Through the spring, it was a rare day when more than two or three masons were at work on the promised addition to Madonna Valentina's balcony. Consequently, the working area was sealed off with canvas and screens, and life went on as usual, more or less, in the lady's bedchamber.

The Genoese delegation arrived, listened sullenly to the duke's explanation of the death of Maria Chigi, repeated the accusations passed to them via Lucrezia and Cesare Borgia, and attended the long, lavish, and ritualistic requiem mass at the basilica. The ceremony was performed, as the duke promised and the Maestro foretold, by no less than three cardinal celebrants, plus four deacons, four subdeacons, and a platoon of altar boys. The delegation then returned home with the body of Maria Chigi and a request from Il Moro for an additional loan to pay his troops and prepare his defenses against the coming French invasion.

Nevertheless Niccolo, the Maestro, and most of the court were aware that the Whisperers and da Corte's agents outside the castle were not only continuing their efforts to identify the seducer of the young lady but actually intensifying their efforts. It was apparent that the duke suspected that some of the Genoese delegation had been sent to San Sisto to verify the Borgian charge that Maria Chigi had been seduced and abandoned while a ward of the Milanese court, and he was prepared, if so charged, to present a possible scapegoat as the girl's seducer.

Niccolo, in one of his late night wanderings down the secret passageway to the kitchens, overheard a conversation between da Corte and one of his agents. From what Niccolo could discern, the security man had acquired what he sought, a scrap of message that indicated that someone had ordered the murder of Galeazzo, and therefore Captain Francesco had been killed by mistake. The writer's identity remained a mystery, of course, but the stableman who received the document had been put under surveillance. It was da Corte's hope that he might lead his agents to the Griffin.

But before da Corte's agents could identify the leader of the assassins, the blond stableman was kicked to death by the duke's nervous stallion, Neptune, one night in the stables. Maestro Ambrogio ruled it an accident, but Maestro Leonardo told Niccolo that there were marks on the dead man's wrists that indicated he had been bound, spread-eagled and suspended, and the horse goaded into kicking him.

The examination of the body in the Maestro's workshop was cursory, and within an hour da Vinci had ordered it removed to the salt cellars and prepared for burial, because the preparations for the festival were demanding more and more of his time.

Finally, during a brief lull in court life, the dwarf once again pressed the Maestro to let him fly once more, and, to his surprise, the artist turned on him in anger.

"You flew, didn't you? I said you could, and you did. So now we know it is possible. But there is nothing further to be learned by repeating the process of hanging beneath curved wings. Perhaps later, if I can find the time, we will try the same thing with a machine I am designing which requires muscle-powered flight with pedals and link chains. A series of gears and belts to flap the wings might solve the problem of simply riding the wind's back and actually propel the driver. When we do that the great bird will take its first flight, filling the whole world with amazement and its fame, and it will bring eternal glory to the nest where it was born. But for the time being, we have done enough. Now we move on. There are other matters to consider. Other problems and possibilities. So, please, please, cease this constant pleading and rejoice in the fact that you accomplished something no other man has ever done before you—with the possible exception of the mythological Icarus. That should be enough for you."

At first Niccolo thought the Maestro was disturbed by the rash of violent deaths at the court and the press of the festival arrangements, but he soon realized that what actually concerned Leonardo was his commission to complete the great equestrian statue of Francesco Sforza.

"Casting such an enormous statue is a problem," the artist told the dwarf as he sketched a horse, upside-down, its legs stretching to the sky. "But only if the problem is considered using the traditional manner of casting metal. When the customary methods seem inapplicable to a new situation, it seems logical to me that new systems should be considered." Suddenly the inverted horse grew a series of uprising pipes, reaching to a horizontal bar. "If we buried the molds upside down and between circular ovens, the molten bronze could be poured through these tubes into the molds." He completed the sketch and sat back wearily in his chair.

"That's remarkable, Maestro," said Niccolo. "When do you begin?"

"I don't," sighed Leonardo. "It would take an immense amount of bronze, and Il Moro needs every particle for his cannon." The artist threw the sketch aside, and nestled his bearded face into his hands, rubbing his eyes. "Cannon!" He sat silently for a moment, and then he whispered, "There—there is a new problem with my fresco," he groaned.

Niccolo knew the master referred to his commission for a wall painting depicting the last gathering of the apostles and Christ at a meal prior to his crucifixion. For the past two weeks the artist had gone directly to the refectory of Santa Maria delle Grazie when he had completed his work at Sanseverino's new palazzo.

"I've never seen your 'Last Supper,' " the dwarf murmured.

The Maestro studied the young man for what seemed a long time, and then he rose and said, "Then come and see it. Perhaps you may provide an answer for my problem."

For the first time, and the last, Niccolo was to view the masterwork in all its brilliance.

The fresco was both an exercise in forced perspective, showing Christ and His apostles seated behind a long table set in a large room, and a sample of what the Maestro called "narrative painting." The upper room stretched back to a distant wall containing two windows and an arched portico. Through these openings a misty landscape could be seen. Each of the side walls contained what Niccolo took to be four large openwork screens, and the top of the dining table, which stretched across the width of the pictured room itself, rested on the top edge of the doorsill leading to the monastery kitchens.

Niccolo was astounded by the variety of expression and postures. No two figures were remotely similar. Christ was centered, of course, and looked out of the frame to his left. Two apostles were plainly discussing Christ's prophecy that one among them would betray him. Of these two, one held a knife in his hand, apparently having just sliced some bread on the table. Another apostle, also holding a knife, had apparently wheeled in surprise and knocked over a glass. One apostle still held a hand on his goblet as he turned toward the Christus. Another seemed to be wringing his hands and turned, frowning, to his neighbor. A third spread his hands widely, exposing the palms, and shrugged his shoulders in astonishment. One placed both hands on the table and stared straight ahead. One leaned forward to have a better view of Christ and shaded his eyes with his hands as if the central figure was surrounded by a blinding aura, invisible to the viewer. One drew back, and another bent forward.

"It is a mistake to repeat the same movements, the same faces, and the same style of drapery in one narrative painting," the Maestro murmured at the dwarf's side. "Choosing the proper face is very important. One might deceive oneself and choose faces that closely conform to one's own.

"The problem is: such painting requires thought which, in turn, requires time. But to paint in fresco, on freshly prepared plaster, demands immediate application of the paint to the wet plaster before it dries. I find this unacceptable. Diligence before speedy execution. So I have been experimenting with various mixtures of oil paints. That way I could come, revise, do a little something here, something there, until my vision is all there, spread, as I conceived it, across the wall."

"Your colors are brilliant."

"Yes," sighed the painter, "but come here." He led the dwarf up the ladder to the scaffolding. "See? Look." He pointed to a segment of the painting depicting a bright blue outer robe of one of the apostles. To Niccolo's surprise, as the Maestro lightly touched the wall, a small section of the painting crumbled and fell away.

"It is blistering," he said. "It is doomed."

Niccolo was overwhelmed with a great wave of melancholy. What must he be feeling? he thought. His two major commissions: the huge statue and this fresco, one delayed for God knows how long by the needs of war, and the other beginning even now to disintegrate.

To his surprise, the Maestro turned his own compassion to another.

"The poor duke," he said. "He is in danger of losing his state, all of his possessions, and his liberty, and he has seen none of his commissioned works completed." He sighed again, and then asked softly, "Well? What do you think, little friend?"

"I—do not consider myself a competent judge," the dwarf stammered.

"Neither do I," smiled the artist. "But nothing deceives us more than our own judgment, and while a friend could be deceived, it is better than the opinion of a courtier or a patron. Such people flatter and praise the early stage of a good work, and that only blinds the painter to the faults."

The dwarf felt the artist really wanted his judgment of the work, and, spurning what he had just been told, the young man said simply, "It is a masterpiece, Maestro."

The artist stared at the dwarf for what seemed an eternity.

Finally he sighed, his eyes misty under the heavy brows, and he whispered, "Yes. That is the tragedy."

"No! It is a comedy!" Piero Tebaldeo thundered at his cast. "A farce! We are portraying life as it is, not as it should be. The romantic view of mankind belongs to the old morality and miracle plays where Everyman has only Good Deeds to take with him for the last judgment. We commedians see with the pauper's eye. Life to us is absurd, irrational, totally and completely mad. The world is an asylum where the inmates keep the warders in their place. In our plays, the meek may inherit the earth, but then they have to pay the taxes. In our plays, the poor in spirit may see God, but they also die in their misery. It is our mission to reveal that the honored banker is a thief and an embezzler. The bemedalled hero is hollow and crumbles before the shadow of a threat, or he's a butcher who considers a human life of no more value than the sweat of his horse. In our world the lecher is impotent, and the reformer a drunk. The priest is a seducer, and the benevolent prince a petty tyrant. And, despite this view of mankind and his world, we make people laugh at it."

The tall leader of the troupe paused then, glanced around the large ballroom, and then continued, "Our work lately would be better performed in a sepulcher. They are tragedies or melodramas!" Then he added quickly, "Now, let's us try again."

Niccolo was the only member of the court permitted to be present in the great hall while the players practiced their improvisational techniques. He had even been invited to participate, calling out a situation which the actors immediately and hilariously turned into a complete playlet with a beginning, a middle, and an end. There were times, of course, when the entire framework collapsed in a whirlwind of nonsense, followed by a cascade of accusations, threats, insults, and obscene gestures.

It was Niccolo's friend, Rubini, who yelled to him now, "Ey, Niccolo! Give us a situation!"

Delighted, the dwarf shouted back, "The general is building his new house!"

The actors laughed, and Piero nodded. "Clear enough. All right. As the Captain, I am discussing the plans with my banker, Pantalone; my master-of-works, the Doctor; and his clerk, Arlecchino."

Marco Torri as Doctor Graziano threw a sheet over one of the tables and began to study the emptiness as though there were a million small details etched on it. Instantly Turio of Verona as Pantalone bent over beside him, and the Captain shoved his way between them. Simone Corio as Arlecchino stood behind the Doctor and pretended to be taking notes and keeping the accounts.

"What is this?" asked the Captain stabbing at the sheet.

"The solarium," replied the Doctor.

"What is a solarium?"

"A room for the sun."

"I have no son. Make it a bedchamber for my daughter."

"We have a bedchamber for your daughter."

"Then give her another. That way the linen has to be changed only every other day."

"It will add to the cost," chirped the Doctor.

"How much?" inquired Pantalone.

Arlecchino showed the old man his pretended figures, and the miser promptly screamed. Then his face slowly distorted with pain and anguish, and he began to weep softly.

"Where are the cannons to be placed?" demanded the Captain, ignoring him.

"Cannons, sire?"

"How do I defend my castle without cannons?"

"There is a moat and a drawbridge."

"Not enough," growled the military man. "My enemies swim like dolphins in heat and train by climbing greased poles at carnival. To be on the safe side, add three more moats and twelve drawbridges."

"Three more moats and twelve drawbridges," echoed the Doctor, and Arlecchino scribbled away at his imaginary tablet.

"How much?" wheezed Pantalone.

Again Arlecchino showed the old man his tally. The miser's eyes widened and a loud groan of pain escaped him. Then his weeping and groaning rose in intensity and volume.

"There is not enough room to add moats and drawbridges, sire," the Doctor explained patiently.

The Captain peered at the cloth. He stabbed another finger at it. "What is this?"

"The village."

"Move the village."

Turio laughed at the quip, the body of the old banker shaking on the floor and effectively ending the sketch.

"Well, that's the problem," sighed Piero, also abandoning the characterization of the Captain. "It's simple enough to start an improvisation, but a snappy finish is always a problem."

If anything could divert the attention of the Milanese court from the recent violence and the impending war, it was the weeks of eager anticipation for this great festival honoring Sanseverino's new palace. For weeks prior to the event, the partially completed building was inundated with pork and sausage butchers, roasters of poultry and game, pastry cooks and confectioners, bread bakers and specialists in sauces. From Sicily came a special chef who created wonders of ice cream and ices, "which," he assured Galeazzo, "even the damned French have never seen."

During the week of the celebration, carts and wagons formed an endless procession at the palace's entrances, unloading tubs of fresh butter and large containers of ass's and cow's milk. Galeazzo went to great lengths to satisfy the palates not only of the Italian cardinals, but those of the French and German as well. Consequently, an army of vinters rolled great casks of Falernian, Moriveaux, Anjou, Graves, Corsican, Nerac, and Orlean wines up the ramps into the kitchens, and a special shipment of Malvesian, known as Malmsey, arrived from England. From the Hospices de Beaune on the Côte d'Or came barrels of Burgundy, and burly men rolled and wheeled casks of Pauillac and Medoc from their heavy wagons into the new domicile of the captain-general.

From the seaports to the south came barrels of oysters,

crates of whale meat, crayfish, salmon, turbot, brill, salted and unsalted herring, and crab. Live lobsters arrived in small bronze tanks, and great haunches of venison and whole carcasses of sheep, lamb, swine, and cattle came from Pavia on the shoulders of brawny herdsmen and hunters.

The master chef became a general in command of platoons of cooks and bakers. Mountains of veal were boiled in sage, coated with cinnamon and saffron, stiffened with eggs, and encased in delicate pastries dotted with dates. Bread bakers worked in clouds of flour as they jiggled and tossed their sieves like carnival jugglers. The huge kitchen, nearly two stories tall, became a bastion of scents and aromatic smoke as meats were marinated in sauces of parsley, garlic, quince, pear, and wine and slowly rotated over glowing coals. Continents of venison were cooked until the flesh fell from the bones and then powdered with ginger, as foretold to Niccolo by the Certosa cook. The tongues of whales were roasted, bathed in orange sauce and trimmed with chopped cloves of garlic which were touted as a preventor of disease.

In the main hall, scented wax candles were fitted into chandeliers and candelabras. Long, embroidered cloths were spread over the many tables, and napkins were ceremoniously folded in myriad shapes including graceful arches and towering columns. The head table was raised and positioned under a canopy of gold cloth, decorated with the heraldic arms of each of the cardinals and nobles in attendance. Each corner of the great room contained a platform decorated by Maestro Leonardo to suggest the four seasons. Here choirs and musicians would serenade the guests as they dined and play for the dancing that would follow. For days prior to the feast, the musicians practiced the *bassa danza,* a slow dance currently popular in the courts of Europe, as well as the more lively *moresca* and the *cantionne alla piffarescha,* written especially for the woodwinds. Singers, including four castrated young men, capable of hitting the highest notes of any soprano since having their manhoods mutilated, rehearsed the secular songs known as *frottola*.

Maestro Ambrogio became annoyed that Maestro Leonardo was consulted on more matters than he, and proclaimed this injustice to the duke who, in turn, informed his captain-general. Galeazzo then prudently asked the court physician and astrologer to determine if the stars were in a favorable position for the celebration. The old man wisely said they were, knowing full well that the event had already been scheduled and to change the date at this point would be an impossibility. He then proceeded on his own to advise the cooks how to prepare the fish in aspic and to instruct the bakers how to create a tart of chestnuts and cheese, because "the stomach needs warmth and very little agitation, otherwise it is unable to produce digestive juices." He continued to make a nuisance of himself in the kitchens as he proclaimed his thesis on the "science of the gullet," insisting that the sauces be organized to "arouse and stimulate the appetite rather than to merely gratify it." He demanded that salads be prepared "according to seasons," specifying which should be served warm and which cold. At last, the master chef demanded that the physician be removed from his kitchens, or "I promise you, he will be baked into a Neapolitan pastry with wine, grapes, and capers."

Galeazzo forced the masons and carpenters to complete at least the great ballroom and fourteen smaller rooms which da Tuttavilla labeled *"chambres séparés"* implying, with tongue planted firmly in cheek, that only the immoral French would make use of such rooms furnished with pillowed lounges and designed for more intimate celebrations. Two of these rooms had walls made entirely of wood veneers fitted into mosaics which drove the carpenters slowly mad, and others were lined with heavy damask draperies and tapestries intended to muffle personal conversations and small noises of passion. All were furnished with gilded trees on whose branches garments could be suspended, and each was illuminated with scarlet or amber colored globes containing scented oils in which a burning wick could be floated.

In the Castello Sforzesco, the ladies spent all of their time examining and debating linens and silks, satins and laces. A "shaved" velvet was passed from hand to hand, and bolts of floral silk damask were draped from throats to the floor in an attempt to envision a gown cut from it. Arm's lengths of velvet that contained loops of gold were cut and stitched into daring gowns that would reveal "appropriate" expanses of breast and shoulder. Rich overgowns were lined with ermine and silver fox, trimmed with jewels, and long columns of pearls marched around the hems and bordered the bodices. Underlinens were trimmed with delicate lace and shamelessly chosen for easy accessibility. Leagues of ribbons were attached to sleeves and bodices and used to gather colored stockings around ivory thighs. Bracelets and necklaces and tiaras were cleaned and polished, and gems chosen for their fires and lightnings. Hair was washed, combed, puffed, piled, twisted and braided and loosened again and bound with diamond clips or decorated with ivory or jade combs.

Madonna Valentina managed to keep secret the design and creation of her long overgown, a garment made of cloth trimmed with emeralds. This was no small miracle since there were bitter accusations of this lady or that "spying" on another in the women's quarters and stealing designs or materials for their own gowns. These recriminations grew more frequent and more violent as the festival day approached with the result that Madonna Dorotea had to overpaint the bruise below her left eye and spend the day before the event with ice pressed against her cheek to control the swelling.

Maestro Leonardo, as usual, decided on a long black robe and soft velvet cap, but violated his own standard of simplicity to add a gold chain and a medallion bearing the Tuscany arms.

Madonna Valentina was given a sum of money to see to Niccolo's wardrobe for the occasion, and the dwarf's new doublet and hose were gold to match his lady's overgown. Her emeralds were echoed in the dwarf's green velvet cap, and Niccolo's new boots and belt were of Spanish leather trimmed with gold studs. He wore his sword, of course, and the jeweled dagger and submitted, unhappily, to a powdering and mild rouging by his lady which he felt was demeaning and which the lady thought maternal.

The day of the celebration, Niccolo was surprised at his morning dose of Epictetus which read: "Banquets of the unlearned and of wicked ones should be avoided. But, if you must partake of them, keep attentive, lest you slip into evil ways. For be assured that a pure man cannot escape defilement if his associates are impure."

Defilement, he thought to himself, that's the thing.

That evening Galeazzo himself appeared at the door of his palazzo in gold armor emblazoned with his coat of arms, alternating horizontal yellow and red stripes on one half of a shield and a modified, red "A" on the other half. He greeted each of his guests arriving by carriage and coach while banners and crests fluttered in the foyer. Niccolo easily identified Cardinal Ippolito d'Este's two-headed eagle and Count Barberini's five blue diamonds descending on a white field posed against three golden horseflies on a blue field. It was Maestro Leonardo who noted a banner tucked between the alternating crosses of the Cavalcanti of Florence and the coat of arms of the Alidosio, a phoenix in flames encollared by two coronets. The partly obscured banner depicted a porcupine with two fleur-de-lys and nine ermine tails, and the Maestro whispered to Niccolo that this seemed an inappropriate insignia, considering the times, because the lilies and the ermine tails were the heraldic elements of Louis of France and his personal badge of merit was the Order of the Porcupine.

The Maestro pondered how the banner was acquired, by

whom, and why was it included among the heralds of the Milanese court?

Maestro Ambrogio made a spectacular entrance in blue velvet with a cloak displaying the insignia of the Apothecaries guild: Apollo standing on a serpent.

Madonna Dorotea's formal gown bore the insignia of the Spada family, three swords in bend sinister, points downward, which, Madonna Valentina pointedly explained, proclaimed the number of bastards among Madonna Dorotea's clan.

Madonna Terese also displayed a gold and enameled pendant bearing the heraldic arms of her family, the Ottoni: an eagle over a checkered shield.

The Countess Bergamini arrived in a coach and four accompanied by her husband who was customarily dull and drab in gray satin. The countess swept into the ballroom on a cloud of white silk and lace sprinkled with silver sequins that glittered and sparkled around her, appearing to Niccolo as an angel floating through a field of stars. Her customary headband was replaced by a diamond tiara, but her ermine choker aroused in both Niccolo and the duke sweet memories of Maestro Leonardo's famed portrait of the beauty.

Il Moro reverted to his traditional black velvet trimmed in silver as if to remind everyone that both the state and the court were in jeopardy. He was escorted by da Corte and Cossa, dark shadows trailing in their master's footsteps. For the evening, and to assure Galeazzo of his confidence in him, the duke's armed guards were dismissed.

The opening pageant and procession were staged with pomp and formality. Everyone agreed that it was no one's fault that the pageant wagon had trouble with the highly polished floors, slid a little now and then and resulted in Madonna Terese's pillar of fortitude nearly impaling Madonna Valentina.

The spectators, nevertheless, proclaimed the entire proceedings "glorious" and excused the gray horse for defecating with every other step of the procession. The noble guests and their small armies of hangers-on, already infused with great quantities of wine and swept away on a wave of general good feeling, generously applauded and lauded the mythological and religious themes as if they understood them.

The members of I Comici Buffoni, scheduled to perform following the feast, were isolated in a side chamber of their own lest they contaminate the guests with bawdy language and worse behavior. This proved to be a wise step, for the troupe was the first of the assembly to float on a mist of sweet fermentation, and Piero Tebaldeo was beginning to suspect that the performance would be even more outrageous than usual when Francesco suggested that the male lover might prove more amusing in female dress, and Prudenza of Siena decided she would play Colombina bare breasted.

"For comic effect I suppose," Rubini observed drily.

The feast itself continued with the format of innovation. In place of the huge platters of meat or cauldrons of stew, the army of servants carried in tureens of minestra and platters of lasagne and ravioli, heavily flavored with garlic and sprinkled with grated prugnoli, the small, delicate mushrooms favored by the Tuscans, a touch that made Maestro Leonardo melancholy for his birthplace.

The solid gold forks were either completely ignored or used to gesture elaborately, thus demonstrating that the bearer was acquainted with this new development and understood that this was a tool of genteel nobility. Half of the cardinals used them, and half utilized their fingers which, as Cardinal Celano observed "were made by God before these tined contraptions of the devil." Most of the ladies and the courtiers struggled with the new utensil in an attempt to appear sophisticated and worldly, occasionally resulting in an accidental stabbing of the outstretched hands of other guests dipping into the platters.

The actors in their sequestered room, used both hands to eat and slipped the gold forks into their tunics for later sale.

❖ ❖ ❖

The initial serving was followed by a parade of salads displaying a menagerie of citron animals and castles of turnips and lemons surrounding slabs of ham and herrings with small piles of anchovies, olives, and caviar. There were flowers spun of candy decorating venison molded into the form of gilded lions, pastries shaped like black eagles, white peacocks or pheasants, statues of marzipan depicting mythical personalities, and a sampling of donkey meat, currently coming into favor with some of the aristocracy, although Niccolo found no stomach for it.

The diners at first flirted and fondled one another between servings with some degree of discretion, but as the evening wore on, and they wallowed in rivers of wines, they became more intense and more obvious in their seductions. They loudly exchanged stories and jests that became increasingly bold and suggestive, and, in general, responded to their host's generosity as expected. Only once was Galeazzo seen to wince, and that came when Cardinal d'Este insisted that the goblets of Venetian glass should be shattered against the walls after each toast "to express our joy and simultaneously show our sworn hostility to the Venetians."

Maestro Ambrogio succeeded in boring most of his tablemates with long-winded analysis of the eight books on dining by Apicius newly published in Milan. He went on to the more familiar text, *The Fifty Courtesies of the Table,* that advised, according to the maestro, that "one must not stuff too large mouthfuls in both cheeks" or "keep one's hand too long in the platter." Eventually his neighbors either dissolved into a drunken stupor, slipped beneath the tables for their own purposes, or simply ignored the old man.

Niccolo was seated to the right of Madonna Valentina who was, in turn, seated on the duke's right. He devoured mounds of jellied and smoked meats and poultry, but drank cautiously of the select vintages, although with deep appreciation of the quality. His attention was primarily focused on the shadowy canyons between the breasts of the serving girls, and he was certain that one in particular deliberately brushed against his arm in subtle invitation. Consequently, plotting to enjoy a brief moment with the young girl who was only a head or two taller, he decided to keep his wits about him. The problem, as he saw it, was to slip away from Madonna Valentina who paraded him about as Madonna Dorotea did her cheetah.

Niccolo, like many males, was slowly transformed during the meal from a nervous and uncertain young suitor into a cunning, sharp-minded seducer. After the final course, the assembly moved into a nearby chamber for the performance by the comedians, and Niccolo took advantage of the confusion to drift into the kitchens. Here he encountered the pretty young girl who was about to clear the tables, and, with the assumed authority of Il Moro, ordered her to accompany him into the gardens to "gather fresh berries" for the ladies, declaring that his mistress and her friends would be "devastated" without fresh fruit.

They had no sooner entered the gardens, however, when the serving girl, whose name turned out to be Ellie for Eleanor, was told to abandon her gathering bowl and to take the dwarf's hand "lest you get lost among the hedges and shrubbery."

The soft light of the torches that illuminated the gardens also produced deep caverns of shadow, and Niccolo cunningly maneuvered himself and Ellie into such a dark area to "gather the sweets," despite the girl's protest that she could not see the berries. After Niccolo supposedly lost his footing and fell against her, resulting in both of the young people stretched against the cool carpet of grass, it became only too obvious to which "sweets" the dwarf had referred, and who was to do the "gathering."

But the maid was willing, partly from curiosity concerning the anatomy of a dwarf and partly because she, like all the servants, had been "sampling" the wine throughout the long evening. Now, on her back and facing the wide tapestry of starry sky, she felt Niccolo's agile fingers untie the laces of her blouse and the cool breath of the night air brush against her nipples. She inhaled the scent and tasted again the wine on Niccolo's lips, and then flushed and gasped as the dwarf's mouth fastened itself on her left breast. She felt the cool fingers of the nocturnal wind creep slowly up her bare legs and thighs as she knew her skirt was being lifted and Niccolo's goal revealed to him.

Niccolo himself was awash in a maelstrom of lace, linen, ties, flesh, stars, grass, and new sensations. His mind quickly retraced all he had learned from the illustrations in the forbidden books of the Certosa library, and he struggled with his own clothing in an attempt to prepare himself for penetration and still sustain a mood of romantic love for the girl beneath him.

He soon learned a basic truth of seduction: it is difficult to paint a beautiful picture while fumbling with the brush.

At that moment, in the aviary of the Castello Sforzesco, Guarino Valla, the falconer and one of the assassins of Vanozza de Faenza's late lover, scrubbed the last of the blood from the claws of the two Alfanechi falcons, checked their beaks one more time for any shred of incriminating flesh, and, satisfied, removed the hoods and placed the birds in their separate cages. He took the shredded remains of the tattered shawl and threw it into the stove that provided the warmth for the birdhouse. Then he extinguished the lamp, slipped through the door and strode up the pathway to the stables. He knew he had only a few moments to mount and return to Sanseverino's palace where he would join his fellow servants in rowdy celebration and, if possible, drink too much, pass out, and give himself an alibi.

"She has permitted me to loosen her bodice," murmured the cardinal to Galeazzo di Sanseverino outside the door of the small, intimate chamber, "supposedly to bless her breasts, but she seems reluctant to go any farther."

The host had abandoned his heavy armor and was dressed only in a white blouse, sash, boots, and tights. He placed an arm around the prelate's pudgy shoulders and passed him the small vial.

"Here, my friend," he whispered, "slip this into the lady's chalice before you pour the wine for her. I have already chosen a vintage widely reputed to be capable of arousing passion in a Mother Superior, and I reserved one bottle for myself and had this last bottle placed in your chamber. This cantharidine powder will stoke the already glowing coals of the lady's desire and let the flames arise and devour you both."

"Oh good, good, good," smiled the chubby Cardinal Albizzi. "I have been the lady's confessor occasionally, and I know she is capable and somewhat experienced in the ways of love. Unhappily she is also devout, and my clerical scarlet seems to have a restraining effect on her. I assured her that lying with a cardinal is not a mortal sin, being neither of grievous matter nor of sufficient reflection, but, on the contrary, a sincere expression of the Christian love and charity between the shepherd and the lamb." He shrugged. "I don't think she believes me."

"Use this," Galeazzo murmured, "and she'll be too much in heat to notice what you're wearing—or what you are not."

The portly cleric giggled, took the vial, and disappeared behind the door. Galeazzo's smile slowly faded, and he paused a moment to rest one ear against the closed portal. Then he turned, crossed to the small balcony, and watched as couples or small groups of guests slipped away from the dancing and drinking in the ballroom, now emptied of tables, and closeted themselves, amid giggles and whispered conversations, in the small antechambers. He noted that Madonna Dorotea, desperately clutching the sleeve of Count Davigno to keep from falling, selected a door, opened it, found the room already occupied, and continued down the corridor until they both disappeared into an empty room, leaving the forlorn cheetah to form a circle within himself and go to sleep.

He smiled to see Il Moro bow stiffly to the Count and Countess Bergamini as these two guests prepared to leave the palace, and he knew that the duke wished with all his heart that he could be the one on the arm of the lovely young woman.

Idiot, he reflected. To let any one woman ensnare you like that.

He was suddenly conscious of someone behind him and wheeled to face Madonna Terese weaving unsteadily in the doorway of the small room. The rosy, flickering light of the interior threw the lady into silhouette, but the captain-general could tell she was still naked.

"Horsey?" she squealed, waving a wine bottle over her head, and then she weaved back into the room in a shower of giggles.

Galeazzo removed his leather quirt from his waistband, slapped it once against his thigh, and entered behind her.

The celebration of I Comici Buffoni, following their performance, was classic in form and structure. Intoxicated to the point of collapse, each of the troupe nevertheless took a turn to entertain the others with songs or dances, recitations and acrobatic demonstrations, and did so with such a high degree of discipline and skill that it produced wonder among the servants, nobility, and workers who had chosen to spend their evening with the theater crowd. Being unacquainted with the more glorious, but secret, traditions of the art, they were not aware that a truly gifted actor, removed from reality by alcohol or weariness or an aftermath of an evening of passion, is still capable of reciting a hundred lines of dialogue without a single lapse of memory or a faltering delivery. Indeed, it had become a widespread phenomenon among the theatrical that some performers were only at the peak of their abilities when their consciousness was dulled or absent.

This was not the case with their leader, Piero Tebaldeo, who had trained with professional mummers and court performers and who stressed discipline above all. It was Tebaldeo who kept insisting that playing comedy was second in difficulty only to mounting a horse by leaping over his head. It was Piero who demanded constant improvisational exercises and who soothed the innumerable small wars that always erupt among creative and egocentric individuals.

This was certainly not the state of mind of Prudenza of Siena who was once again locked in the torrid and burly embrace of the chamberlain of the Castello Sforzesco. The official had to divest himself of his escort for the evening in order to renew old passions with Prudenza whom he remembered with delight from the troupe's previous visit to Milan, and she, in turn, had prepared herself with enough wine to dull her occasionally abrasive nature and to loosen her few remaining inhibitions and her remarkably talented tongue.

Isabella was, as usual, surrounded by a legion of courtiers. These noble gentlemen, like most theater-goers, failed to separate the woman from the role, and, assuming that Isabella was the lady she portrayed on stage, treated her with respect and genteel admiration. She, on the other hand, would indulge herself with this little game for the first several hours, and later would slip away with one of the tall and handsome grooms from Sanseverino's stables to enjoy several more hours of uncontrolled and obscene amusement in the haylofts.

The third female member of the troupe, Anna Ponti, reverted to her role as the songstress and introduced the revelers to a barrage of sea chanties, drinking songs, and bawdy ballads that constituted her offstage repertory. Eventually she went off with one or two fellow musicians and developed an entirely new concept of counterpoint.

Niccolo's closest friend in the troupe, Rubini, the former high-wire walker, went scurrying among the ladies of the court for a possible partner since his taste ran to nobility, and found it in Madonna Valentina who had been abandoned by Il Moro for a new conquest from Cremona. In a surprising mood of discretion, Madonna Valentina took Rubini back to her own rooms in the Castello Sforzesco, reasoning that this would be the safest place in the world for a brief romantic encounter since most of the occupants would remain at the Palazzo di Sanseverino until the late morning hours.

They had disembarked from the lady's carriage at the postern gate rather than risk entering by the main entrance and being recognized. This forced the couple to cross through the ducal gardens where the torches that lined the pathways were extinguished for the night, and they had to grope their way through this tenebrae toward the women's quarters. They paused from time to time in the shadows to resume the anatomical groping that had begun in the performers' room and continued through the rapid ride in the carriage.

It was after one of these passionate pauses that Rubini, customarily light-footed and agile, tripped over something lying in the pathway and propelled both himself and Madonna Valentina into the shrubbery. After a brief match of delighted wrestling and wet kisses, they resumed their upright stature and turned to examine what was blocking their passage.

It was an unidentifiable mass of torn clothing and stripped human sinew and cartilage, floating on a sea of blood.

Madonna Valentina turned into the shrubbery and donated her dinner to the hedges.

It was deep in the afternoon of the following day before Maestro Leonardo was able to identify the body as that of Vanozza de Faenza, the pastry cook in the Castello Sforzesco. It was nearly twilight before Leonardo's careful diligence and powers of observation were able to separate a single item, a piece of feather, from the shredded face and hands of the victim and could attribute the death to an attack by one or more falcons.

When confronted with this information, Valla the falconer could only shrug and say he found no indications that any of Il Moro's hawks had found prey in their nocturnal forays. He informed the duke that it was customary to release some of the falcons at night to forage for rodents and small animals and so encourage their natural instinct for hunting.

"They always return to the aviary," he said.

The senior handler went on to explain that it was most unusual for hunting hawks to attack a human, but, of all the breeds, the Alfanechi were notorious for unprovoked aggression. He explained in tedious detail how this breed could be attracted by almost anything, a sudden flash of light, an abrupt movement, but there was nothing tangible to indicate that it was Il Moro's falcons that were the killers of the pastry cook. Knowing that the hawks, if found guilty, would probably be destroyed, Valla suggested that the killers might have been someone else's hawks or wild birds of prey.

The duke agreed but seemed to give some consideration to his own birds. "I have heard others claim it, and I have said it myself: Russian hawks are unpredictable."

It was, of course, Maestro Leonardo who offered an alternative explanation to Niccolo that same night.

"Falcons, especially the hunting breeds, are trained killers, but their victims are usually chosen instinctively, like small rodents or other birds. But they can be trained to attack other things, a specific post or an article of clothing draped on it, and if they are so trained, they will repeatedly attack the item when they see it. If Vanozza's shawl, for example, disappeared for a while and was used by someone to train falcons to attack it, the lady would be an appropriate prey when the hawks saw her wearing it again."

"But this is only conjecture," argued the young man. "I mean, you have no proof."

"No," the Maestro agreed, "but I did find the shreds of a shawl imbedded in the flesh, although the shawl itself could not be found."

"Then you are implying that this is murder?"

The Maestro sighed. "As usual."

The death of Vanozza de Faenza held the attention of the court for less than a day.

On the afternoon of the second day following the festival, the servants of Cardinal Albizzi discovered that their master was dead. His naked body had been noted the morning following the celebration, but it was assumed from the scattering of clothing and the disheveled bedding that the cardinal had returned to the Castello Sforzesco after some traditional wild cavorting with a lady or two at the orgy, and, weary and drunken, had fallen into a deep sleep. It was customary for his servants on such occasions to let him sleep until he aroused himself and rang for them, but when the hours went on with no sign of His Eminence awakening, his body servant discovered that the corpse was cold and hardening.

Masters Ambrogio and Leonardo were both dispatched to the cardinal's bedchamber to conduct their examinations. A slight trace of white froth on the lips suggested poison to Leonardo, but the physician insisted that the corpulent cardinal had simply attempted too many bouts with cupid, and his overworked heart had surrendered to the ultimate exhaustion.

The lady who was the object of the cardinal's lust following the dinner was questioned with utmost discretion and gentility by both da Corte and Maestro Leonardo and weepingly confessed to "three or four" brief bouts of love during the evening. This suggested that the cardinal had been chemically primed for the evening, and Maestro Ambrogio ran through his library of aphrodisiacs including mandrake root and ginseng, but there was nothing lethal in that list. He did remark to Leonardo that the cleric had access to a garden of herbs and medicines that included colchicum or autumn crocus seeds for his gout, squill for his heart, tansy for worms, ephedra for coughs, rhubarb for his bowels, and fennel and senna for digestion. The aged physician also volunteered the information that there had been a sudden demand for rue and savin among the ladies of the court following the festival under the impression that either or both would induce miscarriages. There had also been several requests, Ambrogio said, for rauwolfia which was reputed to calm nerves and was often given to madmen.

Then Galeazzo di Sanseverino stepped forth to volunteer the information that the cardinal had petitioned the host for an aphrodisiac to lure the lady into a more obliging state on the night of the festival, and that he had, indeed, provided the portly cleric with a vial of cantharidine powder.

Once again da Vinci presented Niccolo with an alternative explanation.

"It is true that cantharidine powder is commonly used as an aphrodisiac in small doses, but in larger amounts it is deadly. It is possible that the cardinal took too much."

"Is that likely?" asked Niccolo. "I mean, the cardinal's reputation was somewhat shadowed, wasn't it? I would imagine that a man of his wide experience would certainly know the proper dosage for an aphrodisiac."

The Maestro nodded. "He would. Therefore, if his death was deliberate, he would have had to imbibe even more of the powder following his usual dosing."

"You mean forcibly?"

"No," the Maestro shook his head. "No signs of bruising or violence on the body. I would think that the best way to induce the poison was to put a normal amount in something else that the cardinal would consume in the evening, a bottle of wine perhaps."

Niccolo then shook his own head. "No," he said. "Galeazzo says the powder was to be given to the lady to arouse her passions. If the lady took the vial of powder, plus some from a bottle of wine, then she, too, would have died from an overdose."

"Very good," smiled the Maestro. "You're thinking. And there are two possibilities from your premise. Either the murderer was perfectly willing to have the lady die as well as the cardinal, or the powder given to the cardinal to put in the lady's goblet was not cantharidine."

Niccolo frowned, and the Maestro continued.

"Let us assume that the killer knew the cardinal would take his normal amount of the aphrodisiac prior to the evening's adventures. Maestro Ambrogio says he had a full complement of herbs and powders. Suppose the killer then provided a bottle of wine for the lovers that was saturated with cantharidine, and a vial of harmless powder for the lady. She would consume only that amount of the aphrodisiac that was in the wine which would loosen her passion and produce the result that the cardinal desired. He, however, would be consuming twice the amount, a fatal portion."

Niccolo blinked in astonishment. "Then you're saying it is another murder."

"I think so."

"And you are also implying that the killer was the one who provided both the wine and the fake aphrodisiac, Sanseverino!"

"Yes," the Maestro nodded. "But," he added quickly, "there is another possibility."

"Of course," sighed the dwarf.

"It is possible that Galeazzo di Sanseverino was not aware that the powder was false or that the wine was loaded with cantharidine. In that case, the real killer was the one who provided the general with the powder in collaboration with someone on the serving staff who prepared and provided the wine."

"A conspiracy?"

"A possibility," said Leonardo. "We must bear in mind that

there remains the mysterious Griffin who oversees assassinations, and cantharidine has a somewhat unusual history. No one seems to know exactly how it is prepared. There is a rumor that it is made of crushed beetles and another that it is distilled from the froth emitted from the mouth of a poisoned bear suspended upside-down from a rafter. The only thing we know for certain are the circumstances under which cantharidine was first used and by whom."

Niccolo was forced to wait for the answer.

"The Borgias."

The death of the amorous cardinal, however, coupled with the memory of the murder of Captain Francesco in Madonna Valentina's bed, produced both a sudden drop in sexual adventuring of the women of the court and a renewal of the vows of chastity among the clergy.

Niccolo, himself, learned a lesson. Three days following his own excursion on the seas of passion, his groin began to itch, and a rash appeared that nearly drove the dwarf insane. This time, however, it was not Maestro Leonardo who provided relief, but his assistant, the yellow-haired Salai.

The two young men had gradually come to an understanding as Salai slowly realized that the dwarf was in favor with the Maestro and could do him harm. From time to time they had encountered one another and attempted a fragile cordiality which had evolved into a mutual tolerance.

Now they had been left alone in the workshop and had spent an hour or two exchanging the stories of their romantic exploits on the evening of the festival. Neither of them, in a surprising display of gentlemanly behavior, named names, but expressed only their feelings and passions during the encounters.

It was then that Niccolo, embarrassed, confessed to the rash.

"Relax," laughed Salai, "it isn't the French disease. That makes itself evident in a totally different way." He went to his chest, opened it, and threw a small container to the dwarf. "Rub this balm on your crotch four times a day," he advised, "and by week's end, you'll be yourself again." He returned and sat beside the young man. "And the next time, use a length of sheep's intestines."

"What?"

"It's called a sheath, and you wear it over your dagger."

"My dagger?"

"Your prick, you idiot!" laughed Salai. "It stretches and is sealed by heat at one end. It will keep the girl from getting pregnant and you from getting whatever disease she's dispensing this week."

"That's amazing," said Niccolo. "Did the Maestro invent that?"

"Not likely," the assistant laughed again. "The Maestro had enough turmoil when he was younger and accused of homosexual conduct by an ecclesiastical court. He was tried three times and acquited all three times, but he swore that the pleasure was not worth the pain and the interruption to his work. Since then I believe he has been celibate."

"Then where did these—sheaths—originate?" asked Niccolo.

"From the same source as the disease," said Salai.

"The French."

Captain Agostino Porco lay on his belly and peered cautiously over the crest of the ridge. Below him on the French approach to the Little St. Bernard Pass, he could see the camps of the Gascon troops and the Swiss mercenaries. His trained eye easily discerned that there were at least four companies of cavalry whose picket lines held strings of identical black geldings, hundreds of pikemen and archers busily sharpening and adjusting their weapons, battalions of workers attending the oxen used to pull the carriage-mounted bronze cannon complete with "dolphins" for hoisting and quadrants for determining elevation. There were columns of hooped mortars with detachable powder chambers, some cast in bronze in two sections for easy transport. Beyond, there were columns of mules and supply wagons.

The army was at rest, and still on the French side of the Alpine passes, but their numbers and their very presence were enough to assure Captain Porco that they were merely awaiting a signal to begin their ascent into the mountains, down into northern Italy and across the Lombard plains to Milan.

A professional soldier, Captain Porco knew that his scouting report must be relayed to the captain-general, Galeazzo di Sanseverino, as soon as possible, but, at the same time he knew that the temperamental senior officer had a reputation of being hard on bearers of bad news. This was not surprising, for the classical response to ill reports was the execution of the messenger. So Captain Porco wisely chose a lieutenant, Antonio Bendinelli, to take the report to Milan.

Lieutenant Bendinelli, of course, was a veteran himself, and he prudently relegated the responsibility to a junior officer who, in turn, passed the report to a noncommissioned officer who passed it to another soldier of lesser rank. There was now a delay of two or three days while the rolls were consulted and analyzed to find the most gullible, the least experienced member of the army.

Finally the report ended in the hands of young Annibale Mancascivolo, who was a drummer boy for his regiment. This new recruit was mounted on a stallion and pointed toward Milan, but on arriving in the city, he guaranteed his future in the army by simply handing the report to a guard at the entrance of the Palazzo di Sanseverino and wheeling the horse back in the direction of the Alps.

The guard passed it to a page who, unaware of the contents of the epistle, took it directly to Galeazzo and rapidly departed.

The passing process resulted in a delay of nearly a week,

including the half day that Lieutenant Bendinelli had let the report rest on his cot while he prayed for enlightenment.

None of the Milanese scouting party had a way of knowing, of course, that by the time Galeazzo di Sanseverino had the packet delivered to him, he had already been informed through his uncle, that the French were mobilized and ready to march. His reaction, however, was somewhat unpredictable. He calmly read the contents and then crossed to the fireplace in the bedchamber of his newly completed palace, and fed it, page by page, to the flames.

Simultaneously, from the convent of San Sisto, a courier galloped toward Genoa with another packet containing signed testimonies of the Mother Superior and two nuns that Maria Chigi had, indeed, been delivered of a son. Included in the packet was an order banning any further loans or financial assistance to Duke Ludovico Sforza, Il Moro, lord of Milan.

In Milan, in his quarters in the Castello Sforzesco, Niccolo the dwarf rubbed the balm given him by Salai on his enflamed crotch while he perused his copy of Epictetus.

The passage read: "There comes a sudden storm, the ship flounders. What matters it to me? My part was to choose the master and the crew. Now the matter is in the hands of the great Master of the sea. All I can do is drown without fear, without tears, without cursing God, remembering that all that is born, dies, I am not eternal, but a human being, a part of the whole, as an hour is part of a day, and, like the hour, I must pass and be forgotten."

Somehow, he did not find this comforting.

Chapter 6
A Plethora of Plots

"Some man may be chosen who,
by reason of his inadequacy,
may cause your descendents to revile you and your age,
judging that this epoch was badly provided
with men of good judgment or good masters . . .
This dishonor would be occasioned if,
by your negligence,
you were to put your faith in some braggart
who by his wiles . . . would beget
very great and lasting shame
to himself and you . . ."

**Letter from Leonardo da Vinci
to the Magnifici fabbricieri
of Piacenza Cathedral
c. 1493**

The funeral mass for Cardinal Albizzi was even more elaborate than the one afforded the hapless Maria Chigi. The cardinal's coat of arms was prominently draped over the coffin: a hound standing on his hind legs, claws extended, with a coronet wound around his neck like a collar.

Niccolo glanced across the basilica to where Maestro Leonardo was sandwiched between Maestro Ambrogio and Marchesino Stanga. While the other two sat with bowed heads, either asleep or deep in religious meditation, the artist seemed to be focusing on the banner as if he were mentally sketching it.

Now what is on your mind? Niccolo wondered.

"What were you thinking of? Why wasn't I informed of this days ago?"

Il Moro roared at Bernardino da Corte and stabbed a finger into the chest of Salvatore Cossa as they stood before him in the Salla della Palla.

"An entire mercenary army is massed on the French side of the Alpine passes with artillery and cavalry! They have been there, in plain sight, for months! Months! And I only receive a report from our agents this morning! How is that possible?" The duke began to pace the floor. "When the Genoese decided to cancel my credit with the Bank of St. George, I received *that* message fast enough!"

Da Corte shrugged. "I can only assume that the report went to General Galeazzo, and then, by some misfortune, it was lost in transit between the Palazzo di Sanseverino and here. We received this report through da Tuttavilla only this morning."

The duke slammed the parchment on the table. "Well, we cannot correct the past, can we, eh?" He wheeled on his assistants. "Tell Galeazz to mobilize our armies immediately. Have the castle's forces prepare for siege and break out our own cannon and catapults. I will go to Vigevano to inspect our other defenses, and I will declare a state of emergency in Milan. Close the gates to the city."

He came around the desk and close to Cossa. "Perhaps it may not be too late to smooth things with the Genoese and have my credit reestablished. After all, I don't imagine that they have a guarantee that the French won't sweep in and commandeer all their wealth. I have instructed da Tuttavilla to see what he can do about reopening the channels of communication. You, Salvatore! I make you personally responsible for locating the seducer of Maria Chigi. Are we any closer to solving that little problem?"

Salvatore Cossa nodded. "There is a lady in court, a Madonna Louisa, who has been telling me interesting stories that I think will lead us to the seducer."

"When?"

"I can't say, Your Highness," he murmured. "Perhaps a week?"

The duke slammed his hand on the desk top. "Perhaps three or four or five? My God, sir, the French are breathing down my neck, and I need money! Not next week or next month, but now, sir! Now! I give you three days. Just three.

No more. Find the man who seduced this child and bring him to me! Mind! I don't want a dead man, Cossa! I want a live man and a written confession!" He turned and headed for the door. "I did what you requested of me earlier," he roared at his assistants over his shoulder. "Now do what I expect of you!"

He paused at the door, turned and announced, "I need some diversion."

And he was gone.

"My God," whined Salvatore. "Three days!"

In the Salla della Palla the commedians met for their daily exercise in improvisation, and Niccolo sat in a shadowed corner with a bowl containing three of the twelve apples he had dispersed to the troupe.

"Is everyone here?" asked Tebaldeo.

Simone scanned the assembly. "Rubini's missing."

"We see less and less of him," grumbled Isabella as she polished an apple against her skirt.

"That's fine with me," said Turio who was sprawled over a chair devouring the fruit. "He's become an arrogant ass, always posturing and bragging how many friends he's made at court."

"He is popular," sighed Francesco. "I understand he also had a private audience with the duke." He lowered his voice. "It concerned Madonna Valentina."

"The duke!" growled Tebaldeo.

There was no disguising the disapproval in Tebaldeo's tone, and Niccolo gasped and sat erect as Il Moro suddenly appeared in the doorway.

The dwarf made a loud and obtrusive clearing of his throat, and the company turned. Instantly the troupe bowed as one to the Milanese prince.

Il Moro crossed to the small assembly. "Sit down, sit down. Be comfortable." He turned to Tebaldeo who remained standing. "I take it you disapprove of dukes, Messer Tebaldeo?"

The captain lowered his head. "Your Highness . . ."

The duke took a chair and waved his hand. "No, go on. Go on. Say what is on your mind. I promise you I will not take offense, and it may take my mind off my problems at present. What have you against dukes?"

It was some time before Tebaldeo said anything, and Niccolo felt uneasy. The leader of the troupe looked at the duke as if he were judging whether he was really being given leave to speak freely, but nothing could be interpreted from Il Moro's countenance.

The company's Captain sighed and said softly, "I have nothing against dukes, Your Highness. Not if they are good men. I believe every man should be a duke, or a king, if his vision is clear, and his heart is pure."

Il Moro laughed. "Yes," he said, "Well. That's a trifle romantic, wouldn't you say, my dear Captain?"

"Yes, Your Highness," he responded, "But I am a romantic. I'm of the theater."

In his shadowed corner, Niccolo smiled.

"I will accept that," said the duke. "But are you certain your dislike for nobility isn't merely a jealous rebellion against wealth and power?"

"I don't consider wealth and power blessings, my lord."

There was a slight flurry of laughter from the other members of the company, but Niccolo, fascinated, leaned forward and began to bite into his apple.

"Oh?" the duke commented drily.

"I wouldn't mind suffering a little of both," laughed Anna.

Tebaldeo turned his head to glare at her. "I mean it! Wealth and power are curses attached to ruthless ambition and dominating pride, the common qualities of kings!"

The smile vanished from the duke's face, and Niccolo feared the leader of the troupe had overstepped his liberties.

Softly, softly, he whispered to himself.

"My dear Tebaldeo," said the duke softly, "doesn't a strong society need strong leaders?"

"I can't dispute that, Your Highness," Tebaldeo admitted. "But I think the people should have the right to choose those who lead them."

"No, no, no!" Il Moro snapped. "A democracy is mob rule, mindless and directionless. If the rabble had their choice of leaders, it would be some handsome and amusing fellow—like you, Tebaldeo—or Francesco there! And, meaning no offense you understand, such people are usually incapable of governing themselves much less a state."

"But that shouldn't exclude attractive individuals from leadership positions," Prudenza grinned.

"God forbid," murmured Isabella.

"I agree to that in principle," Tebaldeo responded. "I think the qualification for kingship should be that the candidate is a good man."

There was another ripple of laughter from the company, and this time Il Moro laughed with them. "Oho! Dangerous territory, my friend." Then he added, "Suppose you define this idealized Good Man for us."

"One that's hard to find," laughed Isabella.

"One that's hard," observed Prudenza.

"I'll tell you," Tebaldeo began quietly, forcing a silence on the duke and the company.

In his corner, Niccolo, intrigued and afraid for Tebaldeo, momentarily forgot his apple and concentrated on the assembly.

"The Good Man doesn't live in a castle or hide behind moats and drawbridges. He has nothing worth stealing, and what he has, he is willing to share with those who are in need. He remembers that the purpose of a home is to shelter himself and his loved ones from the elements. He has no need for fifty rooms!"

"Don't let Galeazzo di Sanseverino hear you," laughed Simone.

"Suppose he has fifty children," asked the duke.

"Unlikely."

"I have fifty children," said the duke, leaning forward and speaking with a new earnestness. "More. Hundreds. They are courtiers and ladies, servants and servitors, grooms, cooks . . ."

"Meaning no offense you understand, my lord," said Tebaldeo. "They are not your children. Most of the courtiers and ladies are parasites, and the others look after you, not you after them."

"A nice distinction," nodded the duke, "but let us say the arrangement is mutual. Servants need an income, and a lord needs servants to bathe and clothe him, to tend to his horses and carriages . . ."

"The Good Man doesn't need an upholstered coach and four. He knows that the purpose of a horse or a coach, like his own two legs, is to merely carry him from one point to another. Somehow the opulence of the carriage now supersedes the basic need of the passenger. It has become a symbol of power and wealth."

"Come," the duke persisted. "You must admit that traveling by coach is less tiring."

"And your clothes don't get dusty," added Turio.

"Cleanliness is important," agreed Tebaldeo. "But the Good Man isn't concerned whether his clothes are gorgeous or fashionable. His clothing is only there to protect his skin from the elements and to prevent embarrassment to others."

"Or, in the case of Marco, embarrassment to oneself," laughed Anna. The company's Doctor, who seldom spoke, merely sniffed and focused his attention on the small black book in his lap.

"Come, Captain!" caroled Isabella as she raised her skirt to reveal a decorated red petticoat. "A little lace in the right place does wonders, darling."

"The Good Man doesn't need lace on his cuffs any more than a lady needs them on her petticoats," argued Tebaldeo. "And he doesn't need his meals elegantly prepared by seven chefs over a period of days. His food must taste well enough to get past his tongue, satisfy the empty feeling in his belly, and provide enough nourishment to keep him alive."

"Oh now, Messer Tebaldeo," the duke objected with a smile. "You must admit that our Italian cuisine is an art form!"

"And there is much to be said," offered Turio, "for an elaborate and delicate meal by candlelight with an attractive young woman . . ."

"Then food becomes an instrument of seduction," growled the Captain. "The Good Man doesn't need elaborate food and potent wines, or for that matter wealth or power, to provide himself with an occasional bed partner. Mutual needs attract."

"That's so," cried Simone, trying to lighten the mood, "I needed discipline . . ."

". . . and he got me!" roared Prudenza imitating the crack of a whip to the laughter of the company.

Niccolo noticed that only Tebaldeo didn't laugh. Or smile.

He means what he is saying, thought the dwarf.

"And the Good Man doesn't need praise and adulation to assure himself that his work is quality," he continued solemnly. "He has no appetite for awards or subsidies, especially since these usually emanate from people who neither understand nor appreciate the nature of the art. It is a subversive form of flattery, and it can be death to an artist."

"Oh bullocks!" roared Marco to everyone's surprise. "Applause and a few coins never hurt!"

"Of course," Tebaldeo nodded. "But it is quite enough for the Good Man that his work is pleasurable, that it keeps him occupied and alert, that it provides enough income to assure him and his loved ones of adequate food and shelter. It is even better if his work helps others."

"Ah, but what of the ultimate award? What of fame, eh, Tebaldeo!" thundered Simone leaping into the argument. "Think of having your name on every tongue!"

"Like a blister from sampling a hot beverage? For that is all fame is: a temporary flame, blinding and warming, and then quickly gone to ashes!"

The duke sighed, rose to his feet and said quietly, "Well my friend, you have no need for kings, dukes, chefs, coachmen, compliments, or heralds. What else do you think society can do without?"

"Cardinals."

"What?" whispered the duke. "Take care, my friend. The church has a million ears, and even I could not protect you from an ecclesiastical court."

"Or rabbis, monks, or prophets," the tall leader of the company pressed on. "The Good Man doesn't need another man to advise and instruct him on the proper path. The Good Man lives with his God constantly, in genuine love and humility. He speaks to Him in the wind. He admires His handiwork in the changing of the seasons, in the profusion of animals and birds, in an exquisite sunset."

The duke studied the Captain for a long while. "I think the Vatican wouldn't know whether to burn you, my friend, or canonize you, although I suspect it would be the former."

"I don't mean to be heretical, Your Highness," sighed Tebaldeo. "All I am saying is that such a king, or a duke, or a prince, would govern his people without ruling them. He would guide by example and love his people whom he recognizes as his peers and not his servants."

"I'm afraid that the reign of such a king would be limited to the time alloted him by mad assassins and belligerent neighbors."

"Perhaps," Tebaldeo admitted, "for behind every assassin is a powerful, and usually wealthy, force that strongly opposes the values of a Good Man. But belligerent neighbors may be dissuaded from conquest if they only stop to remember that a happy and peaceful nation, with the values of the Good Man ever before them, may be invaded, but it can never, never be conquered."

The duke turned away and started for the chamber door.

"Well, my dear Tebaldeo, I hope you are right for we are about to be invaded. I am also enlightened. Not concerning the qualities of kings as much as the romanticism and idealism of the creative artist. I am now thoroughly convinced that actors would make terrible rulers."

"Perhaps."

Il Moro nodded to Niccolo in his corner as he turned at the door. "In any case, it brings me to my reason for coming here to you. You are now, of course, free to leave the court since the festival is completed, but I feel I should warn you that the French are definitely on the march, and northern Italy will soon be enmeshed in total war. If you feel you might be safer here in my castle, you are free to continue to draw upon my hospitality."

Tebaldeo stepped forward, "Thank you, Your Highness. And I hope what I said did not offend you."

Il Moro managed a thin smile. "No. I have heard it all before, my friend." He smiled and whispered to the tall leader of the troupe, "In the book assembled from the words of those men you say we do not need."

He turned and nearly collided with Rubini who stopped and bowed stiffy to the duke. Niccolo thought he saw a trace of a smile on Il Moro's lips as he faced his rival for the affections of Madonna Valentina. But the duke said nothing, nodded and entered the corridor as Rubini rushed into the room.

"I'm sorry I'm late," said Scapino. "Did I miss anything?"

"Only a long-winded gospel according to Piero," murmured Marco turning his attention back to his book.

"The duke says the French are coming," sighed Anna, rising from her chair and stretching. "He says we may stay here if we choose."

"Considering all the people dying in grotesque ways around here," said Rubini. "We might be safer on the road."

Marco put aside his book. "I agree. And if the French are

coming through the Little St. Bernard Pass to the west, isn't it better for us to go east, and as quickly as we can?"

Tebaldeo shrugged. "The question is: how far could we get before the French were on us? How fast are they coming?"

"Why are we so concerned about the French anyway?" declared Isabella. "We've done nothing to them."

"I agree," said Turio. "It seems more dangerous for us to stay here and be associated with Il Moro. It's the duke that Louis wants. Not a troupe of actors."

"If it were a political matter, fine," argued Piero. "But when mercenaries pour into a city, there is no discipline, no questions asked about politics. They just rape and plunder. That's how they get paid. And we are nobody, so we would all be vulnerable."

"To what?" asked Anna. "Rape?"

"Certainly for you women," Rubini interjected, and then with a laugh, "and perhaps for the rest of us. Some of these Swiss and Gascon bowmen have perverted tastes. One never knows."

Tebaldeo signaled for silence. "The thing is: I think we should stay together. So either we all go, or we all stay."

"Well, I can't speak for anyone else," said Rubini stretching out in one of the upholstered chairs. "But I have become attached to the abundance of good food and drink. I rather like not having to plod beside the wagon in the rain and mud. There is something to be said for having a roof over your head and a warm fire when you change your costumes."

"You're not objective," sniffed Francesco. "You have an arrangement with Madonna Valentina. That's the nourishment you don't want to leave."

"I left it before, didn't I?" snapped Rubini. "When have I ever put my own needs and wishes before those of the company?" He drew himself into a sitting position. "I simply don't want to return to working the fairs. I don't want to find myself back on the high wire." Something in his voice alerted Niccolo. "I feel if I go back to the wire, I'll die there."

"You won't have to go back on the wire," Piero promised.

Suddenly Isabella stood and turned to face all of them. "Am I the only one who suspects that, well, that perhaps we are not here merely because we are entertainers?"

Again Niccolo found his attention focused on the troupe. "What?"

"What do you mean?" asked Anna.

"I'm asking why the duke suddenly sent a courier to us and invited us to perform for the festival," Isabella inquired. "He didn't seem enthralled by us during our initial visit."

"Perhaps he was," shrugged Turio. "Perhaps he is one of those people who laugh on the inside."

"An audience like that," Prudenza grumbled, "and we could switch to tragedy and no one would ever notice the difference."

"I don't know what you are implying, Isabella," Turio called to her, "but if you suspect something, say it straight, so we can all consider it."

"I'm not sure of anything," Isabella replied. "I just asked: why do you think Il Moro requested a troupe of new *commedia* players to entertain? There are jugglers and mummers throughout northern Italy who are better known than we are. There are court plays and players like those of Cardinal Bibbiena. Why did he invite us to entertain?"

"Perhaps he didn't," said Anna. "Perhaps he just responded to a request from the actual host, Sanseverino. It was really his festival. Maybe he requested us, and the duke merely sent word."

Marco shook his head. "No. If there is one person who has less of a sense of humor than Il Moro, it is Sanseverino."

"All right," Piero interjected. "We have to decide. We must choose. Let's go with the hands. All in favor of leaving, let me see them."

Isabella and Marco raised their hands.

"Unhuh. All opposed?"

The majority elevated their hands.

"Well, there it is," announced Tebaldeo. "We stay."

"Good," roared Rubini. "I was getting hungry."

As the troupe began their exercise, Niccolo quietly rose and slipped from the room. Three things he had heard troubled him.

The first was a statement by Tebaldeo. Behind every assassin is a powerful, and usually wealthy, force.

The second was a paraphrase of Isabella's insinuation. Were the commedians invited, not to entertain, but to be in the court where they could be readily available? And, if so, to what purpose?

And the third was the most intriguing. Could an actor who proclaims revolutionary views regarding princes and kings be moved, perhaps, to assassinate a duke?

Later Niccolo made these concerns known to the Maestro, and the response was more puzzling than the original question.

"So," Maestro Leonardo smiled. "Someone in the court has finally learned how to count backward."

In the Palazzo del Verme, Countess Bergamini reflected on her words as she looked from the large window at the spring flowering in her garden. Then she turned, dipped the feathered quill in the ink jar and began to write.

"Dear friend," the message began, "I am happy to learn from Niccolo that the death of the stableman aroused no great concern at the court, and that Cossa did not consider it worth investigating. Though my small friend tells me that Maestro da Vinci found something that suggested the man was deliberately killed. Still, no one will listen to the Maestro, so you did well. I am displeased, however, that Captain Francesco had to be sacrificed. We must be more careful, If our subject realizes he is in danger, he may arm himself or, God forbid, hasten the proceedings which would result in the fall of Milan and all our deaths. I must ask you, therefore, to proceed immediately with our plan, with greater care, but with increased dedication. I promise you a reward beyond your dreams if we succeed. Your friend . . ."

She made a rapid sketch on the bottom of the letter, depicting an eagle-headed lion, and then she folded the parchment and sealed it with her signet ring. She rose and crossed to the door. Just outside the portal stood a mercenary, and the lady handed him the parchment.

"The usual method," she said. "For the falconer, Guarino Valla."

In a small, still-unfinished antechamber in the Palazzo di Sanseverino, Galeazzo was also bent over a writing desk. He occasionally mouthed the words as he slowly inscribed them on the parchment, writing hurriedly and stopping only long enough to dip the feathered pen in the ink jug and then resume his frantic scrawling.

"My gracious lord," he wrote. "I feel certain you must be concerned about the recent occurrences at Pavia and in Milan, especially at the tragic events following my festival. I hesitate to say so, but I think there has been a rupture within the organization. The attempt on the life of Il Moro at the Certosa was more than a bungled assassination attempt. I am now convinced that the block of marble was not intended for the duke but for me, for I was the one whose horse bolted as the stone fell before us, and the duke was still some distance back. What this implies, of course, is that the Griffin has ordered my death for some reason I cannot discern, although I am not in a position of such great power that I could do harm to anyone on his level.

"Nevertheless I have proceeded with my duties and performed what was expected of me. The surviving assassin was no sooner buried, however, when another attempt was made on Il Moro's life, although this time it was Captain Francesco who was killed. Upon careful consideration, I came to the conclusion that this second attempt was certainly not meant for the duke. Madonna Valentina was out of favor with His Highness at the time, and it was an open secret that I had replaced him. Therefore it became clear to me that I was the intended victim, and that the Griffin was definitely trying to murder me and not Il Moro.

"I tell you this by way of explanation for the resulting events and to assure you that my loyalties remain, as always, to you and to your cause. I will continue to press forward with our original plan. I am aware that the time has already been extended, and that your patience must be wearing thin. I promise you that the ultimate action will be successfully carried out within a fortnight, and I remain your obedient servant, Galeazzo di Sanseverino, by the grace of God captain-general of the armies of Milan."

He quickly folded the parchment, sealed it with wax and imbedded his signet ring on the cooling surface. Then he rose and crossed to the door where a courier stood waiting.

"Quickly," commanded Galeazzo. "Get this to him as quickly as you can."

The courier took the parchment, saluted, wheeled smartly, and left the room.

Within half an hour, he handed it to Bernardino da Corte.

The chief of security waited for some response from Il Moro as the duke sat behind his desk in the room adjacent to his bedchamber and read the letter by candlelight. He had already listened as da Corte read it to him, and finally, Il Moro passed the message back to da Corte.

"What does this imply," he asked, "other than the not-surprising fact that my captain-general has become frightened and believes he is the target for the Griffin, and not me?"

"It is the tone that disturbs me," da Corte said. "Expressions such as 'the tragic events following my festival.' To which events does he refer? The death of the pastry cook? Cardinal Albizzi's overdose of aphrodisiacs?"

"Is that important?"

"It could be. And what of this phrase?" He unfolded the parchment and read: 'My loyalties remain, as always, to you and to your cause'? Unless the letter is addressed to you, who else commands our general's loyalty? The French? The Venetians? The Vatican? The Geonese? Who?"

"To whom was the courier to deliver the letter?"

"To a second courier, and I have no doubt, on to perhaps a third and fourth. There is no name inscribed on the letter, but I will have the courier watched as he passes it to someone, and then have that one followed until the letter gets to the one for whom it was intended. That will mark the power behind this Griffin."

The duke sighed. "I admit the letter offers some basis for confusion, but unless you can present something more tangible, I cannot believe Galeazz is an assassin. We have been friends long before I became duke. He has saved my life on several occasions. I need something much more damning before I accuse him of betraying me." He stood and came around the desk. "And what of that scrap of parchment you found in the stable? The figure drawn at the bottom was a griffin, wasn't it? Isn't that what you told me? Yet the scrap seemed to be a commission for the murder of Galeazz. At least that is what you deduced. Did my general order his own assassination then?"

"No, Your Highness," da Corte whispered.

"Then find something definite, something beyond a doubt,

that links Galeazz to this conspiracy," the duke demanded. "Then I will take some action."

Da Corte grimaced, bowed smartly and murmured, "Well, I only hope, Your Highness, that I can supply you with the dagger before we pull it from your back."

In the hidden passageway, Niccolo closed the spy hole and went first to relay the news to Maestro Leonardo, and then to inscribe it in his weekly report to the countess.

The burly man with the shaven skull worked his dagger around the edge of the padlock on the wooden door. "Why do we have to do this?" he grumbled. "Where is the key?"

"Lost," shrugged the old man whose gray mustaches reached below the level of his chin. "Our orders are to open the dungeons, all of the rooms, every one! We are to light the torches and prepare the equipment for use."

The muscular man picked at the rotted wood, and the latch began to be freed from the door. "That spells trouble for someone, Giorgio," he murmured. "Mark my words. Someone is about to end their days screaming down here where no one can hear them."

Giorgio nodded. "It has been months since the place was used, thank God for small mercies," he said. "But now, Lucio, now I hear the rumors that the Whisperers are looking for some rapist or something, and the duke needs information, so . . ."

Lucio succeeded at his labors, and the padlock fell to the floor. "There!" he crowed. "That does it!"

The old man and the stocky one both pressed their shoulders against the door and it slowly swung open. Instantly both men recoiled and backed away, choking, into the corridor.

"Hell fire!" wailed Lucio. "What a stench!"

Giorgio snatched the soft cap from his head and held it against his nose and mouth with one hand as he seized the torch from the iron ring in the wall. He kicked at the door which swung open a little farther, and he slowly entered the dank chamber with Lucio close behind him.

The light danced around the walls and frightened the fat rats that turned and glared at the intrusion, their eyes glittering beads in the light of the torch. Then they scurried away, shrieking at the interruption, and the torch illuminated a collection of bones, gelatinous matter, and shredded clothing lashed to a table.

The missing kitchen worker, Mino Spinolo, had been found.

"He knew she was missing?" da Corte asked.

The beautiful yellow-haired girl sat sobbing in the armless chair, and the chief of security lowered himself to one knee to console and reassure her. "There is no reason to weep, Madonna Louisa. I merely wish to understand. You will be doing a great service for your late friend, I assure you." He stood erect. "Now, once again, you say that His Eminence knew Madonna Maria was, as you put it, missing from the court?"

The young woman nodded.

"And His Eminence, Cardinal de Celano, had been her confessor?"

The sobbing grew in intensity.

"No harm will come to the good cardinal if he is innocent," da Corte declared drily, "and if he is guilty, I am certain you would wish to see justice done to this blackguard who harmed your friend."

Madonna Louise nodded again.

"So," barked da Corte as he returned to his own chair facing the girl. "Cardinal de Celano was Maria Chigi's confessor, as he was for you. And you say he administered 'unusual' penances? Could you, that is, can you bring yourself to be more explicit? I take it these penances were not the customary decades of the rosary or recitations of the litany of the saints?"

Madonna Louisa dabbed at her eyes with her lace handkerchief and nodded.

"Were they, ah, would you say they required, how shall I say this? Physical actions?"

Madonna Louisa wailed, but eventually she nodded.

"With His Eminence?"

She nodded again, and the wailing swelled.

"I understand," da Corte sighed. "But I must pursue the topic in more depth, Madonna, if you don't mind. Did these 'penances' require, ah, relationships with the cardinal? That is, were they, pardon my necessity for using the word, sexual?"

Madonna Louisa shrieked, nodding violently.

"Ah good! Good!" caroled the inquisitor. "Now, do you imagine that the cardinal made such demands of Madonna Maria Chigi as well? That is, do you believe that he required her to become, ah, a lover?"

Suddenly the sobbing stopped, and Madonna Louisa stared at her interrogator. "Of course!" she snapped. "What are you implying? That I was the only one who submitted to His Eminence? What do you take me for?"

"I . . ."

"I'll have you know I come from a long and distinguished line of Tuscan nobility, sir! My mother is a marquesa, and my father a count! I was only sent here to Duke Ludovico's court, because they wished me to acquire a more cosmopolitan polish than accessible in our city, a more thorough knowledge of the ways of the world, and to increase my poor abilities to cope with them!"

"I did not intend to imply . . ."

"If I say Cardinal de Celano took advantage of his position and his stature within the hierarchy of the church to prey upon young and inexperienced women of the court, such as I, then you may rely, sir, on the absolute truth of that statement! I am not some wanton who has a perverted hunger for men in ecclesiastical scarlet! I have been taught from childhood to respect and honor the clergy and certain nobility but to remain quite distant from them, and I . . ."

The young woman continued her harangue as a courtier entered, bent over da Corte and whispered something in his ear.

"My God!" da Corte suddenly cried, standing erect and frightening Madonna Louisa, effectively damming her torrent of words.

"Who now?"

Maestro Leonardo was mercifully spared having to examine the remains of Mino Spinolo, but, at the master's insistence, Niccolo and he began to spend more time in the spacious kitchens of the castle, supposedly to conduct sanitation checks for Il Moro, but actually to gather information that the Maestro quickly inscribed in a small red-backed book.

As the bakers kneaded their bread prior to making it into loaves, the Maestro peered into corners, rubbed a gloved hand across tabletops and demanded the flour be sifted twice in his presence.

"It is imperative that cleanliness be maintained at every stage of the food preparation," the Maestro lectured the cooks. "The late pastry cook was especially aware of this, and, I am told, prepared her delicacies in immaculate receptacles."

"To whom do you refer?"

"Signora Vanozza de Faenza, of course."

The baker laughed. "The woman had no talent for baking, and no more regard for cleanliness than a cesspit cleaner. When the duke annoyed her, she used to spit in his dumpling paste. She and Dino used to catch flies and throw them into the raisin puddings!"

The Maestro smiled at Niccolo. "You are enlightening, sir," he said. "Were she and this Dino accustomed to working together?"

"They did everything together," murmured the head baker,

and then, to Niccolo's shock and surprise, he winked and nudged the artist.

"I am shocked," declared the Maestro with no trace of surprise. "This Dino, isn't he one of the men who was recently murdered?"

"Yes."

"This late kitchen worker, Mino Spinolo, wasn't he a friend of this Dino?"

"Not at all!" cried the baker. "Who has been putting such ideas into your head, sir? There was bad blood between Mino and Dino since last Hallowmas! Mino was always sulking about and glaring at Dino when he wasn't sneaking off and playing at dice with one of the falconers."

"A falconer? Which falconer?"

"The one that used to be a favorite of the duke's mistress. Before his marriage, of course. Valla, I think."

Niccolo became bored with these shadowy interrogations and began to pick at turnovers fresh from the oven. He reveled in the smell of the new bread and the warmth of the large ovens. He entertained himself by watching the chefs and their assistants scurrying here and there carrying pots and jars and tureens.

Then he spotted her, halfway in the shadows of an archway that led down to the wine cellars.

Now in an apron bearing the crest of the Sforza, Ellie the carrier of rashes, was watching him.

He was at her side in minutes. She did not hide or try to run, but stood there as if she fully expected him to come to her. Before he could even express his anger and disappointment with her, the pretty kitchen wench said, "I have something for you."

"Really?" sid Niccolo, glaring at her. "And what are you dispensing today? The pox perhaps? The falling sickness?"

She withdrew the small jar from her apron pocket and

handed it to him. "It's for the ... Well, by now you know what's it for."

"Yes, I do," he snapped. "Fortunately someone else was inflicted with the same thing, quite possibly from contact with you, and he gave me some of this balm."

This time the girl returned his glare, and her voice took on an acid tone. "I don't care what you think, but I never knew I had it! Sweet mother of God, what kind of a person do you take me for? And you needn't be so damned arrogant! You knew I wasn't a virgin, didn't you? And the way you maneuvered me into the garden to pick berries by the dark of the moon certainly told me a lot about your character, my little lord!"

She softened a little then, and said quickly, "Not that I owe you any explanation, but I must have gotten it from Guiliano, the butcher's boy, while we were preparing for the festival. Like the others, I had been sampling the new wines my lord had ordered all through the afternoon, and I wasn't quite—well—I was not in my right senses. He cornered me in the potato bin and practically raped me!"

"He raped you?"

"Practically."

She began to cry, and Niccolo, unaccustomed to the devious ways of young women, placed an arm around her waist to comfort her. She buried her head on his shoulder, and the dwarf felt his previous passion for the wench slowly resurrected.

"He was my first," she said between sobs. "Well, the first with whom I did the—whole thing, you understand? And—and you were my second, only it was different with you. It was beautiful and gentle."

Niccolo slowly lowered the palm of his hand from the girl's waist to her buttocks.

"Not here," she whispered. "I am newly attached to the duke's staff, and everyone is watching me. After the festival, my lord, Galeazzo di Sanseverino, found that he did not need all the servants he had hired for the celebration, so he sent me and two others here. Come! Let's go into the wine cellar."

"No," Niccolo whispered. "I have a better idea."

And so another person learned of the secret passageways in the castle. Niccolo showed her how to enter from the kitchen and follow the upward path to the bedchamber of Madonna Valentina. He showed her how to look through the spy hole first to make certain there was no one in the Madonna's quarters, and then they stepped through the hidden doorway, crossed through the bedchamber to the dwarf's quarters, and prepared for the inevitable.

The girl was already unfastening the ties of her skirt when she paused and slipped something into Niccolo's hand.

When he opened it, the flickering light of the fireplace revealed the nature and purpose of her gift.

It was a section of sheep's intestines, washed, stretched and sealed at one end.

"What do you mean, he did not come?" the countess demanded.

"I mean, I put the letter where we agreed, where we have always placed the messages," said the courier, "but the next day I returned to see if there was a reply, and your letter was still there, hidden behind the stone in the wall."

"What did you do?"

"I left it there, thinking perhaps the falconer was busy or something and would pick it up later. I couldn't be seen standing around the wall without arousing suspicion and having to answer a lot of questions. But when I went back the next day, it was still there!"

The countess frowned and pressed her lip between her teeth.

"I couldn't ask too many questions," the courier went on, "but I understand that the falconer hasn't been seen for two or three days."

The countess wheeled and crossed to the window that looked down into the garden. "My God," she whispered. "Could he have been discovered? Could da Corte have him in the dungeons?"

The courier shrugged.

"If so, we are all in danger," she murmured. Suddenly she turned on the servant. "Have my coach ready immediately after dinner tonight," she commanded. "Tell no one, and try to be inconspicuous. If Valla has fallen into the hands of the duke's men, he will be able to tell them everything, and it will only be a matter of hours before Il Moro sends someone for me! I have to make certain the falconer is safe!"

Never before had Niccolo felt so safe, so confident, so wrapped in his own little cocoon of sheer masculinity. The boy was gone, and only the man remained. He reviewed his life since leaving the Certosa. In service to the duke of Milan, lord of Lombardy, the legendary Il Moro. In secret service to the beautiful Countess Bergamini. He was at this time a veritable treasury of information, a man of growing wealth from his spying activities, and a confidante to one of the most intelligent and gifted men in Italy.

Now, to complete the circle, he had a beautiful and young lover with worlds of experience, a conclusion he could no longer deny even to himself, who frequently slipped through the passages and into his bed in the early morning hours, always departing for her own small room off the kitchen just before dawn. He had discovered a secret known to males from the earliest days of mankind, that there is nothing like frequent pleasure with a beautiful woman to reassure a man that he has power and vitality, even at advanced ages, and that life, indeed, has purpose.

So now, as he awaited his "kitchen kitten," as he had taken to calling Ellie, he smiled and stoked the fire. Madonna Valentina was, he imagined, bedded somewhere with Rubini, and the duke was at Vigevano making certain that the defenses of his model city were prepared for the impending invasion. The dwarf had pleaded stomach distress so he could be left behind.

Now he heard the soft padding of feet in the next room, and he deliberately stretched the open collar of his blouse to reveal more of his chest. He turned slowly, not too quickly to expose his eagerness, and he smiled. The woman in the shadows made a small sound.

A gasp perhaps? At the sight of so much virility in one so small, Niccolo thought.

Then she stepped forward.

"Promising," said the countess, "but we really won't have the time tonight."

Quickly the countess explained that something had happened to Valla whom, she explained, was one of her principal agents in the Castello Sforzesco. She made clear to the dwarf that her ladies had heard nothing of the man, and he had now been gone for three days. She asked if Niccolo had heard anything about what might be occurring in the dungeons, but the dwarf could only say that the body of a kitchen helper had been discovered there, and that the four rooms had been cleaned and prepared for some future interrogation. It was whispered through the court, Niccolo told her, that da Corte was beginning a series of "questionings" at the prodding of the duke, who was growing visibly more nervous, but since both men were away inspecting the defenses, it was doubtful that anyone was being held in the torture chambers.

He told the countess he did not know why or which members of the court were to be put to the torture upon their return. He reassured her, however, that he had heard nothing of the falconer, but he would investigate the matter if the countess so desired.

"Thank you, my small friend," the beautiful lady smiled, and then she bent and kissed him lightly on the mouth. He sucked in the sweet aura of lilac.

"Well," came the icy voice of Ellie behind them, "has the bed schedule been changed?"

High in the madman's tower, even at this hour of the darkness before dawn, Maestro Leonardo dabbed at a page of the small book bound in red leather. He had sketched a bare tree with many branches and limbs jutting in all directions, and near each of these branches he had inscribed a name. The trunk was marked with a "G."

"Some trees and their branches," he wrote in his backward lettering, "proceed to grow in a perfectly natural way, but some are hindered by natural deficiencies, some break under the lash of lightning or by winds and storms, and some fall short of their natural size by being cut off by men.

"The branches will be most misshapen that grows furthest from the trunk."

The "gift" of a private balcony for Madonna Valentina had been delayed for more than four months due partly to the fact that most of the carpenters and masons had been involved in preparing the Palazzo Sanseverino, and partly due to the duke's annoyance that Madonna Valentina had left the festival with Rubini and then they stumbled over the body of the pastry cook. To Il Moro this constituted a double insult in that his acknowledged mistress did not wait patiently while he dallied with the female guest from Cremona and that, when she did choose to abandon him, she did not run off with another noble, but one of the members of the disreputable vulgarians of the *commedia* troupe.

Consequently the duke, in order to teach Madonna Valentina a lesson, had seen to it that the balcony construction, which had resulted very early in a massive hole being gouged through the outer wall of the lady's chamber, was delayed far beyond the normal time required. In between his efforts to mobilize his defenses against the French, placate the Geonese and deal with the fear and anxiety that gripped the residents of the castle, Il Moro had seen to it that a dispute concerning the funding for this new addition blossomed between his secretary, Bartolomeo Calco, and the Milanese minister of public works, Marchesino Stanga. Since the balcony was a part of the Castello Sforzesco, the funds should have come from the duke's own purse, but Ludovico cleverly dispatched a series of memoranda to Stanga suggesting that the funds come from the general treasury of the city, arguing that the castello was a part of Milan and therefore should be considered a "public building."

Already hard pressed to underwrite the numerous commissions for statuary, tombs, equestrian statues, as well as the maintenance of the city's water reserves, the connecting canals with the Ticino, and the rapidly decaying streets, originally laid by Roman legions, Stanga rebelled and accused Calco of trying to rob the people of Milan.

Calco, unaware of Il Moro's dispatches, ranted against the minister for "implying that the Sforza possessions were any less important to the Milanese than the stinking sewers you call canals."

It was well into summer before the duke decided that his mistress had been appropriately punished for her indiscretion, and agreed to yield to her constant requests to come to the women's quarters to inspect the construction.

Accompanied by Galeazzo, da Corte, Cossa and Cardinal d'Este who still insisted on serving as the duke's personal bodyguard on occasion, Il Moro swept into Madonna Valentina's bedchamber one late afternoon. Niccolo and the lady were waiting, since the time of the visit was common knowledge, and they bowed and curtsied abjectly to the lord of Milan. Niccolo kissed Il Moro's ring to the annoyance of the cardinal who felt such an act of homage was due only to ecclesiastical authorities.

"They'll be asking the duke for absolution next," grumbled the prelate.

"I am so grateful for your presence, Your Highness," the lady whined. "You have no idea how difficult it has been to try and rest comfortably in these quarters with that enormous chasm in my bedchamber wall. The canvas covering does not prevent much of the wind from entering, and the screens do little to disguise the ugliness left by the masons, the surveyors, the rude plasterers, and God only knows who else. I appeal to you, my lord, to at least alleviate some of the traffic connected with this enterprise. I hardly have a moment of privacy for spiritual contemplation when someone wanders through with an adze or a chisel and mallet or some terrifying axe."

Il Moro tried not to smile at the "spiritual contemplation" of the lady which, he knew, still referred to an occasional liason with Rubini. He had made it quite clear to the actor in a private conversation that he had no objection to the acrobat romancing the lady, but he had to insist on complete and thorough discretion, for the mingling of classes could only result in even more turmoil in the court. Furthermore the troupe's Scapino had to agree to stay away every other Monday which was to be the duke's turn with milady.

Da Corte and Cossa removed the screens, and Galeazzo ripped away the canvas. The room became filled with warmth and sunlight, and the duke had to observe that "the hole is an improvement, I think, Madonna."

"Only in the summer," glared the lady.

A small scaffolding of three or four planks had been erected on the level of the bedchamber floor and rested on two projecting poles set into holes in the stone wall. A web of heavy ropes and pulleys used to carry building materials and tools up to the construction site dangled on either side.

"When completed, the view should be magnificent," declared Galeazzo as he stood aside for the duke to step out and see for himself.

But it was Niccolo who brushed past the duke and stepped out on the scaffolding. "If it were extended on either side, my lord, by a handspan or two, it . . ."

He did not have time to finish the statement for there was an ominous sound of cracking wood, and the planks began to buckle under the dwarf's feet. Instantly, a moment before the entire flooring fell away beneath him, Niccolo reached out and seized one of the ropes.

The daily prayers of the Certosan monks for the young man's safety must have met with a divine response for the chosen rope was attached at the opposite end to a large basket filled with stone, and as the dwarf's weight was added to one end of the hawser, the basket slowly rose. Niccolo, terrified and clinging for dear life, was lowered gently to the earth. There two carpenters rushed forward as he arrived, seized the rope and slowly lowered the basket back to the base.

In her bedchamber, Madonna Valentina screamed and, in the best tradition of genteel womanhood, swooned. The cardinal rushed forward and pushed the captain-general aside in his attempt to place himself between the duke and the gaping hole. Cossa seized one of the duke's arms and da Corte the other to gently back their lord from the edge of the precipice, and Il Moro, ashen and shaking, stood murmuring, "My God! My God!"

Galeazzo was on his knees peering over the edge and announced, "The dwarf is fine. He seems to be resting on the ground, and there are two servants with him." He pulled himself up, slapped at the dust on his uniform, and turned back to face Il Moro. "But this is an abomination! An outrage! The carpenters and masons responsible for erecting such a flimsy and dangerous scaffolding should be put to the torture."

"Indeed," murmured Bernardino da Corte who had dropped to one knee and was inspecting the broken ends of the two hole posts. "Especially since these supporting posts have been sawed halfway through." He stood erect and turned to the duke. "We were fortunate the dwarf chose to go first. If a man of normal weight had gone out there, he would have dropped instantly, without any warning."

The duke took a tentative step forward and glanced at the two stubs projecting from the bottom of the hole. "Are you sure?"

"You can see for yourself," the security chief gestured. "The top half of each supporting post is smoothly cut, and the bottom half broken and ragged. Furthermore, the scaffolding boards should have been fastened to those posts, but apparently the nails have been removed, and the planks merely set upon them."

Il Moro wheeled, his fright now fury. "Get me the foreman!" he thundered. "And the scaffold builder! I want everyone connected with this project before me within the hour!"

He stepped over the body of Madonna Valentina and headed out the door, followed by everyone except the cardinal who felt it was only Christian charity to pay some attention to the fallen woman. D'Este raised the lady to a sitting position as the duke's voice echoed back from the corridor outside.

"See to Niccolo!"

And then, from a distance.

"And get me a brandy!"

The latest attempt on the duke's life, for it was determined that he was the intended victim, caused another ripple of activity to spread through the court. Guards blossomed like armored scarecrows at the sill of every door. Women went nowhere unescorted, and, if possible, tried to avoid being in attendance on Il Moro lest by happenstance they found themselves in the path of an errant arrow. Food tasters were conscripted from the kitchen help, and Niccolo was momentarily alarmed when Ellie was chosen to taste for Madonna Valentina. But then the young man reasoned that the least likely victim of assassination at court had to be Madonna Valentina whose protectors, he imagined, were legion.

The dwarf was honored for once again saving the life of the duke, who was slowly disintegrating with anxiety and fear, and, in gratitude, Il Moro presented him with a tailored suit of silver armor trimmed in gold.

"Considering the frequency of accidents here," sighed the duke when he gave the present to Niccolo, "and your tendency to be present to save me from them, this gift seems especially appropriate."

Niccolo was also released from his personal servitude to Madonna Valentina and placed in direct service to the duke himself. This merited private quarters for the young man in the Rochetta, the most heavily armed section of the castle, but when Niccolo discovered that these new quarters did not provide access to the secret passageway, he pleaded with the duke to let him retain his old room, and, considering the circumstances, Il Moro had to oblige the dwarf.

It was on the day of his reception of the silver armor that Niccolo raced to tell Maestro Leonardo of his turn of good fortune. As he dashed down the corridor to the tower he glanced to his left and stopped in his tracks.

Mother of God, he prayed, who is it now?

And the black banner rustled in the summer wind.

"He is Guarino Valla, the head falconer," the Maestro said as he lifted an edge of the sheet that covered the body. "They discovered him when the smell of the guano took on a different stench. They searched through the dung of the birds and found him at the bottom."

"How did he die?" asked Niccolo.

"Suffocation. Possibly he was held under the guano until he died. There are traces of bird dung in his nose and throat."

Niccolo tried to restrain himself from appearing too eager for the information as he asked, "Was he—was he tortured?"

The Maestro shook his head. "No," he said softly. "It appears to be a branch from another arm of the tree."

* * *

Niccolo did not understand the metaphor, but he was relieved that the countess was in no danger. He excused himself and descended the secret passageway to the kitchen. Here he stepped through the hidden door, beckoned to Ellie with whom he had been reconciled when the countess explained her presence in his bedchamber, and gave her a message.

Within the hour Ellie, mantled in a hooded cape and carrying a container of honey intended for the Countess Bergamini, departed the Castello Sforzesco and made her way to the Palazzo del Verme and to the woman who had become her new friend and her confidential employer.

Oddly enough, another murder did not disturb Niccolo, and he wondered whether it was the frequency of these deaths that dulled him or if, in the normal passage to manhood, he had just accepted a termination of life as a natural occurrence, no matter how bizarre an end. Despite the loss of so many servants and high churchmen, the dwarf rejoiced in his own continued existence, his passion for Ellie, his acquisition of armor and florins and friends, the memory of flight and the challenges put to him by Maestro Leonardo.

That evening Niccolo found his Epictetus open on his desk to a page chosen by the passing wind. He picked up the small book and smiled at what was written there.

"No evil can happen to me. For me, there are no robbers, no earthquakes. All things are filled with peace and tranquillity. This one supplies me with food, another with clothing, another has given me perceptions of sense and primary conceptions.

"So who is the rich man?

"He who is content."

Chapter 7
The Little Wars

"(To represent a battle)
show the victors running . . .
indicate the spot where the (fallen one)
has slithered in the dust
now turned into a bloodstained mire . . .
Show a horse dragging along its dead master,
leaving tracks where the corpse has been hauled
through the dust and mud . . ."

Leonardo da Vinci
"How to Represent a Battle"

Milan, in the approaching autumn of this year of Our Lord fourteen hundred and ninety-nine, went mad.

War, which the Maestro described to Niccolo as a "bestial madness," is always preceded by a kind of general insanity. The fear of death or injury lies just below the surface of the fiery oratory, the calls to nationalistic defense for the protection of one's home and family. There is a scent of forboding in the air that is as strong and persuasive as any perfume. Banners blossom like ornate flowers from windowsills. Summoning trumpets echo through the streets. The tattoo of drums mimic the racing pulse. Horses are groomed and shod anew. Leather harness and saddles are stroked with a softening oil. Bridles and bits are polished. Ropes are woven and stretched. Bayonets, daggers, and swords are sharpened until their edges are razor thin. Men, who in their normal daily apparel would attract no attention, are suddenly transformed into demigods by elegant uniforms with brass buttons and colorful sashes, and the quiet apathy that surrounds their daily lives is magically replaced with symbolic courage and defiant resolution. Women who would stoically defend even the most tarnished honor against further assault, now open themselves to tearful farewells and the desperation of the seized moment.

In Milan bronze cannon rattled and clanged on their horse-drawn carriages as they raced through the piazzas and the narrow streets. Old men who had fought their wars now resurrected their ancient animosities and cried once again for the blood of the invaders. The graphic verbal reports of the atrocities and the humiliations of the preceding French invasion, only five years earlier, were stoked and blown into glow once more until imaginations flamed and wills were hammered into resolve.

In the Castello Sforzesco, the "long guns" with thick barrel walls and straight bores were wheeled into the bastions and towers where their fire could break up siege batteries. Gunners inspected and, when necessary, repaired their iron-shod traversing spikes, their sponges, their quadrants and "dolphin" elevators, rammers and powder ladles. Breech-loading mortars on fixed carriages were wheeled into position to fire over the high parapets or the lower walls.

The earlier invasion of Italy by Charles VIII had changed the face of war. The mobility and destructive efficiency of their cannon and mortars permitted the French siege train to keep pace with their armies and leveled the enemy. Duke Ludovico the Moor, lord of Milan, studied reports from Francesco Guicciardini, diplomat and papal governor of Parma, who stated flatly that "before the French invasion, wars were protracted, battles bloodless and the besieging of towns slow and uncertain. Artillery was managed with such lack of skill that it caused little hurt. But the French with their use of brass cannon charged with heavy iron balls and mounted on carriages harnessed to horses, not oxen, can plant their weapons against the walls of a city with such speed and fire so rapidly, that surrender comes in hours, not days or weeks."

Il Moro reviewed the inventory of his own weapons which included only three or four "full cannon" known as culverin, but several half and quarter cannon which were shorter and had thinner barrels. This did not alarm the duke for his officers reported that the heavy artillery was cumbersome and expensive. On the other hand, they were less prone to blow up under a heavy charge and kill their own gunners.

The more traditional methods were not ignored. Hoardings were installed around the tops of all the walls and towers. Food and grain poured into the storage rooms. Arrows were made, and boulders collected for dropping from the walls. Vertical stone spikes called finials were mounted on every battlement. Mercenaries prepared crossbows, maces, and battle-axes. Armor was polished and oiled.

The harried duke issued commands to his troops, who obediently marched to the perimeters, and to his mercenaries, who refused to move until they were paid. He sent his captain-general, Galeazzo di Sanseverino, to the bordering towns to examine and strengthen these perimeters. He dispatched emissaries to his relative, the Hapsburg emperor; to potential allies to the south and east; to the enemy courts of France and Venice for explanations and conditions; and especially to the bankers of Genoa and Florence—for war is an expensive hobby and requires vast amounts of money.

Il Moro pleaded with his mercenaries to be patient, but their wages were now three months overdue, and the soldiers knew their cannon and lances were all that secured the safety and preservation of Milan, so their individual requests became, under the banners of war, a single, thundering command.

"Pay or perish!"

"I have succeeded," the venerable diplomat advised the duke. "Genoa has agreed to return a delegation to Milan to hear our side of the story and to decide whether to advance us the necessary funds to defend the city. I argued that the Borgias have hidden motives for spreading the rumor that the seduction of Madonna Maria Chigi was due to a slackening of morals in our court, and I deflected their suspicions to Cesare

Borgia, saying that we have reason to believe he deliberately sent an agent to Milan to do just what he did, seduce the girl so that the Bank of St. George would sever our traditional friendly relations and withhold our credits."

"Incredible," marveled Il Moro. "I never cease to be astounded by the turns of your mind, my friend. The lie about Cesare is masterful!"

Da Tuttavilla stood erect. "I never lie, Your Highness," he lied. "I practice a form of diplomacy called broad mental reservation, and I merely say what I believe. Fortunately, I am gullible."

The duke rose from behind his desk and stepped around to embrace the diplomat. "However you do it, my dear Girolamo, please continue to do it." He slowly escorted da Tuttavilla toward the door. "My responsibility now is to produce the seducer, preferably with a signed confession."

"Preferably a cardinal, so we can link Cesare Borgia as the instigator of the seduction," added da Tuttavilla.

"Of course," the duke agreed. "My agents tell me they now believe Cardinal de Celano is the seducer. Cesare Borgia was himself a cardinal at the time, and since he is the son of the pope, who holds absolute authority over the cardinals, that connection will be emphasized."

Da Tuttavilla bowed smartly from the waist, and the duke closed the door behind him and leaned wearily against it.

"Now! How does one prepare the fatted calf for the sacrifice?" he pondered.

In the Palazzo del Verme, the countess Bergamini pondered her own mystery. She sat before the great floor-to-ceiling window that looked down on her gardens and reread the latest report from Niccolo that announced the death by suffocation of her agent, Guarino Valla. She read again the statement that there were no signs that the man had been tortured.

Who killed him then? she wondered. If it was the duke of

his men, because they suspected his part in the murder of Captain Francesco, why wasn't the agent tortured to find out who employed him? And if the falconer had fallen into the hands of Galeazzo, who may have suspected that he was the intended victim, again, why was there no torture? Was her connection with Valla already common knowledge? Were they playing some sort of cruel game with her?

And if so, would they soon come for her?

She rose and crossed to her desk where she let the parchment slip from her fingers.

The French are coming, and the perimeters will not hold, her husband had told her. We should consider leaving as soon as possible and take refuge with my relatives in Bologna.

Not yet, the countess said to herself. I have not yet learned all I must. Until I do, the lessons must continue.

Niccolo and the Maestro were able to ignore the war gathering beyond Milan by drifting into a perfect educational process, partly because da Vinci sensed the keen intellect and curiosity of the dwarf and, as is often the case with dedicated teachers, he imagined these qualities might be the wellspring for creativity.

But he also devoted more time to instructing the dwarf, because of a growing frustration with his assistant, Salai, whom he called "a thief, a braggart, an obstinate liar, and a glutton."

Niccolo was present that morning when the Maestro caught Salai in yet another theft of his materials. The artist had seized the blond young man by the back of his neck with one hand and brought him to his knees screaming in pain. Then he had dragged Salai to the doorway of the studio and hurled him through it, banishing him for yet another week from the workshop.

So da Vinci shifted even more of his attentions to Niccolo and the Maestro's other young assistant, Giovanni Francesco Melzi, a handsome and cultured youth who was as opposite from Salai as one could get. Melzi was well-born, obedient, trustworthy, generous, and soft-spoken.

Consequently Niccolo found him boring, and he rejoiced when the youth was constantly being called home to assist his nobleman father and thus was absent from the workshop.

The dwarf began translating the artist's written commentaries into Latin and showed the Maestro how to develop phrases and construct sentences in the proper tense and mode. He instructed the artist by working with him on the translation of *Perspectiva Communis*, a text by John Pecham on optics, and Pliny's *Historia Naturalis*, a treatise on the depicting of animals and birds in nature.

Da Vinci, in turn, grasped the young man's right hand in his own left and traced the fluid motion needed for broad strokes. He examined and evaluated the dwarf's sketches and demonstrated the different strengths and weaknesses of varied media. With charcoal and chalk he showed the dwarf the principles of highlighting and shadowing to create the depth and dimension that Niccolo had seen that first day in the Maestro's sketch of the Virgin and St. Anne.

"Small children," the Maestro told him as they reviewed the sketch together, "should be depicted as lively, wriggling creatures when they are seated, and timid and fearful when erect. Women should be depicted with modest actions, their legs and arms together, their heads bowed and inclined to one side."

He gave the dwarf the assignment to sketch some grotesque, mythological creatures. "If you wish to make an imaginary animal seem natural," he lectured the young man, "use natural components; for example, a serpent with the head of a hound, but the eyes of a cat and the neck of a turtle."

Niccolo took his sketch board and the parchment to the top gallery that ran the entire length of the castle wall where he could utilize the northern light, as the Maestro suggested, and where he would not be in the way of the soldiers preparing the defenses. He was seated on a bench there, sketching, when Salvatore Cossa suddenly materialized at his elbow. Niccolo was aware of the man's presence before he spoke since the Whisperer was addicted to heavy perfumes.

"He uses it to disguise the stench of pain and death from his work," the Maestro had maintained. "Blood, urine, and decay."

"That is a bizarre lion," Cossa murmured without interest.

"It is not a lion," Niccolo responded. "It is a griffin."

He sensed the sudden shift in intensity and concentration in the torturer. "A griffin?" Cossa repeated.

"A lion with the head and wings of an eagle," Niccolo said arrogantly, wanting to demonstrate to the Whisperer that his intelligence was superior to Cossa's, despite his smaller stature. "Although it is sometimes depicted with the body and head of a lion with the wings and claws of the eagle. As in the coat of arms of Cardinal Castagno."

He had no sooner heard himself make the statement then he wished he could withdraw it.

God's blood, he thought, why can't I remember the advice of Epictetus?

Cossa stood erect with that sly smile he displayed when he had caught someone in a lie or extracted valuable information. "Cardinal Castagno has a griffin in his coat of arms?"

Niccolo instantly regretted having made the observation and tried to modify it. "There are many with a griffin in their arms," he said quickly. "It is not as common as the lion or the unicorn, but I remember reading a book in the Certosa that listed a menagerie on family crests including goats, boars, leopards, horses, even a rhinocerus. There are dogs depicted in the crests of both Francesco Sforza and the late Cardinal Albizzi. It only means that the bearer is considered to have some of the qualities of the animal depicted on his arms."

"Really?" smiled Cossa. "And what are the serpent qualities in our lord, Duke Ludovico, would you say?"

Niccolo flushed. "Serpents have an undeserved reputation,

because of the biblical narrative. I assure you that they have many good qualities. They rid domiciles of rats for one."

So be warned, he added silently.

Cossa grinned, enjoying the boy's discomfort. "Of course," he hissed. "Now tell me, who else in the court has a griffin in his crest?"

Niccolo knew he had talked himself into a corner. "Well," he murmured, "no one else that I know of. But that doesn't mean that someone else's arms don't carry the image. I'm— just not aware of them."

Cossa smiled again, which Niccolo did not find reassuring, and then he deliberately tousled the black curls of the dwarf as one would with a small child, a gesture which he may have considered friendly or paternal but which Niccolo found patronizing and insulting. He wanted to lash out at the Whisperer, but Cossa quickly strode down the gallery and was soon out of sight.

Hell fire! Niccolo cursed himself. Why can't I learn to keep my mouth closed and my eyes open?

He hurried to the Maestro's workshop to report his error, but the large room was empty. Niccolo noticed that the dust cover was raised on a painting the Maestro had been daubing at earlier in the day. He went to check that the pigment was dry and to lower the cover when he stopped in amazement.

The painting, which he had never seen before, depicted an angel announcing to the Virgin that she would soon be the mother of Christ. It was a variation on an earlier painting on which the artist had collaborated when he attended the school of Verrocchio. The Virgin was caught at a loom, weaving, when the visitor arrived, but her face wore an expression of total peace and contentment, an absolute surrender to the will of God.

But it was the angel that startled Niccolo.

He was shown genuflecting before the lady, his great white

wings stretched and glowing in the light of the sun. One hand was upraised as if in salutation.

But the face!

The face of the angel was beautiful beyond description, pure and guileless, youthful and innocent, a vision of comfort and quiet joy. The hair was brown and hung below the shoulders, but Niccolo instantly recognized that it should be golden.

For this was, unmistakably, the face of Salai.

My God, the boy whispered to himself, would that I were so loved!

"Are you certain?" snapped da Corte to the chief of the Whisperers who leaned across the table to him. "I have no great love for Cardinal Castagno, but he is widely respected."

"The dwarf told me," Cossa replied. "He recognized the animal in the Cardinal's coat of arms as a griffin. What would be more natural than a man choosing a code name from his own arms?"

"And what could be more obvious?" da Corte responded.

"It wasn't obvious to me," Salvatore snapped. "Or you apparently! Or anyone else at court!"

Da Corte leaned back in his chair in the antechamber and stared at the fire. "How often have I seen the coat of arms of the cardinal? He is not like Albizzi who had his arms embroidered on his cardinal's robes. Still," he pondered, "if I remember correctly, Cardinal Castagno's mother was French, and he has a brother who lives in Venice."

"I don't care if his mother was Hungarian and his whole family lives in China," Cossa growled. "What choice have we? We have now settled on Cardinal de Celano as the seducer of Madonna Maria during one of his perverted penances, and the only missing element is the identity of the Griffin. Il Moro is getting impatient. He wants someone, preferably someone who could be aligned with Cesare Borgia, to present to the Genoese as the despoiler, and he wants this Griffin out of his hair. What harm would it do if we present both prelates as our choices?" There was a slight pause before the Whisperer added, "Especially if they are dead and cannot refute our claims eh?"

Bernardino stroked his beard in contemplation. "All right," he said finally. "I will inform the duke that we are now convinced that Cardinal de Celano is the seducer and Cardinal Castagno is the Griffin. You are right. God knows we have to present him with someone quickly, or we will be the ones screaming our lives away in the dungeons."

The security chief rose and went out the door behind him, and Cossa rose and crossed to the opposite door. The Whisperer opened it and signaled to a large man with a bushy black beard waiting there.

"Perelli, is it?"

The sullen man nodded.

"Perelli, I have an assignment for you," Cossa whispered. "And here is the symbol of my trust in you to perform it well."

He handed the dark man a small leather purse that jingled in the assassin's hand.

In the corridor on the opposite side of the small antechamber, da Corte was passing a similar purse to another, younger, man, a thin wraith with eyes like slits cut into his skull. "Remember, Napoli," he warned, "make it seem an accident."

The thin man suddenly genuflected and kissed the hand of the chief of security.

"Yes, yes," Bernardino murmured, quickly drawing the hand back and wiping it against his hose. "Move! And report to me when it is done!"

It was the following morning before Niccolo could report his slip of the tongue to the Maestro who sat writing with intense concentration in the small red book. "I'm sure that

Cossa now thinks that Cardinal Castagno is the Griffin," the boy wailed. "And it is all my fault!"

"Perhaps not," the Maestro murmured. "Or perhaps it's true that the cardinal is the Griffin."

"He's not!" the young man almost shrieked, and then realizing that he was losing control, he softened his tone. "Well, I don't think so. Do you know what I think? Do you know whom I think the Griffin might be?"

"I promise not to take another breath until you tell me," the Maestro said drily, continuing his frantic writing.

"The countess Bergamini," said Niccolo. "She has a network of spies already working within the castle, including me, and I saw that scrap of paper da Corte has. It has the sketch of a griffin on the bottom."

"And why would the countess want Il Moro dead?" the artist asked. "She told you herself that as long as the duke lives, he will continue to support their son, Cesare. She lives for that boy. What would she gain by the assassination of the duke?"

"Perhaps she didn't order the assassination of the duke," the boy offered. "Perhaps Galeazzo is right when he suspects that the Griffin is really trying to kill him."

Da Vinci turned from his writing to focus on the boy. "You accuse me of making simple things complicated," he said. "Will you listen to yourself?" He put the pen down. "Why would the countess want Sanseverino murdered?"

Niccolo frowned. "I don't know," he mumbled. Then, inspired, he announced: "Unrequited love!"

The Maestro stared at the youth for fully a minute before a small smile creased his face. Then he did something that neither Niccolo nor anyone at court had ever heard the Maestro do.

He chuckled.

After an eternity of deep, throaty guffaws, the artist wiped his eyes with his right hand, and said softly, "How romantic! You really must spend less time with those theater people.

What an imagination! If you could channel that wild brain of yours into some sort of creative activity, my young friend, you could startle the world." He stood then, towering over the dwarf who sat perched on the stool especially constructed for him. "As a matter of truth, the countess did order the murder of Galeazzo. That is irrefutable. If I expressed it in the form of an equation, it could be proven mathematically. Not because she is the Griffin, mind, but because she apparently thought Galeazzo was. She came to that conclusion, I would say, because you passed on the information that the assassin was killed by a small metal object inserted in his skull so he could not reveal any damaging information. Galeazzo had assumed command of that interrogation, remember? He was the one with the time and the knowledge and the authority to murder the assassin before da Corte took control of the process. The countess, believing Galeazzo was the Griffin and therefore a threat to the duke, set her agents here in the castello to murder our captain-general."

Niccolo sat stunned at the clarity of it. "But—but what of the sketches of a griffin at the bottom of her orders?"

"A tribute to the lady's intelligence," the Maestro replied. "If any of the letters were discovered, they would be attributed to the man they are already seeking. The Griffin. Not the countess. She merely took advantage of the presence of a mysterious, unknown assassin in the castle to protect her own identity."

Niccolo gave a deep sigh. "Then—who *is* the Griffin?" he asked. "Do you know?"

The Maestro sighed. "Wrong question. Most fallacies arise not from ignorance, Niccolo, but by asking the wrong questions." He crossed to one of the windows and pointed out. "Suppose, for example, I needed to know the height of that tall poplar tree. How would I pose the problem?"

The dwarf, annoyed at the reprimand and frustrated at the apparent change in topic, stepped down from his high stool and followed the artist to the window.

"What is the height of the tree?" he declared.

"No!" growled the master. "How! How! How do I determine the height of the tree? The process! That's the primary question, and the answer will provide me with a formula I can use in the future to determine the height of anything." He placed a hand around the dwarf's shoulders. "Now, Niccolo, how can I determine the height of the tree?"

The dwarf reflected for a moment, and then, still annoyed, he quickly volunteered, "Tie a small rock on the end of a ball of cord. Climb the tree. Drop the weighted end, and where it hits the ground, mark that spot on the cord. Then come down and measure the cord."

The bearded artist shook his head. "Possible, but time consuming. Not to mention dangerous and stupid." He crossed to a table and began to make marks on a parchment. "Establish a ratio."

"What?" asked Niccolo as he followed the master.

"Measure the tree's shadow," Leonardo explained as he sketched a tall tree on the parchment.

"What does that tell me?"

"Nothing yet. But then measure your own shadow at the same time."

"So?"

"Establish a ratio!" the master repeated. He sketched a figure of a man and two shadows stretching from the tree and the stick figure. "You know three of the variables. The tree's shadow, your shadow . . ."

"And my own height!"

Maestro Leondaro clapped a hand on the dwarf's shoulder. "Ah!" he exclaimed. "There is some hope for you!" He returned to the sketch and imposed two triangles over the figures. "Yes! Your shadow is to your height as the tree's shadow is to it's height. See how simple it is?"

Niccolo studied the sketch. "But inaccurate," he said softly.

The artist stiffened. "What?"

"I'm standing erect," the dwarf explained. "Suppose the tree leans in the direction of the shadow?"

Da Vinci gave another deep sigh and sat down. "You're incorrigible," he said. "But intelligent. My point is that you asked the wrong question. The question is not 'Who is the Griffin?' the primary question should be: 'What is a griffin?' "

"We know that," the dwarf replied impatiently. "It is a lion with an eagle's head and wings."

"You see!" crowed the artist. "What did I tell you? There is always another possibility!" The dwarf climbed back onto his high stool, angered and frustrated. "You are supposed to have a remarkable memory! Do you remember that the assassin is supposed to have said that someone whispered his instructions to him? Commands were always verbal. It wasn't until the countess began to sketch your lion-eagle, that the word was interpreted that way. But there is another word. Another 'griffin,' only it is spelled with an 'o' and not an 'i.' A griffon!"

Niccolo was confused and surprised. "What is a griffon?"

Da Vinci smiled again. "Ah! The primary question at last! A griffon, my young friend, is a buff-colored dog, and it so happens that I have seen such an emblem on two sets of arms recently. The first is on a small shield mounted on the perch of the parrot belonging to Cardinal Ascanio Sforza, and it is a derivation of the arms of his father, Francesco Sforza, a dog tethered to a tree. The second I saw two weeks ago, on the coffin of the late Cardinal Albizzi. A dog with a coronet for a collar. A buff-colored dog. In short, a griffon."

"Are you suggesting that Cardinal Sforza or Cardinal Albizzi is, or was, the Griffon?"

"You suggested the link between the coat of arms and the title! I simply say there is another possibility. There is another interpretation of the pronounced word, griffon."

"But surely Cardinal Ascanio wouldn't order the assassination of his own brother?"

"Why not? The cardinal owes his health and power to

Rome and the Vatican, and the pope might have more influence on the man than his brother, the duke."

"Unlikely."

"You love that word, don't you?" the artist moaned. "All right. Let us assume that the dead Cardinal Albizzi was the Griffon. Since the late prelate was poisoned, it suggests that either his identity was known to the duke who ordered him killed, or that he was murdered by one of his own agents who believed the Griffon had turned on him. Using the information we have at hand, we know that Galeazzo's intercepted letter points to that possibility and to Galeazzo as the Griffon's agent in the court. We know from that letter that Galeazzo was unnerved by the bungled attempt on his life that ended in the death of Francesco. Believing that the murder of Francesco was meant for him, Galeazzo wrongly deduced that it was Cardinal Albizzi, the Griffon—with an 'o'—who was trying to eliminate him for reasons of his own, perhaps the bungled attempt on the duke's life at the Certosa. Subsequently the captain-general decided to act first and arranged for Albizzi's death by aphrodisiac. We can also assume that whoever is above the Griffon, the real commander of the assassins, would be distressed at the death of his agent, hence Galeazzo's apology to that mysterious gentleman. Then the general, to reassure this unknown commander that he was still loyal, arranged for the 'accident' at the Madonna's balcony which was intended for the duke, but almost cost you your life."

The artist frowned and arose. "In a sense, the poor duke has brought all this upon himself. Or, at least, he is reaping what his father sowed. For thousands of years, the kings and dukes and emperors of Italy, with the backing of the Roman Catholic church, of course, worked very hard to convince the people that they ruled by the grace and power of God. But along came Francesco Sforza, the duke's father, who took Milan by force of arms and held it against the traditional rulers, the Visconti, who were supposedly God's chosen. You see, you dare not kill a king whom God protects, because the wrath of heaven will strike you down like a hawk falls on its prey. But if it is only a matter of a man with the bigger gun, then I can get a still bigger gun and make myself a king, and God, if there is a God, will only watch. The people quickly grasped and understood that message: it is guns, not divinities, that make kings. So, the Sforzas removed their own best protection: the belief that emperors ruled by divine sanction. Now Duke Ludovico must suffer the consequences."

Niccolo sat silently for a moment, and then he murmured softly, "Then all these murders—all this violence—was ordered either by Cardinal Albizzi or Galeazzo di Sanseverino?"

"No," the artist responded. "That is not the case at all. He rose, crossed to the table and picked up the red book. He opened it to a page and brought it to show to Niccolo. It was a sketch of a tree. There was a large "G" marked on the trunk in it, but on the branches of the tree were the names of the murdered: Luigi, Anna, Dino, Mino, Vanozza, Chigi, Martino, Albizzi, and Valla.

"The branches farthest from the trunk could not possibly be nurtured by it," the artist explained. "The trunk of the tree represents the Griffon, and the victims killed by his command, either by Galeazzo or at Galeazzo's order. They begin with Luigi, the Certosa assassin who survived and who was murdered before he could volunteer damaging information. It is understandable that the Griffon would want him silenced, and it was Galeazzo himself who killed him.

"But the next victim was Anna Spinolo, a house servant. Why was she murdered? How was she murdered? She drank some wine that was poisoned. Who poisoned it? The man who had access to the wine cellars. Dino. But why would Dino want Anna killed? The probable answer: he didn't. He intended the poison for the duke, but here is where the branch separates from the trees. It was not by command of the Griffon. Dino didn't know the Griffon. His position in the kitchens did not reach to the rooms of the cardinals. No.

A COMEDY OF MURDERS 247

He wanted to kill the duke for his own reasons. Why? Because, as we learned from the kitchen help, he was a kinsman to the dead assassin, Alfredo. His motive was the oldest and the strongest in man's history. It is biblical: an eye for an eye, and a tooth for a tooth. It is the summation of Italian history. World history. Vendetta. Revenge. You kill one of mine. I kill one of yours. Dino poisoned the wine to revenge his kinsman, and Anna became the first victim by accident."

He pointed to a large branch that spread to the left of the trunk in his sketch.

"From this branch sprang several other murders. Mino Spinolo wanted revenge for the death of his kinswoman, Anna, and he decided that the guilty one was Dino. Besides, according to the bakers, he hated the gaunt man anyway. So Mino and a friend clubbed Dino and threw him into the cesspit."

The artist pointed to another branch. "But here we have another complication," he explained, "because his friend happened to be the falconer, Guarino Valla, who was also an agent of the countess. Valla and Mino killed Dino, but Vanozza, a proud virago, a woman only Italy could produce, decided to take vengeance for the murder of her lover, Dino, and she left Mino helpless, to die in the dungeons.

"But Guarino, the falconer, was no fool. He knew when Mino 'disappeared' that it had the mark of a vendetta, and he would be next, because he helped murder Dino. He also reasoned that the vengeance would spring from Dino's lover, Vanozza. So he struck first. He stole Vanozza's shawl. He trained his Russian-bred falcons to kill whoever was wearing it, and then he quietly returned it to her room, and when she wore it, the falcons tore her to pieces. This, of course, set in motion an entirely new vendetta, and I assume that one or more of the de Faenza family were responsible for suffocating Valla in the guano stalls."

Niccolo watched as Da Vinci went back to the branch marked "Valla".

"Now the countess had sent word to Valla that Galeazzo should be killed before the general killed the duke whom she was protecting from the first. The falconer and another friend decided to murder the captain-general while he was sleeping with Madonna Valentina, but, as we know, they killed the wrong lover. This, however, led to Galeazzo's obsession with the idea that the Griffon had ordered the general's death, and, like Valla, he decided to strike first. Remember when I told you no one expects a vulnerable man to attack? Galeazzo decided to kill the man whom he knew as the Griffon—with an 'o'—before the Griffon killed him. So he murdered Cardinal Albizzi by pouring cantharidine powder in the wine that he sent to the cardinal's chamber, knowing Albizzi had already dosed himself with the aphrodisiac earlier in the evening. He knew that if the powder he gave the cardinal was really cantharidine, the lady would also die of an overdose from it, and that would clearly mark it as murder. So the powder he gave the cardinal was harmless, probably sugar which would dissolve and only sweeten the taste of the wine. Then, of course, he had to apologize to the still-unknown leader for murdering the Griffon.

"But violence breeds violence, especially in those who see revenge as a noble or even sanctified motive for killing a brother. The murder-by-mistake of Captain Francesco, therefore, necessitated the revenge murder of Martino."

"Who is Martino?"

"The stableman who assisted Valla in the attempt. Bernardino and Salvatore had identified him as one of the two men who had killed Captain Francesco, and they were about to put him to the torture when the countess ordered Valla to kill him and make it appear accidental. The result was the 'stomping' to death of the stableman by Neptune, the duke's stallion, although it was well known that the stallion was timid and skittish. I remember how he responded to the boar's attack in Pavia. The horse would never stomp anyone unless he was goaded to it."

Niccolo studied the sketch. "Then that leaves only one murder unexplained," he observed. "This small branch here. Maria Chigi."

"Unfortunate," the Maestro said softly. "Completely political. Despite the duke's orders that the lady be questioned gently, da Corte subjected her to the torture of being beaten on the soles of her feet in order to elicit the name of the man who seduced her. Either she was obstinate under the torture, which I personally doubt, or she did not really know the name of her seducer, because she continually replied, 'The old man.' I suspect the outcry of 'father' was only the appeal of a child for her principal protector and had nothing to do with the identity of the seducer.

"In any case," the Maestro continued, "when the truth came out, and the Genoese delegation was on its way to Milan, the duke could not take the chance that the girl would report the torture to her father, the banker of the House of St. George. So Il Moro ordered her killed. The method was drowning, to make it appear that she had tumbled from the gallery walk at the top of the castle and drowned in the moat. A fainting spell is the sign of a delicate and genteel woman and would somewhat soothe the father's response to his daughter's death."

"Such a tragedy!" the dwarf murmured.

"Why do you say that?" The Maestro frowned at him.

"For one so young to die."

"You value youth above life? Or social status? Is it less a tragedy when an old man is murdered? Should we be less concerned at the murder of the stableman than at the killing of a cardinal?"

Niccolo was embarrassed. "I meant . . ."

"The fact, my young friend, is that murder is never a tragedy. Nothing is ever resolved by murder. All the motives—a consolidation of power, an acquisition of wealth or property, the avenging of another murder—none of these have any permanent effect. Power shifts. Wealth buys nothing of lasting value. The vendettas here in the castle should teach you that one murder does not wipe away another but multiplies it!"

The Maestro sighed and put down the quill. "No. No. A murderer is a fool, and the proper place for a fool is not in a tragedy, but in a comedy."

"But killers should be exposed and brought to justice," Niccolo persisted. "They should be made to pay for their crime. Isn't that what we are doing?"

The Maestro frowned at him. "Is that what you imagine we are doing? If so, you are naive. The monks of the Certosa have deceived you with their lectures on morality. The goal of the man who solves a crime is the same as that of an artist or a scientist: to reveal the truth. The value of the work we do in solving a murder is in the process not in the conclusion."

"But then the killer is free to kill again."

"Yes. You solve nothing by killing the killer—except to bring yourself down to his level. Taking a life is murder, and you do not convince the killer—or other killers—to abandon killing by killing. The way to change the murderer is to uncover the truth. If the killer is revealed to be a fool—as I pointed out he is—and not someone worthy of our admiration, he can change. That is the best we can hope for, and, I might add, it is an act of true morality. It is doing God's work."

The dwarf was adamant. "But—justice . . . !"

"Justice is a divine quality. You will seldom find it in this world. Leave it to heaven and do what I keep urging you to do. Untangle the cords. Illuminate the shadows. Expose the lie. Truth! Truth is everything!

"The tree branches," the Maestro continued, "leave only two more questions to be answered: who was the seducer? And, most important, who is the power above the dead Griffon who set these murderers about their grisly business?"

Niccolo decided to abandon the debate which he did not

fully understand, and he turned to study the sketch. "There are a great many more branches, Maestro," he said, "with no names on them."

"They are the dead-to-come," the master said softly as he took the book from him. "Vendettas are wars in miniature. Little wars. Whenever a killer tells his victim, 'You die, because you killed my kinsman,' it is the pronouncement of doom for the murderer and the victim. There will be others who will die. Those branches, believe me, will soon have names."

As if to verify the Maestro's statement, at that precise moment Giovanni Francesco Melzi burst into the room, breathless and ruffled. Niccolo silently rejoiced to see the usually meticulous young man in disarray.

"They sent me to prepare you, Maestro!" he cried. "They are bringing in another dead man. They found him in the pigsty with his throat cut. They say he is Guiseppe de Faenza!"

The artist-engineer glanced at the dwarf.

"You see?" he said.

Perelli had planned it carefully. The huge crucifix was made of iron and brass. It was suspended between two chains that reached to the chapel ceiling and hung directly over the place where the celebrant of the Mass would bend over the altar table for the consecration. He had been very careful to saw through the links of both chains so that the huge cross was now held in place by a single hawser. One slash from his sharp knife, and the crucifix would come hurtling down and crush Cardinal Castagno—the man suspected of being the Griffin—at his daily mass.

Now, the assassin thought as he hid himself in the cupola, I have only to wait.

I Comici Buffoni were bored and requested permission of the duke to perform once again in the streets, from their wagon stage, for the general population.

"It will ease some of the anxiety," Piero argued, "and perhaps take their minds off the approaching invaders for an hour or so."

"I'm not certain I want their minds diverted from the invasion," the duke responded. He leaned across the huge map spread out upon his desk and measured a distance with a pair of calipers. "I want them straining at the leash like starving dogs so they'll fall upon the French and devour them."

"But no one can be certain when the attacks will begin," the leader argued, "and if we can keep their morale uplifted, they will be in a better mood to defend the city."

Anxious to return to his own preparations for the defense of the city, Il Moro waved an impatient hand at the actor.

"Fine! Fine!" he barked. "Just don't put me in your little entertainment. I have enough trouble as it is."

It had taken Napoli a day to find the apothecary who had the poison he needed, a clear and colorless liquid that smelled lightly of almonds. The man with the narrow eyes was assured that, if administered in the proper dosage, the powder would induce an almost instant paralysis and a quick death that would appear to be a natural result of a weakened heart.

The problem now was how to administer it to Cardinal Castagno without the prelate suspecting anything. Unlike the other cardinals in temporary residence at the castello, Castagno imbibed alcoholic beverages only in moderation, if at all. If the poison were to be planted in his cup at a dinner, he might or might not drink from it, and time was pressing.

Napoli prayed to the god of assassins for enlightenment, and it came to him at the morning Mass.

He would put the poison in the altar wine, and when the cardinal sipped from the chalice at the consecration, he would die at the base of the great iron crucifix.

Napoli replaced the wine cruet with the poisoned one just prior to the Mass the next morning and stood peering from behind the tapestry in the sacristy, the small room just off the chapel altar.

Now, he reassured himself, I have only to wait.

Duke Ludovico seldom came to da Vinci's workshop unless invited, but the press of war demanded that the master's genius be applied to those creations he listed in his letter of commission to Il Moro. Now, more than ever, the duke had need of "portable bridges," "mantlets and scaling ladders," "cannon capable of firing small stones like a hailstorm," and "impenetrable covered vehicles behind which an infantry will be able to follow, uninjured and unimpeded."

The duke reviewed the sketches and designs of the war machines, the chariots with sharp blades fastened to the hubs of the wheels to cut down advancing infantry, the smoke containers that could hide a defensive position but only if the wind was blowing from the right direction, a device to be harnessed before a horse and rider that had four curved scythes mounted on a windlass to revolve as the horse advanced and which, da Vinci assured him, "would cut down the enemy like wheat."

There were covered vehicles run by cranks turned by the occupants who would also fire breech-loading cannon that projected from the conical roof, missiles with directional fins, guns with multiple barrels and small containers of powder-and-turpentine that could be hurled at the enemy and would set them afire.

All of these, of course, would require construction and testing time, and there was none, so the artist smiled when Il Moro commended the mind behind them but rejected the instruments themselves.

"I regret I cannot be of greater service, Your Highness," the Maestro apologized as he studied the appearance of Il Moro.

The duke was visibly coming apart. His usual dedication to

his wardrobe and his appearance had deteriorated in small ways: a button undone, a stain on the sleeve.

"I—ah—I appreciate your dedication, Maestro Leonardo," the duke responded, "but I believe our present defenses will prove sufficient, provided I can raise enough money to give the mercenaries their back pay. Fortunately we have uncovered the seducer of our dear Madonna Maria, and we have reason to believe that the banks of Genoa will once again provide us with the funds necessary to defend our city and our people."

"I am pleased to hear it," the artist said, "and may I ask who the wicked gentleman is?"

"Well, it will be common knowledge soon, because I have already ordered his arrest and interrogation," Il Moro said quietly. "It is Cardinal de Celano. It appears the man imposed unorthodox and scandalous penances upon his female penitents, and poor Madonna Maria was one of his victims."

"I'm amazed," said the Maestro.

"Yes," the duke sighed, "I am afraid we inhabit a wicked and irresponsible world, Maestro. The idea of a member of the hierarchy of the church using his power to . . ."

"No, no," the Maestro interrupted him. "I am not amazed that there is corruption within the church. I would be amazed if there were not, because it is an institution of power and wealth, and those are corrupting."

The duke stared at the bearded artist and shook his head. "You share an animosity toward such institutions with the leader of the *commedia* troupe, Maestro. I received one sermon on this subject and that is sufficient to last me until the next feast of the Nativity."

Da Vinci lowered his head. "I am sorry, my lord," he murmured. "I was just amazed that Cardinal de Celano could impregnate Madonna Maria over a distance of three hundred kilometers. You must admit that that is an exceptional achievement, even for the most ardent and talented lover."

Il Moro's face paled, and Niccolo, watching from his tall

seat beside the study desk, saw him stagger a little as if someone had clubbed him. "What?" he whispered. "What do you mean?"

"The cardinal was not in the court when Madonna Maria was impregnated, Your Highness," the Maestro informed him. The artist turned to Niccolo. "That is what I meant by counting backward." He turned again to face the duke who had collapsed into one of the chairs. "Madonna Maria Chigi obviously was rendered pregnant nine months earlier than her delivery date at the convent. The child was not premature but full term, so, unless the lady had mastered a new gestation technique never before known to man, it would place the conception date during the first appearance of the acting troupe."

He crossed to the duke with a carafe of wine and a goblet. "But you may remember that the cardinal had heard stories of the company's anticlericalism, and he feared repercussions from Rome if he were reported to be in the audience. So he requested permission to go on pilgrimage to his old diocese to avoid being at court when the players arrived. Therefore he was not in the court when the girl was impregnated."

"My God," mumbled the duke as he poured some wine into the cup, his hand shaking. "My God."

"I apologize if I have unsettled things, Your Highness," the Maestro continued.

"No! No!" the duke exploded as he quickly downed the wine and rose rapidly from the chair. "But I have to prevent . . . ! That is da Corte may already have . . . !" He strode toward the door. "I must go!" he shouted.

Niccolo watched with a subdued amusement as his lord swept from the room. The door no sooner closed when the Maestro shrugged and turned to the dwarf.

"I thought he knew," the bearded man commented. "When I learned that the troupe had been invited back to the castle, I assumed that someone had counted back nine months from

Madonna Maria's delivery date and realized that the seducer might very well be someone among the performers."

Niccolo was astounded in turn at this revelation, and his brow wrinkled with thought as he attempted to place this new information into the background of the seduction.

"Which one of the actors?" he asked.

"Not the primary question," da Vinci grumbled, his own brow wrinkling in thought. "If the duke did not send for the company, because he realized that the seducer was an actor, then who sent for them? I wondered why, if the duke suspected them, he hadn't subjected the actors to his torturers. If da Corte or Cossa had arranged for their return, why hadn't they taken steps instead of looking for some cleric as the seducer? No," he reflected, "someone else wanted the troupe returned to Milan, and the duke merely agreed to invite them. The requester, therefore, has to be someone in a high position at the court, someone whom the duke would respect and whose request he would honor. But whom? That is the primary question! And why? Then, finally, we might look at the question of the identity of the seducer."

"Could it be the duke's brother, Cardinal Ascanio?" Niccolo asked.

"Why would that prelate want the *commedia* troupe returned to Milan?" da Vinci countered.

Niccolo shrugged. "Could it have been the Griffon, Cardinal Albizzi? Could he have asked for the troupe to return?"

"Why?"

"He was planning to assassinate the duke, so perhaps he thought he could place the blame on someone in the company."

"Unlikely," replied the Maestro, and Niccolo smiled.

"Then Galeazzo!" cried the dwarf. "Being the agent chosen by the Griffon to assassinate the prince, he may have decided someone in the troupe would be a good scapegoat."

"Possibly," de Vinci acknowledged. "We'll have the answer

when we know who was above the Griffon. Who was the power that placed the cardinal here in the castle and made Galeazzo his lieutenant?"

He crossed to the young man and leaned across the table to him. "The primary question there is: to whom did Galeazzo apologize for killing the cardinal?"

"Cesare Borgia," da Corte announced to the duke. "That is the man to whom the letter was addressed. My agents followed the couriers. The Borgian prince, who is now the Duke of Valentinois and loyal to the French, obviously put the Griffin into this court to have the duke assassinated, and that would be the signal for the invasion of the French. Presumably Louis of France would promptly reward Cesare with the Romagna."

Il Moro sprawled in his velvet chair, one hand shielding his eyes from the light. "My God," he murmured again. "The link with the Borgias that da Tuttavilla conceived has a basis in fact! Well, we can use that information now to explain the seduction of Madonna Maria when her father's delegation arrives. But now the question is: if Cardinal de Celano is eliminated, because he was not in the court at that time, who is left to suspect?"

The security man shrugged. "Perhaps we can tie the seduction to the Griffin. Perhaps we can place the responsibility at the door of Cardinal Castagno."

The duke removed his hand and peered across it at da Corte. "I forgot about him! Where are we on that matter?"

Da Corte smiled. "He is a dead man, sire."

Vittorio Napoli's slit eyes watched intently as the cardinal celebrated the mass. From where he stood, just behind the archway that led to the sacristy that served as a dressing room for the altar boys, he could see everything, and the scent of the incense and the soft flickering of the candles and the chanting of the choir resurrected memories in him that he had thought long deadened. Through the smoke of the incense he could see himself as an altar boy in immaculate cassock and surplice years and years before. His tongue again reveled in the sweet flavor of the Latin responses, and his memory translated them once more.

"I shall go unto the altar of God . . ."

"To God who gives joy to my youth . . ."

My youth, he thought, happy days in the Lombardy countryside. Running barefoot through wide fields under the deep blue sky. Whipping away the rough, homespun peasant blouse to feel again the kiss of the sun upon the young skin.

Then other memories flooded into his vision, less happy memories. A mother lost to the fever that had killed his father years earlier. A strong, young boy on the road to Milan, alone and without funds or hope. The arrogance of the young toughs before the shops of the goldsmiths that he took as an insult to the beautiful young woman. The flashing blade that bit into his left shoulder and resulted in the ragged scar that still smarted from time to time.

Then he remembered the better days. His early years of service to Gian Galeazzo Sforza, duke of Milan and husband to Isabella of Aragon, whom he had defended against the thugs who mistook the lady for a whore, because she had indulged her whim to walk the streets unescorted and clad in less than an opulent cloak. The brief but magnificent moment when he hurled himself into the path of the assassin's knife, saving the life of his patron, but resulting in the ragged scar on his right shoulder which also smarted from time to time.

Then there were the medals, the gold florins, the promotions. Vittorio Napoli was once a genuine hero!

Yes, he was!

I was!

The seasoned veteran was lost in this reverie when something instinctive, something inborn and nourished through experience, alerted him. Almost as if the world had slowed, he saw things happening by flashes of lightning. The heavy iron crucifix trembled, inched slowly forward and down. The cardinal was bent over the chalice below it.

And suddenly ancient trumpets blared in the ears of the once-heroic Vittorio Napoli. Half-forgotten drums rolled, and his blood began to heat again. Within fractions of a second, without another thought to his own safety, the man with the slit eyes raced forward, arms stretched out before him, and propelled the cardinal from harm's way.

Then there was only the brief, crushing pain and the darkness.

Giorgio Perelli, from his hiding place behind the opposite archway, watched in dismay and horror as his intended victim tumbled down the altar steps, and the iron cross crushed the life from the mercenary who saved him. Thunderstruck, he sheathed the dagger he had used to cut the supporting hawser and raced to the fallen cardinal. He helped the shaken prelate to his feet, pretending concern and horror at the accident. Then he turned to look at the broken and bleeding body of Vittorio Napoli.

Sweet Jesus, what a mess, he thought to himself.

His right hand touched the table of the altar, and his fingers found their way around the handle of the gold-and-silver chalice. He was suddenly aware of the dryness in his throat, the trembling of his hand, and, in simple reflex and thirst, he lifted the chalice to his lips and emptied the contents.

He licked his lips which were soon flecked with a white foam.

Then the chapel revolved. Sounds died, and he, too, drifted into the darkness that had already embraced his brother conspirator.

Cardinal Castagno could never be considered a master wit or a clever man. Dedicated, yes, and occasionally even devout, but not exceptionally brilliant.

But on this single occasion, learning that the links in the crucifix had been sawed through and that the alter wine had been poisoned, Cardinal Castagno revealed an intelligence beyond anyone's experience. Within an hour he was embedded between protecting pillows in his private coach, the heavy damask curtains drawn, as it dashed under the portcullis of the castle, out through the square, and away from Milan.

Niccolo and Ellie had developed a taste for making love in the curtained carriage of Duke Ludovico which was housed in the stable area and almost never disturbed unless Il Moro sent word to prepare the vehicle for a ride in the country. Ellie expressed a fondness for the soft red velvet upholstery, and Niccolo realized he had better traction for someone his size if he stood on the carriage floor with Ellie seated.

On the day following the rapid exodus of Cardinal Castagno, the young couple had performed to each other's satisfaction and now reclined in each other's arms, warm and secure and at peace with the world.

Unhappily, the world itself was not at peace, and Niccolo and Ellie could hear the rapid footsteps of the soldiers running back and forth outside the carriage house, preparing their weapons and dragging out the heavy war machines stored in the large empty rooms around the stables.

"What will happen to us if the French come?" Ellie voiced what was on both their minds.

"Nothing," Niccolo lied. "Why should the French be concerned with us? I'm too small to be conscripted and too intelligent to waste as a target for the archers. You're an experienced kitchen worker, and, although you are lovely and desirable, if you smear potash on your face and maybe a little shit on your apron, you'll be so repulsive that even the most lustful Gascon will leave you alone."

"But you're not worried about the war?"

"No."

She sat up and looked down at him. "Then what are you concerned about? You're so distant."

He reached out and brushed the nipple of her left breast. "Well, I can't be too distant. I felt that."

She smiled at him. "I did too, but don't try to change the subject. Something is on your mind."

He took a moment before he sat up beside her.

"I believe someone in the acting troupe was responsible for getting Madonna Maria with child," he whispered.

Her eyes widened. "You do? Who? Why?"

"Well," the young man explained, "if one counts back nine months from the delivery date of Maria's illegitimate child, it coincides with the time when I Comici Buffoni was at court the first time. It was a time of celebration, you see, which is why the troupe was at court in the first place. Il Moro's wife, Beatrice, had requested a festival to lighten her mood in these heavy hours, because she was herself pregnant and about to deliver, and perhaps that is why she had compassion for Madonna Maria when the younger woman announced that she was with child as a result of a brief encounter with some man following the banquet and performance. Unhappily, the duchess and her child both died in the birthing process, and Il Moro had gone into mourning until the following January. The duke still had two sons, but he seemed incapable of consoling them in his time of grief, and he assigned them to the care of the governess. When war threatened, he sent the children to the safety of his Hapsburg in-laws."

"Amazing," Ellie glowed. "You are so bright, you are blinding!" Then she frowned as Niccolo glowed. "But the fact that the actors were here when Madonna Maria conceived, doesn't mean that one of the performers was the father of her child."

"The fact that Madonna Maria didn't seem to know the man's name would indicate it was a newcomer to the court," Niccolo explained. "She certainly would know the names of the courtiers and the cardinals, and the torture to which she was subjected would most certainly have elicited the name if she knew it."

"She didn't name the man?"

"She said only that he was 'an old man,' and that could apply to a number of people."

"Who is the oldest member of the troupe?" asked Ellie.

Niccolo reviewed the names and faces of the company members. Finally he whispered, "Piero Tebaldeo." Suddenly a thought flashed across his mind, and he murmured, "And that is significant."

"Why?"

"Because Piero Tebaldeo, the man who plays the Captain, hates the nobility," the dwarf said in hushed tones.

Could this coupling be an act of violence? he wondered. Was an act of love employed as an instrument of revenge?

Was this, too, another battle in the little wars of little men?

Chapter 8
A Medley of Murders

"If the poet says
I will describe hell or . . . terrors,
the painter will surpass you,
because he will place things before you
which will silently . . . terrify you
or turn your mind to flight."

Leonardo da Vinci
"General Principles"
Codex Urbinas

The dwarf and the kitchen wench elbowed their way through the small but excited crowd of Milanese townspeople gathered around the wagon stage in the center of the Piazza Castello. Niccolo noted that the audience was composed mostly of women and old men with a few small children tugging at skirts or standing hand in hand with their bowed grandfathers.

"I'm glad the troupe isn't depending on what they earn from this crowd," the dwarf whispered to Ellie.

"When you know the earth is going to collapse under your feet, would you go dancing?" asked the kitchen wench.

Niccolo understood his paramour. Behind and around them, columns of carriage-mounted cannon were being hastily wheeled through the streets. The foundaries on the Via degli Armorai belched smoke and anvil noise, and from every livery along the boulevards rose the neighing and whinnying of the war-horses being prepared for combat.

It was, in short, a comedy being performed in an asylum.

Niccolo himself would have preferred to remain in the workshop of the Maestro where he felt most comfortable and safe, but the duke had the artist-engineer working day and night on a mortar with multiple barrels which Il Moro felt could be produced quickly and put into service, so the young man had convinced Ellie to accompany him outside the castle walls to watch the performance which had finally been approved by the harassed duke.

This brief period away from the castle permitted Niccolo some respite, for with the rising number of murder victims and the pressing demands on the duke to prepare his defenses, to locate and punish the seducer of Maria Chigi, and to identify the elusive Griffin, Il Moro's iron hand had come down hard. The freedom of the estate that he had enjoyed at the beginning of his service nearly a year earlier was now a controlled and hostile environment. Spies were everywhere. No one trusted anyone else. Food tasters were now employed by everyone from the lowest courtier to the duke himself. A chance comment or an indiscreet observation on anything could bring rapid repercussions or torture or even death.

More and more Niccolo began to believe he had sold himself into a gentle slavery where he was constantly subject to the whims and desires of a tyrant slowly going mad and who, in turn, provided him with fine clothes and rich foods, rare wines, comfortable quarters, and a swelling purse of gold florins as a compensation.

"Many have settled comfortably into such a slavery for far less," the Maestro had commented when Niccolo revealed his discomfort.

Niccolo had decided to attend the afternoon performance hoping to gather more information on why and by whom the troupe had been invited back to Milan, and, if possible, to warn the actors that whoever requested their return to the court might believe that Madonna Maria's seducer was one of them.

His thought was shattered by a single, loud boom of a bass drum which caused some of the more nervous townspeople to wheel around frantically looking for possible cannon. Immediately following the explosive drum, however, the attention of the audience was again drawn to the stage by the surprising and skillful entrance of Simone Corio as Arlecchino.

The thin man in the patchwork of colorful rags literally leaped through the curtains, did a double cartwheel and ended perched on the lip of the stage, his long skinny legs dangling over the edge. For a long time he looked over the audience, then slowly his face began to twitch and contort and, finally, the ragged man broke into tears, and the crowd chuckled.

"Oh, miserable me," wailed the Arlecchino. "Pantalone is going to marry his beautiful daughter, Isabella, to the Doctor in return for free advice, potent aphrodisiacs, and sweet milk enemas. I have nothing comparable to offer, although I suppose I could administer an enema with the best of them. But, oh! How can I survive without that immaculate vision of loveliness, my beloved Isabella, before me?"

He stood erect and addressed the heavens. "I would rather die!"

A wide grin slowly appeared beneath his black half-mask. "That's it!" he crowed. "I'll die! I'll kill myself!"

He once again seated himself on the edge of the stage, crossed his legs, rested his chin on his hand in a pose of thinking.

"Ah," he murmured, "but how shall I kill myself? It should be something—romantic. Something legendary. Something impressive. Something inexpensive and with a short duration of pain. Suicide makes a statement, but mutilation is an exaggeration." He scratched his head without removing his wide-brimmed cap. "Let me see," he reflected. "There's hanging. That's simple enough, isn't it? I mean, a rope, a rafter, and my neck. Death can't come any less expensive than that, can it?"

He leaped to his feet in a single, apparently effortless motion, and mimed the imaginary death. "I will go to my room, tie the rope to the rafter, kick away the chair, place the rope around my neck . . ."

He stopped then and looked directly at the audience which elicited a nervous laugh. "No," he declared. "That's not right! First I must put the rope around my neck, and then I kick away the rafter." He once again sat on the edge of the stage and scratched his head. "Kick away the rafter? How the devil do I do that?" He shrugged. "No, that's far too difficult to organize, and planning is not my strong point. I must try for something else."

Suddenly he was once again on his feet, his knife drawn from its sheath. "I have it! I will cut my throat!" He then moved quickly to his right and turned as if he were addressing himself. "No, you won't!" He quickly shifted to his left as if taking an opposing stance. "Yes, I will!" Again to his right. "No, you won't!" To his left again. "Why not?" To the right. "It will make you look ugly, all that blood dripping onto your shirt and staining your doublet." Once more he shifted his stance to the left. "You're right! And since I intend to always remain handsome, even in the embrace of death, throat-cutting will not do!"

He replaced the knife in its sheath and began to pace the entire length of the stage, his hands cupped behind his back. Finally he stopped, center, and exclaimed, "Poison! That will do it! A quick sip of lye and . . . aaaaagh!" He made a hideous face as if tasting the poison. "No! Wait! I have a very sensitive palate. I even stuff my pepperoni into oranges to lessen the fire on my tongue!" He began to pace again, and again he stopped center stage. "But wait! Why not something more tasty? Something even pleasant! Yes! Who says death has to be an annoyance?" From somewhere within the folds of his multicolored cloak of rags, Arlecchino produced a bottle. "Three bottles of French wine. That should kill anyone."

The audience laughed nervously at this attack on the invading armies, but Simone pulled the cork from the bottle with his teeth and spit it into the pit where three small children fought to recover it. "Why, then I'll be happy and smiling as I step off the roof of the cathedral to my death! Yes! That's the thing!"

He sat on the lip once more and began to drink from the bottle with loud slurping sounds. He apparently did not see Anna Ponti as Lesbino, the servant girl, who entered behind him and stood watching him for a while.

"What are you doing, Arlecchino?" she finally asked.

Arlecchino put the bottle aside. "Committing suicide."

Lesbino sat beside him on the edge of the stage. "Really?" she said. "What's in the bottle?"

"French wine."

"You're going to kill yourself with French wine?"

"I intend to drink until I am happy and giddy, and then I'll step off the roof of the cathedral and fall merrily to my death."

Anna made a circling gesture to the side of her head to the delight of the audience. Then she turned to the ragged man again. "If you get so drunk, how will you manage to climb the two thousand steps to the roof of the cathedral?"

"I hadn't thought of that."

"And suppose you don't get happy? Suppose you get terribly sick? French wines can do that."

"Oh, I wouldn't want that."

Lesbino took the bottle and almost emptied it in long swallows before Arlecchino snatched it back from her.

Anna wiped her mouth with the hem of her skirt and asked, "So tell me. Why do you want to kill yourself, Arlecchino?"

The man's mouth turned down mournfully under the black half-mask. "Because Pantalone is preparing to depart with my dearest of anchovies, my sweetest of olives, my tastiest of pomegrantes, my . . ."

"Pantalone is giving away a salad?"

"No!" the ragged man snapped. "I refer to my love, my

passion, my angel, Isabella the Fair, Isabella the Beautiful. Isabella the . . ."

"Generous," added Lesbino. "Yes, everyone knows Isabella."

"What?"

"We know of Isabella," Lesbino quickly declared. "So, as I understand it, Pantalone is going to marry off his daughter, Isabella . . ."

". . . the Fair. The Beautiful. The . . ."

"Ever-ready, yes. Well, before he has the wedding performed, why don't you abduct the girl and run off with her?"

"I would if I could get into his house," the Arlecchino wailed. "He keeps his daughter under lock and key, and Pantalone has given his servants instructions to keep me out."

"Then go in disguise," Lesbino whispered. "Pantalone considers himself to be a very moral man. He is superstitious. Pretend that you are a prophet, and that God has sent you to foretell his future. He could never resist that. And once you are inside, grab the girl and run."

"A prophet?"

"Yes," the servant girl exclaimed. "It's simple. All you need is a beard. All prophets had beards." She poked a hand into her apron pocket and brought out a strand of long black hair. She spit on the end and slapped it hard against Arlecchino's bare chin. "There!"

Arlecchino fingered the hair. "This is a wonderful beard," he smiled. "Where did you get it?"

"You'll know when you see your horse's behind."

The audience was laughing quite openly now, temporarily forgetting their worries and the war, and Ellie seized Niccolo's arm and whispered, "Now Pantalone will enter. Isn't Turio amazing? Imagine the youngest member of the company playing that old man!"

Sudden clarity came with the word. Niccolo ran through the statements as though they were factors in an equation.

Turio of Verona, the young man, the youngest member of the troupe. The curly-haired young man equals Pantalone.
Pantalone.
The old man.
The father.

"Don't you see?" Niccolo railed at the artist, hoping for the bearded man's admiration. "Madonna Maria did identify her seducer. She said it was 'the old man,' 'the father.' And Turio of Verona plays that role, the role of the old father. Madonna Maria only knew him by his role!"

"It is a possibility," the Maestro agreed, "but I still believe the girl was calling to her familial protector when she muttered, 'Father.' Still, I suspect that you are right about one thing. I suspect that Madonna Maria's seducer was an actor. But you must view the entire matter from Madonna Maria's eyes. If you were a young and impressionable young woman, perhaps a little disoriented from the wine and the excitement of the festival, which of the players would attract you? And remember, there is an aura to everyone on the stage. That is what makes theater a potent weapon, and . . ."

He stopped then and mumbled, "Weapon."

The Maestro wheeled, grabbed an armful of designs, and started for the door. "I was supposed to explain the workings of the new weapon to the duke," he announced. "Wait here if you wish!"

He disappeared through the door, and the guards stationed just outside closed it.

Niccolo had been so anxious to announce his analytical conclusion to the Maestro, he did not note the eye pressed against the spy hole in the hidden passageway.

But Bernardino da Corte, who had taken to roaming the secret corridors more frequently in his attempt to gather information concerning the Griffin and the seducer of Maria Chigi, heard everything. He turned in the narrow confines of the passage and quickly worked his way down to the chamber of Salvatore Cossa.

Niccolo wandered around the workshop for a few minutes, examining the new, quick sketches for future paintings and the latest inscriptions in the big leather-bound books where the Maestro recorded his observations and conclusions.

The latest was dated that morning, and Niccolo read, "The deluge. Darkness. Wind. Tempest. Rain. Bolts from heaven. Earthquakes. Mountains collapse. Cities are razed. People huddled together on trees which cannot bear their weight. Men, women and children are openly weeping and wailing, terror-stricken by the fury of the winds and the churning waters. Oh, what fearful noises! Many covering their ears with their hands, others covering their eyes in order to not witness the pitiless slaughter of the human race by the wrath of God! They hurl themselves from the rocks, taking their own lives in despair. Others strangling themselves or their children. Some wounding themselves with weapons. And above these accursed horrors, dark clouds are ripped apart by the jagged course of raging bolts!"

Niccolo closed the book and shuddered.

This is not the deluge he is describing, he thought.

This is war.

Later, in his own chamber, the dwarf remembered that his daily dosage of Epictetus had been neglected when Ellie, the pretty servant girl, entered his life, and he realized another truth about the world.

Women can teach you more than philosphy.

Nevertheless, in homage to his long-ago companions at the Certosa, he opened the small book again and read, "Even as bad actors cannot sing alone, but only in chorus; so some men cannot walk alone. In a republic comprised of wise men, there will be nothing to hinder you from marrying and rearing offspring. For the wife will be another self and so, too, will the children be."

Niccolo smiled at the observation and read on.

"But in the world's present condition, which resembles an army in battle array, one ought to be freed from all distraction and given wholly to the service of God. The question at stake is no common one. It is: are we in our senses, or are we not?"

Niccolo closed the book and answered.

We definitely are not.

"Are you mad?" Cossa screamed at the dark-eyed man who stood before him in the Whisperer's small antechamber. "He's dead? What do you mean, he's dead?"

The dark man in the heavy hooded cloak fingered the dagger at his waist. "Cardinal de Celano's dead. Hung. Looks just like suicide. That's what you told me to do, didn't you? You said 'Don't let it look like a murder!' That's what you said. So Timodeo and I, we smothered him a little. Just a little, you see, so he wouldn't struggle and make it harder for us. Then we tied the rope to the rafter, put it around his throat and placed a chair, upside down, under his feet."

The leader of the Whisperers ran a nervous hand across his sweaty brow. "My God!" he lamented. "You idiot! I rescinded that order yesterday! Where were you? We didn't want Cardinal de Celano dead, because the duke discovered he wasn't in the court when Madonna Maria was . . . well, he wasn't at court at that time! And then, to make it worse, you made it look like suicide!"

The dark man scratched his beard. "I thought you'd like that touch," he growled. "I said to myself, I said, 'Franco, if you make it look like suicide, then the duke can say that His Eminence was the seducer, realized the truth was coming out, and killed himself!' That's what I said."

Cossa emitted a deep sigh and groaned. "And did you remember to tell yourself that suicide, in the eyes of the church, is considered the unforgiveable sin? Did you say to yourself,

'You know, Franco, you bubble-headed ass, if it looks as though the cardinal killed himself, the church says he cannot be buried in sanctified ground? Not until a full investigation is made and a decision reached by an ecclestiastical court!'? Did you say to yourself, 'Franco, you moronic spawn of a jackass, the pope himself will send investigators to determine if the cardinal did, in fact, die in despair and was therefore damned'? Did you say that, Franco, you great pile of shit? Did you?"

The assassin frowned and shook his head.

"No, of course, you didn't," Salvatore Cossa howled. "Such a conversation would indicate an intelligence beyond your capabilities! Get out! Get out, you broken prick, and stay away from this castle until I sort this thing out."

The dark assassin quickly genuflected and reached for Cossa's hand to kiss, but the Whisperer quickly placed it behind his back.

"No, you don't," snapped Salvatore. "You'd probably bite it off and swear I preferred it that way! Get the hell out of here!"

Franco rose, pouted, frowned, seemed about to say something, but wisely kept his silence and awkwardly backed from the room.

"My God," Cossa murmured to the figure seated in the shadows. "There is only one way out of this. Franco will have to die, and then we can produce a forged confession that he killed the cardinal and made it look like a suicide. That way, at least, the cardinal can receive the last rites and be buried with full ceremonial ritual."

Bernardino da Corte rose from his chair in the corner. "And the Borgian pope won't have to conduct an investigation," he added. "But Il Moro may still demand our balls for this. Especially after that incredible mess in the chapel where two assassins killed each other and not the cardinal! And, as I just told you, I now believe that Maria Chigi did reveal the identity of her lover under torture. It was an actor, the one who plays the old man."

"An actor?"

"Yes."

"What abominable taste!" Salvatore crossed to the table and poured himself a goblet of the pale red wine. "Well, I hope you're right."

"The delegation from Genoa arrives tomorrow."

Following the initial warning of Epictetus, Niccolo decided not to mention to the duke or the countess his observations and conclusions about the possible seducer of Madonna Maria. He still pondered the question as to which member of the court requested the return of the acting company and why the duke honored it.

The following morning, in the Salla della Palla as the troupe did the physical exercises that preceded their rehearsals, the dwarf mentioned to his friend, Rubini, the Scapino of the troupe, that improvisation seemed to be a difficult way of performing.

"All acting is the same." The stocky acrobat dismissed the dwarf's comment. "You say something to me or do something, and I react. You react to what I do or say, and so on. In scripted plays, the words are the author's, so he is, in a very real sense, talking to himself. But in *commedia dell'arte*, each actor's response is his or her own and is dictated by the nature of the character. By that I mean, Pantalone the Venetian, must always say and do things that show him to be a greedy, narrow-minded, lecherous old man. The Doctor must always respond as a self-glorifying, arrogant, overly educated pretender, a product of the universities at Padua and Bologna. Arlecchino is always the clever servant, sometimes a mooning lover. I, Scapino, am an acrobat and the man off whom the others bounce their witticisms. I am the perpetual adolescent. I think I can do anything and accomplish nothing. I remain an uneducated buffoon from Bergamo, the same birthplace as Arlecchino."

"I still think it requires a rare talent," Niccolo said.

"Well, what do you intend to do with the rhinoceros?" Rubini suddenly asked.

"What?" asked Niccolo, confused.

"The rhinoceros," Rubini repeated. "What do you intend to do with it?" He paused and leaned toward the dwarf. "And how did it get in your bed? And how did you ever teach it to play the lute?"

Niccolo frowned, but he slowly smiled and said cautiously, "I—ah—I mistook it for—my wife."

"I can see how the horny skin confused you," Rubini nodded, seating himself beside the young man. "But surely you won't keep him as pet? I mean, your savage ape will be jealous."

Niccolo laughed but staggered on. "I—have no ape," he said.

"No?" cried the Scapino. "But those heavy brows, the stupid expression, the broad shoulders and the little brain! I thought..."

"Please, signore!" Niccolo trumpeted in mock anger. "My child may not be beautiful, but with a little snip of hair here, some straightening of the teeth and clipping of the nails..."

Niccolo suddenly swung his gloves across the actor's face. "You lie, signore!" he roared. "It is my daughter who looks like an ape. My son looks like a rabid wolf." He struggled to stifle his laugh. "In heat."

"My apologies," Rubini bowed, "Signor...?"

"Panqualirobododo," Niccolo announced.

"Not of the Asti Panqualirobododo?" the acrobat recoiled. "Not of the famed family who produced four popes, six cardinals, three robins, and a bluejay?"

"The very one," smiled Niccolo. "Throughout Italy all the people cry, 'The Panqualirobododo are for the birds!' "

"Not all, signore," Rubini corrected him. "The Borgias say you Panqualirobododo are dirty dogs."

"So that's why Cesare has been sniffing around my daughter!"

But the effort was too difficult, and the pace accelerating, so Niccolo raised both hands in surrender. "All right," he heralded. "Enough. I understand the nature and the difficulty of improvisation."

Rubini smiled and stood erect.

"Fine," he smiled. He leaned closer to the young man and whispered, "But how did you ever teach your camel to bleat the Angelus?"

The six feeders of the animals in the duke's private zoo lugged their baskets of grain and fruit between the cages, and the short, one-eyed supervisor, Antonelli Souza, made a mental note that the python would require a pig within a day or two. He watched as one of his assistants hurled several chunks of raw meat into the leopard's cage and was rewarded with a grateful roar as the large cat ambled over to the meal, reclined, and began to gnaw and tear at his dinner.

Antonelli turned away and glanced at the python's large enclosure, but the huge snake was stretched against the warm stone floor and was not moving. The supervisor moved closer and squinted with his one good eye to bring the serpent into as sharp a focus as he could manage. The large bulge in the great snake indicated that he had already been fed, and Antonelli scratched his scraggly beard and tried to identify which of his assistants might have taken the assignment on himself. With the castle preparing for siege, the food supplies had been checked and rechecked daily to make certain the animals would not starve, and only the one-eyed supervisor had the authority to ration the feedings.

"Well, if bad times do come, sweetheart," the zoo keeper cooed to the huge snake, "you might just keep us from starving."

He chuckled at his little joke, pondering how one would prepare a python for eating.

He turned away from his meditation when one corner of his good eye caught a glimpse of something gleaming in the sunlight at the edge of the serpent's enclosure. He struggled to focus on it again, and he took the handler's pole, slipped it between the narrow openings in the wire and dragged the item to where he could reach and recover it. He replaced the pole against the stone wall and raised the long leather strap to his eye to better examine it.

It was a man's belt, and there was something burned into it. A name.

"Giorgio Adamo," he read.

The zoo keeper thought for a moment, and suddenly the name registered in his memory, and he trembled and grew pale. He quickly moved around the edge of the snake house and saw the small pile of clothing gathered there, and he silently shrieked as he realized what the python was slowly digesting.

Little Giorgio Adamo, the carriage maker's apprentice.

A second cousin to Guarino Valla.

"What about the seducer?" Il Moro asked, his hand trembling even as he lifted the wine glass to his lips.

Da Corte smiled and responded, "I believe he is a member of the acting troupe, the boy who plays the role of the old man, the father. Pantalone."

The duke's eyes became thin slits, and his smile dissolved. "No!" he grumbled. "No. That won't do!"

Da Corte was stunned. "But those were the terms the girl used when questioned about the identity of her lover. 'The old man' and 'the father.' And the players were in the court at the time she conceived. There was a festival, you may remember . . ."

"I don't care if the man himself confesses!" the duke muttered. "I thought we agreed to place the responsibility on Cesare Borgia! I thought you understood that we needed a scapegoat who was in the hierarchy of the church! I am less concerned as to the true identity of the seducer than I am in a scapegoat who will turn the accusations of the Genoese bankers from me to the Borgias!"

They were interrupted by the arrival of Maestro Ambrogio, who came into the room waving a rolled parchment. "Your Highness," he declared, "I have finished casting your horoscope! Your natal sun is being squared and Saturn is in opposition to your natal Neptune! This means that . . ."

The duke waved a hand to stem the flood of omens, and the maestro realized that he was also in the presence of the security chief. The old physician slowed and came to a halt. "My apologies, Messer Bernardino. I did not see you there."

"It is a quality I have carefully developed over the years," da Corte replied drily. Then he turned again to Il Moro. "It occurs to me, Your Highness, that if we have need of a cardinal to present to the bankers from Genoa as the seducer, we can always point to Cardinal Castagno. He fled the city after the attempt on his life, but he could still serve our purposes with Madonna Maria's parents as the seducer."

The duke stroked his beard which had not been trimmed for nearly a week and managed a smile. "Yes," he said softly. "He could, couldn't he? I can present the name to the Genoese delegation this afternoon, and tell them I will take the liberty of avenging their dishonor."

"Cardinal Castagno is gone?" the aged physician asked.

The duke, still smiling, shrugged. "Unhappily, yes."

Maestro Ambrogio frowned. "Well!" He sighed. "Then I suppose I will never be able to cure him, will I? A pity. I felt I was coming so close."

"Cure him?" asked the duke. "Cure him of what?"

"Well, he didn't want it voiced about," the physician whispered, "but since he has fled the city . . . well, for the past three years I have been treating the cardinal for—sterility. That is why he remained in court for such a lengthy period of time. He needed my weekly treatments of mercury and . . ."

"What?" growled the duke.

"Surely you know Madonna Rosemarie was mistress to the late cardinal?" the aged physician continued. "Well, the lady wanted a child to provide a little extra income, you see, and the cardinal agreed, but, alas, he proved sterile, and . . ."

A small groan escaped the duke. "Sterile," he sobbed. "How can I announce a man is responsible for impregnating Madonna Maria when he has been sterile for the past two years?" He sank into a chair and covered his eyes with one hand. "By the Virgin, people are dropping dead around this castle with increasing rapidity, and the court crawls with lechers and libertines, and I can't find one, dead or alive, who could have been Madonna Maria's seducer! Not one!"

Da Corte suddenly snapped his fingers. "Wait, sire! I think I have a possibility! The cardinal Novara! He's very old, but his reputation is scandalous! Remember he was spied behind the arras in the women's quarters only last month, masturbating as Madonna Dorotea bathed. And later . . ."

"Yes, yes, yes," the duke growled. "Do it! Don't tell me! Just do it! But I must have a virile cardinal by this afternoon to present to the Genoese bankers! And a written confession! Both! By this afternoon!"

Da Corte bowed smartly from the waist, wheeled and swept from the room.

The duke groaned.

"Are you sure?" the fat, aged cardinal Novara asked his servant. "My astrologer did not predict any such occurrence for this month. Are you absolutely certain, boy?"

The tall, gawky boy nodded vigorously, kneading his cap in his bony hands. "Lady Leonora overheard Messer Bernardino issuing the order, and she sent her manservant here to tell us, and I am telling you. They are coming for you, Eminence. You are to be submitted to the torture for some reason, by direct order of the duke."

The corpulent cardinal tried to struggle to his feet from the dining table loaded with food and cruets of wine and olive oil, but he no sooner stood when his face paled and strange guttural noises erupted from his throat. His right hand suddenly clutched his left as if to force it to move, and then his eyes seemed to search upward until only the whites showed under his lids, frightening the servant.

"Are you all right, Eminence?" the young man wailed. "Shall I fetch you something?"

Novara trembled and seemed to gesture to something on the table.

"Some mutton?" asked the boy with a swelling anxiety in his voice. "More wine? A knife? What, Eminence? What do you want?"

His Eminence again tried to gesture at something on the dining table before him, but his fat arm waved through the air and settled on no single object. His tongue began to protrude through his thick lips, but the only sound that emerged was the continuing, guttural wheeze.

"Cheese?" wailed the boy. "Honey? An egg? More soup?"

The cardinal seemed to weave like a tower in a windstorm and then, suddenly, and with a resounding crash that echoed through the castle, his great bulk tipped forward, and he fell, face-down in the uncovered tureen.

"It was the soup you wanted then, was it?" asked the servant.

"He dropped dead?" wailed Il Moro at his security chief. "Just like that? He dropped dead?"

"He was an old man and quite fat, Your Highness," Bernardino sighed. "The word must have reached him that we were coming for him, and, well, Maestro Ambrogio said he dropped dead from fright."

"Of fright? That's what Maestro Ambrogio told the Genoese that Madonna Maria died of! Something on the castle walls frightened her and she plummeted to her death in the moat! And now they know that was a lie! Why should they accept this explanation? What are they to think? Has my court become a chamber of horrors? Sweet Jesus," the duke prayed. "There's Albizzi, de Celano, Castagno, and now Novara! Three cardinals dead and one in hiding in almost as many weeks! It is fortunate that I have sent my brother, Cardinal Ascanio, to the Hapsburg court, or your stupid assassins would have served him up to me as the seducer!"

He hurled himself in desperation and anxiety into his chair. "And we have no confession! None! Even if I presented Novara's body to the Genoese as the violator of the poor child, I have nothing to support my statement! And they are here now, in this court, waiting for the audience I promised them!"

Bernardino nodded, lowered his voice, and almost whispered, "Give Novara to the Genoese, Your Highness. I promise you that, within an hour, you will have a signed confession from the dead cardinal."

The duke peered at his protector from between the fingers of his hand. "You promise?"

"I promise you," Bernardino assured him.

Il Moro heaved a sigh and rubbed his hand across his beard. "Then see to it. Have it ready within the hour, and, oh yes, it would be appropriate to have the bells toll for the dead cardinal. For all of them."

The little monk scrambled over the narrow cobbled walkway in the cool air of the early morning and entered the campanile. Brother Angelo felt a great responsibility for the sanctity of the people in the castle and surrounding residences, for it was his special duty to summon the faithful to the morning mass and the evening services. It was his melodic voice in the high bell tower that signaled the Angelus and announced vespers and matins. The arms and upper torso of the little monk had developed into iron bands of muscle from the years of tugging and pulling on the ropes connected to the great bells in the high tower.

Now the assignment had evolved into an exercise of pure pleasure. Brother Angelo would untie the hawsers, lift his arms as far as he could reach, seize the thick rope with both hands and drop to the floor. The reverse action of the tolling bells would then lift the little man high in the air with giggles and a feeling of pure joy.

He prepared himself to pull the rope for the first and largest bell in the tower above him. He leaped a small distance from the floor, grabbed, and was slowly lowered to the floor.

But there was no ringing of the bell.

There was a sound, but not the one the monk anticipated. Instead of the deep-throated bass boom, there was only a muffled thud. As the bell swung back, the monk was elevated again, but again there was only the dull crunch.

The little monk released the rope and tried to peer up through the darkness of the tower toward the bells, and as he did, he felt a drop of moisture strike his forehead. He brushed at the liquid with his hand and drew it down to his eyes where he realized it was deep red.

By this time more of the substance was dripping from the area above him and began to pool on the stone floor. The monk frowned, touched the scarlet finger to the tip of his tongue to reassure himself, and then went screaming toward the rectory in a volley of prayers and oaths.

In his workshop, Leonard da Vinci leaned across his desk, dipped his quill in the inkpot and began to inscribe a name on a limb of the tree sketched in his red book. Stretching from the branch marked Guarino Valla, he drew another limb and wrote above it "Giorgio Adamo."

He then sketched another limb from the branch marked "Vanozza de Faenza" and labelled it "Sebastiano Loncavallo."

"He was another relative of the Faenza," the Maestro calmly announced to Niccolo and Ellie. "He had been stripped, bound, gagged and wrapped around the clapper, upside-down, inside the bell. When the monk pulled the rope, the unfortunate young man's head was hurled against the inside of the heavy bronze bell, and it was, in point of fact, crushed.

"Now," he sighed, "we can expect the madness to spread even more rapidly and in a dozen different directions."

"We can't let this continue!" the duke bellowed at Cossa and da Corte who stood, heads lowered, before him in the Salla della Palla. "Men drowned in cesspits, devoured by rats in a locked dungeon room, suffocated in guano, suspended from bell clappers, fed to pythons! A woman mutilated and killed by hawks! My God!" he shrieked. "If my own assassins showed as much imagination, the Griffin would have been found in the muzzle of a cannon three months ago, and Madonna Maria's seducer would have dangled from a tree in the garden with his testicles stuffed up his nose!"

In Rome, in the Salla dei Misteri della Fede in the Borgian apartments of the Vatican, the tall, portly frame of Pope Alexander VI, Rodrigo Borgia, was anchored in the center of the room as the pontiff reviewed the five mural paintings framed in gold and set against the pale-green background. The bald, hook-nosed man with the sensual lips and dark eyes studied the paintings which allegedly depicted the Nativity, the Epiphany, the Resurrection, the Assumption, and Pentecost. Actually they honored the Borgia family. The pontiff himself, in an awesome telescoping of time and space, was shown witnessing the resurrection of Christ from the tomb, and the ascending Nazarene appears to be blessing the portly prelate. In another painting the pope's uncle, himself a pope, was commemorated through his bastard son, Francesco Borgia, who was shown present and prominent at the Assumption.

The pontiff shuffled into the next room where frescoes of the lives of the saints painted by Pinturicchio filled the lunettes under a marble cornice depicting the bull, symbol of the Borgia family. The pope stopped before a huge narrative painting where St. Catherine of Alexandria demanded that the emperor Maximilian turn from paganism. St. Catherine clearly wore the face of Lucrezia Borgia as that lady appeared at her wedding to Giovanni Sforza, and the emperor was most certainly the pope's son, Cesare.

The pope was conscious, then, of the presence of the real Cesare behind him, and he turned to face the pale countenance, the auburn hair, and the neatly trimmed beard of his son. The Duke of Valentinois wore a doublet of white damask with gold edgings, a black velvet cloak, and a cap with a white plume spangled with rubies which made Rodrigo shake his head in disapproval. His son had already spent over one hundred thousand ducats since his ascendency to the dukedom, and twice the pope had been forced to provide Cesare with additional funds.

The Duke of Valentinois swept the soft cap from his head and stuffed it under his arm. He genuflected and kissed the ring of the Roman pope, but Rodrgio withdrew his hand angrily, and Cesare rose slowly, but smiling.

"Am I in disfavor again?" he asked.

"You waste money, Cesare!" snapped the pope.

"What else can one do with it?" the duke replied. He crossed, without invitation, to the table and poured himself some wine. He sipped it and commented, "Good vintage. Is this part of the settlement of the late Cardinal Campofregoso?"

"No," the angry pope declared as he crossed to his son. "It is from Louis of France. It is a bribe. The king wants his marriage annulled so he can marry his cousin's widow."

Cesare sipped the wine again. "I must side with the monarch. After all, he did invest me with several counties and castles, including the salt deposits. That will most certainly annoy Sforza, because I will start eating into his monopolies. Furthermore, Louis raised Valence to the rank of a duchy for me, which ranks me with the bastard of Milan."

"It wasn't that simple," the pontiff warned him. "I had to make concessions to Milan for the French king's generosity.

I had to offer Cardinal Ascanio Sforza two abbeys. In three years he will have cleared a thousand ducats profit."

"Small compensation," Cesare smiled, "considering we made his pasty-faced brother admit to impotency. I heard bawdy songs about him throughout the Emilia."

The pope locked his arm with his son's and guided him toward the Borgia Tower. "That matter is closed. Giovanni Sforza signed the papers. I annulled the marriage, and at the same time, I remembered to anull Lucrezia's earlier betrothal to Gaspare d'Aversa."

"On what grounds?"

"The poor child had been engaged in haste, under the influence of a passing aberration."

"Really?" smiled the Duke of Valentinois. "What was his name?"

The pope laughed with him, but then the pontiff announced, "You are amusing at times, Cesare, but I want you to know I had a devil of a time covering for you when you cut the throat of that Perotto and threw his body in the Tiber."

"The bastard deserved it for seducing my sister," growled the younger man. "And what about the baby?"

"Oh yes," the pope smiled, "you've been in France, and don't know, do you? I issued two bulls. The first legitimatized the child as a result of a union between an unmarried woman, and you."

"Me?" Cesare glared at his father. "Why me? How does that look with my own new wife pregnant?"

The pontiff chuckled as the two men started up the stairs to the tower. "She'll say nothing. Her father had a good portion of the lady's dowry returned, plus an augmentation, and I made her brother a cardinal."

"For nothing?"

"It's in the family, isn't it?"

The pope shrugged. "By the way, how was your wedding night?"

"Eight trips," boasted the duke.

"To the bed or to the water closet?" the pope asked. "I was told that, instead of the requested aphrodisiac, the apothecary gave you a laxative."

Cesare glared at his father again. "The lady is pregnant, father. That's all that matters."

The pontiff made a gesture of dismissal with his hands and again linked his arm through the duke's. "You're too sensitive, Cesare. It will be your death."

The two men entered the small chamber which served as an exclusive, intimate room for private business. The pontiff gestured his son to one of the two chairs and seated himself behind the desk.

"I will tell you why I summoned you," the pope explained. "I have decided to side with the French. I granted Louis the annulment so he can marry the widow of his late cousin, and I am going to send you back to him with the appropriate papers and a document that verifies my support for his claim not only against Milan but also against Naples."

Cesare accepted the packet which his father passed across the desk, unbound it and began to examine the documents.

"There will be hell to pay," Cesare observed.

"What choice did I have?" the pope snapped. "I know for a fact that the French army has thirteen thousand horse, seventeen thousand mercenaries, and heavy artillery at Asti. They came through the passes earlier this week. At the same time, the Venetians are moving from the east with four thousand mercenaries and heavy cavalry. They have already taken Ghiara d'Adda and Cremona, so Il Moro has instructed his troops to hold at Alessandria. If it falls, and it will, he has only Pavia between his enemies and Milan. But it is inevitable. Milan is doomed. The Moor has already sent his brother, Cardinal Ascanio, to Germany. So it would be foolish for me not to align myself with the winners."

"There will be an uproar, you know," Cesare said quietly. "The people won't like the fact that the Holy Father has encouraged an invasion of Italian soil by French troops."

"The people be damned," the pontiff declared. "I can justify Louis's claims to Milan by virtue of his ancestral ties to the Visconti. And the people may think twice about Il Moro when they learn, as I just have, that three princes of the Church have recently met untimely deaths at the Milanese court and another fled for his life. And one of the deaths is rumored to have been a suicide. I dispatched a demand for an immediate explanation and an investigation, but, whether one is provided or no, it justifies my siding with the French."

"Three cardinals?" Cesare leaned forward and rested his arms on the desk. "Dead in Milan?"

"And one of them was your agent, Cardinal Albizzi."

"I knew of Albizzi's death," Cesare replied. "Galeazzo di Sanseverino poisoned him. Rather cleverly too. Then he sent me an apology. But what of these other deaths? Has Il Moro gone mad and decided to wipe out the college of cardinals? What do you suppose is going on up there?"

The pontiff raised his hands in mock confusion.

"Damned if I know," he said. "But if you wish to find out, you may stop in Milan on your way to the French king."

The pope chuckled. "That ought to keep Il Moro sleepless!"

Galeazzo di Sanseverino peered from behind the tapestry as Il Moro sat down to his dinner. Tucked into his belt was the folded communique from Rome that informed him that Cesare Borgia was on his way to Milan.

He's coming to kill me for murdering the Griffin, the general silently argued with himself. But if I can carry out the assignment and assassinate the duke before he gets here, maybe I'll be forgiven.

The general lifted the crossbow to his shoulder and placed the bolt on the runners.

Easy, he warned himself. Let him get seated, so there will be no other movement.

He squinted down the sights as the duke sat erect in the

high-backed chair and looked at the dishes placed before him. He shook the napkin and placed it on his lap. Galeazzo's finger slowly, slowly applied pressure against the trigger, and suddenly the bolt was released.

Just as Duke Ludovico lowered his head to say grace.

The bolt bit into the back of the chair, sending a few splinters on either side of the astonished duke. Quickly grasping the situation, Il Moro threw himself under the table and overturned it, providing a shield against any further missiles.

But Galeazzo had recognized that the hand of God was plainly at work here, and he was down the narrow steps and through the doorway into the open courtyard. He raced toward the stables for his horse which had been saddled and waiting.

That's enough, he vowed as he ran. When it is a choice between the devil and instant death, I'll risk the devil.

"God's blood! The world is collapsing around my ears!" the distraught and desperate Il Moro roared at his assembled courtiers. "I will not bother to mention my humiliation when the Genoese delegation stormed from the Salla della Palla after I presented them with Novara's confession!"

Bernardino's head was already on his chest. "I had no way of knowing the man couldn't read or write in Latin, and that he had a manservant who handled his correspondence."

"What would you expect from a man who purchased his cardinal's cap with an inheritance?" the duke roared. "And why didn't you think to check whether the late cardinal was left-handed? My God, under the circumstances, that confession wouldn't have fooled a blind man! Especially when his signature was spelled wrong! And now we are left penniless before our enemies! Not only will the Bank of St. George not renew my credit, but they have also circulated lies about me through the banking houses of Germany and the Lowlands!"

"I'm—sorry," da Corte apologized. "What do you want us to do about Galeazzo di Sanseverino?"

"What in hell do you suppose I want done about him? Give him a medal for poor marksmanship? I ought to have him elevated to the college of cardinals! Considering recent events, that would guarantee his death within a matter of days!"

The duke began to pace the room. "First, I want all his servants and followers evicted from his new palace! Then I want—I want all the mules and donkeys, all the chickens and poultry and cattle we have impounded against the city under siege law, stabled in his rooms! Let the shit accumulate until no one can stand the smell! Then—then—I want—I want you to remove the livestock and torch the place!"

He once again hurled himself into a chair. His right eye had begun to twitch a little two days before, and he now covered the trembling lid with his hand.

"It's the end of the world," he mourned.

Chapter 9
The Old Man

"Old men should be made
with sluggish and slow movements,
their legs bent at the knees when they stand still,
both when their feet are together
and some distance apart,
stooping with their heads tilted forwards
and their arms not too extended."

Leonardo da Vinci
"On Painting Old Men"
Codex Urbinas

Despite his deep-chested wheezing and the foam already forming on his flanks, the warhorse of Galeazzo di Sanseverino carried his master another kilometer at the accelerated speed that the captain-general demanded of him. From time to time, the fugitive glanced back along the stony road to make sure no one was following him for he was certain Il Moro would send someone in an attempt to stop him from reaching the French lines. He regretted that he had had no time to arrange for the storage or shipping of his possessions from his new palace or to inform his servants that he was leaving. He thought briefly of the tomb of his late wife, Il Moro's daughter, and wondered if the duke, in his anger and frustration, would desecrate it or, perhaps, remove his daughter's body and have it entombed with his wife, Beatrice, in the Santa Maria della Grazie.

As he approached the perimeter of Asti, an unrecognizable voice aroused Galeazzo from his reverie and demanded he stop and rein in his mount, and after a moment's reflection the captain realized the command had been shouted in the dialect of the Gascons.

"I am Captain-General Galeazzo di Sanseverino," he called to the trees in his limited French. "Commander of the armies of Milan! I seek sanctuary from the duke of Milan!"

"Sanctuary?" a voice responded from the shadows. "We are not a church. Unbuckle your sword and let it fall and dismount."

The weary horse whinnied and nervously pawed the earth, his breath making little clouds of steam in the early morning air. The captain did as he had been instructed. When he stood beside the animal, one arm under and around the warhorse's great neck, Galeazzo watched warily as four or five armed mercenaries drifted down the slopes from between the trees. He was surprised to note that they did not wear the customary armored helmets worn by most soldiers of the time, but soft caps that drooped over one ear and wide-sleeved tunics under a small breastplate.

"Sanseverino, you said?" asked one man with heavy, black mustaches that draped themselves on both sides of his mouth. "Are you a kinsman of Prince Antonello di Sanseverino of Salerno?"

"He is my uncle."

Black Mustache glanced at one of the other mercenaries. "We'll see if he's lying. Where is Prince Antonello?"

"Where is he usually?" the other mercenary smiled. "His tent is in the middle of those of the camp followers."

The mercenaries laughed, and one approached closer and took the reins of the warhorse from the general. Now, in the early morning light Galeazzo understood why these men were not burdened with the heavy plate of full armor. Unlike their Swiss allies, the Gascons carried long-barreled muskets, hand-firing weapons whose balls could easily penetrate plate, and Galeazzo recalled his early prediction to Duke Ludovico.

It is guns that make the king.

The countess Cecilia Bergamini stood like a queen in the middle of her bedchamber in the Palazzo del Verme and directed the armies of servants whirling around her carrying sections of armor, paintings, statuary, and plate. Her long-sleeved dressing gown of black velvet was trimmed with silver, and the jeweled rings on her fingers flashed and flickered as she waved these servants in one direction, others in another.

"The da Vinci portrait of course," she commanded two of the male servants lugging a large, framed painting across the room. "And the two Masaccios, and the della Francesca, but I'm afraid we must leave the Perugino and the Uccello. I never cared for the battle scene anyway, and we cannot take everything to Bologna. We are, after all, coming as guests not as conquerors."

Two other servants struggled past her carrying a large painting of a madonna with a child on her lap. The lady appeared to be seated on a bed of slate rock above a stone quarry.

"No! Yes!" The countess ran a delicate hand across her forehead. "Oh, I don't know. Mantegna. He is so very good at painting family portraiture, and we may have need of that talent in the future." Then, with a wave of that hand, she declared, "I'm afraid it must either be the 'Madonna of the Stonecutters' or the Crivelli 'Annunciation.' We haven't room for both. Let my husband decide."

She swept into the adjoining, larger room where burly, sweating men were busily hammering crates closed and others were carrying them away. Young women in the Bergamini livery were packing gold and silver plates in alternating beds of straw and linen, and a column of male laborers rolled the large rugs and tapestries and tied them with lengths of hemp. Some chattering ladies swept through the room with layers of robes and gowns balanced over their arms, and the kitchen staff rolled barrels of sugar and salt and carried crates of spices past the countess who visually examined everything.

She glanced from the narrow window to the courtyard below where a long procession of horses before two-wheeled carts and four-wheeled wagons waited patiently for their cargo. Grooms were leading strings of purebred horses from the stables under the watchful eyes of mercenaries wearing the livery of the Bergamini. In the center of this bedlam the gray-haired count himself was a rock of tranquility and composure, nodding at this mount, shaking his head at another, and once again the countess found herself admiring this man she had been forced to marry, but whom, over the years, had proven himself to be strong in crisis, faithful in his vows to her, and a good father to the illegitimate son imposed on him by the duke of Milan and his young wife.

"I don't care who fathered him," the count had once whispered to the countess as they watched the boy at play. "It is love that makes the parent, and I will always be his."

The countess found herself smiling now despite the chaos and confusion, and as she turned to continue her decision making, she was surprised to see the two hooded figures standing a little apart from her, one slightly taller than the other, like stationary rocks in a violent sea of whirling servants and workers.

"Niccolo?" the countess asked.

The dwarf threw back his hood, and beside him, Ellie did the same. They both seemed a little awkward and uncomfortable, so the countess quickly crossed to them through the mob of workers and took one each of their hands in her own.

"I was hoping to see you again before we left Milan," she said, smiling. "I'm delighted you came to say good-bye."

"I know you are very much occupied, Countess," Niccolo said. "But I have a—problem, and I thought you might be able to help me with it. You see, the French are coming, and Signorina Eleanor is afraid. I was hoping, that is, if it would not be too much trouble, could you—would you take her with you? She has proven herself to be a very capable and trustworthy servant, and, well, I want her protected."

The countess stopped him with a wave of her hand and smiled at the dwarf who seemed so much taller under the mantle of his responsibility to the young girl. "Of course. Of course." she agreed. "But surely not as a servant. She has been secretly in my employ for some time. For your many kindnesses and your dedication to our mutual cause, Eleanor, now you will be a lady-in-waiting to me."

"Oh no!" Ellie cried. "I would be too uncomfortable in the fine clothes of a lady, and I would prove awkward and embarrass you. My manners would be laughed at, and I—I cannot speak or read Latin."

"Good," the countess declared. "Thank God I will have one in my retinue who can practice the vulgar tongue with me and teach me all the nasty gutter words and phrases shouted in the streets. I hear them all the time, but I do not understand them. You can educate me. Italian is a much more vital language anyway, and I frankly believe that the use of Latin, like the customs and mores of those who utilize it, is declining in importance."

She slipped an arm through the girl's and started to lead her across the bustling room. "As for your manners, we will make a game of them and have ourselves a little fun. When you do or say something that my ladies consider improper or scandalous, I will repeat the action or the words immediately. That will make us appear to be fashionable and everyone else behind the times."

She laughed with Ellie, and then she spied something from the corner of her eye, and she turned to instruct a servant. "Make certain our embroidered napkins are packed away for storage. We will be guests of the Bentivoglio in Bologna whose initial is the same as ours, and I don't want any of our fine embroidered linen confused with theirs."

She turned back to Niccolo. "Now! What of you, Niccolo? Won't you come with us? You know that it is possible that Il Moro may release his frustration and anger on you if he feels your fidelity to me conflicted with the service you owed him. On the other hand, the French may take revenge on anyone who was a member of Il Moro's court, so you may very well be in danger from both sides."

"That's what I told him," cried Ellie.

"No," the dwarf responded, "I am too small to be of much significance to the French. They will probably find me amusing, because I am different, but I doubt that they will hurt me. I may even have some little value for them. And as for Il Moro, I'm afraid our bewildered duke is much too busy trying to locate a possible ally against the French to concern himself with me. But, to reassure you, Countess, if I appear to be in genuine danger, the Maestro and I will simply take a boat downriver to Pavia and seek sanctuary with my old friends in the Certosa."

The countess smiled and crossed to him, placing an ivory hand under the young man's chin and lifting his eyes to hers. "You will be bored to distraction in a monastery," she laughed. "Once one has relished the tangy spices of this world, Niccolo, ordinary salt loses its zest."

"Perhaps." Niccolo returned her smile. "But if I should find my appetite for 'tangy spices' overpowering, and assuming I can work my way to Bologna, would you have room in your court for a little man?"

"No," the countess declared.

Niccolo seemed surprised and disappointed until the lady leaned toward him and whispered, "But there will always be a place for a clever giant who poses as a dwarf."

Ari Biccoca, the red-bearded, ranking kinsman of the dwindling de Faenza family, stood by the large-wheeled carriage of the ponderous bronze cannon. From where he stood on the parapet of the Castello Sforzesco he could look down the wooden incline into the courtyard where armed peasants, including his hated enemy, Piero Sinolo, were stacking spears and pikes and sighting down the length of their arrows to make certain they were not bowed.

How clever I am, he congratulated himself. One yank of the chock and the whole thing will speed down the ramp and crush him! To everyone it will look like an accident, but the damned Spinolo family will know! They'll know who and why it was done!

For the final time, the burly gunner checked the wedges placed under the wheels, the triangular chock that prevented the large gun from rolling backward, the distance from the edge of the parapet to the incline, and the relation of the intended victim to the bottom of the ramp.

A little more to the left, you narrow-assed son-of-a-bitch, Biccoca mentally commanded him. Just a little more.

As if in obedience to the silent command, Piero moved a step to the left to recover a fallen pike, and at that moment, Biccoca gave a quick yank on the rope attached to the chock.

The cannon shuddered and began to roll backward, gaining momentum as it slipped down the incline, and in that brief moment the assassin saw, to his horror, the rider on the white charger who was slowly picking his way between the ramp and his designated victim. The erect aristocrat was followed by a column of armed cavalry, each horseman resplendent in black velvet with the coat of arms of a red bull embroidered on their short capes.

The great charger sensed the danger and suddenly reared, neighing in his surprise and terror, and the rider was forced to lean forward in his saddle and embrace the great horse's neck. He recovered quickly, however, his gloved hands tightening their grip on the reins as the cannon and carriage rattled under the horse's front hooves and sped past the man and his horse and rumbled halfway across the courtyard.

Biccoca stood stunned, uncertain as to what he should do now, but there was so much chaos and confusion in the courtyard that no one thought to look for the man who had set the cannon in motion. The conscripted peasants ran, screaming obscenities and warnings. They knocked over the stacked weapons and then tripped over them and sprawled on the cobbled surface. The armed companions to the leading rider quickly encircled their lord, but they did not look at Biccoca or even at the cannon. Their master, swiftly wheeling his charger around, broke through his own protective circle, galloped under the portcullis and fled the castello. His cavalry, swords drawn and looking in every direction but where Biccoca stood on the parapet, saw their lord gallop away and immediately followed their leader.

God's blood! Cesare Borgia swore to himself as he raced through Milan toward the French to the west.

They must think I'm still a cardinal!

Prudenza of Siena wondered if she should pray or flee. Praying was somewhat alien to her, and fleeing was just not in her nature. When she was commanded to report to this intimate little room off the Salla della Palla, the robust actress had no idea what was of expected of her, and now she found herself closeted with the grinning, elaborately dressed Salvatore Cossa. She quickly observed that the small room contained only a velvet chaise, a small table, and several bottles of wine, and she wondered now if this private interlude was to be an interrogation, a seduction, or a combination of both.

Actually she was close to the truth for the Whisperer had taken upon himself the responsibility for identifying the seducer of Madonna Maria Chigi. The point was moot, of course, for the Genoese delegation had already departed the court, determined to punish Il Moro for the insult by cutting off his funds to wage war.

But for the leader of the Whisperers, the matter had become a personal quest, an individual crusade that would, at least, resurrect his self-respect. Now, as Cosso sat thigh to thigh beside the portly actress on the small chaise, he fixed a mask of sincere empathy on his pale face, leaned across her to the half-filled wine bottle and filled her glass for the fifth time in the past half hour.

"It is a superior vintage, isn't it?" the Whisperer whispered in her ear as she raised the glass to her lips. "The chamberlain—you remember the chamberlain of course? He told me you were particularly fond of this Hospice burgundy."

"Did he?" Prudenza asked suspiciously. "Does a lot of talking, does he? And what else did he tell you about me, eh?"

"Only that you were a very lovely woman of simple beauty, ample endowments, and some, shall we say, 'earthy' experience."

"Well, he's right about the ample endowments, isn't he?" Prudenza laughed as she swallowed huge mouthfuls of the wine, some of which escaped to race down her chin and throat and seek sanctuary between her breasts. "But let's make this clear right now, shall we? I may be earthy, but, by God, I am also particular, signore! I give myself when and to whom I choose, and no man on earth can ever say he took me." She gave a loud raucous laugh. "And no animal either."

She found this so hilarious that she poked a sharp elbow into the Whisperer's ribs to urge him to share in the merriment. Between gasps of pain, Salvatore managed to smile and chuckle.

"You say this wine is made in a hospital?" she asked in wonder, emptying the vessel.

"The Hospice of Beaune," Cosso informed her, "on the Côte d'Or."

"Very nice," Prudenza maintained.

"Yes, indeed. For a French burgundy it has surprising body and an intoxicating bouquet."

"That's what the chamberlain said of me," roared Prudenza emptying her glass and again bayoneting an elbow into Salvatore.

"Is it too—hearty?" asked the Whisperer. "Perhaps you would prefer a blush?"

"I haven't blushed in twenty years," laughed Prudenza. Then, the laugh dying on her lips, she instantly added, "When I was ten."

Cossa filled the glass again, and Prudenza cocked an eyebrow at him. "Aren't you drinking, Signore Cossa?"

"Alas, my physician has ordered me to abstain for a while,"

the Whisperer explained, "but you go ahead and enjoy yourself. This little tête-à-tête . . ."

"Keep your mind off my tetes," Prudenza mock-warned, and then she erupted in another burst of laughter and returned her elbow to Salvatore's ribs with a swift, darting movement. The Whisperer emitted a violent grunt.

"What I meant was, I understand you are accustomed to more—elaborate—affairs."

Prudenza frowned. "What? What affairs?"

"I mean, being an actress, I imagine you prefer the larger, more grand festivals, like the celebration when you first came to the court. When was it? A year or so ago?"

"A year or so," Prudenza agreed. Then she emptied the glass and poured herself another.

"That was a wonderful celebration, was it?" Cossa asked with a sly smile. "Do you remember it?"

"Of course I remember it!" Prudenza snapped. "Why shouldn't I? Listen, did the chamberlain say something about—about that little episode in the water closet? If so, I'll have you know that I kept my wits about me, no matter what he thinks."

Cossa looked confused, but he pressed on. "No. I was just wondering about—well—another incident. I mean, I heard that one of the male actors in the company snuck off with a beautiful, young lady-in-waiting, Madonna Maria. Do you remember that?"

"I wouldn't be surprised," Prudenza nodded. "The males in this miserable company are a sneaking-off bunch. But I think I remember which one of the company went off with the dark-haired lady. She was beautiful and young, damn her eyes. Let me see. Piero, he was sulking in a corner, and Turio, he had passed out on the floor . . ."

Cossa suddenly sat erect. "What? Turio? The boy who plays the old man? You say he had passed out?"

"That's what I said," Prudenza growled. "I forget nothing!"

With that proclamation, she suddenly stood erect, and her

eyes rolled back in her head. She emited a prolonged, deep-bass rumble of gas and weaved back and forth like a tree in the wind. Finally, after a moment, the lady collapsed. Her head came crashing down against the tabletop, and then her hefty torso slid from the chaise and deposited itself in a single bulging lump on the thick rug.

"Hell fire!" growled the Whisperer.

"Is that all she said?" Benardino da Corte asked.

The security man paused in his pacing to face Cossa across the small desk.

"All," replied Salvatore. "Then she became a pale shade of green and deflated. It was useless to question her further." He sprawled in the velvet-upholstered chair and swung one leg over the arm of it. "The young man who plays the old father could not have been the seducer of Madonna Maria Chigi, no matter what Maestro Leonardo thinks, because he passed out early." The Whisperer sighed. "I suppose it seems silly to go to all this trouble since the Geonese bankers have already returned home and cut off Il Moro's financing."

"Ah, but there are one or two other possible allies who might come to the duke's defense," Bernardino declared. "For one, there is Rome and the Borgia pope. Rodrigo has seven or eight armed companies already in the field. If Il Moro can secure the pontiff's backing, we may yet have a chance against the French. To do that, however, the duke must convince the pontiff that the seduction of Maria Chigi had nothing to do with his court. If we can prove it was an outsider, one of the actors, it would serve his purpose. Of course, Il Moro must also produce a plausible explanation for the death of the three cardinals." He stroked his short beard and chuckled. "And to that end the duke sent a messenger to Rome declaring that the cardinal killer was none other than Galeazzo di Sanseverino."

Cossa grinned. "No," he said.

"He did," da Corte insisted. "He told the pope that

when he discovered the horrible truth he drove the murderer from the city, and the French promptly gave him refuge, exposing the invaders as protectors of the wicked and treacherous."

The Whisperer smiled. "The duke has an amazing mind."

"He regrets, however, that Cesare Borgia turned from the castle so soon after his arrival," Bernardino remarked.

"The conscripts say the duke of Valentinois was almost trampled by a runaway cannon or something. In any case, he didn't say or do anything. He simply turned his mount and headed west."

"Unfortunate," sighed the chief of security.

"Not at all," Cassa disagreed. "I understand that Cesare Borgia has his own methods for extracting information, and if there's one thing we don't need in the court at this moment, it is another inquisitor." He swung his leg from the arm of the chair and bent forward. "Besides," he whispered, "I have heard that the pope is already supporting the French."

"I have heard that rumor, too," Bernardino nodded. "But we've received no definite word. Da Tuttavilla says he has heard nothing. He believes Rodrigo Borgia will wait before he decides to wager on the next roll of the die."

"Do you think someone could have tried to assassinate Borgia the moment he arrived?"

"None of my men!" declared da Corte. "How about yours?"

Cossa shook his head. "No," he said. "I didn't order it. Perhaps it was one of the Borgia-haters. That number is swelling with potential assassins. The Orsini. The della Roveres."

"Well, whoever did it, he would have had my blessing if he had succeeded," the security man said. "Since he didn't . . ."

"Of course," Salvatore acknowledged. "But at least we have learned a little about the possible seducer. Prudenza admitted that it was a male in I Comici Buffoni who was seen with the Madonna. It just wasn't Tebaldeo or Turio of Verona."

"What kind of a name is that? Turio of Verona?"

"It is a name taken when they become actors. They do it so their disgrace will not reflect upon their families. There are three such in the company. Francesco who plays the male lover. Rubini who plays Scapino, and Prudenza of Siena who plays Colombina."

"I remember something I overheard Maestro Leonardo tell the dwarf," Bernardino said, beginning to again pace the floor. "He said, 'Put yourself in the girl's place. Which of the actors would you choose for a lover?'"

Cossa shrugged. "I don't know. The handsome one, perhaps? What is his name? Francesco?"

"Quite possibly," da Corte said, nodding.

"Why don't we put him to the torture and see if he'll confess?"

"No!" Bernardino declined. "How would it look if he is the wrong one? The duke already considers us a pair of bumbling asses, why compound it? Besides, I think the less we resort to torture, the better. I for one would hesitate to go down into those chambers again. God knows whose mutilated body might be waiting for us there."

Cossa stood up and stretched his arms. "Well, give me one more afternoon with one of the other actresses, and I'll have the name of the seducer, and then we can arrest him."

"Oh?" asked Bernardino. "What is your plan, Salvatore?"

"I have only one."

"I thought you were interested in Prudenza," Anna Ponti, the songstress, cooed to Salvatore Cossa as they sat side by side on the chaise. "Or are you planning to seduce all three of us? If so, you could have saved some time by inviting all of us here at once. That, at least, would have indicated some imagination and daring, wouldn't it? But, frankly, I think I should warn you that Isabella Corteze is not what she appears to be. You understand? Watch your step with that one. She'll eat you alive."

This seemed to amuse the actress who erupted with a deep-throated laugh like a horse's whinny.

Cossa refilled the two wine glasses.

"I'm not interested in Signora Isabella," Salvatore replied. "You are the one who fascinates me. I just wanted to take the opportunity to have a little chat with you before the French arrive, because, well, we've had so little time to—mingle, have we? And I imagine your troupe is now planning to leave the castle before the French arrive?"

He handed her the glass.

"Mama told me never to drink alone," she commented.

Cassa forced a smile and raised the other glass to his lips.

This will take you a little longer than you planned, Whisperer, Niccolo thought to himself from his hiding place behind the wall.

Then the dwarf closed the spy hole and worked his way back to the madman's tower.

The Maestro listened to Niccolo's description of the near-tragedy with the cannon, the departure of the Bergamini from Milan, and the attempt by Salvatore Cossa to elicit information from Prudenza and Anna concerning the identity of the seducer. The dwarf explained that even now the Whisperer was continuing to use his charms and the remaining stock of French vintage wine on the hapless songstress.

The Maestro did not respond as he carefully placed his paints and rolls of blank canvas in the large barrels and crates. Finally, as he looked around at the rapidly emptying workshop, the artist sighed and shook his head.

"It is the hour of desperation," the Maestro declared. "The duke has only two potential allies left, his relative, the German emperor and the pope. The pope holds the most power in Italy, but the Hapsburgs have huge armies of mercenaries ready to pour through the Alps and help the Milanese if Maximilian gives the word."

"Hapsburg mercenaries?"

"Highly trained and professional. Even the Swiss fear them. You see, Louis's Swiss mercenaries are largely conscripts who are well paid for their services, but the Germans are disciplined soldiers of fortune. The Swiss fight for the money, but the Germans actually enjoy the battles. And while the Germans have developed light cavalry, improved their muskets, and made their artillery more mobile, the Swiss are still relying on pikes and swords."

The Maestro said nothing for a while, but stood looking from the tower windows at the chaos in the courtyards below. Finally Niccolo heard him murmur, "So many changes. So many truths. So many lies." He turned to look at the dwarf who had perched himself on the high stool. "One doesn't know what to believe anymore."

"You once said that the only truths were those that were provable by mathematics," the dwarf reminded him.

"And you said that wouldn't apply to spiritual matters," the Maestro responded. "I'm tired, Niccolo. I don't know what I believe anymore." He picked up the heavy Bible and placed it delicately on the straw as if it were the Christ child himself,. "Certainly I have come to question the age of the earth as dictated in the Bible, and the account of the Flood, and if these stories are less than truth, what of the rest?"

"Father Abbot once told me that the Bible was not meant as history, but as a testament to the faith of the writers."

The Maestro added another blanket of straw above the thick tome, and turned to the dwarf. "Do you know what I think now, Niccolo? Do you?" he lowered his voice. "I have come to believe that the earth is alive, a living thing, and its rivers are like the arteries to a human being."

Niccolo glanced around the workshop nervously. "You shouldn't say things like that," he warned. "You could be brought before an ecclesiastical court."

"I have stood before an ecclesiastical court," the Maestro said, gathering an armful of rolled parchments and placing them in a barrel. "Three times. It is useless to try and debate matters when one side begins with the assumption that they, they alone, hold the truth. My trials were the most humiliating moments of my life. And the most frustrating. The inquisitors began with the warning that any word spoken against what they believe would be considered heresy. Where can argumentation proceed from that?"

They both were suddenly aware that someone else was in the workshop. The dwarf turned on his stool as the figure slowly stepped from the shadows into the light of the oil lamps.

" 'Cuse," muttered Prudenza.

She was mantled from head to toe in black, but the whites of her eyes were streaked with red, and her voice had become a rasp. "You'll have to excuse my appearance," she groaned. "I'm—in mourning."

"For whom?" asked the dwarf.

"My mind," replied the portly woman crossing to the table. "I lost it somewhere between the third and fourth bottle of Frenchy wine, and I'm afraid I said something I shouldn't."

Niccolo smiled and wanted to reassure her that he had heard everything from his hidden perch in the secret passage, but he remembered his initial warning from Epictetus and said nothing.

"I came to ask a favor of you, Maestro Leonardo," she curtsied to da Vinci.

"Of course, Signora," the artist responded graciously.

From somewhere under her great traveling cloak the troupe's Colombina produced a silver goblet which she set on the table. "Each of us has one," she said, "except Piero who took two. He said the nobility have a responsibility to share their wealth with the less fortunate, even if the less fortunate have to steal it to balance things."

"I don't understand," the Maestro frowned.

"Ten goblets. Heavy. Pure silver with the inside of the cups coated in gold. When—well, when we were here the first time—we, ah, we were very poor and, ah, facing a hard winter, you understand? The chamberlain had the ten goblets cleaned and wiped following the festival honoring the duchess, and, well, they looked to be very valuable, eh? I mean, there they were, just sitting on a table. The money from selling them could last us a long time, and we were leaving within the hour, so—well—I had, ah, been rather friendly with the chamberlain the previous night, you see, so I was assigned to—distract—him while the others stole the goblets."

The Maestro stroke his beard and smiled. "I see," he said. He wheeled suddenly and crossed to the table where the only remaining item was the red book, an ink jar, and his quill pen. He quickly opened the tome to an empty page and began to write.

"When we returned here," she continued, following behind the Maestro, "and I—ah—saw the chamberlain again, I got the impression that he knew where the goblets had gone, and he began to ask some questions. Fortunately, he was overcome by the wine and my—ah—endowments, and we ended the evening rather pleasantly.

"But now"—Prudenza turned to Niccolo—"I think maybe the duke is going to cause us some trouble over this little theft. That beanpole Cossa tried to get me drunk so I'd confess, I think, but I passed out before I did any real damage. At least, I hope I did. Now the company is planning to get away from the castle and Milan before the French come, and I thought, maybe, if at least one of us brought back a goblet, the duke might, you know, let us go with just a warning. I hadn't sold mine, so—well—there it is."

She tried to peer over the Maestro's shoulder, but the backward writing both confused and alarmed her. "Are you writing all this down?" she wailed. "Are you going to expose us?"

"No," the Maestro assured her as he continued writing. "This is a private journal. You have just supplied a part of the puzzle, and I am entering that information in my ledger. The primary question was: who was responsible for the troupe being invited back to the court? Now we know! The chamberlain! I thought you were brought back, because one of you had something to do with the seduction of Madonna Maria, and someone had realized that. But I was wrong! I gave them credit for some intelligence. It now appears that the chamberlain, who is personally responsible for the duke's goods, reasoned that it was one or more of the *commedia* company who had stolen the ten goblets, so he went to the duke and asked him to invite you back, hoping to recover the chalices before the duke discovered them missing. Since the chamberlain had something of an emotional attachment for you, my dear lady, he may have only told the duke some fanciful story, reasoning that he could get the goblets back quietly by renewing his relationship with you."

Prudenza smiled. "You think so? You think he didn't tell the duke? Because he liked me?"

The Maestro turned to her, his eyes smiling under his bushy brows. "When you arrived the second time, the duke didn't put you to the torture or imprison you, did he? I think he didn't know about the theft, because the chamberlain didn't tell him, because the chamberlain was taken with you." He smiled and said softly, "How could he do otherwise, Madonna?"

Niccolo smiled, too, and Prudenza actually glowed, even the tiny red veins crisscrossing the whites of her eyes seemed to radiate with a new warmth.

"My!" is all she could whisper.

"You're certain he is in there?" da Corte asked the tall guard in the livery of the Sforza.

"The tall one, you said? The handsome one?" the guard

asked, and da Corte nodded. "Yes, Signor Bernardino. I could swear to it. I saw him enter about a quarter hour past."

Da Corte nodded again, drew his sword, and motioned two of the armed men to the opposite side of the door. Then he suddenly wheeled and kicked at the handle forcing the door to fly open with a loud crash.

The noise alarmed and alerted the two naked young men in the bed. Salai recovered more quickly and grinned at the security chief and the four armed guards staring at them.

"You really will have to await your turn," he smirked.

Da Corte glanced at the frightened Francesco who was clutching the linen sheet to his bare chest.

"Hell fire!" he muttered.

At that moment in the workshop, Prudenza watched as the Maestro entered her commentaries in the red book.

"Francesco couldn't have been the seducer," she smiled. "He prefers boys. I've never understood how he does it, but onstage, he is all passion and lust for Isabella, but offstage, well . . ."

"That eliminates three of the six men," Niccolo observed. "Piero was sulking. Turio had passed out, and Francesco's taste runs to other men. That leaves Mario Torri who plays the Doctor, Simone Corio who plays Arlecchino, and Rubini. Rubini. Is that his real name?"

"Oh no," Prudenza smiled. "His real name is . . . now what is it again? He hasn't used it in over a year. Let me see. Oh yes! Paulo! Paulo Vecchio!"

The Maestro looked up from his writing. "What? What did you say his name was?"

"Paulo . . ."

"Vecchio!" he cried. " 'The old man' in the vulgar tongue, Italian!" He turned to Niccolo. "Do you understand now? Maria Chigi knew her seducer and did identify him, but the torturers misunderstood and thought she was speaking Italian. That's a common failing in those who generally converse in

Latin. The torturers asked her, 'Who was your lover?', and she replied, 'Vecchio' which happens to be the gentleman's name! It also happens to mean 'the old man' in Italian. The torturers translated the word rather than taking it literally."

He wheeled then and began to enter this new information in the red book.

"Have you been recording everything that happened at the castle in that book?" asked Niccolo.

"Of course," the Maestro replied, bent over his work. "It is, in a sense, a protective shield." He looked up and stared at Niccolo under his thick eyebrows. "I know, young friend, that many will say this is a useless work, perhaps even a dangerous one, but good men possess a natural desire to know the truth. Men who possess a desire only for material wealth scorn truth and wisdom which is the wealth of the mind, but this book will enable good men to distinguish the true from the false as to what occurred here at the Castello Sforzesco.

"Besides," he added, "the lifeblood of an artist is observation, and one cannot trust everything to memory."

"You are correct when you say it is dangerous," Niccolo responded.

Suddenly the dwarf was alerted by something, some rustling behind the walls. He slowly slid from the stool and put a finger to his lips. He walked to the west boundary of the room, placed his back to it and began to work his way toward the panel that was the doorway to the secret passageway. As he came to it, he reached for the serpent motif and began to slowly turn it.

Almost at once everyone in the room heard the rapid footsteps receding down the passageway. Niccolo swung the door open and darted after the eavesdropper. He did not have time to light a lamp, but he could see the light bobbing ahead of him and hear the rapid footfall down the narrow corridor.

Then, suddenly, he heard nothing.

He's gone to tell the duke, the dwarf thought.

At that moment the young man imagined he heard someone caroling. No. Not caroling. It is too raucous, too blaring and rowdy. It is pirates, he thought, or, at least one pirate.

The baying seemed to be coming from his left which, he knew, was the "intimate chamber" where Cossa had tried to lure Prudenza into revealing the identity of the seducer. Niccolo put his eye to the spy hole, laughed at what he saw, and then he slowly opened the door and stepped through it into the room.

"How did you do that?" asked Anna Ponti, pausing in her concert.

Niccolo crossed to where the woman sat on the chest of Salvatore Cossa, her red petticoats gathered around her waist and her pretty long legs straddling the unconscious Whisperer. Cossa was spread-eagled on the thick rug with empty wine bottles placed like votive candles at his head and feet.

"What happened to him?" asked Niccolo. "Is this some sort of religious ritual?"

"The gentleman has a drinking problem," the songstress smiled. "He can't do it."

With that she launched into another sea chanty about a voyage on a boat filled with lusty and lustful men whose masthead was a naked prostitute lying "abed."

"Listen," Niccolo interrupted the chorus. "Someone has been listening to a conversation we have been having with Prudenza in the tower. I think the spy is going to report to the duke, and that will put all of us in a great deal of trouble. You must go to Tebaldeo as fast as you can, and tell him to get the company out of the castle at once. Do you understand, Lesbino? Out of the castello at once!"

"You may call me Anna," she cooed.

Prudenza had already warned Tebaldeo and the others in the company by the time Anna weaved her way back to the Salla della Palla.

"Quickly!" the Captain commanded, throwing items into a

burlap sack. "Take the masks and the costumes! The wagon is still in the courtyard, but the two mules are in the stables! Marco, you and Simone run down and get them into harness! Prudenza, you and Anna and Isabella check the costumes and props! Let's go! Hurry!"

The lanky Arlecchino and the Doctor ran to the two great doors of the spacious room and threw them open to face two stocky guards who wheeled on them with their three-bladed pikes. The two actors smiled, nodded to the sentries, backed into the room and slowly closed the doors.

At the opposite end of the room, Isabella opened the smaller door and a detachment of six guards pushed her aside and rushed in with drawn swords. Barking commands, they herded the members of the troupe to the center of the room.

"We couldn't have left anyway," Isabella whispered to Tebaldeo. "Rubini's missing."

Duke Ludovico the Moor, dissheveled and distraught, nervously rubbed a hand across his brow and gestured to the bloodstained sack before his chair. "It is the head of my messenger," he moaned. "The damned pope has sent me his head as a warning that he has decided to side with the French. Now my only hope is the German mercenaries, and, in order to raise them, I will have to go to Emperor Maximilian myself and plead my case." He looked at the two men who stood before him. "You must do what you feel best, but I would like you, Bernardino, to remain here and assume command of the court. If the French can be delayed long enough at Alessandrina, I may be able to ride back to your rescue with the Germans."

"I will remain," da Corte replied softly. "I am not afraid of the French. But you should know that Messer Salvatore and I have finally unraveled the truth concerning Madonna Maria Chigi. She was seduced by an actor, the one who calls himself Rubini. We are holding the company prisoners in the

Salla della Palla, but Rubini is not among them. I have my men searching the castle."

The duke seemed to be deep in thought. The slight trembling in his right eye becoming more frequent. "An actor, humm?" He stroked his short beard. "That could serve me. It shows that the girl was not violated by a member of my court. Capture this Rubini and extract a confession from him if you can. If you can't locate him, torture each of the actors until they tell you where he is. One of them must know."

Da Corte nodded. "I also have to report that Maestro Leonardo has been keeping a record of everything that has happened in the court since last September. It is detailed in a small red book in his workshop."

"Everything?" thundered the duke, rising from his chair. "The seduction? The assassinations? The murders?"

Bernardino shrugged. "I have not seen it, but my spies tell me that the Maestro has annotated everything. Everything."

"My God," the duke groaned collapsing back into his chair. "If the emperor should get his hands on that! What could that bearded old fart have in mind, doing such a thing? You must seize it at once! At once! Do you understand, Bernardino? No matter what you have to do, no matter who has to die, you must seize that book and destroy it!"

"I understand," the security man said.

The duke rose abruptly. "I must leave immediately, but you have all my authority to command the castle guards! Take as many as you need and see to it at once!"

He started for the door to the salon.

"But if possible," the duke intoned solemnly, "make it look accidental."

He turned at the door.

"Ask some of the servants how to do it."

Niccolo returned to the workshop to find Salai rummaging through the last barrel which had remained opened to receive any last-minute additions. As Niccolo quietly stepped into the room, he saw the blond apprentice bobbing into the barrel. Finally Salai emerged with the red book, smiled at his new possession, wiped away some of the straw and turned to leave the workroom.

"Give it to me," Niccolo demanded softly, putting out his hand. "It's not for you, Salai."

"If it is what I think it is," the young man replied unsmiling, "and if I can deliver it to Il Moro, it is not only my guarantee of safe passage from this damned castle and from the service to the old miser, but it will enable me to return to my friends in Florence with a few florins in my purse."

"You're not leaving this room with it," Niccolo said coldly.

Salai put the book under one arm, and drew his dagger from its sheath. "Don't try to stop me, grotesque. I've just grown to tolerate you a little, and that's about all I can stand of you. If you get in my way, I'll have to slice off your nose and complete the monstrosity that God did not finish creating."

The yellow-haired young man started to walk slowly toward the dwarf who drew his own dagger and took a wide stance, arms extended on either side. The apprentice gave a small laugh and slowly swung his blade before him in wide arcs. Niccolo elevated his right arm at an angle in front of his body to either block the thrust or to accept it and spare the more vital areas of his torso. He maneuvered himself between the blond young man and the door, and shifted his weight back and forth like a sailor on a rolling deck. This apparently amused Salai even more. Once again he emitted a small laugh, and then, suddenly, he gave a loud cry and leaped forward, arm and dagger fully extended before him.

Niccolo rolled to one side with the easy rhythm he had learned from the *commedia* actors, drawing back his arm a few seconds before the blade sliced through the empty air. He did a quick pirouette as the apprentice's momentum carried him past the dwarf and into the shadows. Salai's knife embedded itself to the hilt in a panel of the false door to the passageway.

Assuming that the dwarf would quickly counterattack, Salai tried to remove the dagger, but in his anxiety and desperation, he pushed the hilt to one side and snapped the blade. At the same time Niccolo placed both hands on the hilt of his own dagger and brought it down, pommel first, on the back of the young man's neck. Salai dropped like a sheep struck between the eyes with a stone hammer, a horrifying sight Niccolo once saw when the Certosa cooks were preparing to kill and dress the animal for a visitor's feast.

"Well done," said the Maestro as he stepped through the secret doorway and worked the broken blade from it. "Ten centimeters to the left, however, and the apprentice would have abruptly cancelled his education."

Later that evening, the Maestro went to arrange for some workers to carry the sealed crates and barrels to the wagons. Salai, bound and gagged in a corner, was softly groaning, and Niccolo opened his Epictetus and read by the light of the solitary oil lamp.

"Kings and tyrants have armed guards to chastise certain persons, although they are evil themselves. But to the questioning man, conscience gives him this power, not arms nor guards . . ."

Chapter 10
The Flight of the Fugitives

"Amid much wailing and weeping
were men and women and children,
all terror-stricken . . . by the corpses . . .
Huddled together in fearful union . . .
were wolves, foxes, serpents
and all manner of fugitives
from death . . ."

Leonardo da Vinci
The Deluge
Codex Urbinas

The Father Abbot stood with Brother Pax on the observation platform at the top of the Certosa, both men wrapped in hooded cloaks, and watched the rising clouds of dust to the north.

For three days and three nights the sounds of bombardment had echoed over the Lombardy plains, and by night the distant fires had told the story of the capitulation of Pavia. By the end of the first day a thin stream of refugees found their way to the monastery and were given sanctuary in the refectory and bedded in the storage rooms. The monks treated the wounds of the injured as best they could, administered the last rites to the dying, and consoled the widowed and orphaned. The monks of the carpentry shop brought out the wooden toys that were normally set aside as gifts for the feast of the Nativity and gave them to the refugee children.

There were two baptisms of newborns. Confessions were heard and absolutions granted. One young and desperate couple were married by the Father Abbot following an emergency dispensation of the customary announcement of the bans.

Now that the bombardment had ended and the silence returned to Lombardy, it was clear to the Father Abbot that the perimeter to the south and west would not hold, and Milan would fall. From information he had gathered from the refugees, only a small corridor to the southeast, toward Cremona, remained open.

"They have swept through Vigevano," the old cleric commented to Brother Pax. "Maestro Leonardo's model city has been totally destroyed, so we can expect at least one detachment of Swiss or Gascon mercenaries to come here within the next day or so."

"What should we do?" asked the deep-voiced monk. "Do you think they will take the refugees? Desecrate the monastery?"

"Of course not," the Father Abbot insisted. "Louis of France would not dare to sack a Catholic monastery or violate the traditions of sanctuary. He knows perfectly well that the pope's legions are formidable, and if the pontiff should request it, every Catholic country in Europe would rise against vandals, even if they, themselves, are Catholic. That's the power of the pontiff."

"Small consolation to the dead victims," Brother Pax grumbled.

The Father Abbot turned away and started for the shadowed door that led down to the refectory. "The most we can expect from the French," he said softly, "is a request to quarter some of their men and horses here for a limited time. A request that we will, of course, honor."

Brother Pax waddled behind the superior. "Then we take the usual steps for invaders?"

The Father Abbot nodded. "Yes. Move the better wines to the burial vaults, and hide them behind the skeletons. Distribute the smoked meats and the wheels of the best cheese among the clerical wardrobes. Gather the jeweled and gold chalices and monstrances and hide them under canvas and straw and animal waste in the stable area. Move our goats and cattle to the breaks beyond the river where the trees will obscure them and stake them there where they will have grass and water. Break out the poorer cheeses and the rancid butter and cut back on the number of loaves baked daily. When the French arrive, we will give them a demonstration of the true monastic life and show them how we would honor our vows of poverty if, when necessary, we pushed that observance to the extreme."

Brother Pax smiled and whispered, "I give them one week before they run screaming for Milan."

The Father Abbot took one last glance toward the distant cloud and whispered, "Poor Niccolo."

"My poor city," the duke groaned softly. "My poor people."

"There is nothing we can do. The perimeter did not hold, Your Highness," the captain whispered to Il Moro as the two men watched the French cannon and horses race past their shadowed hiding place among the rocky ledges approaching the Alpine passes. "The mercenaries deserted. If Pavia has fallen, then Alessandria is isolated, and our forces are cut off to the south. They will link with the papal forces from the south and the Venetians from the east. By tomorrow or the next day they will start bombarding Milan—unless, of course, the people open the gates to the invaders."

"And they will," the duke prophesized. "They bear me ill, because of the taxes, but they should look at my treasure vaults! Just one year ago I had over a million ducats in gold, gems, and plate! The Venetians were awed when I showed it to them. That was my mistake. It also made them greedy and treacherous."

He turned from looking at the valley below and rested his back against a rock. "If the French control both the Great and Little St. Bernard passes, and the Venetians have cut off access to the Brenner to the east. How can we break through to Germany?"

"There are only one or two more encampments between

us and the St. Gotthard Pass, and at Andermatt we can cross the Devil's Bridge to Goscheren and board a ship going up the Rhine."

Il Moro turned again and watched sullenly as the long procession of cannon, horsemen, and marching pikemen rumbled past them in the valley below. Suddenly he seized the captain's arm and whispered, "Wait! Look!"

Below them a contingent of Gascon musketeers marched past, preceded by two regal horsemen and a familiar banner of alternating red and yellow stripes.

"Galeazzo!" hissed Il Moro. "The bastard and his uncle! What I wouldn't give for a marksman and a musket!"

"No, Your Highness," the captain responded. "It would only put an end to one of your enemies and reveal our hiding place. Just remember that you will pass this way again shortly with a German army, and Milan will be liberated. Then you can demand payment for past debts."

Il Moro continued to watch until his former captain-general rode from sight.

"I'm coming back, you son-of-a-bitch," he whispered to the back of the departing officer.

"And then you'll start your term in hell."

"It is hell! Hell!" the weary and filthy messenger reported to Benardino da Corte in the small room in the bustling Castello Sforzesco. "Bombardments every day and all night. Fires everywhere. Bodies in the streets, under the rubble, everywhere. That beautiful city that Maestro Leonardo built with the network of the canals like a pattern of lace has been totally leveled. The sluices were destroyed the first day, and the grain fields are all under water. The old Roman forum that Maestro Leonardo rebuilt is in ruins and Bramante's tower is broken and lies shattered along the banks of the Ticino. The creamery, the big farm, the whitewashed houses, everything, all gone."

Within the hidden passageway, Niccolo overheard the news with a sinking heart.

Vigevano. The Maestro's city of tomorrow.

He closed the spy hole and rested his head against the wall. He had seen the designs and plans for the canals and the conduits for waste. Now it was gone, as the Maestro's masterwork, "The Last Supper" was doomed to go.

What can I tell him? Niccolo asked himself. How can I bring myself to tell him?

"It is quite simple," da Corte addressed the twenty armed soldiers in the livery of the Sforza gathered in the corridor with Salvatore Cossa. "Listen to me. There is a book. A red book. It is valueless to anyone but me. Half of you will come with me to retrieve it from the madman's tower. The other half will go with Messer Cossa and hunt down this actor, this Rubini, whom, we are told, is hiding somewhere in the women's quarters."

One of the soldiers mumbled something, and some of the others laughed. When da Corte challenged him to repeat it, the guard shrugged and said, "He picked a good place to hide."

"I've heard of this Leonardo," a tall, dark junior officer said. "They say he's got magical powers. My pike and sword won't do much good against magic. And they say he can bring the dead to life up there in that tower of his. Suppose he has an army of dead men up there? How can you kill a dead man, eh? I'm no coward, and I'd face the devil himself if I thought it was a fair fight, but magic ...!"

Da Corte raised a hand to silence the swelling voices. "Maestro Leonardo has no magic. He is a man like you or me. A little older, but just an ordinary man. It's true he has dead bodies brought to his tower, but there is no magic connected with what he is doing."

The rumble of protest grew louder.

"He only cuts them open to study the muscles and things

inside!" the security man shouted. "He has never brought one back to life. Never!"

"What's in this book then?" asked another of the guards. "Is it the devil's book? I won't have anything to do with the devil's book!"

"It is a simple red book with backward writing, and . . ."

"Backward writing?" shrieked one.

"The devil's book," the junior officer repeated. "I told you, didn't I? It's the devil's own book, and that devil in the tower is the only one who can read it!"

The rumbling grew louder.

"Listen!" Bernardino trumpeted. "To every man who goes with me into the tower, I will give two gold florins."

The rebellion subsided, and da Corte smiled to himself.

Oh yes! Magic chants are terrifying, but the comforting sounds of money overpowers them every time.

Just before the detachments were divided into two forces, da Corte took Cossa aside and whispered, "The book could be our salvation! If we seize it and present it to the French as an indictment against Il Moro, we can say we only stayed behind to secure it so that Louis of France had proof of the wickedness and debauchery of the Milanese court."

"And if the Maestro won't give it to us?"

"Kill him!" da Corte instructed him. "And the dwarf, too, if he gets in the way. We can always say that the duke murdered them before he fled the city."

Cossa nodded. "I understand."

"Then I'm for the book," Bernardino said, drawing his sword. "You get this Rubini and put him with the others of the troupe in the Salla della Palla."

"And then?"

The chief of security rubbed a hand across his forehead. "Turn them over to the guards," he said. "They can use the men for archery practice, and the women for themselves."

He started toward his detachment.

"I never thought they were funny anyway."

In the Salla della Palla, Tebaldeo and seven members of the I Comici Buffoni sat on the sacks that held their meager supply of props and costumes. The five soldiers that were assigned to guard them encircled the small band, two men at the main doors, one at the door opposite, and one each leaning against the remaining walls. Tebaldeo noted that their principal weapons were swords and pikes, but they wore the Sforza serpent on their crests, so they were not mercenaries.

"If we could get out of here," he whispered to his troupe, "they'd have to run us down, because they don't have bows or muskets, and, with a little luck, we could divide and run in different directions, and that would confuse them. That way, at least, some of us might survive."

"Why not wait a little?" Marco suggested. "Maybe they'll let us go. We've done nothing to them."

"We know about the murders and the seduction and torture of Madonna Chigi. They can't afford to let us live."

Simone shook his head. "I often thought I would be killed for my poor acting, never for what I know."

"Rubini is still not here," whispered Isabella.

"He's on his own," the Captain growled. "But, on the other hand, his absence buys us a little time. According to what Prudenza says, Rubini is the one they really want. They won't do anything to us until they find him."

"Or until they don't find him," Marco murmured. "Then they'll start on each one of us until they find out where he is."

"We could rush them," Simone said softly. "We're equal in numbers. They have five men, and we have five."

"Why this sudden revival of chivalry?" growled Turio. "Why don't we include the women in this plan, eh? In fact, why don't we just let the women rush them?"

"Or the women could seduce them," suggested Francesco.

"So could you," snapped Prudenza.

"You're prettier," mocked Anna.

"We won't do anything rash or violent." Piero insisted. "They are trained professionals attached to the court. One move toward any of them, and we'd be impaled on those pikes."

"Well," Anna murmured, "What can we do?"

"What we do best," smiled Piero. "Use our heads and our gifts. As I said, these are professional soldiers. Their weapons are pikes and swords. Let's see how they stand against lies and cunning."

He turned and looked at each of the guards in turn and decided that the one leaning against the south wall was the ranking soldier.

" 'Cuse, captain!" Tebaldeo called to him. "While we're waiting to die, have you any objection to our working?"

"I'm not a captain," the soldier growled. "And what do you mean by working?"

"Rehearsing," explained Tebaldeo. "Perhaps the duke will reconsider and let us go. After all, we are only actors and of no value to anyone."

"True," snarled another guard at the door. "I've seen them play."

The mercenaries laughed, and Piero laughed with them. Then he continued his plea.

"If we're released, we'll have to earn our bread by acting again, and theater is a disciplined art, like soldiering. So we need to practice, to rehearse. To keep our skills sharp, as I imagine you soldiers do."

"To hell with our skills," the door guard growled again. "We keep our blades sharp, and our skills take care of themselves."

The others laughed again, and the soldier addressed as "captain" stood erect and exchanged glances with the others to his right and left.

"What do you want to do? Rehearse what?"

"What we always rehearse." Piero smiled and waved his

hands. "We are comic actors. We make people laugh. We tell stories, make jests, fall on our behinds, steal kisses, lift petticoats, get slapped! We ridicule and mock!"

"You also talk a lot," grumbled the door guard.

"Our blessing and our curse," Piero acknowledged.

The "captain" approached the group. "What do you need for this rehearsing? You can't have any weapons, and you can't leave this room."

"Of course not. But, you see, we are accustomed to performing on a small stage. We will just set our props to approximate the floor areas of our wagon, mark the boundaries with our bags, and we will not go beyond them."

As he said it, some of the male actors began to smile and place the burlap sacks some distance apart to mark the imaginary edges of the stage. Anna and Isabella began to adjust their costumes, paying particular attention to their gartered thighs, which caught and focused the attention of the guards who smiled and stood upright.

"Well, all right," murmured the "captain."

Turio, Marco, Simone, and Piero put on their half-masks. Francesco adjusted his hair and loudly cleared his throat. Turio slipped into his great long coat and affixed the fat leather purse to his belt. Piero withdrew his cape of colored rags from one of the bags and whipped it around his shoulders.

"What shall we rehearse?" Prudenza softly asked the leader of the troupe as she helped him fasten the clasp of the cape.

"The Invasion!" Piero announced loudly.

The title caught the interest of the guards who focused all their attention on the players. Piero noted that they were beginning to smile and assume more relaxed positions a little apart from the walls.

That's it guardians, he thought to himself. Relax. Enjoy yourselves.

The actors moved to the edge of the marked perimeter to

sit on the floor, but Piero seized Turio's long-sleeved robe as he passed and pulled him into the center of the group.

"This man," Piero exclaimed in his booming theatrical voice, "is Signore Pantalone of Venice!"

Two of the guards laughed.

"He is a miser, and in that great purse at his waist are florins and ducats and lire and contracts and broken promises, unfulfilled ambitions and shattered dreams. He is old beyond his years, has nothing to anticipate but death, and nothing to remember but missed opportunities and friendless festivals. Despite his appearance and his history, he imagines himself to be a shrewd man of business, an untiring lover, a valiant protector, and a wise father. And yet his partners cheat him and are quietly embezzling his funds. No woman loves him, although one or two now and again may pretend affection in order to steal his money or to have their way with him. Everything frightens him, and he mistakes discipline for parenting. He is, in a word, a fool."

"Certainly! He's a Venetian!" yelled one of the guards and the others laughed.

That's it, Piero thought. Get into the spirit of it.

"On this occasion," the leader declared, "Pantalone sits alone and lonely in the largest room of his castello, very much like this one. In the distance, there is a threatening boom of cannon."

Piero separated from Pantalone and sat beside Isabella on the floor as Simone and Marco went "Boom! Boom!"

"It is the end of the world," cried the old miser in character.

He drew a voluminous handkerchief from the sleeve of his great robe and blew his nose in it, creating such a loud and obscene noise that the actors laughed along with the guards.

"The city is invaded," Pantalone wailed, "and as the leading citizen, I am afraid the enemy will force their way onto my estates, intrude on my peace and confiscate my goods and rape my horses." The soldiers laughed, and Pantalone crossed to the one addressed as "captain" and snapped, "Well, they're French, aren't they? Don't you remember the last invasion? The court was a mess! Men and women played cards and ate in the presence of their king! The stables were filthy! Revolting!"

He began to pace in an ever-widening circle, forcing some of the actors to move their burlap sacks and themselves back a step or two.

"Arlecchino!" he suddenly bellowed. "Where the devil is that insolent fellow? Arlecchino!"

Simone and Anna suddenly were on their feet and in a passionate and foolish embrace that set the mercenaries to laughing and whistling and shouting obscenities. Pantalone, his back to the couple, suddenly wheeled to face them.

"Ah! There you are, you shameless servants!"

Arlecchino and Lesbino broke the embrace and looked at each other, and then the man in the rags of many colors said quietly, "So we are." And they resumed the wild embracing, pawing each other with reckless abandon and making sounds of intense passion.

"Stop that!" screamed Pantalone. "Stop it this instant! You are obscene! Scandalous! Disgusting! Don't you know the French are almost upon us?"

Lesbino pulled back a little to say, "Then they'll just have to wait. Arlecchino got here first."

Pantalone took the heavy leather purse from his waist and swung it against Arlecchino's back. The lovers instantly separated.

"You, Arlecchino! Fetch my account books, so I can adjust them to reflect my poverty! You, Lesbino, bring me my jewel case at once! Go!"

Simone instantly crossed to one corner of the imaginary stage, picked up one of the sacks and withdrew a large black-bound book. When he placed the sack down again, he set it another foot toward the wall. On the opposite side, Anna took a small chest from another bag and also replaced it a little farther back from where it had been marked. The two servants then crossed, center, to where Pantalone was again pacing.

"Your accounts, Signor Pantalone," Arlecchino declared, passing the book to the old man.

"Your jewel case," Lesbino announced as she placed the small chest on top of the account book.

"Good! Good! Now you, Arlecchino, take this jewel case and hide it somewhere, and you, Lesbino, take this account book and stick it—some place where the French are unlikely to find it."

Simone instantly crossed to the opposite side of the stage, picked up the sack, placed the chest in it, and then dropped the bag still another step or two away from the center of the room. Lesbino, at the same time, took the account book and shoved it under her skirts. Tebaldeo smiled as he saw the guards move closer to the actors for a better view of Anna's red-stockinged legs.

That's it. That's it.

Prudenza looked up at one of the guards who had moved closer and she patted the sack beside her, inviting the infantry man to sit. The soldier glanced at the others and then sat down.

In the meantime Pantalone had swung his purse against Lesbino's backside, forcing her to drop the book from under her skirts.

"No, you slut!" he croaked. "I said put it some place where the French were unlikely to find it! Not in the first place they'll look!"

The guards laughed, and across the arena from Prudenza, another of the soldiers sat down beside Isabella.

Tebaldeo had stuffed a pillow under his costume and suddenly leaped into the acting area as the Captain. With a great deal of difficulty he managed to draw the absurd wooden sword from his sash and waved it about, startling both Pantalone and Lesbino. The female servant shrieked and ran away from the playing area. Then she sat beyond the area marked by a bag and pulled it toward her. After a moment, two of the guards moved and sat on either side of her.

"*Voilà!*" bellowed Tebaldeo as the Captain "*J' arrive!*"

Pantalone quickly went up to the mock officer. "Please to meet you, Signor Jareeve! My name is Signor Pantalone di Venezia!"

"Quiet!" thundered the Captain. "I am the captain-general of the armies of all France, including a little bit of northern Spain around the mountains of Navarre and the western edge of the Dutch country! Also foreign colonies and, hopefully, Milan and Naples!"

One of the soldiers shouted an obscenity, and the others laughed.

"Assemble all your workers and family immediately to hear my instructions!" shouted the Captain.

Instantly all the actors were on their feet around the Captain and Pantalone. "These are my servants, Arlecchino and Lesbino. This is my wife, Colombina, and my physician, Doctor Graziano, a specialist in enemas. A lovely touch. Lovely. This is my daughter, Isabella, and her worthless friend, Francesco."

The Captain stepped forward and seized Prudenza by one hand and pulled her to him. "You, woman! You stay with me! You, Arlecchino and Lesbino, run and bring me all the cash boxes and jewel chests in the house! You, Isabella and Francesco, bring me all medallions, brocaded capes, and the best wines!"

The Captain then threw Pantalone at the doctor. "You, Doctor, take this worthless piece of shit and bring me all the paintings, statuary and valuables, and someone bring me a shank of mutton, not too much fat, roasted on the outside but just pink on the inside, and wrap it in a slice of buttered bread! Hurry!"

The room became a whirlwind of confusion. The actors dashed in front of each other, reversed direction, ran toward the opposite corner, yelling commands and screaming instructions.

The guards by this time had all reclined on the floor to watch the proceedings as the performers whirled around them. In the center of this bedlam, the Captain was slowly raising Prudenza's skirt with the tip of his sword which focused the attention of the soldiers. They did not notice that with each rapid medley of crisscrossing maneuvers, one of the actors slowly disappeared through the doors until the Captain and Prudenza were alone with the guards.

"What do you think, my friends?" Tebaldeo yelled to keep the guards attention centered on Prudenza's legs. "Is this high enough?"

The guards shouted their approval and instructions, and Tebaldeo obediently raised the skirt a little higher. This process continued for some moments with the soldiers calling for more until the Captain noted from the corner of one eye that one of the great doors was opened and Turio and Isabella were gesturing to him.

"My God!" the Captain suddenly cried. "That girl is totally naked!"

He pointed in the direction opposite to the great doors, and as the guards turned or stood to look, Tebaldeo seized Prudenza's hands and raced for the open door.

They just cleared it when the guards realized the deception, grabbed their weapons and started after them. But as Piero and Prudenza ran through it, Turio and Isabella slammed the door shut, snatched the metal javelin from the armored figure beside it and slipped it through the handles of the door, effectively locking it. As the soldiers pounded on the portal and shouted muffled oaths, the actors raced down the corridor.

"Everything is in confusion in the courtyard," Turio yelled to Tebaldeo. "Francesco and Simone have the wagon out and the animals harnessed. No one will pay any attention to us, but there is no sign of Rubini!"

"Damn his eyes to fourteen kinds of hell!" snapped Tebaldeo. "What is he up to now?"

Had Piero the eyes to see through and beyond the walls of the Rochetta to the women's quarters, he would have seen Rubini's hand halfway up the bare thigh of Madonna Valentina.

"You really should be going," sighed the lady.

"Why?"

"The French will be coming," she explained.

"Not as often as I did," the actor laughed.

She laughed with him, but their merry mood was shattered by the loud thunder outside the locked door and the shouting of Salvatore Cossa.

"Come out, Rubini!" the Whisperer screamed.

"What now?" the actor cried as he leaped from the bed and began to put on his boots. "Do you have a husband?"

"No," Madonna Valentina assured him, frantically rising from the opposite side. "That is the voice of Messer Cossa! You must have done something wrong!"

"I thought I was doing everything right," wailed Rubini. "I didn't know there was a court criteria for making love!"

The thunder at the door became a rhythmic, steady pounding as Cossa's men began to break through the portal. Madonna Valentina was out of the bed and hurriedly donning a robe.

"Go! Go!" she demanded.

"Go where?" Rubini asked.

The sharp, high-pitched whistle from outside the room came as if in response, and Rubini threw the screen to one side and whipped back the canvas which masked the still unfinished balcony. He stood in the large opening in the bedchamber wall and looked to where Turio's head seemed impaled on the outer curtain of the castle, some distance away.

"Hurry!" yelled the company's Pantalone, his green half-mask perched on his forehead. "We have to get away from here!"

"How?" shrieked Rubini.

Turio pointed, and Rubini leaned out to see what he was indicating. When he realized what it was, he paled.

"Oh no. God, no," he murmured.

Stretching from the top of the hole in the wall to the outer curtain was a slick, slightly angled, tightly coiled rope. From it dangled a wooden container used to carry waste stone from the project to the outer wall where it could be dumped.

"Hurry!" Turio screamed. "They want to kill you!"

Rubini sighed and quickly glanced around the room. A rack of several wooden shafts used for scaffolding were propped against one corner of the room. The actor quickly crossed to them, weighed two of three of the long poles in his hands, and then selected one.

The door to the bedchamber was already cracking and splintering under the pounding from Cossa's men, and the Madonna, in her best form, had responded traditionally to this new crisis by fainting in front of the door, forming a human barricade.

Rubini quickly crossed to the hole, wrapped a silk sash from the Madonna's discarded clothing around the center of the pole and slung it over his back. He then leaned from the hole, seized the rope in both hands and somersaulted himself above and on it. He placed one steadying hand against the stone wall, and slipped the long pole from his back. He was aware of his own labored breathing, the cold on the back of his neck, the dryness of his mouth. He held the long rod in one hand, judging the center of it, and then, when he felt he had located the middle point, he very slowly placed his feet parallel to the rope and cautiously removed his supporting hand from the stone wall. He could feel the perspiration moistening his forehead and his hands, but he sighed, focused his attention on the other end of the rope and began to walk.

Beneath and behind him, workers, soldiers, and servants

watched and held their breath. Cossa, the first of the pursuers to reach the hole, observed the slow movement of the rope-dancer with awe and annoyance. Far below stray dogs stared up at the man in midair, growled and barked and leaped about in confusion.

Ahead of and below Rubini, straddling the wall, were Turio and Simone, one hand each outstretched to seize the rope-dancer when, and if, he came within arm's reach, but for Rubini, all of his concentration was fixed on the next step, one by one, as he slightly adjusted the long pole to compensate for a tremor in his stance or a wobble of the rope.

Halfway across the actor suddenly became aware that the angle of the rope was more acute than he had first thought. He was slowly being propelled forward, forced to walk faster than he wished and, just as Cossa reached above his head to shake the rope, Rubini felt himself begin to slide, at first slowly, and then accelerating, until he quickly plunged down the remaining length and into the waiting arms of Simone and Turio, almost carrying them off the wall with him.

"Bravo, Rubini!" Simone cheered him. "I never saw you do that ending before! What do you call that?"

Rubini wiped the sweat from his forehead and grinned at him.

"The slide for life," he murmured.

Beyond the outer curtain of the castle, Cossa could hear the cheers of the actors, and then he realized that the soldiers and workers were cheering too. The Whisperer wheeled suddenly, shoved the grinning armed men to one side, and swept from the room.

In the abandoned bedchamber of Il Moro, a serving maid who was packing away some of the linen before the French arrived, swung open the doors of a high cupboard, and was almost crushed under the falling body of Gaetano Dominici, first cousin of Vanozza de Faenza.

He had been suffocated and the head of a decapitated falcon had been stuffed in his mouth.

Almost at the same moment, at the opposite end of the castle, a cavalryman lightly held the reins of his nervous mount and wondered why the horse would not drink from the trough. When he peered into it, he saw the wide-eyed, vacant stare of the dead Tomasso Falcone, a distant relative of Guarino Valla. The man had been stripped and drowned, his body weighed down with heavy rocks in the watering trench.

Within hours, men and women were being stabbed, strangled, hurled from windows and poisoned throughout the castle as the venedetta that began with the death of Anna Spinolo ran its inevitable course.

In the madman's tower, Niccolo and the Maestro heard the insistent pounding against the doors and knew that Bernardino da Corte had come for the red book. Salai, still bound and gagged and propped in one corner, writhed in a frenzy of frustration and fear.

The dwarf turned the insignia of the serpent and opened the door to the secret passage. "Quickly, Maestro!" he called. "This way!"

Da Vinci made no sign of movement. He picked up Niccolo's small edition of Epictetus and seemed totally engrossed in it.

As Niccolo demanded that he hurry to the hidden passage and as da Corte's men battered against the door, the artist calmly read, " 'Fly, you tell me. Fly. Where shall I fly? Can wings take me beyond the limits of the world? It may not be, but wherever I go, there shall I still find the sun, the moon, and the stars. There shall I find dreams and omens and be able to converse with God . . .' "

At the open door to the passage, Niccolo heard the echo of running footsteps down the hidden corridor and suddenly remembered that da Corte also knew of the passageway. Obviously he had sent some of his men to cut off this avenue of retreat.

Niccolo quickly closed the panel, wedged an iron crowbar left behind by the servants against the serpent handle and crossed to the Maestro.

"They're coming up the secret passageway," he reported. "What shall we do?"

The dwarf was surprised and a little annoyed at the complacency of the Maestro as he closed the book, smiled down at the young man and said softly, "Why, you will fly, Niccolo."

The dwarf realized at once what the Maestro had in mind even before the artist crossed the room and lowered the great dragon wings from the ceiling.

"But you . . . ?"

The Maestro led him to the harness and began to strap him into it. "Don't you realize that what they want is my red book? As long as that book is in hands other than da Corte's, they will not dare to harm me. You are the only one light enough to use the wing. You've done it before, and you've been at me to let you do it again. All right. Now you have the opportunity."

He completed the harnessing and led the dwarf to the tall, arched windows. He threw them open and helped the young man mount the sill.

"Keep the book safe. It is our protection. Remember that."

He handed the dwarf the red book and the Epictetus.

"No," Niccolo quickly whispered. "You keep the Epictetus. Practice your Latin, and I, I promise to study Euclid."

The smile bloomed under the beard and mustache, and the eyes glittered under the heavy brows. Behind them the panel of the door to the passageway was splintering.

"Will I ever see you again?"

"Likely," smiled the artist. "But if not, remember what I taught you. Do not assume. Do not jump to conclusions. There is always another alternative."

Niccolo felt the heavy pressure of his hand against the

small of his back, and he was instantly catapulted out and away from the tower. He placed his feet across the bar behind him and began to adjust the steering ropes.

Once again the exhilaration rose in him, the sense of being one with the sky and the cloud, and he deliberately forced the wing to take him higher and higher as he began long, slow circles that carried him first nearer, and then farther from, the castle. Below him there were scenes of hysteria and confusion. He heard no bombardment, but he could see in the distance the clouds of advancing calvary and cannon, and he knew that the Milanese had capitulated. The gates to the city would be opened to the invaders to prevent the destruction from cannonade and violent reprisals. The French would enter the city as conquerors, without a struggle.

Niccolo began to adjust the wing for a gradual descent. He passed over the great square and the shuttered shops. Here and there he saw small strings of carts and wagons carrying fugitives east, apparently unaware that the Venetians would be coming from that direction. The dwarf soared to his right, away from the advancing columns of the French and their mercenaries, heading southeast, parallel to the Corso Porta Romana, in the general direction of Lodi and Cremona, the only possible opening between the pincers being applied to the Lombardy plains.

Within minutes he saw the wagon. Even at this height there was no mistaking the colorfully painted vehicle carrying the I Comici Buffoni away from Milan. The dwarf beneath the dragon's wing soared over the wagon, and it was Rubini, perched on top, who recognized the contraption and its occupant.

"It is Niccolo!" he called. "It is the Maestro's little man!"

The dwarf continued to descend, speeding ahead of the wagon and then sharply banking to his right as he realized he could not land on the roadway which was crowded with fleeing refugees. He chose instead a newly harvested field beside the road, and removed his feet from the bar, tilted the wing, and ran with it for a short distance, before he tripped and fell facedown into the soft earth.

Within minutes the actors were around him, undoing the straps and lifting the little man from under the great wing.

"What a thrill!" they chorused. "Imagine! Flying!"

"Shall we keep this wing?" asked Rubini.

"No," Niccolo said softly, checking to make certain that the red book had not slipped from his doublet. "It's part of the past. The Maestro has another idea."

As the performers escorted him to their wagon, he explained, "It is a sort of revolving wing, like the spiral of a screw.

"The magic of it is: it can lift one straight up from the ground."

Da Corte was the first man through the broken door, and one glance told him that he had been too late. One of the guards crossed to Salai in the corner and untied the ropes and the gag.

"He sent the little bastard off with the red book!" the blond assistant yelled. "He harnessed him to that wing of his and threw him from the window!"

Bernardino quickly ran to the open window, but all he could see of the wing was a distant flash of yellow and gold against the deep blue sky. Beyond he saw the advancing French column, and he wheeled to face da Vinci.

"You treacherous old fart!" he snarled. "That book could have saved all of us! What can prevent me now from running you through and blaming it on Il Moro, eh?"

Da Vinci glared at him, drawing himself up his full height, a head above the security man.

"The fact that Niccolo has the book," he responded coldly, "and the fact that if anything happens to me, he will take it to his friends at the Certosa. They, in turn, will see that it safely reaches the pope who will surely inform the Genoese family of Maria Chigi who it was who tortured and murdered her."

Da Corte glared back at the dark-robed artist.

"On the other hand," the artist continued quietly, "if you will permit me to leave before you simply turn the Castello Sforzesco over to the French, you may be confident that your secrets will be safe with me and Niccolo. As far as Louis is concerned, you were only an obedient servant to a rascally master, and loyalty is commonly recognized as a virtue—even among enemies."

The torturer wavered as if he were about to collapse, but his cheeks flushed, and he suddenly sheathed his sword as Giovanni Francesco Melzi rushed into the room.

"Master! Master! Are you all right?" the apprentice called. "My father has sent some men-at-arms to bring you safely to our palace!"

Da Corte glared at the young nobleman and gestured to his men to leave. As the last one stepped across the broken portal, the Maestro called to the torturer.

"Please, Messer da Corte," he said loudly, "take your offal with you."

He gestured to Salai who stared at the Maestro and then smiled.

"You'll send for me," he said softly. "You will always send for me."

With that he followed da Corte from the room.

The artist emitted a deep sigh and sat on the edge of one of the crates. "Thank your father for me, Francesco," he said. "But leaving the castle with men-at-arms would only attract attention. However, ask him if he could provide some men to remove my things and store them for me."

The young assistant nodded. "Of course," he said.

The Maestro rose. "And may I ask something else of you?"

"Anything."

"There will be a man traveling with the French, a Count

Louis de Ligny. Find him, please, and give him a message for me."

"Yes, Maestro. What is the message?"

The instructions poured from the tall bearded artist. "Find Ligny and tell him that I have given you permission to wait for him in Rome and then you are to go on with him to Naples. See that his donation for my needs is made in your name. You should bring with you our braziers from the Santa Maria delle Grazie, and see if you can find the rascal who stole one and make him return it. Sell whatever you cannot carry. By all means sell the scaffolding. Buy some tablecloths, napkins, cloaks, caps, shoes, four pair of hose, a doublet of chamois, and some hides to make others. Have two boxes made. Bring the muleteers blankets, although the three bedcovers would be better. One of these I will probably leave at Vinci."

He placed one strong hand on the young man's elbow and walked with him toward the broken door, through it and out into the corridor.

"Take with you the Witelo book and our measurements of the public buildings. Pick up the plans of the theater at Verona from Giovanni Lombardo. Don't forget the lathe of Alessandro. If you have the time, ask Jean de Paris—he will be traveling with the French too—to tell you his secrets for coloring, so I might paint a fresco without hurrying the execution, and with white salt, and how to make coated paper. Oh yes, and pick up his box of colors. Ask him how he makes flesh colors in tempera and dissolves gum lac. Don't forget to bring the *fotteragi* seeds, and the parsnips and garlic from Piacenza. Remember to bring the Pelacani treatise on weights, *De Ponderibus,* and the works by Leonardo of Cremona. Remove Giovanni's little furnance. Bring with you the seeds of lilies, lady's mantle, and red byrony, and all our surveying tools, and see if anyone can determine how much ground a man can dig in one day."

Melzi had begun inscribing all these instructions in a small book as they walked, his lips moving as he tried to remember and repeat everything.

"As for me. I am going to Florence where I anticipate a commission from the Servites for the completion of 'Saint Anne with the Virgin and Child' and another from Francesco del Giocondo who wants a portrait of his wife . . ."

The words were still cascading from him as the two men came to the end of the corridor, turned abruptly, and disappeared from sight.

In the courtyard, the Maestro pulled his hooded cloak around his shoulders and stopped momentarily to survey the scene. Three or four bodies were scattered around the courtyard, although there had been no sounds of gunfire or armed conflict.

"Vendetta," he sighed and shook his head. "The idiots."

He went under the portcullis and into the public square. He quickly covered the ground to the Santa Maria della Grazie, dodging children and dogs who ran ahead of the approaching column to announce its arrival. He entered the dimly lit church and went directly to the refectory.

The large fresco of "The Last Supper" loomed before him over the door to the kitchens, the scaffolding still in place. The artist walked slowly toward the ladder, climbed, and leaned into the painting. He lightly touched the pigment, and the plaster beneath it made a slight cracking sound.

"Doomed," he whispered to himself.

He slowly climbed down from the scaffold, turned, did not look back, and left the refectory and the church.

Once again in the bright sunlight he heard the cry and cheers of the male voices, and as he rounded the corner, he saw what had aroused the watchers.

Gascon and Swiss archers were using the Maestro's great clay model of the mounted Francesco Sforza for target practice. The towering figure was already disfigured and resembled nothing so much as a giant hedgehog. Even as its creator watched, the model trembled from a rope thrown across the neck of the clay horse, and the mercenaries began to tug at it to bring it down, aided by scores of townspeople.

Da Vinci did not wait to see the end of the destruction. He understood the rage of the commoners against the Sforzas for bringing them to this state of humiliation. He felt cold despite the heavy cloak, and he stared without intent or feeling at the wet, cobbled roadway as he pushed his way through the wild and raucous crowd assembling to watch the Sforza monument tumble and shatter.

All of it, he thought. Everything. The fresco. Vigevano, and now the great statue. All of my work for nothing. Nothing.

He found he could not move, his legs refusing to carry him farther, and he slipped into a doorway as the conquering procession entered the piazza and passed by him. Without emotion or interest, he watched as Cesare Borgia rode before a small congregation of nobles and ladies. Among them, the Maestro recognized the Marquesa of Mantua, Isabella d'Este, accompanied by her husband, Francesco Gonzaga, captain-general of the armies of Venice. Behind them rode the marquesa's brothers including Cardinal Ippolito d'Este who had once sworn to protect Il Moro with his own life. Behind the brothers rode the cardinals d'Amboise and Giuliano della Rovere, the man also secretly struggling to bring down the Borgia family.

The Maestro waited until the collected enemies of the Sforza family had passed. He leaned back against the cold stone wall of the entryway and wondered if he would pass out. He placed a hand in a great pocket of the cloak and his fingers closed around something.

He drew it out and stared at it.

It was Niccolo's edition of Epictetus.

Almost without thinking, the Maestro thumbed through the pages until he stopped at a passage and read it.

"Remind yourself that what you love is not your own. It is given you for the present, not irrevocably or forever, but even as a fig or a grape, for an appointed season. All these changes are not destruction, but an ordered process. So, leaving things behind is of small account. It is a little death, death being an even greater change from what is now, not to what is not, but to what is not now. You will continue to be, but something different, which the world will need."

His eyes misted as he read the last line.

"For you were not born when you chose to be, but when the world needed you . . ."

Epilogue

*"This will be a collection without order
drawn from many pages . . .
according to the subjects with which they will deal
and I believe before I am at the end of this,
I will repeat the same things many times
for which do not blame me, reader . . ."*

**Leonardo da Vinci
Florence, March 22, 1508**

The conventional biographies of the Renaissance artist report that Leonardo da Vinci went home to Tuscany after the fall of Il Moro, then to Florence, and returned to Milan under invitation from Cesare Borgia.

It seems that, when the Duke of Valentinois examined the captured workshop of the Maestro in the Castello Sforzesco, he was fascinated by the war machines left behind when the castle was abandoned to the French. The Maestro, who had once denounced war as "madness," was invited to make maps and design weapons for the new duke, and he agreed. When Cesare was defeated, da Vinci returned to Florence.

Eventually he found himself, an old gray-bearded man, in residence at the Chateau de Cloux near the Loire where he daubed at three paintings, and worked on designs for a new royal residence for the new French king, Francis I. Here, Salai, who had returned to his service when the Maestro worked for Cesare Borgia, finally left him forever.

Giovanni Francesco Melzi, however, stayed with the great artist to the end when, according to the conventional biographies, the Maestro died asking God's forgiveness for not "using all the resources of my spirit and my art."

The red book of Leonardo da Vinci, however, was carried by Niccolo for the rest of the dwarf's life. He continued to make entries in it from time to time, and according to this text, the great painter-engineer sent for his small friend upon his return to Milan.

Then, no one knows why, it disappeared for nearly a century.

Late in the seventeenth century, the red book containing Niccolo's later chronicles were reportedly in the hands of a private collector who claimed to have received it from his grandfather who allegedly received it from the hands of the dwarf himself. The red book and Niccolo's narrative about those days in the Castello Sforzesco were largely ignored, because of the great wave of publicity that was accorded the *Codex Urbinas,* a compilation of the Maestro's own words that was published in Paris in 1651 with illustrations by Poussin.

This was unfortunate, because Niccolo's additions to the Sforzesco chronicles detailed events in the Maestro's later life which remain, even today, largely unknown to the world. There are, for example, the years with Cesare Borgia and Machiavelli that were listed as "The Maestro and the War Machines"; the amazing adventures the Maestro had in Rome which Niccolo entitled "The Maestro and the Chamber of Lies"; the episodes in Florence which were labeled "The Maestro and the Arno Serpent" and many more.

Niccolo notes in the red book that the Duke Ludovico Sforza returned briefly to Milan with the German armies of his in-law, but he was forced out again and died in prison. The dwarf maintains that, when the end came, Il Moro was a raving maniac who kept seeing dead cardinals murdered by bizarre methods, in the shadowy corners of his cell.

The dwarf always maintained that Galeazzo di Sanseverino served the French with a dedication he did not bestow upon the hapless Duke of Milan, his father-in-law, and he argues, in defiance of the conventional histories, that Salvatore Cossa and Bernardino da Corte both died under torture at the hands of the Inquisition when they could not respond to the questions of the judge, because they could not speak Spanish.

The moral that the dwarf drew from this tragedy is that, in a troubled world, bilingualism is vital to survival.

Niccolo himself was taken south with the *commedia* troupe, and when the company played their final performance in Padua, he left to join the court of the countess Bergamini at Cremona and was reunited with Ellie.

He was now, however, no longer a bizarre figure to be gawked at, but a knight and courtier, and Ellie became a lady by virtue of marriage. For the remainder of his life, Niccolo slept in big beds, this time with a woman of his own, dressed in embroidered silks and satins and, unhappily, continued to steal food from the kitchens just to keep a grip on the happier traditions of his youth.

He died, according to the final entry in the red book, in the arms of his beloved, and was interred at the Certosa in a deceptively long, six-foot grave with a towering seven-foot, marble headstone depicting an angel writing in a book. The inscription, from Epictetus, was ordered by the dwarf before his death, as a testament to what he had learned at the Castello Sforzesco.

"Forgiveness is better then revenge."

I Comici Buffoni, in the best tradition of all good theater troupes, was forced to dissolve when the performers were offered more money by rival companies that were now welcomed in the courts of kings and emperors and, on rare occasions, even sanctioned by the church.

On that fateful date, Simone as Arlecchino took the stage in Padua for the last time, bowed to the laughing audiences who had just witnessed the final performance, ignored the scattered coins which included three or four gold florins, and pronounced an epilogue.

"A theater," he proclaimed to this last audience of the Buffoni, "will always find its audience! Do not weep for us!

"As long as there is life, my dear friends, laughter will be the weapon of we who mock it even as we struggle to understand it."

Then he whispered his final words and removed his black half-mask to reveal the single tear on one cheek, a symbol that would become his own when his character evolved into the French Pierrot.

"The comedy," he said, "is finished."

CHARACTERS

The Milanese Court

Nobles
Ludovico Sforza, duke of Milan
Giovanni Sforza, lord of Pesaro, the duke's brother

Court Officials
Girolamo da Tuttavilla, senior diplomat
Bernardino da Corte, chief of security
Galeazzo di Sanseverino, captain-general of the armies
Maestro Leonardo da Vinci, artist-engineer
Maestro Ambrogio da Rosate, chief physician and astrologer
Count Belgioioso, Milanese envoy to the French court
Salvatore Cossa, captain of the Whisperers
Francesco da Bicocca, captain of the guards of the women's quarters
Bartolomeo Calco, the duke's secretary, arranger of celebrations
Francesco da Casate, one of the advisors
Marchesino Stanga, Minister of Public Works

Court Ladies
Madonna Dorotea Spada
Madonna Terese Ottoni
Madonna Valentina Gaddi

Madonna Maria Chigi
Madonna Anna da Casate

Workers
Dino Spada, a kitchen worker
Guarino Valla, the head falconer, an agent of the countess
Giacomo Salai, da Vinci's assistant
Giovanni Francesco Melzi, another da Vinci assistant
Mino Spinolo, a kitchen worker
Anna Spinolo, a servant girl, first victim of the vendetta
Vanozza de Faenza, a pastry cook, Dino's lover

Clergy
Cardinal Ascanio Sforza
Cardinal de Celano
Cardinal Belgado
Cardinal Ippolito d'Este
Cardinal Castagno
Cardinal Albizzi

Milanese Nobles
Count Bergamini, lord of the Palazzo del Verme
Countess Cecilia Bergamini (Gallerani), mother to Il Moro's son
Count Della Torre

The French Court
Louis de Valois, Duc d'Orleans, king of France
Antonello di Sanseverino, exiled prince of Salerno
Shara, a courtesan

At the Certosa
Alfredo Coelci, an assassin
Luigi Manetti, his assistant
Father Abbot
Niccolo, a dwarf
Brother Pax, the librarian
Brother Antonius, the chief cook

A COMEDY OF MURDERS

I Comici Buffoni

Simone Corio who plays Arlecchino
Piero Tebaldeo who plays the Captain
Turio of Verona who plays Pantalone
Francesco who plays the male lover
Rubini who plays Scapino
Marco Torri who plays Doctor Graziano
Prudenza of Siena who plays Colombina
Anna Ponti, the songstress who plays Lesbino
Isabella Corteze who plays the female lover